THE MIDDLE FORK

■   A GUIDE   ■

CARREY
&
CONLEY

THE MIDDLE FORK

■ A GUIDE ■

JOHNNY CARREY & CORT CONLEY

Third Edition

Backeddy Books
P O. Box 301
Cambridge, Idaho 83610

Bibliography: p. Includes Index. 1. Salmon Valley, Idaho—
History 2. Salmon Valley, Idaho —Description and travel.
3. Tukuarika Indians—Wars, 1879. 4. Boats and boating
— Idaho — Salmon River. 5. Hiking—Idaho—Salmon
Valley.

ISBN 0-9603566-1-4

Without history we are little higher than porpoises.
                              William Sonnichsen

The only thing new is the history you don't know.
                              Harry Truman

*Men travel far to see a city, but few seem curious about a river.
Every river has, nevertheless, its individuality, its great silent
interest. Every river has, moreover, its influence over the people
who pass their lives within sight of its waters.*
                              H. S. Merriman

FOREWORD

This book was written as an historical guide for persons who float or hike down the Middle Fork of the Salmon River. Of necessity its scope has been limited to sites and events close to the river.

Significant new information and more than seventy additional photographs have been added to this edition.

While not intended as a guide for getting down the river, the Forest Service chart with information on river rapids has been included as a convenience for some readers.

Our hope is that by providing this history we may contribute in a small way to the preservation of the past and thereby fulfill a responsibility to the future.

Please refrain from removing any article or artifact from sites in the canyon. What may be only a souvenir to you might be of great interest to the next party. Inconsiderate visitors have already inflicted irreparable damage.

Cort Conley

CONTENTS

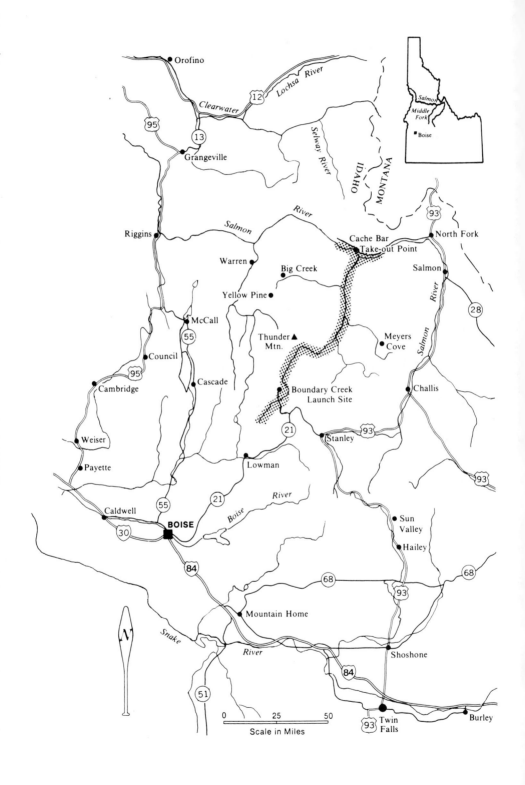

Orofino

Lochsa River

Clearwater

12

95

Selway River

13

Grangeville

IDAHO

MONTANA

93

River

Salmon

Cache Bar
Take-out Point

North Fork

Riggins

Salmon

Salmon

Warren

Big Creek

Salmon River

Yellow Pine

28

McCall

55

Thunder ▲
Mtn.

Meyers
Cove

Council

95

Cascade

Boundary Creek
Launch Site

Challis

Cambridge

21

93

Weiser

Stanley

93

Payette

Lowman

Caldwell

55

21

Boise River

30

BOISE

Sun
Valley

84

Hailey

68

68

Mountain Home

93

Snake

Shoshone

River

84

51

93

Twin
Falls

Burley

0   25   50
Scale in Miles

N

HEADWATERS

Imprints of travel...

A brigade of forty Hudson's Bay Company trappers, together with Iroquois trappers, under Alexander Ross passed through Stanley Basin in September, 1824—they had come north up the Big Wood River, over Galena Summit, and went down the Salmon River below Challis, eventually encountering Jedediah Smith and his band of trappers ascending the Lemhi River toward Lemhi Pass.

The scarcity of beaver caused other trappers to avoid the area until 1831, when Warren Ferris trudged up the Salmon River and camped in the Basin for ten days. He clubbed salmon in the streams for food but found the same streams more bereft of beaver than when Ross's party waded through. The Ferris brigade left the area with the remark that their "visit to this now interesting country was a complete failure..."

In 1832 John Work brought his Snake River trapping expedition through Bear Valley and Stanley Basin, and the same year Captain Benjamin Bonneville spent Christmas Day with a band of fourteen trappers, and Nez Perce Indians, feasting on elk and mountain sheep. Washington Irving wrote in his account:

"Here, then, there was a cessation from toil, from hunger, and alarm. Past ills and dangers were forgotten. The hunt, the game, the song, the story, the rough though good-humored joke, made time pass joyously away, and plenty and security reigned throughout the camp."

It was over thirty years before any Euro-Americans visited the area again. This time the visitors were in search of gold.

In 1863 John Stanley's prospecting party, about seventy-five strong, set out from Warren's diggings (just

Stanley, 1930.

Salmon gigging, Bear Valley, 1939.

northeast of present McCall) after celebrating the Fourth of July with a ten-gallon keg of whiskey at Three-Finger Smith's saloon.

The expedition prospected through Bear Valley and around Stanley Basin. Uneasy about Indians, the group separated, and all but ten went back to Warren. Frank Coffin, who later ran the Pioneer Hardware House in Boise, was one of the ten and left a reminiscence of their expedition:

"After we left the separation camp, we went along about fifteen miles. Coming around a point of rocks we run onto about a hundred Indians camped on the creek below us, drying fish on cedar racks. They disappeared in a hurry in the timber behind them, and we went back on the trail behind a rock to consult, hold a council of war I suppose you would call it. We were talking a little while when we heard an Indian whoop, and six of them had ridden out on a point. One got down off his horse, laid his blanket and rifle on the ground and made signs for us to come down, send a man down to meet him and have a talk. Old [John] Stanley sent me down. I was a boy then and had to do all the running around, run the errands, and then I had a little knowledge of chinook, a little more than the older fellows, and could talk a little Indian sign language. Anyhow, they made me ambassador, so I went down and met the young Indian standing there, and I tell you he was a magnificent specimen, young and supple as a leopard. Old Stanley had told me, now you negotiate peace at any terms down there if you can, we don't want any trouble with those Indians, so after I went down we talked with a good deal of signs and a good deal of grunting, and a little chinook mixed up. The young Indian would refer back to an old Indian on the hill for advice, while I would refer to Stanley on the other side. There was a good deal of side talk, and it was an hour and a half before we got through. Old Stanley told me to insist upon their coming out of the timber and come back to the fish racks, and that when they did that we would go on. After a long time they finally came trailing back out of the timber, and we went on as agreed."

Stanley's party crossed the Sawtooth Mountains and enroute southwest to Idaho City discovered what would become known as the Atlanta Mining District on the Middle Fork of the Boise River. (Stanley Basin mining did not become prosperous until after 1900.)

Exit pursued by bear...

In July, 1881, another prospector in Bear Valley had a less fortunate encounter. His story was reported in the *Wood River News*.

"A prospector by the name of H. A. Johnson came down from the mountains on yesterday morning's stage. From the crown of his head to the soles of his feet he was the worst patched-up and "bent" prospector we have looked upon for many a day—in fact, he was but a wreck of his former self. A *News* reporter interviewed him and learned that since he left Bellevue he had taken in a great deal of the country north, and was prospecting on the Middle Fork of Salmon River. Late last week he started out mining with his prospecting tools, his partner going another way, and fell in with a fellow from Bonanza or Challis, who called himself Barber, or a similar name. They were passing through a little park when a monster grizzly bear was seen a short distance off. Barber recommended that Johnson take a shot with his Remington rifle. Johnson jumped from his horse and with a rest over his knee turned loose. The grizzly caught it and started for the party, when Barber straddled Johnson's horse quick as a flash and darted away. Johnson shouted his protest, but he had no time to fool away, and kept upon his knee, pumping shots into the advancing grizzly at [a] lightning-stroke rate; in fact, the grizzly got five shots in his carcass—one between the eyes and one through the heart—and he still kept coming. When the bear was about 25 feet off Johnson gave up experimenting and dashed for a tree. He sprang high, but the bear caught him at the left hip, tearing away the clothing and bringing down Johnson to the grass. As he fell, the bear caught him on the scalp and tore the whole business loose from near his forehead to the back of the crown. With his right hand Johnson fastened to the beast's nostrils and hung there for a moment, but he was getting weak and soon lost his hold. By this time the bear's eyes were getting glassy, but when Johnson attempted to move away from him he was roused to three severe attacks, once catching Johnson in the left shoulder; next in the left forearm, breaking both bones, and again above the elbow of the left arm, causing a serious flesh wound. That was the last nip of Mr. Grizzly, and he rolled over dead upon Johnson's gun. Now was the pluck of the hunter tried. His left arm and leg were lacerated and bleeding; his shoulder was bare and torn open, his left arm was broken in two places and seriously ripped open in another, his right hand was split by a tooth of the savage beast, and his scalp was hanging down on his shoulders, and he was alone. He had two miles to walk to his camp and then find his partner away, in all probability. He was getting dizzy, but roused and went to camp, splinted his arm, put snow about it, and started for Bellevue, accompanied by his partner.

Johnson is now under the care of Dr. Thiele and, owing to his remarkable care for himself in all the days of travel between here and [the] Middle Fork, the doctor predicts a speedy recovery. From the scene of the fight to Bellevue it cannot be less than 170 miles, and this had to be traveled over by the wounded man on horseback.

Middle Fork affords not at all a healthy climate for Mr. Barber, and at the rate he was traveling when last seen, no bear will ever catch him. The bear would weigh about 900 pounds, but Johnson carries the beast's scalp in his pocket to-day."

When there were foresters...

Because avaricious timber barons had become more serious and widespread than a plague of western pine beetles, the Forest Reserves Act of 1891 authorized the president to set aside timbered portions of the western public domain. Presidents Cleveland and Harrison reserved 33 million acres.

In 1905 the Sawtooth Forest Reserve was established by President Roosevelt—the same year that reserve management was transferred from the Department of the Interior to the Department of Agriculture, thereby giving birth to the U. S. Forest Service. A year later the Reserve was increased to 3.3 million acres; the following year it was renamed the Sawtooth National Forest. The SNF-West was managed from Boise; the SNF-East was managed from Hailey. While the Sawtooth included Stanley Basin and Bear Valley, the Middle Fork lay outside its boundaries. At present, four national forests—Boise, Challis, Payette, Salmon—portions of which were carved out of the original Sawtooth, include reaches of the Middle Fork.

During the early 1920s, officials of the Idaho Department of Fish and Game, and of the Salmon and Payette national forests, sought to increase the amount of game on the upper half of the Middle Fork by protecting the winter range. In 1925 they established the Middle Fork Game Preserve, which extended downriver to Marble Creek and up Camas Creek for several miles.

In 1930, at the urging of the visionary and astute Intermountain District Forester Richard Rutledge, Governor H. C. Baldridge selected a committee to consider a draft proposal for preserving the Middle Fork country as a "primitive area." The committee recommended the concept by a unanimous vote.

Regional Forester Rutledge then forwarded the document to the Chief Forester in Washington, D. C. In 1931 the Chief signed the Idaho Primitive Area Report. The goal was

"to make it possible for people to detach themselves, at least temporarily, from the strains and turmoil of modern existence, and to revert to simple types of existence in conditions of relatively unmodified nature [and] to afford unique opportunities for physical, mental, and spiritual recreation and regeneration."

The Idaho Primitive Area covered slightly more than 1 million acres and included the Pistol Creek and Indian

Creek drainages. Domestic sheep grazing was eliminated west of the river and north of Sulphur Creek, and the Game Preserve was allowed to expire in 1933.

In 1968 the Middle Fork was included in the Wild and Scenic Rivers Act. A dozen years later, the Primitive Area was subsumed when President Carter signed the Central Idaho Wilderness Act, establishing the 2.2 million-acre River of No Return Wilderness—one that includes the entire Middle Fork of the Salmon.

Settled lives and livestock...

Prior to the Forest Reserves Homestead Act of 1906, citizens could not legally file for a homestead in Stanley Basin, Bear Valley, or along the Middle Fork on land inside the reserves. Nevertheless, settlers squatted on the land in anticipation of the new homestead act. Often they sold their "squatter's rights" to newcomers willing to await the arrival of a surveyor.

The new Act permitted settlement and development of agricultural land (160 acres) included within the national forest. Because of the mountain climate and the thin soils, however, agricultural land was uncommon in the area. Local history recounts that early homesteads in Bear Valley were disallowed on grounds the land was "unsuitable" for farming. Old cabins were burned, leaving a residue of bitterness.

Over 100 applications were filed in the Middle Fork drainage, where conditions were somewhat milder, but only one-half were "proved-up on" (patented). Approximately two-thirds of the applicants were single; about two-thirds of the applicants who were married had children. Only three of the applicants were women. Generally, homesteads on the east side of the river were patented first, and two-thirds of the patents were issued between 1920 and 1930.

The grass in Sawtooth Valley, Stanley Basin, and Bear Valley attracted sheepmen. (Cattle, never a factor in the

Sheep outfit leaving Andy Little's ranch in Cascade for Bear Valley, early 1900s.

Stanley Basin, only arrived after lower, more accessible regions were denuded.) In 1887 sheep began grazing portions of the range now within the Sawtooth Forest. Bands were herded from Idaho City, Emmett, Cascade, and even from the Snake River country. Competing woolgrowers sheared as early as possible in the spring, then raced each other for the more desirable areas, following the retreat of the snow all summer, then trailing their bands out in the fall.

The stockman's objective was not a fat lamb; rather it was to keep the wethers growing for market as three-year-olds.

As with most agreeable arrangements that require self-restraint, the system was soon abused. In 1910 there were 334,000 sheep permitted on the Sawtooth Forest. Pioneer sheepman Ben Darrah reflected,

"The way we were ruining the country...some sort of regulation was necessary....Very few wanted government regulation, but most of us knew we needed it, and eventually all fell into line....If the (Sawtooth) national forest had not been created, the area it now embraces would soon have been a dust bed, and good range would no longer have been available."

By 1933 the number of allotted sheep on the forest had been reduced one-half. Today Idaho has fewer sheep than at any time since they were introduced to the state, and with the establishment of the Sawtooth National Recreation Area, even cattle numbers have been reduced in order to protect streambanks.

Good-bye, thanks for everything...

Mining returned to Bear Valley—and consequently the Middle Fork—again in the 1950s. Steve Bagwell, one-time editor at the *Idaho Statesman*, has written a summary of that visitation that makes a telling argument against the industry:

"When Porter Brothers Corporation began dredge-mining the uranium-rich black sands of Bear Valley Creek in 1955, it vowed to keep the pure high-country water "crystal clear," to protect some of the richest salmon and steelhead spawning beds in the entire Snake-Columbia system, and to mount a reclamation effort afterward that would eliminate all trace of its presence.

Safeguards would exceed requirements. "In a few years, it will never be evident that the area has been dredged," the firm told *Mining World* as it phased down its tax-subsidized operation in 1958 ($12.5 million).

Well, it's been more than a few years, and the devastation is incredible. Money has been poured into cleanup and reclamation plans for twenty years, only slightly diminishing the mess. Meanwhile, millions have gone into restoring fish runs, but with only limited success, mostly downriver.

The damage will still be evident 100 years from now.

Richer deposits of uranium for the nuclear defense industry were readily available at lower cost from friendly nations. However, the Atomic Energy Commission was so intent on securing a domestic supply, on national security grounds, that it brokered development of Bear Valley and about two dozen other U.S. sites.

The project was wildly uneconomical, even with 900 acres of public land free for the taking under the Mining Act of 1872. The AEC not only financed the entire mining and refining effort, but agreed to purchase the output at a fixed price well above market rates.

Miners diverted creeks and tributaries into canals and dredged channels out of existence. They shipped the radioactive ore to a mill in Lowman, Idaho, for processing.

Spawning gravel was scooped out and dumped. Forest cover was stripped. Groundwater that charges the South Fork of the Payette River was compromised.

Radioactive sediment was sent streaming down the creek, suffocating spawning beds, clogging rearing pools and muddying the Middle Fork downstream. It will be decades before the last of the excess is flushed.

Agencies have created a stack of studies. But little has happened on the ground, either in the valley or in town.

The creek is gradually cutting a new channel. The canals have been filled and the mill site fenced. Yet three decades after mining ceased, the ponds, tailings, and sediment remain while most of the fish do not."

The coming of the roads...

For many years the only road into Bear Valley was over Nip-and-Tuck grade, just northeast of Stanley.

In 1915 the District Forester in Ogden, Utah, was informed by letter from the Payette Forest Supervisor Guy Mains, "that the road from the Main Salmon through Stanley to the head of Bear Valley, a distance of approximately fifty miles, was completed by Boomer and Parsons under contract, with yokes of oxen and teams of horses, the grade being laid out by the state engineer's office."

The Forest Highway route from Boise to Stanley (Highway 21) was much longer arriving. Construction began in the 1920s. The portion from Boise to Idaho City—following the route of the Intermountain Railroad—was gravelled by 1925 but not paved until 1942. Work slowly proceeded toward Lowman and up the South Fork of the Payette; however, it was 1965 before the road opened as a through route.

The road from Ayer's Meadow to Dagger Falls-Boundary Creek was scraped out in 1958-1959 in order to haul materials for a fish ladder built alongside the falls. Once construction was completed, the road reverted to the Forest Service.

BOATMEN ON THE MIDDLE FORK

The Shootist...

Nearly 9,000 persons are waterborne through the Middle Fork canyon every summer, most of them in surety and comfort. In at least an historical sense, they are warmed by campfires they did not build and drink from creeks they did not find. To whom are they indebted? Who demonstrated the passability of this canyon and its river?

Before 1925, there is only tantalizing silence. Those who might have known have gone to bed with the shovel long ago—their tales retreat into fog.

The keelwork of the boating era, so far as *can* be known, was laid in 1926, when river-running was unarguably a nascent sport or recreation. The story begins, aptly enough, in Idaho. And it begins with a man fiercely committed to the current of the world, a remarkable omnicompetent.

Henry Weidner came west by wagon from Iowa to New Plymouth, Idaho—where he met his wife-to-be Hallie—and then to Payette, in southwest Idaho. Although of Pennsylvanian Dutch-German descent, he was an archetypal Idaho individualist.

For several years Weidner made his living as a trapper along the Payette and Snake rivers. He was also an adept carpenter; when Hallie accepted his marriage proposal, he set to work on an elaborate house in Payette. During construction, a steel flake from a nailhead cost him his sight in one eye; thereafter he wore a glass eye.

Over the next fourteen years, Hallie gave birth to a son and two daughters. Henry, ever busy, had turned to beekeeping for their principal livelihood . He had 650 hives distributed between Payette and New Meadows, ninety miles north. The honey—alfalfa and clover—was marketed under the name "Sungold" in Lewiston and Spokane.

On his return trips from those towns, Weidner's trucks carried lumber. Told he had to have a license for such hauling, he promptly opened Weidner Lumber, as well as Weidner Motors, a dealership for International trucks and Hudson automobiles, in Payette. Additionally, Weidner ran a photography studio on Main Street and served as a dealer for Shakespeare fishing gear.

At home he practiced taxidermy, did realistic oil paintings, made his own wooden furniture and boats, tanned leather, collected bird eggs (displayed in cotton nests), grew a garden, and experimented with hybrid irises.

All the while, he was an ardent and consummate hunter and fisherman. (His family credits him with being among the first to introduce pheasants to Idaho.) And even with the loss of one eye, he managed to remain a crack shot.

Henry appears to have had an instinctual affinity for water: he was a proficient swimmer, canoeist, and fisherman. In 1911, at age twenty-three (and married), he built a seven-by-twenty-four-foot sweepboat and spent three months running the Salmon River from Salmon City to Riggins, without serious mishap. He reported at the time that he already had some experience boating swift streams.

When the Weidner house in Payette, along with all its furnishings, burned, Henry built a second house, less expansive, which still stands. It was 1921, however, before he had time to make another extended river trip. He returned to the Main Salmon, traveling by train and stage to Salmon City. He brought along a greenhorn friend from Portland who "did not mind to wash dishes, which to my way of thinking is the most desirable trait to have in a fellow camper." And he brought an unusual craft: a folding canvas boat fourteen-feet long, weighing eighty-five pounds. (A year earlier he had paddled the boat on the Snake River from Glenns Ferry, Idaho, with a portage at Swan Falls, to Huntington, Oregon—about 150 miles.) This Salmon River voyage proved to be as exhilarating and no more stressful than the first.

Two visits to the mouth of the Middle Fork at its inviting canyon-confluence with the Main Salmon proved formative: Henry Weidner toyed with an idea. The motivation is clear enough in his diary of 1921:

"I suppose my main reason for wishing to run this rough piece of water with a light boat is because so far as I could find out it had never been done and the "Genus Homo" is very prone to try something new; especially if it is difficult of accomplishment."

Weidner had become increasingly fascinated by photography: he had numerous cameras, took portraits at his studio, and there did exacting color tints of scenic photographs.

Only ten years earlier, with D.W. Griffith's *The Birth of a Nation*, the motion picture had come of age, and with it came an audience for realistic films. Henry bought a hand-cranked motion-picture camera. It weighed fifty-five pounds, but he lugged it about, photographing birds and animals. He developed the negatives, printed the film, projected the results, studied them, gained competence. The idea teased his mind: Why not make his own movie of the Idaho backcountry—the Middle Fork canyon with its wildlife—and show it in the new theaters that had popped up in every town?

It was 1926 and Henry Weidner had charted his course. He selected a crew of three to accompany him: his sixteen-year-old son Wesley, a non-swimmer and green as a new foaled colt; Roy Herrington, a friend from Fruitland principally interested in prospecting; and Harold Mallett, a rancher from nearby Ontario, Oregon, who at thirty-six was two years younger than Henry.

Weidner settled on two canoes, eighteen-feet long, of maple, spruce, and canvas: an Old Town that weighed eighty-six pounds, and a Mullens sponson-type designed for still water. (Mallett had not seen the Mullens until the put-in and said it was given to Weidner "by someone who must have had a grudge against him.")

On July 2 the men arrived on Marsh Creek, a headwater tributary of the Middle Fork, in Bear Valley. It was a low-water year. Mallett looked over the Mullens canoe and said he would like to ditch the whole deal despite what he had invested in it. Weidner replied that then the trip

Weidner trip on
Marsh Creek,
1926.

would be over because neither Wes nor Roy could handle a canoe in rapids. Mallett relented.

They loaded several hundred pounds of supplies stored in waterproof bags into the canoes. The most valuable part of the cargo, the camera gear and film, went in the Old Town with the Weidners. Mallett and Herrington were sentenced to the Mullens. Mallett observed later that the sponsons kept the canoe from sinking but were a liability in fast water: "It would upset if you shifted tobacco from one side of your mouth to the other."

At dawn on July 3 the four-man navy launched. "Most rivers are toughest at their source," wrote John McPhee. The Middle Fork is the rule, not the exception. At first, Marsh Creek scarcely looks like it has ambitions to be a river, but the shallow, twisting stretches shortly give way to water that moves with rapidity. Weidner and Mallett felt they were at least seniors in the class of river running; soon they realized they had not gotten even an

elementary education. Despite early miscues, however, after thirteen miles the party finally reached Sulphur Creek Falls (now renamed Dagger).

They frogged the canoes around the falls and pushed on down the unpathed waters. Henry had 4,000 feet of film. His photographic method (before the telephoto lens) consisted of setting out salt blocks and then hiding in a blind until game animals discovered the salt. A tedious process. Often the noise of the hand-crank spooked the quarry. Diary entries at Pistol Creek total up to a ten-day wait for deer.

At one point, part of Weidner's film was spilled from his canoe in a hole about fifteen feet deep. Reported Mallett, "We could see those cans and Henry would try to get to them holding onto a rock as big as both of us could lift, but those eddies are strong and we had to just leave the film."

Weidners in camp, 1926.

Wes Weidner, age sixteen, tying on a fly.

On wilderness trips forced idleness is as much a psychological danger as forced hardships. Prolonged delays for filming began to take their toll on the other members of the group. After a quarrelsome session, Herrington announced that he was departing. He left the expedition at Survey Creek (mile 75), intent on hiking out by way of Big Creek. The rest of the party felt a surge of relief: Roy was a poor swimmer, he had served largely as ballast; moreover, with only three of them left and meager supplies, they were free to abandon the loggy Mullens canoe. (Herrington, sustained by settlers and trappers he met along the way, walked nearly a hundred miles to Cascade, where he hitched rides back home. He told Mallett afterward that it was the only part of the trip that he enjoyed.)

With shared apprehensions, the three-man party entered somber Impassable Canyon, recalling how often strangers had regaled them with the hyperbolic perils of this reach. By now, however, they had knocked the velvet off their antlers and felt a growing confidence. They chose to ignore the stories and trust their skill.

(It should be noted here that at least one man already had claimed to have taken a boat through Impassable Canyon. The Challis *Silver Messenger* [17 November 1896] reprinted an account from the Spokane *Chronicle* of a resident prospector J. W. Proctor, who had just returned to the city. The report said in part, "Proctor came near to losing his life on the way home. He started down the impassable canyon on the Middle Fork on October 1, and everything went well until he got to the mouth of Fiddle Creek twenty-five miles above the White Bird [on the Main Salmon], when the boat capsized. He lost everything and if he had not been an excellent swimmer would have lost his life.")

The Weidner party shot deer, sheep, bear, and an elk to supplement their dwindling larder. Weidner was getting good footage of mountain goats and mountain sheep. They spent three weeks in the gorge, and it was the end of September before the men decided to push on to the confluence with the Main Salmon.

Their craft pitched like a cayuse through House Rock and Jump-Off rapids, then floated the silky-swift last three miles into the River of No Return. Paddling strenuously, they crossed the stout current and landed on the far shore: from uncertain freshmen in the quickwater college of river running, they had just graduated *cum laude*.

Henry had exposed about 3,000 feet of film, he had 1,000 feet left, and Henry was nothing if not pertinacious. When they trailed upriver to Shoup (twenty miles), they found Monroe Hancock and Jack Cunningham moored there in charge of a sweepboat destined for Riggins (125 miles).

Weidner and Mallett sent a telegram to Mallett's mother in Ontario asking her to dispatch a man with a truck to pick them up—they would pay the $125 expense (it was a seven-day round trip).

Weidners on the Middle Fork.

William Rhodenbaugh, a fruit grower from Middleton, Idaho, and Joe Quist, an Ontario, Oregon, beekeeper took the shuttle job. The truck developed mechanical problems and they left it at Shoup, traveling down to the Pope Ranch at Colson Creek, three miles above the confluence of the Middle Fork and the Salmon, where the boatmen were waiting for them. (Weidner had visited the ranch in 1921.) The drivers were obdurate about not returning to Ontario unless either Weidner or Mallett went up to Shoup and fixed the truck.

Inside the house, Quist overheard Weidner persuading Mallett "that it was as much benefit to Mallett as to himself for Mallett to go on out with the truck, while he went on down the river to use the rest of his film." Rhodenbaugh recalled that Mallett said he would like to go down the river. "Weidner told him that if he could go down the Salmon River he could use the balance of the films they hadn't shot and complete the pictures which would be an advantage to both of them." Mallett with reluctance eventually concurred. The sweepboat cast off; the truck, once repaired, headed for Ontario with camp equipment and a steamer trunk full of Weidner's exposed film.

Weidner and his son, with the guidance of Hancock and Cunningham, floated through to Riggins and got back to Payette on October 20, three and a half months after their departure for the Middle Fork.

As word of their success was reported in area newspapers, requests to see the movies began to arrive. Henry was invited to a banquet given by the sportsman's club of Caldwell, Idaho. At the dinner, Jim Gipson of Caxton Printers in Caldwell was so captivated by Weidner's journey that he approached him with a suggestion: he offered to pay the expenses of a Salmon River sweepboat trip if he could accompany Weidner on it. Apparently Henry was disappointed in the results of some of the footage he had developed, for he readily accepted Gipson's proposal.

On March 27, 1927, Henry Weidner, his son Wes, cook Vern Ivey, and guides Hancock and Cunningham met in Salmon. They had timed the trip in order to photograph game at mineral licks along the river. The guides had a twenty-eight-foot scow named *Weidner* ready for departure. On March 30, with a ton of supplies aboard, the barge cast off from below the Salmon City bridge.

They floated to Cunningham's quarters at Butts Bar on the Main Salmon, about seven miles below the mouth of the Middle Fork. Weidner learned that last fall Hancock had lined his own canoe back up the Middle Fork, found the abandoned Mullens canoe, loaded its bow with a boulder, and towed it out!

Hancock, Weidner, son Wes, and Gipson took a canoe (the diary does not say which one) and pulled it back up the Salmon to the mouth of the Middle Fork, then on April 5 began lining it up the Middle Fork to Stoddard Creek (about seven miles), where for two weeks Henry photographed mountain sheep, deer, and the Indian pictographs.

While encamped, Gipson in his diary made a revealing assessment of Henry Weidner:

"4/16 Hank, from what he has dropped from time to time, is a universal genius. He has been by turns cow puncher, farmer, trapper, hotel man, artist, photographer, interior decorator, carpenter, cement man, moving picture photographer, fisherman, beeman, big game hunter, and boatman and is good at everything. He is doing something every minute that he is awake, and when he has no duties he goes to bed."

Henry Weidner, cameraman. Camera weighed 55 pounds and was hand-cranked.

They broke camp on April 19, all four men piling into the canoe with several hundred pounds of dunnage, and stroked for the Main in a driving snowstorm. That evening, short of their goal, Gipson made another disclosure:

"I have had quite an education in the matter of taking good moving pictures of nature subjects. It involves waiting in a cold blind by a lick, hour after hour, cramped, silent and lonely, without the solace even of tobacco. It necessitates hard and dangerous climbs to get scenery, and waiting for hours for the proper light and cloud effects. It calls for infinite patience and rare judgment, as well as extraordinary artistic ability. All of these my friend Weidner possesses in an extraordinary degree."

The scow in the practiced hands of Monroe Hancock made the trip down the more lenient Main Salmon without difficulties, while Henry augmented his now consider-

able footage of sweepboats, rapids, and wildlife.

Wesley drove the car from Riggins to Payette in six hours, two hours faster than the truck. (The same drive today requires just over two hours.)

Weidner's weathervane now swung toward the movie business. Once he had developed his film (at a cost of over $500), imposed captions, and edited the footage, he titled the one-hour feature *Trip of a Thousand Thrills*. Gipson at

Caxton Printers lithographed 10,000 handbills and window posters. Governor H. C. Baldridge gave it a puff. Weidner did not lack for bookings: the movie opened in Nebraska, Montana, Wyoming, Utah, and Oregon. It played in Chicago and Philadelphia. Every town in Idaho, from Ashton to Preston to Middleton, was eager for a showing. Henry was on the road for weeks at a time.

But "the unexpected floats the river like an alligator bent on mayhem." It was 1928, less than a year before the Great Depression. The price of a weekend movie matinee was twenty-five cents, an evening performance forty cents. Theaters demanded sixty percent of the gross; if the gross

Wes Weidner with 29-inch Dolly Varden, 1926.

Weidner camp,
Middle Fork.

exceeded $100 the split was 50-50, but it seldom exceeded $50. An eastern distributor in Denver defaulted on his contract. The Portland film lab dunned Henry for $317 owed for processing. Outdoor Life Publishing Company had obtained copies of the film to show to sportsman organizations in exchange for a column of free advertising for the "Salmon River Hunting and Fishing Club" that Weidner was trying to establish. Wesley wrote saying he needed $12.50 a week to keep the bee business afloat. In mid-July, the Weidners had to execute a chattel mortgage pledging all their beehives, honey crop, truck, and personal and household goods to secure a loan of $2,100 from the Payette State Bank.

Then the alligator flipped Henry Weidner's canoe bottom-up. As he watched Weidner's apparent success, Harold Mallett chafed at his own "honor without profit." Mallett had decided to marry a woman in Corvallis, Oregon, at November-end, 1927. On October 29, 1927, he filed suit against Henry Weidner for $1070. Mallett asserted that he had been orally promised a one-quarter interest in the film. A notice of attachment was published for the same property as that described in the chattel mortgage. In early December, Weidner filed an answer and a cross complaint for $283.

On May 2, 1928, a jury trial was held in Payette County before Judge Jay Downing. Eleven witnesses appeared for plaintiff Mallett: they included his two brothers, and Herrington, Rhodenbaugh, and Quist.

Mallett asserted two causes of action: that he had been hired for the trip and his services were worth $100 a month ($450); that he had advanced Weidner money for supplies and had paid certain labor and transportation bills in the sum of $620.

Weidner denied that Mallett performed any services or furnished any support or was ever employed by him. He alleged, moreover, that he took Mallett on an "excursion and pleasure trip down and along the Middle Fork," furnished a boat and equipment, and acted as guide at the

Lining canoe up Middle Fork, 1927.

"special ...request of...Plaintiff." His damages included Mallett's abandonment of the canoe ($78), a loan ($60), and unreturned camping equipment ($145).

The evidence exhibited by the plaintiff contained cancelled checks totaling $100 written by himself to Weidner, as well as checks of $80 for transportation and other expenses.

Unfortunately, the trial record was written in Pitman shorthand—the precursor to Gregg—and thus is difficult

to decipher at this time. (Trial records were not usually typed unless an appeal was taken.) The judge's instructions to the jury, however, reveal much about the case:

"The Court instructs the jury that if you find from the evidence that Plaintiff performed services for the Defendant between about July 1, 1926 and November 1, 1926, or any time between said dates, in assisting the Defendant in connection with the taking of photographic and moving pictures along the Middle Fork of the Salmon River in Idaho, and that such services were performed by the Plaintiff with the Defendant's knowledge and consent, and that the Defendant voluntarily took the benefit thereof and accepted said services, then the law will presume that the Plaintiff should be paid by the Defendant for those services unless the contrary is shown by the evidence; and if no contract is shown fixing the price, then Plaintiff would be entitled to recover what said services are reasonably worth.

The Court further instructs the jury if they shall find from the evidence that on or about the 15th day of May, 1926 Plaintiff and Defendant entered into an oral agreement under the terms of which the Defendant employed the Plaintiff to go with and assist the Defendant in taking photographic and moving pictures of scenery of the river and wildlife along the Middle Fork of the Salmon River in Idaho, during the summer of 1926, and under said contract of employment the Plaintiff was to furnish one-fourth of the expenses of transportation and supplies and his own services and was to get in pay for money and supplies furnished and services rendered one-fourth interest in all pictures that might be taken,

and if Plaintiff did furnish money and supplies and transportation and did go with Defendant and assist in the work of taking said pictures, and thereafter Defendant refused to deliver and give to Plaintiff any interest in said moving pictures taken during said period and denied that there was any agreement between himself and Plaintiff,

then the Court instructs you that the Plaintiff is entitled to recover from the Defendant the reasonable value of the services rendered by him for the Defendant, and of all moneys and supplies and transportation advanced by him to the Defendant in connection with and in assisting in taking said photographic and moving views of said scenery and wildlife."

The jury deliberated until 2:30 AM. They found for plaintiff Mallett and assessed damages at $770 plus $84 in costs. Judgment was filed and entered nine days later.

"One woe doth tread upon another's heels so fast they follow." The size of the judgment at this time must have staggered the Weidners. (Including his own legal fees, it was the equivalent of about $6800 today.) The stock market crash was still a year away, but hard times were already being felt in rural areas. (In 1930 the average family income in America was less than $800 a year.)

Henry had shipped copies of the film to a Denver distributor two days before the trial. He now apparently disposed of his remaining copy, as family members never saw it again, and the children sensed that it was not an acceptable topic of conversation. (Neither the Weidner nor the Mallett children know whether the judgment was satisfied.)

Henry Weidner

Henry continued in the bee business. In 1930 he applied to Governor C. Ben Ross for a job as a state game warden, a position he did not get. And while there is no record that he ever ran another river, he remained an enthusiastic hunter and fisherman until his death in 1954.

Wes and Hallie ran the "Sungold" honey business until 1965, when Wes died. Roy Herrington disappeared from Fruitland with no forwarding address. In 1975 Harold Mallett died in an Ontario nursing home, having lived most of his life on the land homesteaded by his parents.

Their deaths leave some many-tentacled questions: Who has Weidner's journal? (It existed.) What *was* the arrangement or agreement for that trip? Why did Mallett wait a year to file suit? Where did all the copies of the movie go? Perhaps the grappling hooks of time and chance may yet turn up some answers.

One thing more: In 1930 the United States Geological Survey crew attached Weidner's name to a rapid in Impassable Canyon, publishing it on their map in 1932. It has been supplanted by the name "Cliffside." Yet boatmen who now know the story might restore it by common usage—an altogether appropriate memorial.

Sweepboat King...

"Captain" Harry Guleke, well-known sweepboat pilot on the Salmon River, probably made a trip down a portion of the Middle Fork. As early as 1896, Cap Guleke was running his thirty-five-foot wooden scows down the Salmon River from the city of Salmon to Lewiston, Idaho, on the Snake River. The Middle Fork must have beckoned to him as he passed its confluence, and he would not have lacked the courage to attempt it.

The Salmon *Recorder-Herald* quotes Guleke as saying he had come down the Middle Fork once on a homemade raft. He remarked, "I knew I wouldn't get into a place I couldn't get out of. Sometimes I was on the raft and sometimes I was under it. But I was never afraid. And until a man is afraid, he'll be all right."

With Guleke's death in 1944, details of this trip have been lost in a haze that cannot be dissipated now (one informant guessed he might have begun at Elk Bar [mile 79] and that the year was 1925). The most plausible theory is that he moored a sweepboat at the mouth of the Middle Fork, hiked up the canyon as far as twenty miles, then being an experienced boatbuilder and able to read water, decided to cobble a raft together and go back the easy way. Obviously he lost his footing a time or two. (Guleke retired

Cap Guleke (right) running front sweep, Main Salmon, 1917.

from boating in 1933, although he did not make his last trip until 1939.)

Utah Pards...

In late July, 1935, six Utahns arrived at Bear Valley Creek with two wooden boats. Characters even in a day when individuality was normal, they were already experienced boatmen, and they planned a complete transit of the Middle Fork.

Their story begins at the Uintah County jail in Vernal, Utah. Enoch Franklin "Frank" Swain owned a brickyard in town and was deputy sheriff and undertaker. He was double-tough. At rodeo time in Vernal he put thirty-seven men in jail single handedly—about half resisted arrest. (Said Swain, "I looked like I'd been working as a meat cutter at Safeway.") He once put his own brother in jail for fighting. He acquired the nickname "Hush": when he walked into a bar, men would say, "Hush, there's the bastard now."

In 1929, Loretta Luck came to Swain and swore out a warrant for the arrest of her husband, alleging he had abandoned her and her two children. The husband was arrested in LaSal, Utah, and Swain drove down to take custody. The prisoner was Parley Galloway, a beaver trapper who used wooden skiffs of his own design to trap inaccessible reaches of the Yampa, Green, and Colorado rivers. In 1927, having learned the boatman's skills from his father, Parley had guided the Clyde Eddy party through Cataract Canyon and the Grand Canyon of the Colorado.

While incarcerated in the Vernal jail, Parley told river stories to Frank Swain and his cousin Robert "Bus" Hatch, and eventually to Bus's brother-in-law Royce "Cap" Mowrey. As Bus remembered it, "We spent as much time in jail as Parley did." Sensing opportunity, Galloway set the hook. If the cousins could help collect $250 still owed him by Eddy, he could make bail, then help them build a Galloway boat and teach them the wiles of whitewater.

A letter from the sheriff to Eddy must have been persuasive. But once out of jail, Parley vanished like a spooked trout. (He died of starvation and exposure near Richfield, Utah.) The cousins considered: they had lost their handhold, but the tug of unknown waters was as strong as ever. Hatch and Mowrey were experienced carpenters—it was their livelihood in Vernal. They could build their own boat with Parley's sketches, and they could teach themselves to run it.

Their first craft was eighteen-feet long with a four-foot beam and no decks. They launched it in late summer, 1931, on the Green River in Utah and ran Lodore Canyon and Split Mountain gorge—an instructive experience involving a capsize, a hole in the boat the size of a pie tin, and the loss of most of their food, which had been packed in jars. But they were not discouraged.

Hatch, with Mowrey's assistance, redesigned two boats. They were three feet shorter, with watertight compartments, and for food storage held carbide cans with lids that screwed flush with the deck. In October they were back in Split Mountain testing the improved version. They were pleased with the results.

Frank Swain had gone to work as a security officer for Utah Copper Company in Bingham, Utah. (He worked there for twenty-nine years without a single sick-day.) He became friends with the company doctor Russell Frazier, and with Bill Fahrni, a storekeeper in nearby Lark. Both men were invited to join the crew on a Green River–Lodore Canyon trip. Despite some difficulties, Frazier was captivated by the river and the camaraderie—he offered to finance other expeditions.

The group acquired knowhow rapidly: 1932, Lodore Canyon; 1933, Desolation, Gray, Labyrinth, and Stillwater canyons of the Green River, and Cataract Canyon of the Colorado; 1934, Grand Canyon of the Colorado. By now they had rowed over a thousand river miles and they were ready for the Middle Fork of the Salmon.

Doc Russell "Big Joe" Frazier had learned of the river from Austin Lightfoot, an Idaho hunting guide. Frazier found it easy to entice Hatch, Swain, Mowrey, and Hatch's brother Alton to take him down the Middle Fork. Fahrni came along, too.

They arrived at Bear Valley Creek on the headwaters of the Middle Fork in mid-July, 1935. Their boats were veterans of the Grand Canyon voyage: the *Lota Ve* (after Alt's oldest daughter) and *Helldiver* (Swain said it was under the water more often than on top).

As anyone who has run it knows, the Middle Fork is not a mudwater river. The top end, above Dagger Falls, is tricky with loaded craft at any stage of water, and to complicate matters, 1935 was a low-water year. They made less than seven miles the first day. On the Mohs scale, Middle Fork granite is harder than Utah sandstone. The bottoms of the boats took a stone stropping. Alt Hatch wrote that the creek "was one continuous rapid and too shallow and rocky to get boats through without pushing and leading." Mowrey remarked that it was "like running a wheelbarrow down a stairway to put a boat through this canyon."

The men struggled four days to make their way over rocks and trees that interrupted the narrow, twisting channel. Twice Hatch and Mowrey repaired the floors with wood split from jack pines. As their tar supply ran out, they reached Sulphur Falls (now Dagger Falls). The water was low enough that running the falls was out of the question ("Rocks were sticking up like tombstones," recalled Swain).

Three cowboys on horseback, pushing cattle through to the meadows, happened by, and the boatmen asked them if they might use their horses to help drag the boats around the falls. The cowboys obliged, and the horses lunged the loads up and along the slope to a point where the boats could be slid back down to the river. At this point the crew called a huddle. It had taken four days to get this far. They concluded that the better part of wisdom would be to cache the boats above the falls for the winter and come back earlier next summer when the flow would be more favorable.

They hiked out to a ranger station and sent a message for a packer to come and get their supplies. Neither daunted nor dispirited, the men were persuaded only timing had affected the outcome. They would return.

Meanwhile, back at the Main...

In the fall of the same year, the National Geographic Society set off on a scow trip down the Main Salmon River. At the confluence of the Main Salmon and the Middle Fork they met Clyde and Don Smith, river people with a cabin on the downstream side of the confluence. Hoping to discover one edge of the Idaho Batholith, the Geographic expedition made arrangements with the Smiths to take a wooden boat up the Middle Fork.

With Clyde Smith standing in the bow of his boat fending off rocks with a pole, the four other members of the party roped and lined the boat upriver better than three miles. They camped for the night.

Horsing the boats
around Dagger
Falls, 1935.

Smiths pulling boat up Middle Fork, 1935. In 1937 they used the same method to go as far as Elk Bar.

The next morning, without having found the desired geological evidence, they had to turn back. With Don and Clyde Smith running oars like sweeps off the front and rear of the boat, they slipped back down to the Main. Boatmen were probing the Middle Fork from both ends.

Return of the Pards...

In late winter Frazier inquired about the depth of the Idaho snowpack and since Lightfoot gave him an encouraging reply, the Utahns made plans to renew their effort. Frazier obtained some conveyor belting in Bingham with which to cover the bottoms of the boats left above Sulphur

Middle Fork crew, 1936: (back row, left to right) Royce Mowrey, Bill Fahrni, Alt Hatch, Frank Swain; (front row) Wallace Calder, Bus Hatch, Russ Frazier.

Falls. Hatch and Mowrey built two new boats, only fourteen-feet long and forty-two inches wide and, to save weight, left them undecked. ("Light as a cork," Mowrey said.) The bottoms were fashioned from three-quarter-inch plywood, the ribs from oak, and the sides were waterproof Masonite. Straps allowed the oars to pivot against a rowing pin. They named the new boats *What Next* and *Who Cares*.

The group, which had added Wallace Calder, a dentist from Vernal, departed Bingham, Utah, for Stanley, Idaho, with two cars pulling the boats on trailers. They arrived at Bear Valley Creek above Cape Horn in early July, a week earlier than the previous year, and one glance told them that the water was higher.

They slid the new boats into the creek, tied them against the tug of the current, and loaded just enough food aboard to see the crew to Sulphur Falls. Bus Hatch was to take one boat with Calder, and Swain the other accompanied by Austin Lightfoot, while the rest of the group traveled by horseback to the falls. The boatmen cast off at 5:00 AM on July 7 (1936) and were swiftly pulled down-

40

Same group, (front row) Blackie Marshall.

stream. Their new boats took to the creek like goslings to water. A day and a half later they arrived at Sulphur Falls, well ahead of their pards. Compared to the year before, it was a boatman's holiday.

After setting up camp, Swain began cooking dinner. Lightfoot was sick and apprehensive. He lay under a tent fly, while a light rain fell. Hatch, as usual, went off to catch fish for dinner.

When he returned he brought two men with him, their story of interest in its own right.

John "Blackie" Marshall had come to Murtaugh, Idaho, from Iowa at the age of four. John Cunningham, an early Salmon River sweepboat pilot, befriended him. (Cunningham, in fact, had been one of the boatmen on the National Geographic probe in 1935.) On a hunting trip, Marshall had gotten interested in floating the Middle Fork. A friend informed him it was too rough for a canoe, but he did not dismiss the idea.

Bus Hatch nailing conveyor belting on the boat bottom, 1936.

Depressed by the unhappy end of a romance, and now
thirty years old, he built a cedar plank boat and decided to
run the Middle Fork with it. His concerned parents had
insisted that he take along a friend of their choosing: O.
W. "Atrie" Hestbeck. Blackie agreed.

Once they launched the boat in Bear Valley Creek it
became obvious that his parents had sabotaged the trip.
The first time Hestbeck got the oars he deliberately took
the boat into a rock, wrecking it beyond repair. They were
able to salvage some groceries. Marshall shrugged and
decided they might as well backpack down the Middle
Fork. Still despondent, he encountered Hatch and Swain.
Since they had decided to let Lightfoot return to Clayton,
they invited Marshall to join them. Said Swain, "We'll kill
you and it won't cost you a cent."

When the rest of the party arrived, they portaged the
new boats around Sulphur Falls—the only portage of the
trip—and while supplies were ferried, Hatch and Mowrey
worked over the bottoms of the *Lota Ve* and *Helldiver*.
They applied the conveyor belting to the boat bottoms
rubber-side-out, fastening it with tar, screws, and nails.

Lightfoot and Hestbeck headed back out with the
packstring.

Cap Mowrey with Bill Fahrni took one of the new
boats; Alt Hatch with Dr. Calder took the other. Frank
Swain rowed the *Helldiver* with Doc Frazier as his passen-
ger, alternating leads with Bus Hatch who carried Blackie
Marshall in the *Lota Ve*. The rest of the boats shirttailed
along behind. (Hatch [age 34] and Swain [age 36] being
the most experienced boatmen, took the worst boats,
thereby establishing a tradition which has been studiously
ignored by second-generation boatmen ever since.) Whenever Bus hung up, Marshall jumped out and pushed, while
the other boats, thus alerted, sought a slightly different
channel. For the first two days he was as wet as if he had
fallen overboard.

Events proceeded smoothly enough. The river continued to pull them downstream: nine miles, twelve miles,

twenty miles. At the Indian Creek guard station, Frazier mailed a letter for the Vernal Express through the Forest Service patrolman:

"Boys have we got this river under our belts! The two old boats are in good shape and with new bottoms we should have very little trouble making it from here on out. The river is a little lower than we had planned but with Frank Swain and Bus Hatch as lead-off men, the rest of us should be able to follow. This Vernal crowd is some water outfit and are by far the best fast-water boatmen in the world."

Trout were thick as shingles on a barn roof and deer as common as roofing nails. On different days Calder, Frazier, and Fahrni were each pitched head over ears into the river, but there were no wrecks. They stopped to visit the George Crandalls at Brush Creek (now the Flying Resort Ranch), and later Earl Parrott at his cabin above the river. In six days they arrived at the confluence with

Bus Hatch restoring his oar in Velvet Falls; Blackie Marshall restoring his equilibium. Hatch died in Utah in 1967; Marshall in Idaho in 1981.

Frank Swain, Middle Fork, 1936. Lids of carbide cans used for food storage are visible on aft deck.

Cap Mowrey in
Waterwheel
Rapid.

the Salmon River and called on the Smiths, who occupied
the cabin there. The group was out of flour because Frazier
packed it in paper bags, which quickly absorbed water.
They traded whiskey and lard for new flour. That night in
camp Marshall was made a member of the Colorado River
Club. The river had treated them leniently.

They pushed on down the muscled current of the
Main Salmon until misfortune overtook them for the first
time. Coming around a bend in the river, they spotted a
bear and her cub feeding on berries. Thinking they might

capture the cub by separating it from its mother, Swain and Mowrey started rowing to head them off. They were holding almost even as the bears scrambled along the bank. Suddenly the roar of water told them they were bearing down on Big Mallard Rapid, too late to dig for shore. The hole behind the large boulder on the left shore yawned. Swain's boat got out from under him as he went in. Mowrey went right over the rock and spilled as well. He got tangled up in an empty five gallon tar can and his leg was broken by the edge of the boat, probably as it slammed a rock. Bus and Alt had held back in case the cub retreated. Now, seeing the men in trouble, Bus rushed to the rescue but also overturned. He and Marshall managed to get their boat ashore, as did the others. Alt and Calder lined their boat through. Needless to say, the bears were long gone.

Since Frazier's plaster of paris got wet in the turnover, he was unable to set Mowrey's leg. Instead, Frazier took over as Mowrey's boatman. They pulled into Riggins two days later, three and a half days from the Middle Fork, having completed the second documented full-length run of the river. (Mowrey's leg did not get set until he got back to Vernal.)

They gave two of the boats to some folks in Riggins. The *What Next* was later traded for beer at Boulder Dam, and the *Lota Ve* seems to have gone the way of most old boats.

Russell Frazier wanted to run the Middle Fork again in 1937. Bus Hatch and Royce Mowrey built him two new boats but were too busy with a construction contract in Bonanza, east of Vernal, to get away for the trip. When the party arrived at Bear Valley Creek, they found the water much higher than the previous year but set out anyway. Swain, however, was the only experienced boatman. (Marshall and Fahrni were along, as was Hack Miller, a writer for the Deseret News of Salt Lake City.) They soon felt like they were riding a ducking stool. Furthermore, according to Miller, once the Masonite and mahogany

Ill-fated boat, 1937.

were exposed to water, it proved weak and brittle com-pared to plywood, and after some consultation the men prudently decided to abort the trip. Blackie Marshall was sent to get a packer for their supplies.

During the evening, following a bit of Rocky Moun-tain cheerwater, partly out of frustration and disappoint-ment that all his pards had not come on the trip, Doc took an axe to the sides of the boats. He had paid for them, of course, and no one said anything. Marshall returned the next day to find the boats ruined and everyone rather disgruntled.

The *Deseret News* later reported that the boats had problems. This caused some hard feelings on the part of Hatch and Mowrey, who believed the boats as worthy as the ones used the year before and those boats, in the proper hands, had been adequate for the conditions. Sensibilities were eventually mended between Hatch and Swain, but the relationship was never really repaired with Doc Frazier. (When Blackie Marshall died in 1981, the last of the Hatch-Swain-Frazier crew was gone.)

Ghost boat...

The summer of 1937 coincides with a boating enigma on the Middle Fork. Its source is a paragraph in *Foldboat Holidays* edited by Jack Kissner, owner of Folboat Corporation. W. S. "Stu" Gardiner contributed a five-page chapter. Gardiner was a rock climber and foldboat paddler in the 1930s-1940s, who worked at the Zion Savings Bank in Salt Lake City. That summer (1937) he paddled his foldboat from North Fork on the Main Salmon down to the mouth of the Middle Fork. At the foot of the first big rapid below the mouth of the Middle Fork, he wrote:

"...there were two fellows in a small scow. They had just finished bailing water out of their boat so they helped me dump the water from mine and then we continued downstream together. The super-streamlined foldboat presented a strange contrast alongside the square ended scow. These fellows had run the wild Middle Fork River from the headwaters and were now heading down the River of No Return in their strange looking craft. Before they left us at the end of the road I procured some valuable data on bad spots of the Middle Fork of the Salmon which I hope to be able to run next summer. From the reports which they gave, this should be an ideal fast water trip for foldboaters."

Nothing else. The guest book at the Hood Ranch sheds no light. Who they were and what they were doing is simply another Middle Fork mystery.

Very hard work, 1939...

In 1939 Swain and Frazier succeeded in running the river again. They took five wooden boats. Hack Miller of the *Deseret News* was along. So was Amos Burg, who ran a rubber boat built by the Air Cruiser Company, the first raft to run the length of the river. Willis Johnson, who had

been with Burg and Holmstrom in the Grand Canyon the
year before, was a boatman on this trip.

Charles Kelly, age fifty, a writer from Salt Lake City,
kept the most interesting journal of the voyage. Born in a
Michigan lumber camp and maltreated by his preacher-
father as a child, Kelly had a rather negative outlook. But
he learned music and the printing trade from his father,
served in World War I, and after a stint of college at
Indiana, moved west to Salt Lake City and married. In
Utah, Kelly became a passionate amateur western historian, writing a half-dozen books and scores of magazine
articles. On the eve of World War II, he and his wife
moved to Fruita, Colorado, where he was employed as the
first custodian of newly established Capitol Reef National
Monument, a position he kept for eighteen years. In 1958
he retired to Salt Lake City, where he pursued his interest
in history until his death in 1971. Kelly's journal is worth
quoting here because it conveys the laborious effort re-

quired to get the wooden boats down the first fifteen miles of the creek-river, and because he comments about people along the river.

"Left Salt Lake Friday morning, June 23, 7 a.m. riding truck with three boats and all equipment. Party consisted of Dr. R. G. Frazier, myself, Frank and Gib Swain, Hack Miller and Bill Fahrni. Two truck drivers from Bingham. Reached Ketchum, Idaho, late that afternoon. Visited Sun Valley and met Harriman and his daughter. Nice people. Took a lot of pictures leaving Sun Valley. Met Amos Burg and Willis Johnson here. Burg had some trouble getting his films out of the express office. Spent some time at Lightfoot's gambling joint. All slept in a cabin. Had been invited to stay at Sun Valley, but [we] looked too tough.

Frazier-Swain-Miller trip, 1937.

Sat. 24th—Loaded everything and hit the river about 10 a.m. Slept cold. The Middle Fork here is shallow and full of rocks. Water very cold. Within an hour we had to stop, unload Frank's boat and caulk it with strips from my sheet. Took over an hour. The boats are stuck on rocks half the time and we have to lift and drag them along. I am riding with Doc. Burg's boat floats over everything. About a mile above Marsh Creek we struck a deep hole full of big salmon. Frank snagged one and we baked it in dutch oven for supper. Very fine. We made camp just above mouth of Marsh Creek. Everybody hungry, cold and tired. Doc says the worst is over. We have all been ducked several times stumbling over the slippery rocks. We have rubber soled shoes without hobnails, and slip at every step, bruising our legs. At mouth of creek just above Marsh Creek we found the two old boats Doc abandoned last year and he decided to take them on through. Willis Johnson takes the old "Deseret News" and Gib Swain takes the "Blue Goose." We have enough extra oars. They are

Not
like Boundary
Creek!
Unloading boats
Bear Valley, 1939.
Cars were Fahrni's
Studebaker coupe
(left) and Miller's
Ford sedan.

water tight, though warped. A short distance below we found the remains of the paper boat plastered against a rock and battered to pieces. Amos Burg stepped out of his rubber boat tonight with dry feet. Burg and Doc took some shots, I got a few but was too busy with the boat to take pictures.

Mon. 26th—Came down to about 1 and 1/2 miles above Sulphur Falls. Tried to make the falls, but it got dark on us and everybody was worn out. Made camp in the brush. Everybody was wet to the neck. Traveled about 12 hours, literally carrying the boats most of the way. I am riding with Doc. Hack takes the Polly alone. Gets stuck often and is worn out. The rubber boat slips over everything. Amos got his feet slightly wet today.

Tues. 27th—Everybody sore and stiff. Started late. Went down about a mile when Hack got his boat stuck between two rocks and it filled. We all went back to help get it off and in trying to move it the weight of water

Barrel contained salt for preserving fish. Ranger on the far right was nicknamed "Bisquick" because he did not know how to use sourdough. Photo courtesy of Hack Miller.

punched a hole a foot square in the bottom. Had to un-load it and dry most of the bedding on the bushes. My bedding and pack kept dry. Left it overturned in the river and went on down to Sulphur Falls. Found Bill Fahrni and Prigmore. Neldon, one of the drivers, had come down the river with us, while Bill went around with Prigmore to show him the way to Sulphur Falls. They had been expect-ing us and were worried, especially when they saw part of the boat bottom come floating by. We unloaded the boats and got one of the horses brought in by Bill and Prigmore to pack the stuff to camp at the falls. Hack took a horse and went back to the Polly for his bedding and mine. I rested most of the day. Laid in the sun to take the soreness out of my legs. Hack, Bill, Frank, and Prigmore fished. Amos took his boat over the falls while I shot movies for him. Boat got caught on a boulder in the lower falls but pulled off without damage. Amos has plenty of nerve. Frank will try to take the wooden boats over the falls tomorrow and pack the stuff down on horses.

Willis Johnson, Bear Valley, 1939.

Amos Burg and first rubber raft, 1939.

Wed. 28th—Found some discarded shoes full of
hobnails. Pulled them out and drove some in my shoes,
also Doc's and Frank's. Ought to help. Salmon started
biting on salmon eggs, and they caught five. Lots of ex-
citement and some pictures. Neldon and Prigmore started
back about noon with a load of fish, taking out letters and
some films. They have about 10 miles to pack out to the
nearest ranch where they left the truck. After lunch we
started letting the boats over the falls. First was the Blue
Goose. Let it down the left chute O.K. but it got caught in
the boil at the bottom and wouldn't float away until it was
half full of water. Took the others over a smaller trickle
mostly by main strength. They were dumped in the pool
below and caught by Doc and Willis. When they were all
down we let them over the second drop and landed them
below camp. All done in 3 hours without undue strain or
accident. Amos photographed most of the operation and
says it will be the highlight of the picture.

Thurs. 29th—Warmer last night. Slept good. Just
after I went to sleep Willis asked Doc to pull a tooth for
him. Doc tried the pliers but they wouldn't work, so he

pushed it out with his thumb. Very painful. This morning his face is badly swollen and he suffers considerable. This morning we packed all the stuff down to the boats and reloaded them. Willis rides with Amos on account of his tooth. I take the old tub. Shot several rapids O.K. but just above Sulphur Creek I went around a boulder and landed on a log sticking out from shore. The boat filled and I climbed out on the log. We couldn't work it loose, so Hack started chopping the log on the downstream side. Then he started chopping on the upstream side. By that time all the rest, including Amos, were on the bank above ready to take photographs. After four or five strokes, the log broke off like a match, dumping Hack in the river. He lost the axe. When the log gave way I tried to ride with the boat, but it was waterlogged and turned over spilling me into the river between the boat and the log. I managed to get free and floated down to where the boat caught on some rocks in shallow water. Nobody hurt. But none of the photographers got any pictures. Made camp just below Sulphur Creek and stayed the rest of the day to let Willis rest, as he is in bad shape. Doc gave him a lot of pills and he slept for three hours. Most of the others went fishing up Sulphur Creek. Caught a lot of small trout. Here we met an engineer who spends his summers in this section. He had a movie and got some pictures as we came down. Doc walked with him downstream about a mile to where a big slide had choked the river. Says we have some hard work ahead. Just before the spill we passed a cable. Old Dodge, a miner, lives here, and Mr. and Mrs. Madden. Latter looks like an outlaw, but the woman is rather good looking. Have comfortable cabins. There is more water in the river now, but it is almost one continuous rapid.

Friday, 30th—Came down a mile to the rock slide. It came down (with several others) last summer in a cloudburst. Had dammed up the river for a quarter mile. Slide was 20 feet deep. The stream here was full of big rocks. We lined the boats down. Very hard work. Took a lot of pictures. A mile further was another nearly as bad but with a more open channel. Frank took all the boats through in about an hour. We then came to Velvet Creek and Velvet Falls, a 5 foot sheer drop. All the boats shot over it nicely, but Amos was out of film and didn't get it. We then had several miles of good going. Below Soldier Creek we got into some fast ones with big waves. Frank broke an oar, hit a rock and dumped Bill Fahrni, who swam to a rock and was rescued later with a rope. Finally got to Sheepeater Hot Springs which was a nice camp. Some old cabins on the flat below the spring. All took a hot bath and felt better. I rode with Amos all day in order to get pictures. The rubber boat runs over everything smoothly. Amos wrenched his back again. Willis took the old tub today. Everybody badly stove up. I got some new bruises. Tick bite has become infected and is quite painful. Got an infection in my eye first day and it is still sore. Stopped at Soldier Creek but no one was there. Hack's shoes have gone to pieces. Frank killed a young deer tonight. Bear tracks seen on the hill. Fine mess of trout for supper. No salmon seen today. Had a long conversation with Amos coming down. He thinks he might make a colored short of the Great Salt Lake, and possibly a Navajo picture in color. We could work together on both. Warmer today, good weather, more water. The worst is supposed to be over now. Boats all leak badly and need repairs. Will soon be short of oars. Jack Crane, now foreman at Bingham, built these cabins years ago. Still comes here every summer. The main cabin is papered with Sat. Eve. Posts dating March to June, 1911 advertising Apperson cars, etc.

July 1—Joe Bump came to camp from his place a mile above. Has some mining claims in here and has been here 15 years. A few years ago he tried to take a raft of lumber and pipe down from Sulphur Creek, but it broke up and he lost nearly all of it. He says there are 2 more slides below. We had to repair the boats and didn't start till noon. Had some exciting going, punched holes in bottom of two boats, had to unload to repair them. Mahogany is too brittle for bottoms. Passed two small slides, then half a mile of still water, and then a hell of a slide. Lined boats

through. Amos ran it. Two trees at top of channel and one at the bottom. Came down with good going to Pistol Creek falls. Amos ran it as usual but we had to line through on account of a bad turn and logs lodged below. Camped just below falls on sandy beach. Fire warden's cabin here, and cable bridge. Doc called out on the forest phone line. Had venison steaks, potatoes, and gravy, and biscuits. Very good. About a mile above here we passed a new placer camp, with water wheel, fine cabin, garden, and log footbridge. Tick bite sore and makes me groggy. Eye still sore. New bruises today, and a bad muscular strain in the belly. Too sore and tired to enjoy anything.

 July 2— Left Pistol Creek 9 a.m. and came down to Loon Creek. About 40 miles (?). Good going. Lined one

Regatta, 1939: (lower right, clockwise) Doc Frazier "Stefansson"; Hack Miller, "Polly B"; Charles Kelly, "Also Ran"; Amos Burg, "Charlie"; Frank Swain, "Rimrock"; Gib Swain, "Blue Goose"; taking picture, Willis Johnson, "Deseret News."

small chute. No broken oars, no trouble. Everybody rowed all day, all tired. Not many pictures today. Timber thinning out, hills red granite. Just above Marble Creek Amos picked up Mary Madsen, walking down from Pungo Creek, 7 miles, with mail. Her stepfather is Milt Hood, runs a small dude ranch. She will teach school this fall. Her mother has not been out for 2 years. Nearest road is 18 miles. P. O. is Cascade, Idaho. Stopped at the ranch for half an hour. Fine garden. Mary rode on the front of rubber boat and got her pants wet. Mr. and Mrs. Lovell have a nice ranch at Loon Creek, acres of hay. Been here 11 years. She is a nurse for the surrounding country. Nice cabin and garden. They rent horses to occasional hunters and dudes. Fixed a canvas over the rear of the old tub to keep out the waves. Works fine. Venison steak and gravy for supper. Amos eats four times as much as me, twice as much as Doc. Weather warm, plenty of water now. No new bruises today.

Lining at Dagger Falls. Photos courtesy of Hack Miller.

July 3—Came down to Crandall's ranch. Good going, only one falls and a few narrow rapids. Fishing most of the time, didn't make many miles. Dark day, few pictures. Timber mostly gone, canyon steep and barren. Crandalls have been here 12 years. She is about 73, and he is 53. They run some cattle and dudes. Have handled 800 hunters in 12 years. She is very shrewd. They own several ranches and have money. Forest airfield near here. New cable bridge, brought in cables by plane. This ranch was started about 50 years ago. Across the river is Mormon ranch, which has always been run by Mormons. It is older than this place. A suicide, lunatic, and murderer are buried over there. It is 20 miles to a road at Wilson's ranch, "The Cove," and 60 miles to a store. An old orchard here. We had some fine cherries. The old lady came down to camp after supper to visit.

July 4—Mrs. Crandall rode through one rapid with us in the rubber boat. Said it was the thrill of her life. Came down to the hermit's at Parrott Creek. Dark day, few pictures. River runs into Impassible Canyon, steep walls, narrow stream. No trail along the river in here. We made no portages or linings, but had several tailtwisters with the last water, big rocks and high waves. Two miles above Parrott's Amos saw two mountain goats. After we passed we heard two shots. Doc said he saw a man on the mountain with a gun, he waved at them and then shot at them. Frank says he was shooting at the goats. Stopped at the hermit's river cabin. No sign of recent occupation, no fresh workings. Nothing in the cabin, but grub cached nearby in the bushes. Poison sign over the door and on the cache.

July 5—[See Mile 89.9, Nugget Creek, for entry involving visit with Parrott.] Frank and Gib killed two mountain goats.

July 6—Parrott had supper with us last night, then climbed back up to his cabin. Came down again just as we finished breakfast. Seemed more friendly. Doc gave him a keg of salt, and some gallon tin cans with lids. I gave him a box of cigars. Seemed to enjoy them. Posed for pictures.

Marshall's boat as it appeared three years after his wreck. New York Explorer's Club flag waves from the stern of Berg's raft.

Rescuing the "Also Ran"—not one of the new boats.

Panned some gold for us... [he] Came down to Butts Bar and met John Cunningham. Some nice rapids in Middle Fork, good pictures. Hit the Main Salmon. It is slightly muddy from placering. Placer miners all along the banks, mostly young men. Plenty of water now, easy going. Stopped to photogaph old miner. Cunningham has a fine garden and orchard. Puts up his own fruit. Has a hydraulic. Is an old river man. Guided National Geographic party a few years ago. Has a big file of Geographics....The young mountain goat for supper was the best meat I ever ate.

July 7—Camped 4 miles below Hancock's at an old diggings. For 20 miles below Cunningham's we passed placer miners. None beyond Salmon Falls. Passed men and women working placer, and below two men with sailboat trying to get upstream. Many rapids but nothing important except Salmon falls. Spent two hours there taking pictures. Some good ones. All came through fine except Johnson who got caught and held in the boil at the base of the falls. Doc broke an oar but had a spare. Made about 30 miles today. Cunningham rode down 4 miles with us to show us some Sheepeater pictographs and walked back from Horse Creek. Roast Mountain goat for lunch. Fine meat.

July 8— Came down to Warren's bar. Passed Big Mallard without trouble. Big waves. River quiet between rapids. Stopped at Ayres place. Fine garden and "Swiss" cabin, with roses. Very picturesque. 3 acres cleared. Has cows and a bull. An old Swede lives with him. Been here 5 years. He is a big man. I worked with Amos boat all day. Still have 45 miles to go.

July 9—Came down to Riggins Hot Springs, arr. 6 p.m. Everybody pooped out. 109 in the shade here, hot wind on the river. Lots of smooth water today, also some bad rapids with big waves. Hit one without stopping to look. Amos was behind. Doc and I got sideways, one wave filled us and the next turned us over. I had indigestion and rode with Doc all day. Amos was mad because he didn't get the picture. So at Carrey Falls Frank and Gib deliberately ran into the biggest waves we had seen, in a narrow chute.

Frank was ahead, nearly overturned, but finally got through. Gib came behind, hit the wave, his boat started back toward the chute, then turned end for end, dumping him head first into the boil. He didn't come up for 50 feet. Came up under the boat, climbed in and pulled to shore. Amos got his picture, also Willis Johnson got one for Doc. I got two shots.

July 10—Pulled the boats out and sorted the stuff. Everybody is glad the trip is over. Left Riggins 2:30 p.m. rode all night, arr. Salt Lake 9:30, July 11."

Willis Johnson, boatman on the journey, made a prophetic entry in his journal:

"We may have rubber boats next year for they add to the thrills of boating, but it will be hard to have a more thrilling or enjoyable trip than this one we have just finished. Although I believe ...open boats can be taken on through, it will be much better to have rubber boats, for Amos Burg has proven them to be far superior to any other kind of boats even though a person will have his share of upsets if he isn't on the alert all the time."

Oregon oars...

In a curious historical coincidence, an independent wooden boat followed three days behind the Swain-Frazier party that year. Woodie Hindman, Texas-born cabinet maker and boat builder from Eugene, Oregon, and his wife, Ruth, were rowing the river on a private fishing trip.

If an "adventure" indicates poor planning, Woodie was no adventurer—he knew fishing and he knew boats. Hindman had been drawn to Oregon from Texas—where he had been a cowboy cook on the King Ranch, and later a hotel owner in McLean—by his fly-fishing experiences on the McKenzie River. He worked for Tom Kaarhus, a Eugene boatbuilder, before opening a boat shop of his own in Springfield, Oregon. Summertime brought him supplemental income from fishermen who wanted a river guide.

A fortunate fusion of interest and skill had prompted Hindman to redesign or modify the McKenzie River drift boat until it was the envy of every hard-hulled oar boat on the water: lighter by 400 pounds than its predecessors, infinitely more maneuverable and wave-worthy than any rowboat or dory.

June, 1939, found Woodie Hindman, along with Ken Taylor and Ed Thurston, guiding the Adolph Spreckels party down the Main Salmon in three McKenzie River-type boats. Woodie noticed the waters of the Middle Fork as he floated past its confluence with the Salmon, and he got a tantalizing glimpse up that undefiled canyon—he decided it looked like a fine fishing stream and began

asking questions. A Forest Service fellow told him there were trails in the canyon but that boating it was a poor idea; Monroe Hancock at Bear Bar said he had run some of it with a boat and it was tough going.

Back home in Eugene, Woodie's wife readily endorsed his plan to boat the unfamiliar stream. They left during the third week of July, with their McKenzie River driftboat (fourteen-feet long, 200 pounds) in tow on a trailer.

Following a 500-mile drive, they stopped at the Cape Horn dude ranch along the road to their camp on Bear Valley Creek. Said the foreman who greeted them: "Where do you think you're going with that boat?"

"Had a fool notion we might run the Middle Fork."

The cowboy advised them to get as far down the canyon as they could before wrecking because then he could charge them more for the pack trip out. (Perhaps he was the same packer who brought Swain and Frazier out in 1935 and 1937.)

Unperturbed, Woodie and Ruth launched their boat that afternoon (July 20). The water was lower than a salmon redd and they made only three miles. They saw the remains of Blackie Marshall's boat transfixed on a rock; a reminder—if they needed one—of the packer's fee.

The second day, with spells of walking and pulling, they reached the confluence with Marsh Creek. The added water was welcome, but there were still more rocks than river. Said Woodie:

"From there to the falls we did everything but turn over. On this stretch of the river from Marsh Creek to the falls, I think anyone looking for rough water won't be disappointed. It is practically an eight-mile rapid. The holes between the rapids are not long enough to give a fellow time to spit on his hands before he is in another one."

That evening they beached the boat, inverted it, and applied three vital patches.

The couple arrived at Dagger Falls the afternoon of day three. Leaving the boat moored to a tree, they went down to inspect the drop. "She was a ragged looking place to try to put a boat through," Woodie recalled. After study, they decided to remove their provisions and line the rapid. With Ruth in the boat handling a thirty-foot fending pole and her husband roping along the bank, they worked their way through. "That boat cut some funny capers but our faces were very sincere until she quit bouncing around at the bottom. We were able to grin a little after that."

A layover day was used to portage supplies. Then they pushed off again. They dodged rocks at the slides, visited miners at Pistol Creek, and the Hoods at Thomas Creek. Cutthroat and rainbow fishing was all they had hoped it would be; grouse and mountain sheep were numerous. In seven days the Hindmans arrived at the confluence with the Main Salmon. They hiked upriver to the CCC camp at Indian Creek, where a telephone call summoned a driver with their car.

The Hindman trip had a significant consequence: It introduced the Middle Fork to a number of Oregon guides—guides who came from a professional whitewater tradition as lengthy as any in the west at that time. Nearly a year to the day of the first trip, Hindman was back in Bear Valley with Prince Helfrich, Harold Dobyns, George Godfrey, and three wooden boats.

Helfrich was a charter member of the McKenzie River Guides Association. Born in central Oregon in 1907, he spent his boyhood in the woods and on the waters, graduating from the University of Oregon with a degree in geology. He had worked as a hunting and fishing guide during college and by the mid-1930s had embraced guiding as a career. Prince was the first guide to boat portions of the Deschutes, Rogue, Blitzen, and lower John Day rivers. His reputation grew with his years.

Harold Dobyns was an employee of the U.S. Fish and Wildlife Service in Oregon, and as far as can be determined at this time, the first man to boat the middle Owyhee.

Prince Helfrich on upper Middle Fork.

George Godfrey was an assistant professor of journalism at the University of Oregon. Though a rubber raft was brought along for Godfrey's use, he quickly decided it was unsuited to this creek, so he rode with Prince. Their journey was without mishap, and Prince's diary reveals that he received a $50 fee.

Helfrich and Hindman got along like a pair of oars. They collaborated in assembling fishing groups, paid expenses and shared the profit. In July, 1941, they ran two Middle Fork trips. Concise notes indicate the charges were $160 and $200 and that a $100 tip was received from the second party. (It is worth noting that these guides, despite unrivaled fishing, already had the perspicacity and sportsmanship to use barbless hooks, realizing the fishery was finite. Had all guides and guests possessed similar insight, the river's cutthroat population would not have been depleted.)

Ivy Leaguers...

In August, 1940, the Middle Fork added some ivy to its genealogy. Alexander "Zee" Grant, a recent Harvard graduate, was the twenty-six year-old son of an affluent Boston family. On a trip to Germany, he discovered the "foldboat" —a framework of replaceable hardwood parts encased in a taut, durable rubber hull. Once having paddled the Isar River there, he became a whitewater convert. In 1939 he ran the Green River through what is now known as Dinosaur National Monument, and a month before he arrived on the Middle Fork he won the first national whitewater championship on Rapid River in Maine, reputedly a formidable river.

Grant had been hired by the Union Pacific as a publicist for Sun Valley. Knowing Idaho meant rivers, he brought his "kayak" —made by Folbot Corp. of N.Y.— along with his luggage. When he learned of the Middle Fork (probably from the manager of Sun Valley, or from Austin Lightfoot, whom he knew), he asked two friends to join him in a descent of it: Rodney Aller, Yale law student and river rat, and Colman Nimick, a rookie recruit from New York.

They arrived at Bear Valley Creek on August 13 in a yellow station wagon with three blue foldboats on top: *Sawtooth Flyer*, *Archduchy of Montenegro*, and *No Name*. Inflated inner tubes were stuffed into the bow and stern of the seventeen-by-three-foot boats, held in place by about 150 pounds of gear in waterproof duffel bags. The bags were covered with inflated air mattresses beneath the rubber decks, which were tied in position "ready to be pulled about our waists with the drawstring that we held in our teeth when plowing through the heaviest water." Red sponson tubes were lashed to the gunwales.

They estimated the five-mile run to the junction with Marsh Creek would be completed by lunchtime. "The best

Zee Grant
assembles foldboat
at Sun Valley.

Rod Aller offers two-for-one.

laid plans gang aft a gley." The creek was river-sized by Boston standards, but the boats often grated over rocks and gravel bars. It was 6:00 PM before they made campfall, just as Nimick was dumped unceremoniously into the water.

By the next day, mountains squeezed the river into a steeper and wilder course. Aller lost an argument with a rock and was "obliged to spend the better part of the afternoon making his boat and equipment seaworthy." The party was amazed by the number of chinook salmon in the creek, but they were unable to hook any.

These boaters needed a stump puller to get up in the morning: for five days they never got out of camp before noon—but then they did not sleep well. Camped below Dagger Falls, Zee recalled:

"...we had our first and only encounter with pack rats. During the night we could hear the tinkle of silverware. We flashed our lights in the direction of our burned-out campfire, but could see nothing. Next morning we found that the rats had been playing games with our cooking outfit. Living up to their reputation as "fair trade" rats, they had taken many things from their places, and whenever they had removed a spoon or fork they had replaced it with an old belt buckle or tin-can top. These large rats are very honest, and in the final accounting there was only one spoon actually lost, in return for which we had been given an old tube of toothpaste."

The river was now augmented by tributaries, and the boaters could drift with the current at times. Then, after lunch, Nimick capsized and the river wrapped his boat around a rock, breaking every rib and cross frame in the center section. Surprisingly, the hull was undamaged and replacement parts got the *Montenegro* back on the water. Zee said that they applied the first of over fifty yards of adhesive tape used on the trip.

On August 17 they paddled "through a small lake about a half-mile long, not shown on the maps." This was the pond behind still-fresh Sulphur Slide. "Through this [landslide] the river has cut a rocky sluice, down which the water caroms between boulders, dropping more than thirty feet." They portaged. During the afternoon, the *Sawtooth Flyer* flipped in the Chutes, ruining Zee's camera and film and washing away the strip map of the river.

They paddled on down the insistent river, reaching Indian Creek on the sixth day. The next day was the longest of the journey—nearly twenty miles. Lunch was

Zee Grant runs
Sulphur Slide.

shared with the McCalls at Thomas Creek, then the men camped the night on an island downstream.

Late in the afternoon on August 21, the three paddlers entered the jagged geography of Impassable Canyon. Since Grant—without maps now—remembered hearing somewhere that the gorge was nine miles long, the party decided to push on and conclude their voyage at the Salmon near dusk:

"Soon we were shooting the rapids in twilight, and then in murky gloom, always certain that the river's end lay just around the corner. On this darkest of moonless nights we dropped twenty-seven feet through the most terrifying cataract of the canyon, Hancock Rapids [sic]. In the quiet pools above the white-water, we would listen and try to place our boats in the deepest part of the stream, farthest away from the rocks. Slipping down the dark "V" above the storming rapids, we would flash our lights on the combers ahead. "Keep her bow pointed downstream and pray"—that's about the only way to get through this type of water at night. It was fortunate, indeed, that in none of the great rapids did we get caught upon a rock."

Fortunate, indeed. It was about 11:00 PM somewhere below Nugget Creek when they decided to camp, just as Nimick stamped his boat in the worst wreck yet. "There were anxious moments before we located him and his foldboat, and we were obliged to camp that night on a rocky shelf under a cliff."

The next morning it took three hours to fix the *Montenegro.* They got it to float, but it could not be taken out of the water without breaking in two. Nimick's load had to be transferred to the other boats.

Day ten. Early in the afternoon they rounded a bend and spotted the canyon of the Salmon River. "Our rejoicing yodels re-echoed from wall to wall of the canyon."

They spent two days with Gus Peebles in the cabin at the confluence while they awaited the station wagon ride

to Sun Valley. Once back at the Challenger Inn, "we celebrated a trip that none of us will ever forget."

Norm Nevills ran a support trip for Zee Grant in Grand Canyon the next year on a flow of about 20,000 cfs. Zee ran numerous eastern rivers after that. In his later life diabetes cost him his sight. He died in 1971, but his foldboat rests in the Park Service museum on the South Rim of Grand Canyon.

First solo...

Additionally, Zee Grant's expedition spawned the first solo-run of the Middle Fork, also done with a foldboat.

Eliot DuBois wakened to rivers as a teenager on canoe trips in northern Maine. He bought a second-hand canoe and polished his paddling skills on the Shepaug River in Connecticut. Eventually he joined the whitewater club of which Zee Grant was president. When Eliot took second place in a race, Zee suggested that he join him on his planned Grand Canyon trip. Eliot declined, feeling he was not yet ready for that. But when Grant described his Middle Fork trip of the year before, the young paddler listened the way a hungry man reads a menu. He decided on a Middle Fork rendezvous the following July.

DuBois was a student at Yale. With America's entrance into the war in December, 1941, his academic schedule was accelerated in order that he would graduate a year earlier, with a one-month vacation in June—before going into the Marine Corps. In June, 1942, he corralled a couple of friends with foldboats and they met in Sun Valley. Since the road to Bear Valley was blocked by snow, they scouted Marsh Creek and found it high but possibly runnable.

On June 14 they launched. The creek was ice cold, swift, and full of concealed rocks. Within three miles the churning current dumped both of Eliot's friends—one boat went on without its paddler, the other boat was gutted on a rock. They had to call it quits.

Stu Gardiner returned to his bank job in Salt Lake City, but Ed Friedman and DuBois visited for a spell with Slim and Mildred Hendrick, managers of the Cape Horn Ranch near Marsh Creek. About a week later, when DuBois and Friedman returned to the ranch house after a day of fishing, they learned that Woodie Hindman had stopped by on his way to run the Middle Fork. The effect of the news is best told by Eliot:

"Instantly my interest in the Middle Fork was re-kindled. I saw a means of salvaging my wrecked ambition to run the river. I would assemble my boat, start down Marsh Creek, join Hindman, and continue with his party on down the Middle Fork. I knew that running any whitewater alone was very hazardous but reasoned that I'd be running only Marsh Creek alone. If Hindman started down Bear Valley Creek the next morning, and if I started down Marsh Creek at the same time, we would arrive simultaneously at the junction of the two creeks. This scheme appealed to me so much that I gave no thought at all as to whether Hindman would agree to let me go along with him down the river."

When he unfolded his plan to Hendrick and Friedman, they both told him "you're just plain nuts!" But DuBois turned stubborn as a government mule. It was what he wanted to do, it was what he came to do, it was what he was going to do.

He threw together his mess kit and some food—
bacon, ham, cheese, pancake flour, bouillon, coffee. Then
he added two sets of clothes, poncho, sleeping bag—all
stuffed into a waterproof bag which was to be tied to the
bottom frame of the boat and carried between his legs.
Supplies and equipment weighed about seventy-five
pounds, the same as the boat.

In the morning he mounted a spray deck on the boat,
threw in a spare paddle, and grabbed his lifejacket.
Hendrick took him by car the short distance to Marsh
Creek.

It was June 22. He pushed off, his paddle taking the
pulse of the current. The water soon accelerated but it did
not carry the velocity of the week before. Eliot threaded
his way down the rock-thwarted stream, finally reaching
the confluence where Marsh Creek marries Bear Valley
Creek to form the Middle Fork. No sign of Hindman.
DuBois made a snug camp, planning a sprint the next day
to catch Hindman at his portage around Dagger Falls.

But at Dagger the next day he found only footprints. The yearling boatman suddenly realized that he might have to run the river alone. He camped below the falls and forgot Hindman.

At daylight he paddled resolutely on. The river toughened, turned boisterous. At Sulphur Slide the river was still at war with its bed. DuBois ran it right-side-up, full of water. Although he scouted whenever he could, his confidence grew.

He camped that night in the spavined shack at Waterwheel Rapid, feeling exhausted. The icy water, wind and rain, and nights too cold for his sleeping bag brought on incipient hypothermia.

A stop at Pungo Creek, where he was welcomed, fed, and sheltered overnight by Ed Budell, was a lifesaver. Other canyon-comers forked out assistance and advice at Hood Ranch, Loon Creek, and Brush Creek.

On day seven he entered gray-cliffed Impassable Canyon. The river was running about 4800 cfs. "Those whom the Lord loves He chastens." At Weber Rapid DuBois got caught by a tumultuous wave in a hole behind a boulder and water became his sky. When he surfaced, he saw his boat upside down a few yards upstream. He finally got it ashore and found the only damage involved the loss of his spray deck, serious enough in that it made the open foldboat as vulnerable as a canoe. He christened the rapid *Lenore* after his girlfriend at the time, then pushed off again.

That night Eliot camped at Nugget Creek, and since his larder now resembled Old Mother Hubbard's, he shot a spruce grouse and gnawed on it for dinner. He slept in Parrott's lower cabin.

At breakfast he finished the last of his pancake flour. Then onward again through more rapids: Weidner, Ouzel, a lengthy, careful scout at Rubber ("I was glad to have come through but grateful not to have to do it again"), and Hancock ("Not as spectacular as Rubber, but one that gave me more trouble").

"I ran the last mile without ... even pausing. When I beached my boat on the left bank, where the Middle Fork emptied into the Main Salmon, it was with a great feeling of relief." The river had loosened its fingers.

Eliot DuBois did not come back to run the Middle Fork again until he was sixty years old, and he subsequently wrote a book, *An Innocent on the Middle Fork*, about the contrast with his earlier trip (see bibliography). At this writing, he lives with his wife in New Mexico.

Postwar flood...

World War II imposed a four-year hiatus on river running—the node between waves of recreational use. Then the Oregonians reappeared in 1946. That year Ruth Hindman ran her own rubber raft down the Middle Fork— the first woman to do so. The only problem to arise was a tube that blew out while the raft was ashore. Since patching material could not be located, they tied a knot in the diaphragm and finished the run without further headaches. Ruth repeated her accomplishment a year later. In the late

Hindman rowing driftboat on the McKenzie River.

1940s, she, along with Ruby Taylor and Coralie Thomson, held professional guide's licenses on Oregon's McKenzie River.

The Middle Fork was acquiring the rhythm of the begattings in the Bible. In 1947 Helfrich and Hindman launched again. Prince's oldest son, Dave, fifteen at the time (and already a licensed guide on the McKenzie) drove the shuttle rig. The next spring, Dave's father told him that if he could follow him down the upper McKenzie from Olallie Creek to Blue River, he could go with him on the Middle Fork.

Someone else handled the shuttle that July, as Dave ran his first Middle Fork trip. Snow necessitated a put-in at Marsh Creek. As Dave fought his way through the rocky garden of quick choices he heard his father remark, "It'll get a lot tougher,"—and he must have felt like the calf being dragged to a branding iron.

Helfrich recalls that their parties always relaxed once they reached Dagger Falls—the hard part was behind. They would stop at Coffee Pot Camp, about two miles above the falls. Early in the morning, the guides would row

down to a point where Woodie had installed block and
tackle and the group would skid their craft up a slope
above the falls. Then the boats were loaded on an iron-
wheeled cart kept there for the purpose, and trundled down
the incline to the pool at the base of Dagger. Hindman and
Prince Helfrich each logged well over a score of trips from
Bear Valley Creek down, before the road was scraped into
Dagger Falls in 1958. (Woodie Hindman died in 1967 in
Parker, Arizona, age seventy-two —after spending the day
fishing.)

Prince Helfrich in
McKenzie
driftboat, Pistol
Creek.

Helfrich and
Hindman line his
boat through
Dagger Falls.

Helfrich and Hindman line his boat through Dagger Falls.

The end of World War II meant inexpensive surplus rubber rafts could be purchased by the public. After Amos Burg and Ruth Hindman, others were not long in testing inflatables on the river.

Andy Anderson, a Utahn by birth, who moved to Challis, Idaho, in 1938, leased the Loon Creek ranch on the Middle Fork from Jack Simplot, and met Frazier and Swain when they camped at Loon Creek in 1945. By then, they were using twelve-foot surplus rubber rafts.

Anderson was intrigued. Although he had been a trapper, rodeo rider, fire-fighter, welder, game warden, and semi-pro baseball player, he had a healthy regard for the power of the river. He went to Pocatello, found a war-surplus raft for $50, packed it on horseback to Loon Creek, and spent ten days in August exploring the river from Loon Creek to the Main Salmon. He made a second trip in September with his wife Melba. During the winter he found two twelve-foot Navy assault rafts in Salt Lake City.

In late August, 1946, he ran the Middle Fork from Loon Creek with his first paying guests: Jack Simplot, Box Troxal, and Leon Jones. After the trip, Andy decided he could make a living as a river outfitter. The Salmon newspaper reported, "Members of the party said they believed this was going to develop into one of the most popular river trips in the northwest. Its recreational advantages are extremely appealing and with proper equipment it can be made in safety and without undue hardship." The dude market was on the rise. With his brother Joe as a partner, he operated out of the Anderson Bar X Ranch at the mouth of Ramshorn Creek in Meyers Cove. Guests were usually met in Sun Valley; supplies and river equipment were packed on as many as eighteen horses and mules from the Bar X to the Tappan Ranch at Grouse Creek. The Andersons used seven-man rafts with oars. They operated on a seven-day turnaround with three of those days spent on the river.

In 1952 they abandoned the packtrains in favor of airplane flights to the Indian Creek landing strip. In August they flew passengers and gear in a Ford Trimotor to

Andy Anderson (stern) and brother Joe in seven-man on Middle Fork.

the Flying B (now Flying Resort) at the head of Impassable Canyon. In 1955 a four-day trip cost $325; a seven-day trip cost $500 (flight included). The Andersons trained a dozen boatmen (one was Andy's son Ted, who would become an outstanding Middle Fork manager for the U. S. Forest Service), and upgraded the rafts with spray shields. The outfit ran between six and eight trips a season.

Anderson ran the river for twenty-seven summers, then sold his business to Eldon Handy. He says, "Those years on the river were my golden years. You bet."

The number of persons floating the river grew with each decade: 25 in 1949, 1,200 in 1965, 4,500 in 1975, and almost 9,000 in 1990.

Memorable runs...

Among numerous feats of boating skill on the Middle Fork, it seems appropriate to include at least three here.

Ralph Smothers was one of the early boatmen with prop motors on the Main Salmon. On May 27, 1957, Smothers, and his father Austin, made a run up the Middle Fork to the Flying B Ranch at Brush Creek using a twenty-foot, fiber-glassed plywood boat designed and built by Austin and powered by a pair of thirty-five-horsepower outboards. It carried 800 pounds, which included fifty gallons of gasoline and a spare motor. With three brief stops, the upriver journey of thirty miles required almost four hours.

Nearly seventy tons of bridge materials had been flown into the Flying B and Brush Creek landing strips by Aircraft Services of Boise to be hauled to construction sites at Big Creek, Waterfall, and Wilson creeks. Included were fourteen-foot steel beams (weighing 640 pounds each), treated timber, cement and a mixer, and construction camp supplies.

The boatmen, with the help of one other man, made an average of five trips a day downriver, carrying about a ton each time.

On June 15, with the job completed, the Smothers returned to the Main Salmon loaded with over a 1,000 pounds of gear, in two and one-half hours. (In 1958 Ralph also ran a ten-man raft rigged with sweeps down the Middle Fork from Fir Creek.)

During the second week of June, 1969, Bob Smith of North Fork, Idaho, set off from Dagger Falls with a large sweepboat. His cargo included a Volkswagen bus. He remembers being unable to pull in before Indian Creek campground. Bob floated the bus sixty miles to the Flying B Ranch.

On August 6, 1977, Al Busby and Mark McKane were guiding for Elwood Masoner. Busby, a biology teacher at Twin Falls (Idaho) High School, had boated the Middle Fork for seven years; McKane, a pre-med student at the College of Idaho, had been on the river for five years. It was a low-water season (2.0 on the marker).

Near Driftwood Camp in Impassable Canyon, Bernie Williams, a teenage girl, had accidentally fallen out of one of the boats and struck her head on a rock. When the party camped at Survey Creek for the night, Bernie, though conscious, had to be carried off the boat. Her parents were on the trip, and her mother was a surgical nurse. The group included a doctor as well. An examination indicated that the girl was not responsive, had numbness in her extremities, and pupil dilation. In event of a head injury, time is critical. The doctor felt it was a serious situation. Busby and McKane, as the most experienced boatmen, offered to take the girl and her parents out. (Time and location made a helicopter flight infeasible.)

They pushed off at 7:30 PM in a Green River raft (with spray shield). Bernie was prone and blanketed on a

Bob Smith departing Dagger Falls for Flying B Ranch, mid-June, 1969.

table in the bow of the boat. Busby rowed downstream, knowing the light would soon be gone. Night caught them before they reached Cliffside.

The men took turns rowing. A party at Otter Bar heard them pass and called out, "Rubber is just around the corner—see you in the morning." Without moonlight the canyon was dark as the inside of a boat pump. The boatmen operated on sound and memory. They avoided all rocks.

Pulling in at the Main Salmon confluence, they walked to Cache Bar where they found a pickup with keys. They drove to Corn Creek and got a Forest Service rig to take them to the hospital in Salmon. There a doctor decided Bernie should be sent to a specialist in Boise, and since it was now 5:30 AM, Salmon Air Taxi was able to take off for the city, where Bernie recovered from her concussion.

The guides stopped for a nap on the way back to Stanley.

DAGGER FALLS TO PISTOL CREEK

MILE 0 *Dagger Falls Campground* (Originally Sulphur Falls) Bear Valley, Marsh, and Elk creeks tangle to form the Middle Fork, and these three streams contribute about fifteen percent of the spring and summer-run chinook salmon in Idaho.

The road to Dagger was cleared in 1958-1959 to support construction of a fish ladder along the edge of the falls. The road opened August 1, 1959, and construction began a few days later. Until that time, there had been an extensive sport fishery at Dagger Falls.

Coffer dams built to dry up the river while excavation took place were washed out by high water in September and twice again in October. The contractor had to use the fishway as a diversion channel around the falls while he built a 160-foot wooden flume, ten feet wide and five feet high, down to the pool at the lower falls. The river then flowed through the flume and the channel while work was completed on the fishway. All cement was in place by November 25, though work continued into December because the cold had caused the river to drop.

Although the runs of Columbia River chinook salmon have been decimated by Army Corps of Engineers' dams on the Columbia and the Snake rivers, occasionally in July it is still possible to see fish lunging homeward up the falls.

Idaho archaeologist Max Pavesic noted that the campground, built in 1964-1965, was located in what was initially a major salmon fishery for the Indians. In 1988, by arrangements with Idaho State University, a sampling excavation (167 square meters) was made at the site. A total of 1,241 lots of artifacts were recovered: projectile points, bifaces, scrapers, drills, gravers, pottery sherds, and ground stone tools. Over ninety-seven percent of the

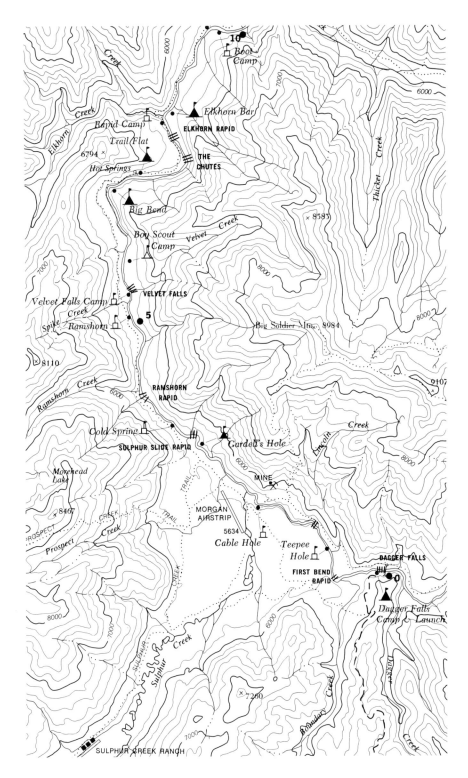

10
Boot
Camp

Creek

6000

7000

6000

Elkhorn Bar
Rapid Camp
ELKHORN RAPID
Trail Flat
6794 ×
Hot Springs
THE
CHUTES

Big Bend

Boy Scout
Camp
Velvet
Creek

× 8583

8000

7000

Velvet Falls Camp
VELVET FALLS
Spike Creek
Ramshorn
5

Big Soldier Mtn. 8984

8000

× 8110

Ramshorn Creek
6000
RAMSHORN
RAPID

9107

Cold Spring
SULPHUR SLIDE RAPID
Gardell's Hole
Lincoln
Creek

8000

Morehead
Lake

8467 ×

MINE

6000

PROSPECT
CREEK
Prospect
Creek

MORGAN
AIRSTRIP
5634
Cable Hole
Teepee
Hole
FIRST BEND
RAPID

DAGGER FALLS

0

8000

TRAIL
TRAIL

6000

Dagger Falls
Camp   Launch

SULPHUR
Creek

Sulphur
Creek

× 7260

BOUNDARY
Creek

DAGGER
Creek

7000

SULPHUR CREEK RANCH

90

Dagger Falls, 1929. Since the 15-foot drop was considered an impediment to fish migration, the U. S. Fish and Wildlife Service spent $181,000 to "improve" passage as part of the Columbia River fishery development. Drilling and blasting removed 20 feet of rock. Fishway completed in 1960.

points were of obsidian, and the closest known source is a butte sixty miles to the southwest. Classified as "Elko" series points, they support a maximum age for occupation of the site of 3,300 years and as late a date as 1,200 years.

They also suggest that the Dagger Falls occupants were more closely tied to the resources of the Snake River drainage, where obsidian is abundant, than to those of the Salmon River drainage. The natives came to take salmon in the summer and fall, returning to the Snake River Basin for the winter with as much dried fish as they could carry.

When the Boundary Creek ramp was completed and opened as the new headwater access in 1978, the log ramp for boat- launching at Dagger was dismantled by the Forest Service.

MILE 1 *Boundary Creek* launch site. On the morning of trip departures, the Forest Service checks permits and assigns campsites at this location.

In the early 1900s, Boundary Creek delineated sheep and cattle range. Sheep were not supposed to be taken south of the stream.

Since much of the Middle Fork has been fire-scarred from 1979 to 1989, and the Boundary Creek area was obviously charred in one such fire (Deadwood), this is the logical place to explain what has occurred.

The Great Idaho Fire of 1910 burned almost 3 million acres and initiated the Weeks Act, which directed the Forest Service to pursue a forest-management policy of fire suppression. With technology, in the last quarter-century the nation has cut its annual fire losses of timber from 30 million acres to less than 5 million. But until the intrusion of "management," fire had been an element of natural balance, removing the buildup of dead wood and decaying plant material. Fire intensity increases in older forests. The instinctive fire suppression response began to be questioned.

In 1972 the U. S. Forest Service adopted a "let-it-burn" policy for lightning-caused fires in wilderness areas, where people and structures were not endangered. Wilderness was a place where the agency could save money on the forest without engendering political heat from the logging industry. For the River of No Return Wilderness, that policy was not implemented in 1985, when the fire management plan was first released, because that was a dry year. (In 1985 the West lost more acreage to fire [2.9 million acres] than at any time since 1965.) One needs little more than sage for brains to understand that wildfire in a drought year can quickly become a calamity.

On July 29, 1987, the Deadwood Summit fire was ignited by a lightning strike about twenty-five air miles east of Cascade, Idaho. Despite being the seventh-driest summer on record in Idaho, Boise National Forest Supervisor Jack Lavin directed that the fire be allowed to burn. Such encouragement was hardly needed: Over the next three months the fire consumed 51,000 acres (an eighty-one-mile perimeter), nearly roasted nine campers and fifteen horses at the Boundary Creek campground, and required $1.5 million in containment costs for belated suppression attempts. (Though costs-per-acre comparisons with other Idaho forest fires are given in the USFS Deadwood fire report, no estimate is given for what containment costs would have been for the first week of August. Ironically, when outfitters whose hunting areas were threatened by the growing fire organized to fight it on their own, they were ordered to desist by the Boise National Forest.)

The Boise National Forest spokesman, whose analysts had predicted a 5,000-acre burn, remarked afterwards, "We made a few mistakes, *maybe*." Obviously, the aesthetic impact of one of the mistakes will be apparent for decades.

In 1988, a drought year, another "let burn" fire consumed 42,000 acres, including five miles along the Middle Fork (see Mile 25. Indian Creek). That year the West set a new record (3.2 million acres) for burned timber. In Idaho, over 300,000 acres of national forest wilderness went up in smoke. The Boise National Forest spokesman observed, "the fire behavior analysts did not do a very good job of predicting the effects of the drought." (The stated attitude of one fire control officer on the forest was, "that's just that much acreage we don't have to worry about burning.") All of which raised questions about the implementation of the "let-it-burn" policy.

As a consequence of these problems and those at Yellowstone, a federal advisory panel in December, 1988, concluding a high-level review of the way the nation fights its forest fires, recommended that government policy be clarified to ensure that fewer naturally caused fires are allowed to burn unchallenged, and called for a "let-it-burn" moratorium until the policy could be revised.

In its report to the secretaries of Interior and Agriculture, the panel reported that the "let-it-burn" policy had in practice often been irresponsibly enforced by fire managers who failed to take proper account of the consequences of their decisions.

In the long term, the panel advised, the government should use man-made fires to serve ecological ends rather than rely heavily on lightning-caused blazes, which are more difficult to control.

Biologist and one-time professor of zoology and forestry John Craighead discussed these issues succinctly in a 1989 university address:

"...research should be undertaken to better understand wilderness ecology, especially fire ecology: the response and recovery of the biota to recent burns; changes in stream flow and sedimentation; nutrient cycling; aquatic productivity; and changes in landscape diversity, to mention only a few areas.

A fire management policy must be integrated with wilderness preservation. Fire, along with climate and soils, determines vegetative cover. When wildfires are effectively suppressed, plant succession throughout the landscape is less diverse, but proceeds slowly to the climatic climax forest. The policy allowing natural-caused fires to run their course permits lightning strikes rather than scientific management plans to determine where successional changes occur, and to a large extent the size of the burn and the type of vegetation that will follow. This is the natural process that existed in Pre-Columbian times. But is it defensible in the late twentieth century, when pristine wilderness areas comprise...less than four percent of our land area in the Lower Forty-eight states?

Lodgepole forests represent a fire climax, that is, a forest destined to burn periodically, a forest that seldom progresses to the 'climatic climax condition.' Small, well-planned, carefully controlled, prescribed burns can provide scenic and biologic diversity, and set the stage for the development of a mosaic of forest communities. Large, intense burns are more likely to set the whole process back 200 to 300 years."

MILE 2 *The Snowstorm* mining claim, located less than one-half mile back from the east bank, was a hardrock gold mine staked in 1927 by Leo Dodge, Joe Fox, and Homer Granger. A cabin and an adit had been established before they arrived; they were unable to learn who was responsible for the work. However, they built additional cabins.

Leo Dodge, from Carmen, Idaho, had worked in the Gibbonsville, Montana, mines as a boy. He met his wife, Emily Schroeder, a nurse, in the Big Hole basin of Montana. They eloped in 1913 to Salmon, Idaho. The couple had two children: Roscoe and Dorothy.

Joe Fox was a friend of Emily; his parents, like hers, had homesteaded in the Big Hole and were friends of the Schroeders.

Fox and Dodge brought their families to the Snowstorm because Homer Granger, who was too elderly to work the claim, was convinced there was a gold-bearing ledge on the property. Fox and Dodge did find some color downstream from the site.

Joe and Lillian Fox leaving Sulphur Creek for Soldier Creek. Joe died in Tacoma, Washington, in 1942.

They worked together until the spring of 1930, when they dissolved the partnership and Dodge acquired the mine by giving Fox all rights to the claim downriver.

The Dodges were at the Snowstorm intermittently over the next twenty years. Sometimes they wintered at Grimes Pass, Idaho; they were in Monterey, California, during the war years. They usually traveled to the property with a packstring from Bear Valley, where a dude ranch run by Bill Bohm, Bud Hoagland, and later, Seymour Hanson, was located. At times, Hanson would send hunting parties down to the Dodges, or rent their cabins for his own parties during the season.

In 1950 the Dodges sold their claim for $6000 to Ben Morgan, who had acquired the Fuller place across the river. He wanted the Snowstorm as a grazing area for his horses.

MILE 2.3 *Sulphur Creek* flows in from the left.

Once congested with spawning salmon, the creek runs through two old homesteads not far from the river. In 1904 Jim and Annazie Fuller took the one a quarter-mile up the creek — though they did not prove up on it until 1930. They had a cabin with a sod and shake roof, as well as an enclosed hot spring wash house. (Emily and Dorothy Dodge would wade the river to take a hot bath at the Fuller's place and were teased about being the only people in the backcountry who would wade a river twice just to take a bath.)

Jim Fuller was born in Nebraska in a wagon train headed for Idaho. As a young man, he was trailing cattle from Sweet, Idaho, to the town of Salmon when he turned down the Middle Fork and discovered his homestead site. He and his wife, along with their four daughters and son, would trail cows for the Sulphur Creek Cattle Association from Emmett Valley down to the creek in the spring, stay there for the summer, and trail out in the fall. They built a transfer cabin in Bear Valley where they could switch from wagon team to horses on their way to the homestead.

Fuller homestead, Sulphur Creek : house-cabin, (right); bathhouse, (center); saddle shed.

Fuller homestead with salmon from Sulphur Creek hanging from the purlins.

Obstetrician Ben Morgan, whose wife Freda, a pilot, and also an obstetrician and anesthesiologist, acquired the Fuller place in 1949, and it is now known as the Morgan Ranch. The Morgans were residents of Chicago. Ben Morgan died in 1980. Freda Morgan and her two children's families still use the site as a summer residence. An airstrip gives access to the property.

Sam Phillips patented a homestead in 1923 a couple of miles farther up the creek. He was already in residence when Jim Fuller came to the country. Phillips had a wife and child and they lived in a well-made cabin. At times Fuller grazed his cattle on their spread.

Ed Parker, and his son Roy, had the Phillips' place in the 1930s; they had been in the area for some time, ran cattle there and put up some hay. The Parkers supplemented their income with the sale of marten and fox pelts trapped in the winter. Ed also made some moonshine during prohibition, and Roy's packstring brought cordial relief to drought-stricken ranchers in the valley beyond Sulphur Creek. Whiskey Cabin, near Landmark, was named by the grateful survivors.

Fuller children at Sulphur Creek, 1942: Nola, Jim, Jamie, Louona.

Jim Fuller, age 76 in 1940, braiding rawhide bridle reins. Fuller often trailed horses across the plains to Kansas and Nebraska. He died in 1957.

The Phillips' place, now referred to as Sulphur Creek Ranch, was purchased by Marv and Barbara Hornback in 1948, the year they were married. Marv, a native Idahoan, had been a cattle rancher in the Dry Creek area near Eagle; Barbara grew up on a Nebraska cattle ranch, attended Boise High, and was working as a legal secretary. The Hornbacks were both pilots—Barbara received her commercial rating before her husband did.

When they first flew to Sulphur Creek, only the Phillip's cabin was still standing on the place. Having decided to convert the location to a guest ranch, the couple had their work cut out for them. Since Marv had tried to walk a bulldozer in from Bear Valley the first spring but rolled it short of the ranch, horses were used to bring in the logs for the barn, lodge, and cabins.

The expansive main lodge was constructed with vertical logs. The floor is concrete. The kitchen on the north end can serve fifteen to twenty guests in the dining hall. Upstairs rooms were quarters for seasonal help. Seven

The Morgan Ranch, Sulphur Creek.

Ben Morgan at his ranch on Sulphur Creek.

Sulphur Creek lodge—inside and out.

Freda Morgan
and her trick horse
"Prince."

Patti Hornback (Reynolds) in 1955 atop her retired rodeo-recovery horse "Dusty," holding her bull terrier "Mike."

Barbara Hornback in 1952, leaving Sulphur Creek lodge on "Breezy."

separate log cabins were built for guests. A Pelton wheel generator furnished power from the creek.

In the winter the Hornbacks would travel to sport and recreation shows to advertise the attractions of their ranch. Gradually they booked hunters, fishermen, and fly-in vacationers. The high-altitude resort drew its share of celebrities, such as Howard Hughes, Fred McMurray, and the Crosbys.

Patti Hornback, age three, one of the Hornback daughters, plays in her swimming pool at Sulphur Creek Ranch. She is now the mother of three children, a pilot, and director of the Idaho Humane Society.

Mark Twain remarked, "A man who has picked up a tomcat by the tail knows more about them than anyone else." Any outfitter knows few occupations impose greater demands on a family than an air-accessible guest ranch. The slender remuneration dictates that the operation be a labor of love. In 1960 the Hornbacks sold the ranch to Gene Barton and Les MacGray from Minnesota, co-owners of Barton Construction, and moved to Pistol Creek (see Mile 22.5).

Eggs and Catherine Beckley managed the ranch for them until 1977, when the owners in turn sold to Boise chiropractor Tom Allegrezza and two partners, who still operate it as a guest ranch and as a base for outfitted hunting trips. It remains accessible only by airplane.

Sulphur Creek lodge and airstrip (right).

MILE 2.6 *Gardell's Hole* is the gravel bar camp on the east side of the river.

MILE 2.7 *Sulphur Slide Rapid* begins at the end of the pool where the river hooks to the left. This rapid formed in 1936, when waterspouts (flash floods) blew out Sulphur Creek, Prospect Creek, and the nearby gulches. The outwash carried hundreds of tons of boulders and debris into the river, dammed it, and formed a lake.

Eventually the river broke through on the east shore, but three vexatious rapids impeded this stretch of river in the 1930s and 1940s. Eliot DuBois gave a good description of the rapid in 1942:

"I stood on the bank and looked, almost in disbelief, at the chute. In a hundred yards, the river made up all of the normal drop for the past quarter-mile of flat water. There

Sulphur Slide, 1938.

were waves everywhere, sharp, frothy waves that seemed to have no pattern. Near the bottom, in dead center, there was a logjam. This place was a greater challenge than anything I'd come through so far. It was far above my ability level. It must have been the spot where Zee [Grant] upset, losing his river maps and damaging his movie camera."

Generally considered most troublesome at low water, Sulphur Slide still partially clogs the channel. In 1953 another flash flood carried new outwash into the river.

MILE 4 *Ramshorn Narrows*
Rapid Named for Ramshorn Creek which enters on the left.

MILE 5 *Second Narrows* or Second Slide (Helfrich) or Hells Half Mile (Shaefers).

MILE 5.4 *Velvet Falls.* The drop over the ledge is not as smooth as its name. "Velvet" in this case refers to the soft membrane covering deer antlers in early summer. Velvet Creek threads in on the right just above the falls. The rapid is not lightly regarded in high water by boatmen who understand the danger of its reversible current at the foot of the fall. In 1952 a boat overturned here and one man drowned.

Some late-June raft trips have encountered water so high that it was necessary to line the boats around the backside of the big boulder on the left bank.

MILE 6.8 *Big Bend Camp* is the spacious opening on the right.

MILE 7.9 *Trail Flat Camp,* known as Waterwheel Camp to Oregon guides, is located up on the bench on the left side of the river. Gear has to be packed up the slope, but at lower water levels there are hot springs accessible at river-edge.

MILE 8.3 *The Chutes* (Anderson, Masoner) or Rickey Rapid (ARTA) or Elkhorn Slide (Hughes), or Snowhole (Oregon guides).

MILE 8.5 *Elkhorn Bar Camp* on the right shore
has space for a large group.

MILE 9.6 *Saddle Camp* is on the left bank in a
timbered flat fifty yards from the river. Named for the
grassy declivity on the ridge above the camp.

MILE 11.5 *Waterwheel Rapid* (Hatch) or Power-
house. The waterwheel, or what is left of it on the right
bank, was built by Sam Sibbitts as the power source for a
one-stamp mill. Charlie Smith and Gene Hussey established the claim at least as early as 1913, according to field
geologist's notes, and worked it for some time. Boating
parties in the 1930s noted activity at the site.

The source of the gold ore was the White Goat claim
on top of the mountain across the river from the mill. The
mine had a vertical shaft with a hoist to raise the ore. The
miners strung a cable across the river to bring the rock over
to the mill. Without a crusher, the rock had to be broken
by hand before feeding it under the stamp.

Fred Paulsen of Challis, Idaho, tried working the claim
for a time in the thirties. He brought in a smaller stamp
mill and packed the ore off the mountain and across the
river by mule.

Fred ran the pulverized ore over copper plates coated
with quicksilver. Since the ore had too much arsenic in it,
it was impossible for the mercury to capture the gold, and
the venture was abandoned.

The cabin which served as living quarters for the
miners stands less than a quarter-mile upstream. The
wooden box used for a wall shelf held evaporated apples,
brought in from Cascade.

By 1986 the mill and cabin had fallen over the edge of
decay. With commendable vision, in 1987 and 1989 the
Middle Fork Ranger District undertook archaeological
stabilization of both structures. Once the debris was
cleared, it was discovered that the machinery of the mill
had never operated: the casting burrs on the cams and
stamps are still present. Estimations of the original height

Smith-Hussey summer cabin used while they worked the White Goat claim.

Remains of the White Goat stamp mill. Wheel was taken out by high water.

Restored cabin.

of the waterwheel led to the conclusion that the wheel probably could have been turned by the river for only a few days a year. In the 1930s the mill building was roofed, but there was insufficient evidence left to reconstruct it.

The Smith-Hussey cabin has one of the more complex roof systems found in the River of No Return Wilderness. It consists of log purlins, to which pole rafters were nailed, to which smaller pole purlins were nailed. Ponderosa pine shingles, almost a yard long, were nailed to the last layer of purlins. The roof was rebuilt as before, and about fifteen wall logs were replaced. All the furniture in the building was repaired, re-pegged, and left for the instruction of visitors.

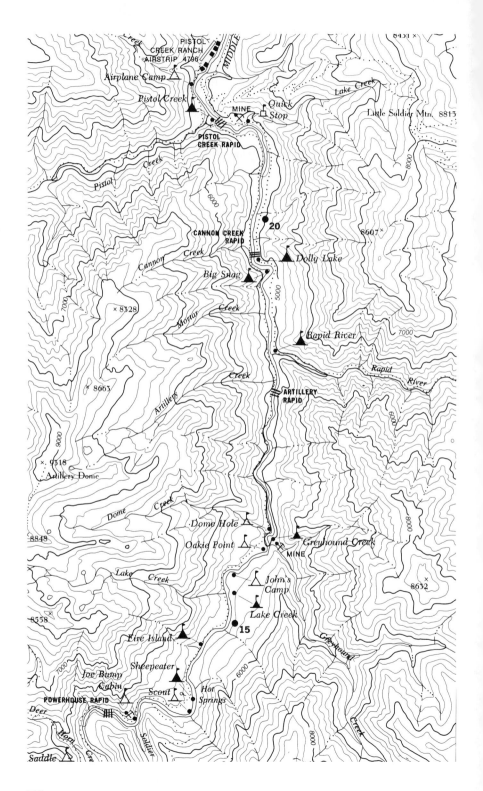

MILE 12.5 *Soldier Creek* comes in on the right. The creek's name is a compliment to Captain Bernard's men who turned up the stream in July, 1879, during the Sheepeater War. Roscoe Dodge found an old Henry rifle (with the breech blown out) in the rocks at the mouth of the creek in 1930—it may have been a relic from the war. Bill Brockman had a promising gold mine a few miles up Soldier Creek. He lived in a cabin there and had a small crew working for him. They drove an adit almost 300 feet into the mountain, but the stone was so compressed they had difficulty keeping an edge on the drill steel. After Brockman's death the mine was abandoned.

The cabin across the river from Soldier Creek was built by Joe Fox and Roscoe Dodge after Fox left the Snowstorm mine upriver. Dodge married Fox's daughter, Alta, and in the early 1930s worked the claim with his father-in-law.

The impressive diversion ditch between the cabin and the river was shoveled out by Fox and Dodge in about six weeks. A wing-dam in the river at the head of the ditch brought water to their placer claim.

Soldier Creek bridge, 1942. High water washed it out.

The two men packed a dozen twenty-foot lengths of pipe, twelve inches in diameter, from Cascade down to the mouth of Sulphur Creek. There they built a log raft and floated the pipe to the claim. They used poles, ropes, and powder to get the raft off rocks and down the channel to their destination. The pipe was used to distribute the ditch water through their placer deposit.

Not much gold was recovered from the effort. "It was a starve-out affair," Dodge recalled. Fox left to placer mine in the Boise Basin, although he lived in the Fuller cabin one winter at the mouth of Sulphur Creek while he trapped mink and marten.

Joe Bump, prospector and packer from Cascade, added the enclosed entry-area to the front of the cabin. Bump knew Fox and Dodge and had done some prospecting with them. According to Charles Kelly, Bump said he had been along the river since 1924. Dorothy Dodge recalled a conversation in which Bump stated he had once been a sheriff in the Black Hills country of South Dakota.

Joe later lost his toes to frostbite in a Bear Valley snowstorm and developed blood poisoning. He had to be taken out to Cascade.

Fox-Dodge cabin with front extension added by Joe Bump. Lumber was rafted from Sulphur Creek.

114

Joe Bump— on a log. Bump spent his last years in a cabin by the railroad alongside the Payette River south of Horseshoe Bend.

After Bump was gone, Elmer Purcell used the cabin. He was a prospector, originally from Oklahoma, in on the mining activity around Meyers Cove on Camas Creek, and he sold a fluorspar claim there for $3,500. That claim was part of the mine later developed by J. R. Simplot.

Purcell moved down by the mouth of Cougar Creek, where he wintered with Charlie Warnock. He spent that winter with only firelight for illumination because he thought the kerosene for his lamps was never delivered by a packer. When the snow melted in the spring, he found the cans by the house, where they had been left while he was away. Snow, sliding from the roof, had hidden them all winter.

When the Warnocks sold out to the Department of Fish and Game, Purcell moved down to Red Bluff Creek to lodge with Fred Paulsen.

Purcell occasionally did some placer mining at the Bump cabin.

Paulsen returned from Indian Creek to the Bump place one evening in May and found Purcell dead in the ditch, where he had fallen from his horse when he suffered a heart attack. He was about seventy-five years old.

Fred went down to Little Creek and got Old Bill Sullivan, Ed Budell and the game warden. After they were deputized by the sheriff to bury Elmer, they returned to the Bump place, wrapped Elmer in a canvas, and buried him in the prospect hole about 200 yards down from the cabin and north of the trail. Sullivan recited the last words and incised a cross on the tree. In 1976 the grave was marked. Proceeds from the sale of Purcell's fluorspar claim collected interest in Custer County Bank until a letter of inquiry came from his sister years later.

In the 1970s Ross Geiling made the Bump place part of his April Showers claim. Geiling was from Pennsylvania, about sixty years old, a veteran and ex-Forest Service employee. He wintered up 44 Mile Creek, living pretty much off the land, and placered for gold in the summer. Owners at Pistol Creek kept track of him and even went together to pay for his hip-replacement surgery. Sadly, in 1989 Geiling took his own life at his cabin.

MILE 13.1 *Sheepeater Hot Springs and Camp* on the left.

Cabins were situated on the upper and lower flat. Gene Hussey and Charles Smith, who worked the mill at Waterwheel, wintered here. They reputedly built the cabins and used them as headquarters for their winter trapping operations. (In 1939, Charles Kelly noted that the walls of the main cabin were papered with pages of the Saturday Evening Post dating to 1911, advertising Apperson cars, etc. He also asserted, probably on the basis of Swain or Frazier's say-so, that the cabins were built by Jack Crane, a foreman at the Bingham Canyon copper mine in Utah, and that Crane was still visiting his claims at Sheepeater every summer.)

The logs around the hot spring are all that remain of a cabin that enclosed it. The room was used for bathing and

Original shelter
over Sheepeater
Hot Springs.

Sheepeater at
present.

Smith-Hussey winter cabins on lower flat at Sheepeater.

Tappan boys swimming in pool behind beaver dam at Sheepeater Hot Springs, 1931.

washing clothes, and water was channeled by small ditches to the other buildings. Evidence of the foundations can still be seen on the flats.

Daisey Tappan recalled that a colony of beaver dammed the outflow of the springs and created a large pond on the upper flat; her boys used it as a swimming pool in the 1940s. In the spring and fall elk are often attracted to the minerals deposited by the waters.

A man who drowned in Velvet Falls is reportedly buried on the Sheepeater bench, but no sign of his grave is apparent.

MILE 14.1 *Fire Island Camp* on the left is grassy with some trees and can accommodate a large party.

MILE 15 *Greyhound Ridge* parallels the river on the right, as does Pistol Creek Ridge on the left. Both are about 8,400 feet in elevation. Ore samples collected on Greyhound Ridge by Colonel Bernard and packer Manuel Fontez during the Sheepeater War were assayed in Boise and showed promise. In the spring of 1880 Fontez led a prospecting party back to the ridge. They found several good lead veins and created enough interest that a few hundred prospectors were on the ridge for several summers.

Galena ore was hauled to a smelter at Clayton, but efforts to develop a road from Cape Horn in Bear Valley to the ridge never materialized, and the national economic panic of 1893 ended investment for decades. A small smelter was finally built on Greyhound, but anticipated values were never realized. The Lucky Lad and Cougar mines on Pistol Creek Ridge produced 1,500 ounces of gold and 24,000 ounces of silver.

All of the creeks draining the Pistol Creek area refer to firearms: Mortar, Artillery, Cannon, Springfield, Winchester, Remington, Savage, Colt, Stephens, Chokebore, Popgun, Beansnapper, and so forth.

MILE 15.2 *Lake Creek Camp* is a small site on the right, across from the mouth of Lake Creek.

MILE 15.5 *John's Camp* on the right, situated on a bench.

MILE 16 *Oakie Point Camp* is located on the left shore. Until recently, this camp was called Lake Creek Camp.

MILE 16.2 *Greyhound Camp* on the right across from **Dome Hole.** Excellent campsite about ten feet above the river and back in the trees. Two cabins occupied this bar when it was used as a placer claim by a man named Hale. Their foundations can still be seen.

Water was brought from Greyhound Creek for a hydraulic operation. Under pressure in the riveted pipe, it was played against the gravel in the gulch to wash out pockets of gold. The nozzle or "giant" from the pipe can be found near the gully.

Dome Hole Camp is just around the curve below Greyhound Creek, on the opposite side of the river.

MILE 17.5 *The Mortar Creek* forest fire, third-largest timber fire in the state's history, began July 26, 1979, near the trail on the left side of the river. The conflagration was started by three campers traveling on horseback who failed to adequately extinguish their campfire. The results of their carelessness are discussed more fully where the fire burned back down to the river (Mile 33.5 Thomas Creek).

MILE 18 *Artillery Rapid*, just above Artillery Creek which flows in on the left.

MILE 18.5 *Rapid River and Camp.*

The camp is on the right just below the mouth of Rapid River, which heads nearly fifty miles from the river. Captain Bernard and his soldiers passed the mouth of the creek on July 1, 1879; they had come up from Camas Creek on their march and were headed back to Bear Valley and then down the South Fork of the Salmon.

MILE 19.3 *Big Snag Camp* on the left. The ponded river here is called Dolly Varden Lake and is a favorite fishing hole. (The Dolly Varden trout is named for a character with colorful petticoats in Charles Dicken's novel *Barnaby Rudge.*

MILE 19.4 *Dolly Lake Camp* is on the bench after the right-hand bend below and across the water from Big Snag.

MILE 19.7 *Big Snag Rapid* at Cannon Creek. Helfrich and other river runners report that this was more of a rapid in the 1940s.

MILE 21.2 *The Huntington Claim*, just above Pistol Creek Rapid, on the right bank of the river. Ed Huntington, R. M. Teachout and E. S. Pickhardt filed this claim October 15, 1938. It covered twenty acres about three-eighths of a mile from the mouth of Pistol Creek. Huntington was from the Great Lakes area and had considerable knowledge of mine engineering. He was about forty-five years old at the time he operated this claim, a capable miner and a superb blacksmith. He sold stock in Michigan for the venture.

The men contoured a ditch around the slope of the hill and into Lake Creek, which drains Little Soldier Mountain.

Hunnington's cabin at Pistol Creek, used while working his claim across the river. Later, summer-kids from Pistol Creek liked to party here.

In 1939 they augered 1,200 feet of pipe in ten-foot lengths made from wood cut on the site. A few pieces were bored by hand before they switched to a small gasoline engine. The pipes were sleeved to fit inside each other and wrapped with wire to help withstand the water pressure developed by the fall from the ditch.

Not much is left of the placering apparatus. The conveyor buckets on the edge of the river were the digging mechanism driven by water power from the pipe. The buckets emptied sand and gravel into a sluicebox arrangement which was used to trap the gold flakes.

Length of log pipeline that carried water from Lake Creek for power at Hunnington's claim. Pipe was augured on site.

Hunnington's
conveyor-scoop
powered by the
pipeline. The river
has carried
away most of the
accessories.

A few feet upstream from the buckets, a chain winch was anchored to pull large boulders out of the path of the scoop, which had to be moved regularly. Another cable was run across the river to a fir tree, but no one ever knew how Huntington planned to use it.

A bridge crossed the river just above Pistol Creek Rapid; Fred Paulsen packed most of the supplies for it. It allowed the miners to reach their cabin, which still stands across the river from their claim. They packed in cement to make a serviceable fireplace.

Eventually Huntington faced serious charges because he had manipulated money from eastern stock promotions. He left for South America and was never heard from again. Little gold was recovered from the operation. Cy Johnson, who had done all the packing for Huntington, was left holding an empty bag.

The bridge, unsafe with age, was burned.

Problem at Pistol Creek on an early trip.

MILE 21.2 The gravel bar on the west bank between the cabin and the river is known as Lower's placer claim. In 1972 the U. S. Geological Survey estimated this bar contains 100,000 cubic yards of gravel with twenty to forty cents of gold per cubic yard, and reported some concentrations are probably present which might be mined economically.

MILE 21.5 *Pistol Creek Rapid.* The rapid occurs on a blind turn. In high water it involves a hard pull away from a cliff and then a pivot-turn into a deep, quiet pool at the mouth of Pistol Creek. (Boaters running the river for the first time on a high stage may want to take the short walk from the Huntington claim to the overlook just downriver.)

MILE 21.6 *Pistol Creek Camp* on the gravel bar to the left. The hot springs three miles up the creek need a lot of work before they will match others on the river.

MILE 22.3 *Airplane Camp* on the west bank in scattered timber. An easy landing for a large camp.

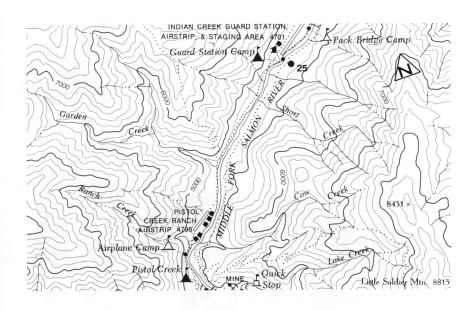

MILE 22.5 *Pistol Creek Ranch-Middle Fork Ranch Corporation.*

The first permanent resident at the mouth of Pistol Creek was Sam Hoppins. The son of a Scotch father and a Cherokee mother, he was well over six feet tall, broad shouldered and dark complected. Sam wore a big black hat, sported a moustache, and always sat straight in the saddle. He made fine horsehair ropes, worked leather, and even wrote some poetry. Those who knew him remember that he was kind and considerate.

Hoppins came to the Middle Fork in 1892. He had a seventy-two acre homestead on Loon Creek at the confluence of Cabin and Indian creeks. At age fifty, when that homestead was patented in 1910, he sold it and moved to Pistol Creek. He built a handsome cabin there, rumped against the hill.

Sam Hoppins in 1910 at his cabin on Pistol Creek.

126

Sam Hoppin's pack string loaded for a trip down Camas Creek and up to Thunder Mountain.

Hoppins was an old-style aparejo packer and did not think much of the more modern methods. While based at Pistol Creek, he worked for Jay Sizick at the Lost Packer mine, running a pack train of big, impressive, buckskin mules.

He spent much of his time hauling supplies for miners and ranchers, then in about 1914 he sold his Pistol Creek place to Eleck Watson. Sam spent the winter of 1926 at Shorts Bar just east of Riggins, Idaho, returning to Big Creek, tributary of the Middle Fork, in the spring.

Hoppins spent his later years on Big Creek, at work on his own mine at Copper Camp. One afternoon, when he came out of the adit, he was shot twice by an incompetent hunter on a hillside across from the mine who thought he was a bear. The shooting cost Hoppins his life; he never fully recovered.

Eleck and Martha Watson, who took over Pistol Creek after Hoppins left, were originally from Texas. They were grandparents of Fred Paulsen and Daisey Tappan on their mother's side. Eleck was a resourceful trapper.

In 1919 the Watsons sold to George L. Risley, age fifty-one, a native of Connecticut, who then filed a homestead entry on 144 acres in 1920, and obtained patent with payment of $1.25 an acre three years later. Risley and his wife lived on the place, cleared thirty acres and cultivated fifteen in hay, potatoes, and garden truck irrigated by ditches from the creek. They had a log house (sixteen by twenty-feet) and barn. Risley and his wife were absent for a year because of a death in her family. In support of the continuity of their homestead claim, the recorder for the Land Office wrote, "The winter season in this vicinity is so severe that nothing can be accomplished by remaining on the land, nor can any work of improvement or cultivation be done." Billy Mitchell from Marble Creek, and Charlie Meyers, who lived across the river from the present Middle Fork Lodge, were their most frequent visitors and served as witnesses for their homestead filing.

The Risleys left to run a dairy ranch near Nampa, Idaho. Following their departure, the ranch sold frequently. It belonged at times to Robert Freeman, Albert Bennett, Marriner Eccles, and W. E. Wayne.

Bill and Adelade Wayne built a two-story lodge at Pistol Creek in the early fifties. Then Wayne was killed in an airplane crash on Elkhorn Ridge. His ashes were scattered over the ranch.

In 1957 Marvin and Barbara Hornback bought the ranch from Adelade Wayne and moved down from Sulphur Creek Ranch before they sold that ranch. (They also had a house in Boise, where their daughters Patricia and Jackie went to school in the winter.)

Between 1958 and 1965 the Hornbacks worked tirelessly at Pistol Creek. First, they extended the landing strip. Then they started out with another hunting and fishing outfit, but in need of operating capital, they surveyed the site into equal-sized lots and began selling them. Most of the purchasers were former Sulphur Creek Ranch guests.

The lots were sold along with a purchase contract for a house. Buyers received a deed, rights to use the private airstrip, and a choice of plans for one, two, or three-bedroom homes. A house could have multiple owners---one triplex had several. Marv hired college students as summer workers, usually supervised by Dewey Heater and his son Don, who assisted with almost every building until 1978. (The Heaters [!] were also winter caretakers at Pistol Creek.) Ferris Lind, originator of the Stinker Stations chain, was the first cabin owner. A two-bedroom house which sold for $8,000 then, sold for $160,000 in 1991.

Six hundred feet of eight-inch pipe was rafted to the site to set up a Pelton wheel generator. "Wild Bill" Watson rafted from Sulphur Creek with parts for a sawmill; other parts were flown in, and the mill was used to cut lumber for the cabins.

Logs were hauled with horses until a John Deere tractor could be brought in piecemeal. The crews dug a septic tank for each cabin, piped water from the creek, and installed propane tubing for lights and water heaters.

The Waynes' log lodge was to serve as the center for the ranch, but in 1958 clothing hung about the stovepipe caught fire and the lodge burned to ashes. Marv's reaction typified his attitude: "We'll build it back bigger and better." And they did.

Once enough houses were occupied, the Hornbacks were in a service business: they offered meals, commissary, and laundry at the lodge. They rented horses, ran river trips, did support for hunting and fishing, and, of course, served as pilots for the ranch, always hauling groceries and propane and people.

Owners came in for a week or a month or sometimes for the summer. It was an idyllic spot for children. Everyone got along well.

Then in October, 1965, while waiting at Strawberry Glen airport in Boise for some passengers for Pistol Creek, Marv was persuaded by an ex-Air Force pilot to take a trial flight in his Stinson Maul. Demonstrating touch-and-go's, the pilot clipped a berm with his tail wheel and both of them were killed in the crash.

Marv and Barbara
Hornback at Pistol
Creek.

Ten lot owners formed a non-profit corporation and purchased the remaining land from Barbara Hornback. (She died in 1971.) The main lodge became a private house. The ranch continues to be operated as a corporation, with twenty-one members at present. Its board of directors meets every Fourth of July at Pistol Creek. And although a river trail passes through the place, the only other access to The Middle Fork Ranch remains a private landing strip.

INDIAN CREEK TO BRUSH CREEK

MILE 25.1 *Indian Creek Campground.*

In 1902 W. B. Patten, who had operated mines in Colorado, Utah, and Montana, spent ten weeks exploring a lode on Indian Creek. In October he took fifty pounds of mineral samples, including wire gold, to Boise, but he was unable to obtain capital from Denver for his prospect.

Indian Creek Bar was first occupied by Eleck Watson, grandfather of Daisey Tappan and Fred Paulsen. He settled on the flat across the river, then decided he preferred the bar. In about 1914 he built several small cabins here.

Fred and Daisey were the only children along that entire section of the river. Miners often left them wild pets. They tamed chipmunks and broke them to pull match-box wagons, sometimes even holding "wagon races." The children trapped ground squirrels for the penny bounty on their tails. (Squirrels or "picket pins" were considered a nuisance in horse country because of their burrows.)

A pilot's view of Middle Fork Ranch (Pistol Creek) and airstrip.

131

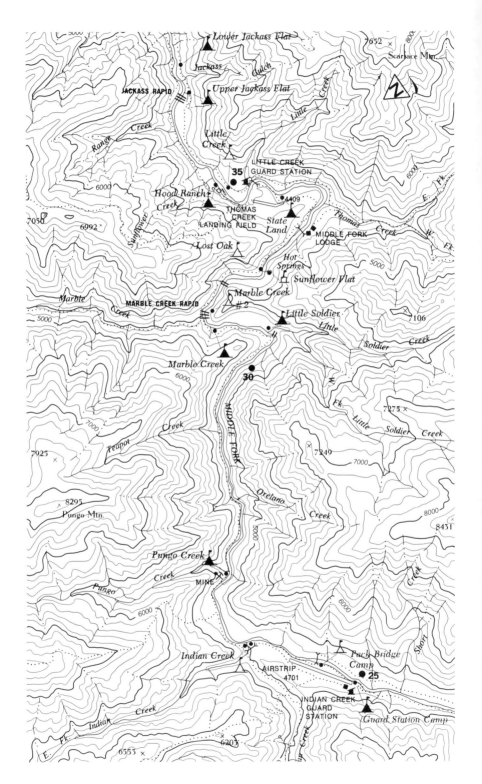

Lured by descriptions from a passing prospector, Watson pulled out in 1919 for Green River, Utah. The children went to school there, but did not stay long. (One of Daisey's schoolmates was Arthur Ekker of Robbers Roost Ranch fame.) They all finally returned to the Middle Fork country. Fred Paulsen worked a mining prospect up behind Indian Creek bar.

Eventually the site was withdrawn by the Forest Service for administrative purposes, and the old cabins were burned.

During the low-water season, Indian Creek is used by boaters as a fly-in launch spot. The wooden ramp running down to the river provides an easier means of getting boats to the river.

The Indian Creek landing strip is large enough to accept DC-3s. (One alighted without lowering its landing gear.) Little Soldier Mountain (8,813 feet) is directly across from the Indian Creek guard station.

The grave among the trees about 200 yards north of the guard station is that of Skipp Knapp, who was a contract pilot for Johnson Flying Service in 1965 and was flying smokejumpers and supplies to the Norton Creek fire. He and the spotter were parachuting tools. They turned to come down Norton Creek, realized they were too low for the ridge, pulled up and entered a high-speed stall. Both men were killed. Knapp's wife requested that he be buried in the backcountry. The line on the grave marker is from one of Skipp's poems.

The small cabin at the south end of the Indian Creek bridge was built in 1950 by Eddie Budell and Shorty Conyers; they roofed it with yellow-pine shingles.

Fire scars evident at Indian Creek, and for five miles downriver to Thomas Creek, where they cross the river, are the result of the Battleaxe fire begun by a lightning strike July 10, 1988. It was another "let-it-burn" blaze that began on the Middle Fork of Indian Creek about seven miles from

Eleck and Mamie Watson's cabin at Indian Creek, 1914. Bessie Watson-Cameron (left); Mamie Watson-Nethkin; Martha Watson.

the river and charred 42,000 acres. In late August the airstrip here had to be closed. The fire made its last run October 20. The scar extends twelve miles north-south and nine miles east-west. Afterwards, the fire management officer for the Forest Service Region Four admitted, "(the fire) is one where we should have taken suppression action earlier."

MILE 26.5 *Indian Creek Camp* consists of sites on each side of the creek; the upstream camp is the larger of the two.

MILE 27.4 *Pungo Creek*

Pungo, spelled Punggo on the 1930 Challis National Forest map, is actually "punko," a Shoshone word for "pet," also used for "horse."

In 1933 one of the old-time trappers on the Middle Fork took up what he believed was a quartz-claim at Pungo Creek. He went by the alias of Harry Jones, but his real name was John Harry Minshew, and he was a native of North Carolina. He had worked through the 1920s as a boiler mechanic at the Union Pacific railroad shop in Pocatello, then lost his job in 1929 during the Depression. Minshew built two cabins at Pungo Creek and had a good-sized garden.

He was primarily interested in trapping marten; there was a good market for the furs at the time, and he could make $500 a season, which was more than enough to get through the year with supplemental hunting and fishing.

Minshew acquired a trapping partner in 1936, Eddie Budell. Between 1925 and 1930 Budell had worked spring, summer, and fall in Chamberlain Basin (northwest of the Middle Fork) as a packer for the Forest Service, and worked winters for open-range cow outfits in the Jordan Valley of Oregon. Other summers were spent packing for the Civilian Conservation Corps in the Middle Fork-Salmon River country. "They were a good outfit," Budell remarked. He looked after Milt Hood's horses and mules at Range Creek downriver on the Middle Fork, and when Hood leased his stock to the Forest Service during the summer, he trusted Budell as wrangler and packer.

Minshew and Budell could usually trap until the end of January, when they had to quit for fear of a starting a fatal avalanche. The rest of the winter could be spent helping the miners work the Lucky Lad adit on the headwaters of Forty-five Creek. That mine was discovered in 1935 by Ben Seward on his way to a forest fire. Bob Johnson of Johnson's Flying Service, Missoula, Montana, furnished money and grub for the crew.

With the outbreak of World War II, both Minshew and Budell went out to see what they could do for their country. Minshew was nearly sixty but again found a boilermaker's job with the Union Pacific in Pocatello, which was important defense work.

Ed Budell (left) and J. R. Minshew at their Pungo cabins.

Both cabins at Pungo Creek, 1938. Potatoes were the major crop.

Budell registered for the draft but failed the examinations. The army rejected him for a preposterous reason: "multiple sclerosis." An extremely intelligent man, tough as an Owyhee County cowboy, and a gifted craftsman—but unsuited for soldiering. Said Budell with an ironic laugh, "That army is a sorry SOB outfit."

Since he had no birth certificate he could not do any other defense work, so he headed back to the Middle Fork. He was forty-two years old.

Minshew had a retarded son, Henry, who enjoyed living at Pungo Creek. He liked to fish, hunt, and trap, and he managed those activities well, so Budell offered to look after the boy.

Henry decided to go see his parents in Pocatello for the Fourth of July, and pilot Abe Knowles, part owner of Webb Flying Service in Boise, was at Loon Creek and offered the boy a flight to Boise. Knowles' controls jammed on takeoff and he crashed into a bluff across the river Although he survived, Henry died two hours later. Budell and Hood packed the body to the Mahoney airstrip and Penn Storr flew it to Cascade and then to Pocatello.

Minshew wanted to investigate matters himself, and Budell loaned him the money for a flight. After he looked things over to his own satisfaction, he gave the Pungo claim to Budell in return for the loan saying, "You might as well have the place, Ed, I won't be coming back."
The war had finished the trapping market, and gold mining too, because gold was not considered a critical metal.

Budell's thoughts turned to that quartz prospect. Minshew, however, had also left him a couple of burros, and one day a district ranger showed up asking if Ed would be willing to cut trail. He said sure. Summers from 1943 to 1950, Budell worked alone cutting trail up Indian Creek and all through the surrounding country. He worked with cross-cut saw and double-bitted axe. "I'm not a modern man," he remarked.

In the winter he had time to explore his claim. He put down a ten-foot shaft on top and sent some samples to American Smelter in Utah. A corporate reply inquired where the mineral was and how much of it existed. Budell immediately became suspicious. He made a trip to the assay office in Boise and took along some samples.

Budell on his way down to the Middle Fork.

The assayer got rather excited and suggested Budell spend $25 to get a spectrographic and quantitative analysis. Budell agreed. The report stated that it was high-grade fluorspar.

Top-grade fluorspar, or acid-grade, is used to make hydrofluoric acid. Demand exceeds supply in this country. Second-grade, or metallurgical grade, is used for steel production.

The assayer assured Budell he had a prospect; the next thing was to determine the quantity of ore. He returned to Pungo Creek and began to work the eighteen-inch lead on the top adit—in width, an encouraging lead. From his Lucky Lad days, he understood how to blacksmith, drill, and blast. Budell hauled his ore with a wheelbarrow. The holding wall was well solidified, but the fluorspar was only five on the hardness scale, and Budell considered that easy drilling. The ore came off in large premium chunks.

Working winters until 1950, he drove the top adit 105 feet, the bottom one 40 feet, and the middle one 65 feet. But the vein pinched out. Budell knew he needed at least 50,000 tons in order to interest anyone in putting a road to his claim. In the meantime he created a seventy-five-ton stockpile on the terrace below the mine.

In 1950 he quit cutting trail and spent the summer prospecting across the river for a continuation of the lead. He never found it but always believed it was there, somewhere under the overburden.

Bob Johnson had some Ford Trimotor airplanes and told Budell he could fly out of Indian Creek to Cascade with 3,000 pounds of fluorspar a trip. So Budell built mule-loading docks on the flat. Then he did some careful figuring and decided all the work would only let him break even. No sense in doing that, especially if he had multiple sclerosis.

In the early fifties Budell sold his claim to the Fluorspar Corporation of Reno, Nevada, for $5,000. They held an option on the prospect and received a Defense Minerals Exploration Administration loan, but the exploration never got underway. The U.S. Geological Survey later estimated the fluorspar resource at the site to contain between 7,000 and 13,000 tons of acid grade and an equal amount of metallurgical grade.

After he quit his claim, Budell began running a pack string for the Challis National Forest. He packed from 1951 to 1965, doing shoeing and blacksmithing as well. In 1965 he ran the last long-string packtrain on that forest. In the fall he had to shoot eight head of stock near Seafoam because the Forest Service had over 100 head of stock to winter in the Pahsimeroi. The horse was giving way to the helicopter.

The Pungo Creek claims were allowed to lapse and the Forest Service withdrew the area from mineral entry for administrative-site purposes. The Minshew cabins were burned as the result of a Forest Service directive.

Ed Budell bought a small place near Lake Lowell, Idaho. He braided some of the finest rawhide bridles and ropes in the country—a craft he learned from "an old cowman friend during the panic years." He continued to cut all his firewood with a crosscut saw. In his last years he suffered a ruptured appendix and prostate cancer. Budell died in 1990.

Budell's loading docks at Pungo Creek. They burned in the 1988 Battle Axe fire. (Historic values are usually sacrificed to the let-it-burn policy.)

Budell (left) with mine inspector Pete Telffer enroute to the Pungo fluorspar prospect.

A couple of years before he died, Budell reflected on his years at Pungo in a letter to Eliot DuBois:

"Pungo Creek made a good home for me as I could get along cheap there having no money or education for any kind of a good job on the outside. I certainly thanked Harry many times for this kind act. I see it was lucky for me I wanted his retarded son to have it and him getting killed and the army not wanting me is what influenced Harry to give it to me. I lived there to the 60's. But it was getting harder every year and I got out of there. Was getting too old for it. Good thing I did as short time after I had to have a serious operation. With no communication you have to have good health to survive there."

MILE 27.7 *Pungo Creek Campground* on the left below the creek. Easy landing, heavily used, lots of space.
MILE 31.3 *Little Soldier Creek Camp* just below the creek on the right. Flat spaces among the trees on the higher benches.
MILE 32 *Marble Creek Camp* on the left, a large bench alongside the big pool.

Billy Mitchell was the first person to settle with some permanence on Marble Creek. He was from Scotland and came into the Salmon River country as a miner near the turn of the century. He located first on the Secesh meadows, building a house there that later came to be known as the Fernan place. Getting the fever again, he mined at Thunder Mountain in 1902, and with Carl Brown at Edwardsburg.

Early in 1916 he started his ranch on the large, open flat on the south side of Marble Creek about two miles from the river. An old cabin was already situated on the meadow. It belonged to an early trapper, Dave Sutton, who committed suicide with his rifle and is buried on the place. Mitchell patented his homestead in 1923 at age fifty.

Marble Creek has seen its share of disappointed placer miners; only the smallest traces of gold were ever found in the stream.

Mitchell's wife, Ora Hughes, came in to the ranch to live with him. For over thirty years he hardscrabbled, maintaining an elaborate irrigation system, going to Meyers Cove for mail, and driving what beef he could raise to market in Cascade.

In 1950 he finally sold out to the Fish and Game Department for $6,000 and moved to Riggins Hot Springs, hoping to

Billy Mitchell at his Marble Creek cabin.

spend the winter with his old friend Andy Casner. In less than a month Mitchell became ill and died in the Council, Idaho, hospital. He was an old pioneer who had outlived almost all of his friends. Few people attended his funeral. His cabin was burned by the Forest Service. The root cellar and irrigation ditches are still visible.

MILE 32.1 *Marble Creek Rapid.* A rock ledge creates an impressive hole from the left shore out through the middle of the river at any flow below high water. The Oregon guides refer to this rapid as "Chipmunk" because in 1954 guide Jack Lowry, while attempting to demonstrate the proper route around the hole, got caught in the reversal and looked like a ground squirrel as he scurried back and forth along his lower sprayskirt attempting to avoid the turnover.

MILE 32.7 *Ski Jump Rapid.*

MILE 33 *Sunflower Campground* on right. The hot spring flowing down the rocks was known as Pottie's Spring; named for Sylvester Potvein, who had his cabin near here. Potaman Peak and Potter Vine Creek are also named for him. The large camp on the timbered terrace across from Sunflower Flat is called **Lost Oak Camp.**

MILE 33.5 *Middle Fork Lodge-Thomas Creek Ranch.*

This anchorhold on the right side of the river, a half-hour flight northeast of Boise, is the Middle Fork Lodge, the most celebrated natural sanctuary and vintage guest ranch on any fork of the Salmon River.

This place is old enough to have a memory of itself. Reportedly, Thomas Creek takes its name from a miner who worked the drainage in the 1880s; tailings are evident along the creek several miles from the river. One hundred yards from the upriver end of the airstrip on the left stands a patriarchal yellow pine with a venerable, in-grown blaze: Idham Lodge 28 SEPT 1885— likely the work of a surveyor employed by the Oregon Short Line Railroad, whose track across Idaho had been completed a year earlier. The OSR, headquartered in Salt Lake City and run by Jay Gould, was looking for a connecting route between Butte, Montana, and Weiser, Idaho. It was never found.

A dozen years later, Jim Voller, an Englishman recently naturalized in Salmon (1889), settled at the mouth of Thomas Creek on the east side of the river and began cultivating the terrace above the present lodge. In 1913, at age fifty-nine, Voller proved-up on his eighty-acre homestead and took title.

Voller had some helpers: Michael James McNerney, native of Ireland, a year older than Voller, tall, lean, with a ready sense of humor; and Charlie Batters, of like age, who had known Voller for several years and lived with him for three. McNerney, by his own account, saw the spot as early as 1895 and visited Voller every couple of months. He and Voller became known as "the Buckskin Boys."

The men dug a half-mile ditch out of the creek and along the skirt of the hill to irrigate sixty acres of "lucerne" (alfalfa) and timothy clover. Busy as the day is long, they hewed a small log cabin and a sixteen-by-twenty-foot barn, and then spanned the river with a 200-foot tramway. They kept horses, cattle, cows, dogs, cats, and chickens—a tireless safeguard against sleeping-in.

Freeman and Mamie Nethkin (left) and Kenny and Bessie Cameron at Little Creek, 1917. The Nethkins' boy, born March, 1919, was the first non-Indian child born on the Middle Fork.

While pitching hay (probably in fall 1915), McNerney collapsed from a heart attack, and his unmarked gravestone on the hem of the hill above Voller's cabin leans now, with time's inexorable tilt, toward the effortless flow of the river. Voller's health soon frayed; he sold the ranch and died in Lewiston some time later.

The Idaho buyers—Freeman Nethkin, Ed Osborn, Henry Clay—stocked the ranch with additional cattle. Nethkin had come into the Salmon River country in 1898 as a miner. He went partners with Fred Burgdorf in a cattle ranch at the mouth of the South Fork of the Salmon—a private resort now known as Mackay Bar. When he and Burgdorf sold their interests in 1910, he used part of his share a few years later to buy the Sater place at Little Creek, immediately downriver and adjacent to Voller's homestead.

Nethkin and his new Thomas Creek partners fought protracted winters and distant, fickle markets. In the spring of 1919 the partners sold out to the Middle Fork Land and Livestock Company, associated with the Overland National Bank in Boise. The Company had expansive plans for a livestock operation—it bought options on ranches downriver as far as Loon Creek (sixteen miles)—but the managers were unfamiliar with the range and its weather.

Summer, 1919: dry as a year-old cow chip; meager hay. Fall, 1919: the Company trailed 1,200 sheep into the canyon, left them, and started out with 300 head of cattle. It was October. Early snowfall raked the canyon; ridges swathed in white. The cattle had not been off the range in six years; they were spooky, ornery, and smart enough not to want to climb toward high country with winter near. Riders pushed the herd upriver toward the Pistol Creek trail to Landmark (7,600'), where they would head west to Cascade.

In mid-November, while trying to break across the divide, a more formidable storm walloped the herd. Snow drifted four feet deep. The temperature dropped like a heart-shot elk. Late calves gave out. No going back. A work horse broke trail. More snow. Fifty, sixty, seventy-five head gave up. Hay was sledded east from Scott Valley. It was Christmas by the time the survivors reached Cascade.

The winter of 1919-1920 became the one against which all others were measured. Deer died by the thousands. Only one-quarter of the sheep in the canyon survived. The Livestock Company went belly-up, the bank failed, and the ranch reverted to Nethkin and Osborn.

No money, no cattle, no hay, agricultural depression. Flirting with insolvency, the partners rented the Voller cabin to the fish and game department as warden quarters. Nethkin put the place up for sale, but there were no offers.

Milt and Mary Hood, having been in the area since the late twenties, moved onto the homestead in the early thirties and established the first commercial hunting and fishing operation on the river. But in 1938 Tom and Nell McCall bought the ranch from Nethkin, forcing the Hoods to decamp downriver to Sunflower Flat, where they ran their business until 1943.

Tom McCall, grandson of the man for whom McCall, Idaho, is named, was unrivaled: he was resourceful, inventive, indefatigable. McCall sold his local Shell Oil distributorship and his flying business and used the money to develop Thomas Creek. His intention was to make the wilderness ranch into a successful lodge for hunters and fishermen—simply a grander version of Hood's dream. McCall herded in thirty-five horses. He flew in the pieces for a sawmill and reassembled them. While he and Nell and six-year-old daughter Bonnie (who was home-schooled until the eighth grade) lived in the Voller cabin, they milled the lumber for a new lodge...and for a new bridge. Nell said that when she arrived at the airstrip and got the courage to cross the old footbridge, she knew the place had to be home because she wouldn't go back over it.

McCall's lodge, Thomas Creek.

The Middle Fork Lodge is blessed with one of the more
splendid hot springs in the West: 135 degrees, abundant, free
of sulphur, pure enough to drink—an earth-gift. McCall
perceived the value of the springs for heating and bathing,
and he had a packer help him train three pairs of mules to
pack sixteen-foot lengths of steel pipe. His mule teams then
hauled 300 feet of pipe from the Greyhound mine above the
Middle Fork down to Pistol Creek. He welded plates over the
ends of the pipe and tack-welded them into rafts which were
floated ten miles downstream to Thomas Creek, arriving
dented but serviceable. Harnessed, the springs added their
spell to an already remarkable place.

In 1955 the McCalls sold the ranch to outfitter-sportsmen
Ken Roundy, Dr. Hugh Dean, and Bill Guth Sr., who continued the traditional business of hunting (deer, elk, bear,
lion) and fishing (salmon and steelhead). Eventually the
partners sold their interests to well-known Idaho outfitter
Rex Lanham.

In 1966, when the U. S. Forest Service failed to exercise
an option to buy the site, multimillionaire Bill Harrah of

147

Harrah's Reno and Lake Tahoe became the new owner, and
the Middle Fork Lodge sailed into halcyon days.

For a man of wealth, Bill Harrah was unusual: shy, considerate of his employees, a conservationist, and devoted to
restoring the outmoded—whether cars, airplanes, or buildings. He hired Bob Cole as manager, a man with most of
McCall's gifts and more of his own. And then McCall drifted
back in and stayed to work at the lodge for another nine
years. Work they did.

At one time Bill Harrah employed six pilots. (Captain
Gordon Hartley, former skipper of the carrier USS Wasp
which was used to recover a half-dozen astronauts, was one.)
Harrah's air corps flew an Otter, a Ford Trimotor, and a
Queen Air to and from Thomas Creek, carrying milled logs
for a remodeled lodge, employee quarters, guest cabins,
fences. Sometimes there were as many as fifty laborers on the
site, some of them sleeping on the floor. By piping water
almost a half-mile from Thomas Creek, a hydropower plant
was brought on line. Diesel generators served as standby. Up
went a five-car garage, barn, shop, a new bridge, a small store
(for river runners); down went a new well, a septic system, a
refinished swimming pool watered by the hot springs. The
Voller cabin was restored; so was the Sater cabin at nearby
Little Creek. Antique cars were helicoptered to the lodge in
order to transport guests in period style. In season, a boating
business rowed the river and hunting camps outfitted in the
high country.

It was during the Harrah-era that the lodge acquired
national notoriety from the celebrities who stayed there: Bill
Cosby, Loretta Lynn, Dick Smothers, John Denver,
Lawrence Welk, Steve McQueen, Sammy Davis, Jr., Glen
Campbell, to drop a few. Daryl Lamonica played touch
football on the lawn; Parnelli Jones was chauffeured across
the bridge in a 1926 Chevrolet station wagon. Even after
Harrah's death in 1978, the attraction remained. President
Carter stopped for lunch in 1979; President Bush (then VP)
in 1984.

Aerial view Middle Fork Lodge; river and bridge in foreground. New bridge was built in 1968 by pulling the cables across the river with a Cat.

Main lodge built by Bill Harrah.

Restored Voller cabin at Thomas Creek.

However, like the rug that gets pulled, other aspects of the place changed once Bill Harrah was gone. The lodge was acquired by Holiday Inn as an appendage of Harrah's Reno and Lake Tahoe, and corporate detachment will never be a match for personal interest. The principal legacies of the Inn years were removal and sale of the antique automobiles, and construction of an incongruous, fenced tennis court on the riverbank.

In 1990 Holiday Inn sold the ranch to the Nature Conservancy, which placed restrictive covenants on the property. Among them: no subdivison or retail sales or herbicides or trapping. Restoration of the hydro plant (which had lost out to diesel generators after the Mortar Creek forest fire and a flash flood) was recommended. Then the Conservancy found a philosophically sympathetic buyer, John McCaw, interested in undoing years of neglect.

McCaw, age forty-two in 1992, is the third of four brothers who own controlling interest in McCaw Cellular Communications (Kirkland, Washington). Their father, J. Elroy McCaw, was a visionary gambler in radio and cable television in the Northwest.

Upon his death in 1969, the young McCaws learned that their father had extensive business liabilities. They labored tirelessly to expand a cable business in Washington and Alaska, and sold it in 1987 to Washington Redskins owner Jack Kent Cooke for $755 million.

The brothers then put cash and junk-bond financing into cellular-phone licenses from coast to coast, and by 1990 theirs was the biggest cellular telephone company in the country—the only national car-phone network—and worth several billion dollars.

The fire scars at Thomas Creek are a vestige of the Mortar Creek fire, the effects of which will certainly be visible for most of a century. Since it was the third-largest timber fire in state history, burning in excess of 100 square miles, and because it received national attention, it seems appropriate to include some information about the event here. The last weeks of July, 1979, brought the most severe fire weather to Idaho in a decade. It was preceded by two winters of abnormally low snowfall.

A week before the Mortar Creek firestorm, twin fires on the river gave ample evidence of the hazardous conditions. A ninety-five-acre blaze on Little Loon Creek was started by a careless backpacker. No sooner had that fire been snuffed by smokejumpers from McCall, than a Boy Scout leader, exercising poor judgment, touched off a second fire that was held at 105 acres by 283 men—assisted by aerial tankers. The two fires nearly conflated. Suppression costs ran $500,000. All but the deaf or skeptical had been put on notice that fire danger in the backcountry was higher than heaven over hell.

Nevertheless, three horseback campers who spent the night by the trail on the upper Middle Fork, between Dome and Artillery creeks, were not sufficiently concerned. They threw some dirt over their fire in the morning and rode away. But "dead things have been known to crawl" —and their fire went on smouldering. It had some help: low fuel moisture and low relative humidity, high temperatures and calescent winds.

At 2:24 on the afternoon of July 26, Tom Harbour was flying fire reconnaissance over the Middle Fork for the U.S. Forest Service. He detected the escaped campfire—now grown ten-feet- square.

Within eight minutes a helicopter left Challis for Indian Creek on the Middle Fork to round out a five-man crew for initial attack. At 3:15 PM a BLM air tanker (a B-26) from Boise was over the fire dropping 1,200 gallons of Firetrol (ammonium nitrate and water).

A second tanker, a DC-6 from Salt Lake City, hit the blaze with an additional 2,200 gallons. Yet in one hour, the fire had already devoured 150 acres and crowned (burning through the treetops). A half hour later it had doubled its size and had spotted-out across the river below Greyhound Creek. Faced with the chance of entrapment, the helitack crew had to withdraw. Smokejumpers flown to the scene were unable to parachute because of the wind conditions they encountered. By nightfall the burn exceeded 1,000 acres, and the Forest Service was moving to establish a fire camp at Bruce Meadows, between Bear Valley and Fir creeks.

Because of steep terrain, inaccessibility, limited visibility, and unpredictable winds—difficulties that were to plague the planners and firefighters for the duration of the blaze—it was almost twenty-four hours before the Forest Service was able to get men back on the fire line. Wind had fanned the flames up Greyhound Creek on the east side of the river, but retardant drops supported by ground work slowed the fire's advance. Only 500 acres were consumed on July 28.

The next day the number of men on the lines was raised to 600; they labored with pulaskis, chain saws and shovels to hold the flanks of the fire and blunt its head. The crews succeeded in establishing a rear line, on the west, just below Artillery Dome.

Monday night, July 30, the fire was declared controlled at 2,250 acres. Mop-up began. It continued for two days. The army of firefighters was reduced to fifty men. If any mistake was made at Mortar Creek, it was this action. As Dr. Kenneth Davis, fire behavior specialist, has written, "The roster of large fires which at one time were believed to be under control, but which subsequently escaped is long and melancholy." On August 2, Mortar Creek was added to the roster.

A short way up Greyhound Creek a small wedge of trees and brush had escaped the fire's fury. A troublesome hot-spot kindled there and the crew called for a retardant drop. They

Mortar Creek fire cloud.

struggled feverishly to get a line around the point. Elusive tongues of flame, spurred by dry winds, bolted past—the fire took off like a bronc coming out of a bucking chute. It would be long outside the corral.

The fire galloped through a thousand acres the next day, caught more wind, and doubled its acreage on August 3. With 7,000 acres on fire, the Forest Service shifted overall control from the fire boss at Bruce Meadows to a general headquarters at Boise. On August 4 the fire had enlarged to 11,800 acres.

The Forest Service at this point had fires throughout the central portion of the state. The Targhee National Forest Gallagher Peak fire, which had begun as a let-burn lightning blaze, was now unhalted and headed for 36,000 acres; the Ship Island fire downriver on the Middle Fork was out of control. A low pressure system in southeast Idaho was pushing high dry winds down to the Mortar Creek fire and propelling flames across ridges at speeds approaching forty miles an hour. Smoke smothered the area, making air support impossible except for brief periods in the afternoon. The slopes were steeper than a cow's face and made ground work difficult and treacherous. Supply logistics were staggering. Despite these obstacles, a massive effort was mounted.

To keep track of the fire, a scanner plane was used above the blaze. It carried special cameras and infrared film (sensitive to long-wave light radiation) which recorded heat images below the smoke. The film was processed on board, placed before a television camera and transmitted to a van at the Bruce Meadows fire camp. There the transmission was recorded on videotape and fire bosses monitored the wildfire's progress on their tv screen. The aircraft made surveillance flights at noon and midnight. On the afternoon of August 5 the convection column over the fire was too turbulent at 30,000 feet to permit an infrared scan. The next films examined on Monday, August 6, revealed the fire had grown at an exponential rate—to 30,800 acres, a leap of 20,000 acres since Saturday night.

Saturday had been an eventful interval beneath the smoke-curtain over the canyon. Professional boaters, committed months in advance to fulfilling vacation plans for numerous passengers, were carrying on their business, though not quite as usual. Boundary Creek launches had dwindled, but Indian Creek was still open. A charter plane from Boise bringing five passengers for a float trip had crashed one and one-half miles from the strip the day before. The passengers were killed and smokejumpers had to fight the fire started by the plane. They rescued the pilot and moved him to Bruce Meadows, where a Forest Service plane flew him to Boise, but his burns proved fatal.

The crash resulted in a temporary air closure of the Indian Creek strip because of fire traffic. Outfitters such as Helfrich, Handy, and Foster, who had started at Boundary Creek intending to meet guests at Indian Creek, had to pick up their passengers at Thomas Creek. But even Thomas Creek was closed intermittently because of poor visibility.

As a consequence of these events, on August 5, Hughes River Expeditions weathered one of the more bizarre experiences in the annals of boating. Outfitter-owner Jerry Hughes had a five-boat trip which was scheduled to depart from Indian Creek on August 6. His sweepboat had been cached there a couple of days earlier in anticipation of the launch. Realizing that the departure point had shifted to Thomas Creek, and that the sweep would have to be moved downriver, Jerry and a helper flew to Thomas Creek with Ray Arnold the morning of the 5th. While Jerry and his swamper packed boat pump and plywood up to Indian Creek to rig the sweep and bring it down, Arnold and fellow pilot Bud Williams brought the rest of Hughes' crew into Thomas Creek, where they began moving their equipment and supplies to the river's edge.

Hughes and helper finished their task at 3:00 PM and pushed off downriver. The convolutions of the fire-cloud could be seen behind the ridge across from Indian Creek. Slow water did not help matters, and Jerry could tell the situation looked marginal by the time he reached the Thomas Creek bridge. At that moment they saw the fire crown at the head of the drainage. A line of flames towered a hundred feet in the air, moving under the power of its own momentum in rushes along the slopes and ridge. A quick check at the Middle Fork Lodge revealed a Forest Service helicopter had just left, after reassuring the people there that the fire could not arrive before the next day.

When Hughes joined his crew on the bank opposite the Little Creek guard station, they had two boats in the water and two to rig, persuaded that they could complete the job in the morning. It was now 8:45 PM.

Hughes was reasonably concerned about the firey advance he had just witnessed. At this point, Ray Arnold's plane circled through the smoke-haze and came in for a landing. The guides went up to learn his estimate of the situation. Arnold was enroute to Cascade from Challis and had decided that Thomas Creek looked so threatened he ought to see if he could help evacuate the boatmen. Williams flew up the canyon and landed to confirm the appraisal, adding that he had just seen the fire jump the river at Mahoney Creek. It was getting late: no time to raft out and little light left for flying. Fire winds buffeted the strip. While Arnold and Williams flew Handy's crew (who were awaiting passengers and boats) to Indian Creek, Hughes' men had ten minutes to sink their boats and gear in the river. There was not much doubt the area would be taken by the sweep of the approaching fire. Arnold and Williams returned, and everyone piled into the Cessnas—there was no room or time for personal gear. The planes took off down river, gaining altitude in the turbulent fire-lit sky, turned and headed back to Indian Creek. Hughes got a glimpse of his new boats scuttled in the river and had a philosophical thought or two about property insurance. (He recovered the boats shortly thereafter.)

At Indian Creek, as fire guard Eli Hill served pilots and guides a much needed cup of coffee, he got a radio call from the Bruce Meadows fire camp: "Did you get the numbers on those damn Cessnas that were violating the air closure?"

Mortar Creek fire, 1979.

Maybe it was too late in the evening, or maybe he knew a couple of pilots had just risked their necks to thwart a disaster of which the Forest Service was not even aware. "Nope, I didn't see them," he replied.

Sunday at dawn the Forest Service dispatched three helicopters with hotshot crews downriver under the layer of smoke. Their mission was to protect the Middle Fork Lodge and Little Creek guard station if possible. The fire had hesitated during the night. Marine pumps were set up, sprinklers activated, and a series of backfires torched along the base of Old Scarface mountain. The backfires caught a draft that the main fire sucked toward itself. Waves of flame met each other, only to collapse for lack of fuel. The strategy worked—it saved the lodge and station, which everyone else had written off.

Mortar Creek was now a "zone" fire. Containment efforts were divided among three teams, each responsible for its own zone, with overall directions from a general headquarters fire team at Boise. About 800 men were on the lines by August 6, with another 500 reinforcements en route. A 150-person overhead crew coordinated and supervised battle tactics.

Transportation and food services were facilitated by 150 members of the Idaho National Guard. Costs were running a one-quarter million dollars a day.

August 7: Wildfire wedded to wind is an awesome natural phenomenon. The Mortar Creek fire engulfed another 10,000 acres—it was spreading like an oil slick. The blaze now had its own well-established microclimate: temperatures of 1,200 to 1,800 degrees sucked superheated air into a convection column where updrafts in the vortex, estimated at seventy-five miles per hour, whorled smoke in the vertical cloud until it appeared to be an everted furnace. Warm air funneled up the steep slopes and canyons at rapid rates, supplying the needed oxygen. At this stage, the fire pre-heated the fuel ahead of itself, and blazing fragments carried forward on the winds ignited spot fires in advance of the main blaze.

If viewers a hundred miles away could only shake their heads in wonder at the thunder cloud of smoke that ascended on the horizon every afternoon, certainly there was not much more the men on the ground could do. They labored on the flanks of the fire, assisted by helicopters and air tankers when the smoke lifted enough to permit the pilots to fly. Nothing yet devised by man could arrest the runaway front.

By the afternoon of August 8 the fire had reached 56,000 acres, but a high skin of clouds began to stretch across the sky. Temperatures lowered and air moisture increased. This slowed the fire appreciably over the next two days, as 2,365 firefighters struggled to take full advantage of the concession.

On the morning of August 11 the cloud layer had darkened. A steady drizzle became a drumming rain by noon—a generous wetness. By late the next day almost an inch of rain had fallen. The flames lost vigor, wavered, and winked out. In the end, nature had handled the situation. Firefighters, lightly clothed, shivered in the cold. The startling reversal was underscored by the evacuation of a hypothermia victim.

The Mortar Creek fire was controlled at 65,300 acres inside 102 miles of fire perimeter.

The most encouraging event in the aftermath was the telephone response received by the Forest Service: callers volunteered to help plant trees—a touching affirmation of the special place the Middle Fork country holds in the hearts of many Idahoans.

MILE 33.5 *Charley Meyer's Cabin.* Charley L. Meyer's cabin and acreage was located on the west side of the river, or the left bank, just below the Middle Fork Lodge bridge. Meyers, born in 1859, came into the Middle Fork from the Squaw Creek and Payette River country in 1893, looking for a place to winter his packstring.

Those who knew him say Meyers was a picturesque old mountain man with hair nearly as long as his beard. (Once a fellow who was helping him throw a diamond hitch pulled the lash rope tight and caught the mountain man's beard under it. Needless to say, the helper's ears got burned.) Meyers was injured in a horse fall while packing to Thunder Mountain, and it left him partially crippled. As a result, he always rode his horse off-center.

Meyers with friend's children at Big Creek.

Charley Meyers,
first settler across
the river from
Thomas Creek.

He built the first cabin, together with a small barn and corral, on the flat across from Thomas Creek. The bar was known as the Start-First claim, but Meyers was not interested in mining or farming. He wintered his horses, trapped, and packed. His only failing, if it be one, was a great fondness for whiskey.

He had been around long enough to have been acquainted with Edward Chamberlain, for whom Chamberlain Basin is named, and with another old-timer, "Trapper" Johnson. Meyers could recall seeing them on the trail, leading to market. a lengthy packstring loaded with their furs

At age sixty-four he was still doing some packing for George Risley at Pistol Creek and brought him his mail "between five and twenty times a year." In his later years, Meyers moved to the Big Creek country and lived in Ed James' cabin up Cave Creek, tributary to Big Creek. He spent several years there looking after his horses. Then he moved to Copper Camp on Big Creek and would follow the summer grass up to Edwardsburg. In the thirties he was taken to Cascade where he died and is buried.

Bill Harrah tore down Meyer's dilapidated cabin to make a garage for the airstrip pick-up vehicle.

Meyers never filed for a homestead. When Jim Voller attempted to add eighty acres on that side of the river to his own homestead filing, the Land Office informed him that he would have to live on it and cultivate it as well, and furthermore, it had not yet been surveyed. Voller did not file on it, and the area is state land.

MILE 34.5 *Thomas Creek Landing Field* on the bench on the left side of the river. This airstrip was built by Milt Hood during the winter of 1934-1935 when he was living at Thomas Creek. It was designated Hood Airport by the state and remains state land. The first plane to land here came from Cascade and was owned and flown by Bob King of Boise.

First plane to land at Thomas Creek: Cabin Waco, four seats, flown by Bob King, Boise. King was the first staff pilot for Standard Oil in South America, where he flew for 15 years.

Tappan family poses with a Beechcraft Travelair 6000, a six-seater, at the Thomas Creek strip.

MILE 36.1 *Little Creek* on the right. Forest Service summer guard station maintained here. The campsite is on a bench downstream and around a bend from the guard station. Take the right hand channel around the island and land just downriver from the island.

MILE 36.1 *Little Creek Bridge*. The Forest Service asked Fred Paulsen if he would pack in the materials for this bridge. He agreed to handle the job. The Service put on a summer crew to widen the trail all the way to the river.

When spring arrived, fifteen feet of snow still blocked parts of the trail, which should have been expected. Instead of waiting for it to melt, the Forest Service hired Bob Johnson to fly in the materials with his Ford Trimotor.

MILE 36.3 *Jim and Belle Hash cabin* on the right.

Jim Hash spent most of his youth on his father's ranch at Idaho Falls. After losing all his front teeth in a fight, when someone hit him with a chair, he always carried two guns.

He was twenty-five when he married Belle, who was fifteen. They never had any children, but they were so busy they could scarcely have had time for any. The couple settled on six acres near the junction of Mayfield and Loon creeks for several years. Then they moved down below Little Creek on the Middle Fork.

In July, 1906, the *Idaho Recorder* in Salmon captured most of what we know about the life of Jim and Belle Hash at this site. It reported:

"J. A. Hash and his wife have been making a living here (on their Middle Fork ranch) about four years. Jim has been in the west over thirty years, but was born in Missouri. Belle was born in Tennesee and has been in the west over twenty-four years—though looks to be thirty-five.

Mr. Hash since he has been in the west was in the motive department of a railroad, but was mired up in the strike some years ago and had to look for other sources of a livelihood. The nearest family resides about twenty miles from the home of Mr. and Mrs. Hash. Game is plentiful;

Frank Gunnison ferry at Little Creek, 1903. Vestiges of the cable remain.

Jim and Belle Hash at Little Creek, 1902, with two of the Beagle brothers from the Mormon Ranch downriver.

First Middle Fork
cable crossing:
Sam Hoppins,
John Sater, Fred
Schiefer, 1913.

Jim Hash (left),
Jenny Laing-Lewis,
Belle Hash in
1903 crossing the
bridge built a year
earlier
near Marble
Creek.

most any time they can see herds of deer from their cabin door. Both being experts with the rifle they have plenty of wild game when in season.

He states that he raised vegetables consisting of potatoes and such other vegetables as he can pack in to Thunder Mountain, which he finds a ready market at five cents per pound.

Last year he raised and packed in about 25,000, but this year he will raise about 40,000 pounds. In addition he cuts hay, and packs it in, which sells readily at $100 per ton. He realizes from his potatoes from $100-$140 per ton."

The Hashes kept a packstring of twenty to thirty burros. They would loose-herd them along the trail, selling their produce from Custer to Thunder Mountain. Packing charges for supplies ran five to fifteen cents a pound. Everyone liked and respected the couple.

The year 1906, however, proved to be the last one before Thunder Mountain and its vegetable market clabbered. Middle Fork ranches tried to market their vegetables in Yellowjacket, but it was neither as big nor as isolated as Thunder Mountain. The Hashes moved on.

By early November, 1906, John Sater, native of Kansas, had settled on the site. He resided there continuously, but his wife took their ten children to school in town for the winters.

Sater had five acres in timothy and clover the first year. By 1916, when he was fifty-six, he had increased the cultivated acreage to forty, irrigated it with two ditches out of Little Creek, and was harvesting about two tons of hay per acre. He had fenced the area, and in addition to their fourteen-by-twenty-foot, two-room house, had a twenty- by-twenty-foot barn. They proved-up on the sixty-two acre homestead that year. Shortly thereafter—perhaps even the same year—Sater sold out to Freeman Nethkin.

The Hash place is now part of the Middle Fork Lodge property, and Bill Harrah directed that the cabin be restored.

Fred Paulsen's parents started the second cabin at Little Creek, but it was never finished. It stands, since roofed, behind the Hash cabin.

MILE 36.4 *Hood Ranch and Campground* to the left of the island.

John Chestnut was the first settler on this bar, and he built a cabin and corral out of cottonwood trees. He planted a peach orchard and sold the fruit in the Thunder Mountain camps.

When Milt and Mary Hood had to move out of the Thomas Creek ranch, they came down to Sunflower Hot Springs, which was state land, and built new outfitting cabins with help from Shorty Conyers. Hot spring water was piped to the cabins. The dead peach trees were burned as firewood.

Milt was born on a ranch near Spokane, Washington. As a teenager he shipped aboard a British ocean liner, but on his return, decided he preferred being ashore and drifted back to cowboying in the Southwest and Mexico. He even tried rounding up wild burros in the Grand Canyon and trailing them for a month to Kingman, Arizona, to sell them to prospectors.

After service in World War I, Hood traveled to the Salmon River country. In the 1930s hardly a forest fire on the Middle Fork could be fought without using packstrings from Hood's herd. Ed Budell remarked that Hood had about seventy-five head of horses and mules which he wintered on Range Creek below Sunflower Flat and hired out to the Forest Service in season.

Milt met and married Mary Madsen, who worked in restaurants in Salmon and Challis. (She had children by a previous marriage.) Together they moved to Thomas Creek, along with a stepdaughter; and after the confrontation with McCall, on down to Sunflower.

The Hoods remained on the Middle Fork until 1943, then left for Seattle, where Milt signed up with the U. S. Trans-

Milt and Mary Hood's cabin built near Sunflower Hot Springs after the move from Thomas Creek.

portation Corps. He was master of an Army tugboat, shoving troop and ammunition ships in and out of harbors. During the Korean War he did patrol work at munition-loading docks on the West Coast. At sixty-five, impelled by fond memories of the Southwest, he retired to Bullhead City, Arizona, although he continued to run safety patrols on the lower Colorado River and Lake Powell as an auxiliary member of the U.S. Coast Guard. After they moved, Mary, who had worked as a mechanic for Boeing Corporation in Seattle, served as a librarian in Kingman, Arizona.

Milt died in 1979; Mary died a few years later.

The land now belongs to the Idaho Fish and Game Department. The agency moved the Hood cabin back from the river bank in order to preserve it.

MILE 36.5 *Sunflower Hot Springs*. Just a short walk down the trail from the Hood cabin.

MILE 37.5 *Jackass Rapid*. A tough pull to the right in low water.

MILE 37.6-.9 *Upper and Lower Jackass Camps* on the right are large, convenient sites but suffered fire damage.

MILE 39.5 *Cameron Creek* on the left.

This creek is named for Kenneth Cameron who had a 147-acre homestead between here and Mahoney Creek.

Cameron was born in Gairloch, Rosshire, Scotland in 1884. In 1900 he immigrated from Glasgow to the port of New York, and in 1922 he became a naturalized citizen at Emmett, Idaho. (His papers describe him as 5' 8", 165 pounds, blue eyes, light complexion, brown hair, missing little finger on left hand.)

He grazed cattle along this reach of the river beginning in 1916; he also worked in the mines, and raised potatoes and apples on his homestead, which he packed to the mines up Big Creek and Rapid River. In 1919 he married Bessie Watson, half his age, who lived at Indian Creek. Their first child, Howard, was born the following year.

The couple had the customary log house and barn.

Their homestead grew from ten cultivated acres in 1917 to thirty-five acres in grain, alfalfa, and potatoes in 1923. They stacked between twenty-five and fifty-five tons of hay each year. Then the Camerons acquired the ranch at the mouth of Loon Creek farther down river and did well there—they were hard workers and fine stockmen.

One fall they headed up Bacon Creek with some mules to put them on winter range. Bessie was out in the lead with the bell mare. When Kenney failed to show up, she back-tracked and found him lying unconscious by the trail. He had a crease along the side of his head above the ear. It was impossible to tell whether he had been shot, struck with a rock, or kicked by a mule. He was taken on a stretcher thirty-five miles to Meyers Cove and was in the hospital for three months before he regained consciousness.

The Camerons eventually sold to the Lovells, and Kenney went to work on the Butte Ranch, north of Emmett, Idaho, raising mules.

MILE 39.5 *Little Loon Creek* enters on the right. Dutch Charlie Rochlan lived up Little Loon Creek about six miles from the river. He had a comfortable cabin in a clearing with beaver dams along the creek; an attractive location.

Rochlan was a fur farmer who began raising foxes and then switched to mink. He had a partner, Fletch Orick, but they argued and Orick left.

Since Rochlan needed a quantity of lumber for his pens and litter boxes, he built a water-powered sawmill. It proved to be slow, but it did the job.

He had an impressive business: bought crippled horses for animal food, and supplemented their meat with rutabagas, spinach, and other vegetables that he raised. Fred Paulsen remembered packing 150 mink pelts out one fall for Rochlan and bringing in a check the next spring.

Rochlan was independent and patient. He served as his own doctor, pulling a tooth when it troubled him, setting his own leg when he broke it. He had a pet marten that he trained to eat at the table with him—an accomplishment, considering the temperament of a marten.

When Charlie Rochlan had to leave the Middle Fork, he was in rather poor health. Then tragically, he burned to death in a rest home.

In 1979 only one of his buildings survived the Mortar Creek fire.

M I L E 39.5 *Cougar Creek Ranch.*

This ranch was long called the "Dutch John place" by canyon residents. The cabin belonged to Dutch John Helmke, although he reported that it antedated his arrival on the site in 1901.

John Helmke was a native of Hannover, Germany, and obtained his U. S. citizenship in 1878 at Carson City, Nevada.

Helmke settled at Cougar Creek in July, 1908. By 1912 he had twenty-five acres under cultivation (watered by ditch from the creek), and harvested eighteen tons of hay, a ton of vegetables, and seventy-five gallons of strawberries. He was sixty-seven years old by then! He packed his crops for sale at the Loon Creek mines and stated that his hay fetched $8 a ton and his strawberries $1 a gallon. He also owned five work horses, six hogs, a cow, and three dozen chickens.

Three graves occupy a spot on the flat below the cabin. One is marked "Jas Cunningham, died 1905," but at this time no one remembers who he was. Maude Garoutte said that another person was already buried next to Cunningham when she first saw the grave as a girl. That was before Helmke's death, and since he was buried on the same spot (sometime after 1922), his is the third grave.

Charley Warnock and his wife Wilma, daughter of Amey Lovell, bought Cougar Creek in 1924 after Helmke's death, along with Mahoney Bar. Warnock was raised in Wallowa County, Oregon, son of Dan Warnock, a prominent Snake River Canyon stockman.

The Warnocks moved in with stock the following year and headquartered at Cougar Creek.

Warnock was an excellent horseman and packer. He raised cattle, horses, and mules. (He helped pack the Zane Grey party in from Meyers Cove to the Mormon Ranch downriver when that writer was working on a novel called *Thunder Mountain.*)

The Warnocks eventually sold their holdings to the state Fish and Game Department and moved to Riggins, Idaho.

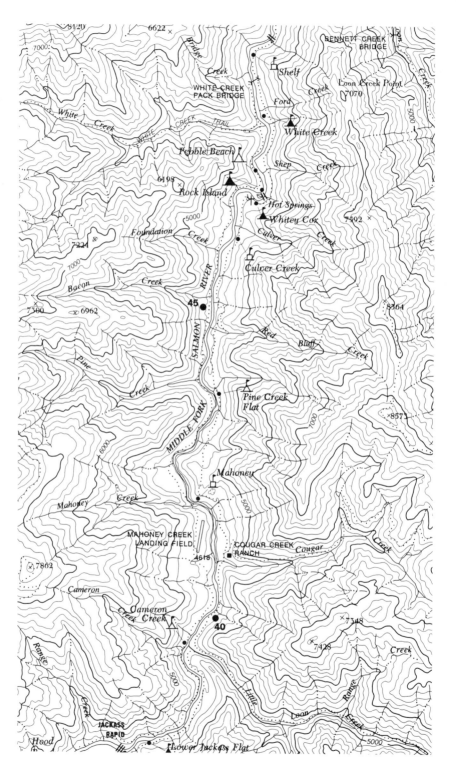

They settled on Wind River. Charley died in 1957; Wilma in 1959, and they were buried in the Riggins cemetery.

The Idaho Fish and Game Department now leases Cougar Creek to a hunting outfitter.

MILE 41.1 *Mahoney airstrip and Mahoney Ranch.*

The ranch and the creek below bear the name of Ray Mahoney, son of E. S. and Alice Mahoney, who were haying a Middle Fork ranch as early as 1903. Mahoney had a two-acre orchard on the bench above the river. Packing fruit trees in one fall, he got caught in a snowstorm and had to cache the trees in a snowbank. The following spring he dug them out, planted them, and saw them survive and bear fruit.

By 1942 Mahoney had married Virginia St. John and was living at the mouth of Owl Creek on the Salmon River, about eight miles upstream from the mouth of the Middle Fork.

Kenny Cameron at Mahoney Creek, loading potatoes for the Snow King Mine.

173

In later years Elmer Purcell tried to farm Mahoney Bar, but his scheme for getting water up from the river never worked out. Water was eventually piped out of the creek and around to the bench.

The airstrip was put in by the Forest Service.

MILE 41.9 *Mahoney Creek* on the left.

MILE 43.5 *Pine Creek Flat Camp* on the right, a sage-splashed bench.

MILE 43.7 *Fred Paulsen's cabin* is up the hill on the right. Paulsen was Daisey Tappan's brother. He spent most of his life in the Middle Fork canyon, at tasks such as packing, mining, and haying. In his prime he stood 6'2" and weighed about 275 pounds. His feats of strength were legendary. He could lift the corner of a hay wagon while someone changed the wheel, or tuck the leg of an ornery mule under his arm to hold it while he shod its hoof.

Paulsen, as much as any canyon-comer, symbolized the best characteristics of the older settlers. He fended off every kind of hardship: foul weather, tight times, frequent tragedies, immeasurable hours—yet through it all he remained

Fred Paulsen at his cabin in 1974, four years before he died.

good-natured and always ready to drop what he was doing to help someone else.

His later years were spent in a cabin on the outskirts of Challis, within sound of running water. He remained active until his death in 1978 at age seventy-two.

MILE 44.3 *The Unfinished Cabin.* Up above the bench, not visible from the river, is an uncompleted log cabin. Phillip Lewis of Boise began it; he owned the forty-six acres at the time.

To visit it recalls a stanza from a poem by David Wagoner:

...no one's going to live there any more.
 It tempts me:
Why not have weather falling in every room?
Isn't the sky
As easy to keep up as any ceiling?

MILE 44.8 *Red Bluff Creek* on the right. Named for the roseate outcropping of stone by the river.

MILE 45.1 *Bacon Creek* comes in on the left.

Joseph "Buck" Culver's homestead was across the river, below Red Bluff Creek. He was seventy-seven in 1916 when he made entry on the forty-six acres. By 1921, when he proved-up, he had at least eleven plowed acres irrigated by several hundred yards of ditch and was growing hay, wheat, oats, potatoes, and a variety of garden vegetables.

Culver, who wrote that he was born in "Misury," claimed to have fought in the Civil War. On the Middle Fork, he packed ten head of burros and used one for his own mount.

One fall, when he was in his mid-eighties, on his way to Meyers Cove to get supplies, he stopped along Loon Creek to open a gate and had a fatal heart attack. His packstring was found a few days later.

The old homesteader was buried on the hem of a hill alongside Loon Creek, but the location of the unmarked grave has been lost.

MILE 45.6 *Foundation Creek.* Named for a cabin that barely got off the ground.

MILE 45.9 *Culver Creek Campsite* on the right. Small, low camp with a few trees.

MILE 46 *Culver Creek* enters just below the campsite.

MILE 46.3 *Cox Hot Springs.* The seep, rather than springs, spreads its way downhill on the left.

MILE 46.5 *Cox Campground-Whitie Cox's Grave.*

Elvis "Whitie" Cox, son of Bert and Martha Cox, was born in Sweet, Idaho. His father, who traveled through the Middle Fork in the early 1900s, was killed in 1926 near Yellow Pine by a bucking horse.

Although Whitie married once and had a son, he was a bit of a loner, and folks who knew him regarded him as something of a charismatic healer.

He was a competent horseman and an exemplary packer. Until the start of World War II, he packed the U. S. Coastal

Whitie Cox at his camp on the Middle Fork.

Geodetic Survey crews through the backcountry. Then he took his pack stock to Wind River near Riggins, Idaho, left them with Charley Warnock, and went to join the infantry. When he returned four years later, most of his stock had winterkilled on the slopes. He went to work for his brother in a bakery at Twin Falls for a period. Finally the call of the Middle Fork grew too strong to resist.

In 1954 he pitched a tent camp at the hot springs and began some placer mining. While digging a ditch to divert water from the hot springs in order to assist with his gold-washing effort, the bank caved in. He might have survived, but it was two weeks before anyone found him. His brother Bud put up a tombstone that was later replaced by the military one. Cox was a kindly soul and still a young man when he died.

Loon Creek Point, elevation 7,070 feet, is visible downriver on the right.
MILE 46.7 *Rock Island Camp* to the left of the island. Large, pleasant, low bench.

MILE 47.5 *White Creek* comes in on the left.

In 1910, when Bert and Clark Cox came through on horseback, George Fox and his partner Shob were living on the flat at White Creek. Fox was willing to talk about himself. He was already an old man—a Civil War veteran on pension— but Shob was taciturn. They both wore long white hair and beards.

Fox and Shob had well-crafted cabins on the edge of the creek. Ditches from the creek watered two fields of alfalfa.

They entertained the Coxes for the evening by singing songs in remarkable harmony. When night arrived, they pulled down mountain goat hides to make a comfortable bed for their visitors.

Lou Hall had a serviceable cabin farther up White Creek where he pastured his horses. When the survey came through in 1917, it found his place was on a school section. So Hall drifted out to the South Fork of the Salmon and his cabin was later burned.

In 1918 Lawrance Phelan homesteaded at White Creek He was born in Oxford, in southeastern Idaho, and was forty years old when he arrived here with his wife May and three children.

They built a three-room log house and a log barn, and eventually cultivated twelve acres of hay to help feed their dozen horses and half-dozen cattle. The Phelans patented their thirty-nine acres at a cost of $49.

In recent times the Forest Service burned the remains of the cabin; it had been damaged by a flood from the creek.

MILE 47.6 *White Creek Camp* on the right just below Ford Creek. Ford Creek takes its name from the old stock crossing about a quarter-mile downstream.

MILE 48 *White Creek Bridge.*

MILE 49 *Jack Creek* on the left, named for a male mule.

MILE 49.6 *Loon Creek-Ramey Ranch-Campsite -Simplot Landing Strip.*

Only Big Creek can compete with Loon Creek as the most historied tributary of the Middle Fork.

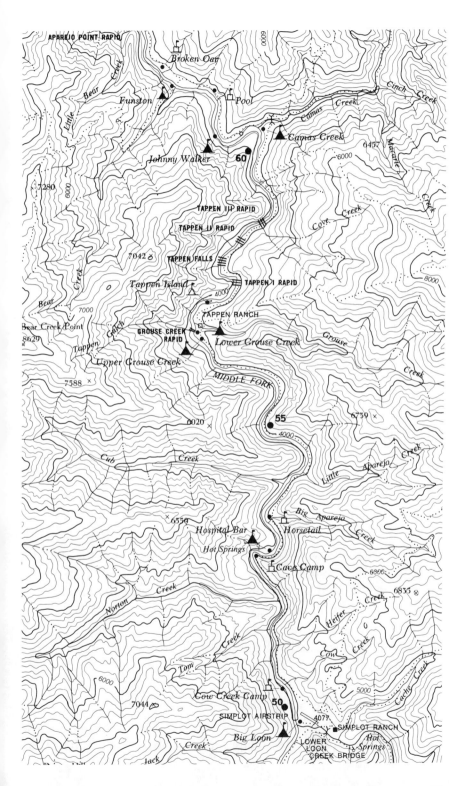

APAREJO POINT RAPID
Broken Oar
Funston
Bear Creek
Little Bear Creek
Pool
Cinch Creek
Camas Creek
Camas Creek
Macafie Creek
6457
Johnny Walker
60
7280
6000
6000
TAPPEN III RAPID
TAPPEN II RAPID
Cove Creek
7042
TAPPEN FALLS
8000
Tappen Island
4000
TAPPEN I RAPID
Bear Creek
7000
TAPPEN RANCH
Bear Creek Point
GROUSE CREEK RAPID
Lower Grouse Creek
Grouse Creek
8629
Tappen
Upper Grouse Creek
MIDDLE FORK
7588 ×
55
6739 ×
8020 ×
4000
Cub Creek
Creek
Little Aparejo Creek
Big Aparejo
6550 ×
Hospital Bar
Horsetail
Aparejo Creek
Hot Springs
Cave Camp
6000
6835
Norton Creek
Heifer Creek
Cow Creek
Castle Creek
6000
Tom Creek
5000
Cow Creek Camp
7044
50
SIMPLOT AIRSTRIP
4077
SIMPLOT RANCH
Big Loon
LOWER LOON CREEK BRIDGE
Hot Springs
Jack Creek

179

Gold was discovered on Loon Creek in the spring of 1869, by Nathan Smith, Elijah Mulkey, and Barney Sharkey of Leesburg, Idaho. Their pans looked promising, and when they returned to Leesburg for supplies, the word soon spread. In a short time there were over 600 claims staked, and by late August an estimated 2,500 miners roosted along the creek. Two outfits were averaging $45 per man-day. By late October, winter weather shut down operations.

The following spring a number of new canvas tents, log cabins, and two hotels were built to service the crowds. Oro Grande became the town for supplies. All of Loon Creek was diverted into a flume to wash the high bar there. Wages were $6 to $7 a day.

By spring, 1872, however, the better placer-ground had been depleted, and Oro Grande's population of seventy-two was half Chinese. Six years later, only five miners were left, and they were all Chinese. In early February they came to a violent end. The *Yankee Fork Herald* carried the following explanation:

" [When] the Chinese were snugly in their warm cabins, with plenty of provisions on hand, Mr. Sheepeater made a call, and not meeting with that hospitality he thought due him on his own land, and his stomach calling loudly for that which he had not to give it, he resolved to do something desperate. After dark the Indians got together, and while most of the Chinese were sitting around a table in one of the largest cabins, engaged in the primitive and fascinating game of 'one cent ante,' the Sheepeaters came down like a wolf on the fold, and the heathen, Oro Grande and all, were swept away as by a cyclone, while the victors returned to the bosom of their families on the Middle Fork to make glad the hearts of the little Sheepeaters with the spoils of the heathen."

While the Sheepeaters later denied any connection with the murders (the work was likely that of white robbers), the action nonetheless precipitated the Sheepeater Indian War of 1879 (see last section of this book). Captain Reuben Bernard's troops camped at the mouth of Loon Creek June 25, 1879.

With mining and military activity, Loon Creek became the major canyon trail used by the communities of Custer, Bonanza, Oro Grande, and later, Challis and Stanley. (Renewed mining interest in Loon Creek accompanied the Thunder Mountain boom in 1902, which was located thirty miles northwest.)

In 1902 Jack Ferguson settled on Loon Creek, ten miles up-creek from the mouth, and in 1908 filed for seventy-three acres, most of it on the west side of the creek. He sold his squatter's rights, along with the sizeable log cabin that he built in 1904—complete with porch and stone chimney— to Lynn Falconbery, who visited in 1907.

Rupert Lynn "Beargrease" Falconbery was born in 1867 in Indiana. In the summer, 1889, while working as a cowman in Nebraska, he stopped at an ice cream parlor and became entranced by an Oregon Short Line railroad map that boosted the Middle Fork country.

Falconbery traveled by horseback to Blackfoot, Idaho, then across the desert to Mackay, then to Challis, doubled back to Clayton, Custer, Yankee Fork, Mayfield, and finally Loon Creek—all with pack stock. Before he acquired Ferguson's spot, he worked as a trapper in the area for several years, establishing a line with a dozen cabins, and taking bear, fox, lynx, bobcats, marten, and coyotes. Billy Wilson recalled that Falconbery averaged about twenty cougars a season, collecting a $50 bounty on each.

He made a homestead entry on the site in 1911, but left temporarily the next summer to work for the Forest Reserve. By 1930 he had thirty acres under cultivation, half of it in hay. He added a root cellar, bunkhouse, storeroom, blacksmith shop, stable, chicken house, and corrals. Willis Jones brought him produce from Grouse Creek a half-dozen times a year.

Lynn "Beargrease"
Falconbery, 1915.

Falconbery ranch.

George and Marie Frinklin lived about four miles farther down Loon Creek at Cold Springs Creek. George was from Syracuse, New York. He and his wife married sometime before World War I, but after duty time in France, where he was wounded and survived a mustard-gas attack, George returned as a disabled veteran. Despite this, they chose to live on Loon Creek and, like Falconbery, Frinklin supported himself by hunting cougar.

Robert L. "Bob" Ramey owned the flat at the mouth of Loon Creek, known for years, naturally enough, as the Ramey Ranch. Bob Ramey was a nephew of John S. Ramey, who guided Captain Bernard through the Middle Fork country during the Sheepeater campaign. His uncle urged Bob to come out from Kentucky and look over the location.

Loon Creek flat was the best ranch site in the canyon: extensive sunlight, ample water, open flats, and an agreeable elevation (4,200'). Ramey took up residence in September, 1909, at age twenty-seven, and filed a homestead entry for 121 acres the next year. He lived in the house built in 1902 by Jack McGiveny, from whom he purchased squatter's rights. McGiveny had raised cattle on the ranch, driving them to Thunder Mountain to butcher for the miners. (In 1904, he and a Mr. Cronan had briefly cornered the hay market there, getting $100 to $125 a ton.)

At times between 1912 and 1915 Ramey went out to work for wages in order to get a mowing machine and tools, but he always left a caretaker on the place. Ned Bennett was one. He helped out at the ranch and once a month would take his horse and a packhorse and make the forty-eight-mile round trip to Meyers Cove for mail. Ned was ninety years old at the time!

In 1914 Ramey's brother Oscar moved to the ranch to live with him. They had seventy-five acres under cultivation, irrigated by ditches out of Cache Creek, and harvested sixty tons of hay each summer. They grew vegetables, too. At first they had no cattle—just packhorses, workhorses, and brood mares. Traffic was frequent, and ready markets lay on the headwaters. Eventually they added cattle, and their herd grew to 100 head at its peak. Mining camps paid them $30 a ton for vegetables and $60 a ton for hay.

In 1913 Bob bought the Mormon Ranch twenty miles downriver. He ran it, while Oscar supervised Loon Creek. It proved too much, and he sold the downriver operation in the fall. Ramey received his homestead certificate in 1916.

Ray Mahoney was the next owner at Loon Creek. He sold to Sam and Amey Lovell. They came in from the Oregon side of Pittsburg Landing on the Snake River, where they had been in the cattle business with their son-in-law Charley Warnock.

The Lovells recognized that the area was splendid horse range: horses could rustle with ease where cows would starve. The new owners trailed in a herd of horses, and from that time on they always outnumbered cattle. The Lovells tapped a busy market selling geldings to the army remount station at Fort Boise. Amey Lovell recalled that their most serious problem was the number of spring colts they lost to mountain lions.

The Lovells pulled out of Loon Creek at the time the Warnocks left Cougar Creek, and lived out their lives near Riggins, Idaho. Sam died in 1950, age seventy-one; Amey died in 1961, age eighty-eight.

Frank Allison was a long-time resident on the ranch from the 1920s to the early 1940s. He had homesteaded on Rams Fork Creek in 1914. In the late 1920s he was advertising in *Outdoor Life*, offering lion hunts with hounds and horses in the winter down in the Middle Fork canyon, and spring bear hunts.

In later years, Tom Brummet had a cabin by the hot springs. He used the hot water to run a placer-mining operation through the winter.

Bob Simplot acquired the Loon Creek ranch from the Lovells and later transferred it to his brother Jack, a wealthy Idaho businessman. Jack Simplot retained the acreage with cabins, and sold the rest to the Idaho Fish and Game Department.

Sam and Amey
Lovell's cabin at
Loon Creek, 1931.
Burned in 1945.

A trail goes up Loon Creek about one-half-mile to a
bridge, and then runs another one-half-mile to the hot
springs on the creek side of the trail.

MILE 51.1 *Norton Creek* enters on the left.
Norton Ridge, at 8,400 feet, runs in a generally north-
south direction from Bacon Creek to Norton Creek. Norton
Lake lies at the north end of the ridge and feeds Norton
Creek.
While the creek is not particularly conspicuous, a story
hangs by the name that is as incredible as any on the river.
Indeed, it is reminiscent of the mountain man saga of Hugh
Glass, or of Jedediah Smith, who, after being attacked by a
grizzly, told his pards to sew his ear back on. The story begins
with an item in the August 31, 1898 issue of the Pocatello
Tribune:

"Charlie Norton, an old-timer in Idaho who has mined in Custer County for twenty years past, died at the County Hospital on August 27 of cancer. He was sixty-five years old and had a most eventful career. He will be missed by many old friends. He has a brother and sister whom he supposed were someplace in California but from whom he had not heard for eighteen years."

Four days later, the *Tribune* elaborated:

A Man of Nerve

"Poor old Charlie Norton, whose death on August 27 at the county hospital in this city was chronicled in our last issue, was one of the pioneers of the Salmon River and Custer mining districts and was essentially a man of nerve. In the early days he was something of a bear hunter and many a cinnamon and silver-tip fell before his unerring aim.

It was about ten years ago that he met a bear that ate him up and left him almost helpless and but the caricature of a man in appearance. He was prospecting in the mountains with but one companion out some 60 miles from Challis when he saw traces of a bear and followed it into some underbrush. He located bruin, took aim and brought him down but at that very same instant a big silver-tip rose up beside him and struck him a blow in the face and broke both his jaws and literally crushed his face in. The bear then chewed him up, mangling him from head to foot and finally went off leaving him for dead.

Here his companion found him later and finding he was still alive, fixed him up as comfortable as possible and started for Challis for help. It was 60 miles to Challis and by the time Norton's partner got back, the flies had gotten at him and blown him and before they took him into camp they took about a quart of maggots from his face and head. A litter was slung between two horses and he was taken to Challis. He still hung onto life and a doctor was sent for 30 miles away. [This should read Custer instead of Challis.]

It seemed impossible that Mr. Norton should recover. The doctor said he couldn't, but went on and fixed him up as well as he could. It was found necessary to take out his whole lower jaw. Norton, however, went right on living and getting better. It developed after awhile that his face would not heal because of its being more or less torn every time he was fed. A hole was then cut in his neck through which he was fed. His face in the meantime healed up. Then it was found impossible to heal the hole in his neck.

Finally Norton was sent to the hospital in Salt Lake and the hole in his neck was sewed up with silver wire and healed up. In the meantime, however, the contraction of the muscles of the face caused his mouth to close so tightly that he could not eat and his mouth had to be cut open time and again. It would always come together again in a short time and the operation would again have to be performed. All these operations were performed without the administration of ether or any other anaesthetic.

Finally, however, Norton left the hospital and went out with a party prospecting. Here his trouble commenced. His mouth grew shut and he couldn't eat. He begged his companions to cut his mouth open but they wouldn't do it and finally Norton found a rock, whetted up his knife, pinning a pocket mirror to a stump, cut his mouth open himself and all was lovely again.

In the meantime a cancer developed in Norton's face and in the last five years he had to have it cut out four times. He always insisted on going through the operations without the use of anaesthetics. It was just before the last operation of this kind a couple of years ago that he met Abe Pierce and was telling him that he was going to the hospital for another operation and as he ended his story he said: "And do you know, Abe, I am getting to be a d— d baby. I kind of flinch when I think of it."

After his years of terrible suffering, after innumerable operations the old man's indomitable nerve was beginning to give away but he went through the operations bravely, and his will kept him up to the end. He died, like thousands of pioneers of this western country—a county charge and long forgotten by his relatives, whose address he himself had even forgotten."

MILE 52.5 *Hospital Bar Campsite* and hot springs. The Hatch boatmen always called this camp the "Tapeats of the Middle Fork" after the Grand Canyon camp that requires a patient wait for the sun to drop behind a ridge. Most persons believe this camp was named for soldiers recovering from the Sheepeater Campaign, but what evidence exists indicates they passed along the opposite side of the river. Hood said the name was already common in the early thirties because Kenney Cameron and Bob Ramey had used the site with its easy ford and good grass to keep their crippled stock.

The hot spring is at the top end of the bar. Hospital Bar is the boundary between Boise National Forest to the south and Salmon National Forest to the north.

MILE 53.3 *Big Aparejo Creek* enters on the right. Aparejo is a Spanish word for a packsaddle used on horses and mules. Aparejos were made of leather and stuffed with red willow withes and grass. Usually they were soaked in a creek and then molded to the animal. It served as a rough cushion for the load and was rapidly replaced by the Sawbuck and Deker saddles.

MILE 53.8 *Cub Creek* flows in on the left.

MILE 54 *Little Aparejo Creek* on the right.

MILE 56.5 *Grouse Creek-Tappan Ranch-Campground.*

Grouse Creek is the favorite campground of many boatmen. In August, 1978, it was one of the two campsites used by President Jimmy Carter on his three-day Middle Fork trip.

The cabin on the upstream side of the creek was already standing when Willis "Bill" Jones, age forty, first settled on the creek in 1917. It may have been built by M. A. Curtis of Challis, who applied for the tract in March, 1910.

Willis "Bill" Jones at his Grouse Creek cabin. Jones said the cabin was there when he arrived.

Jones cabin after the Tappans enclosed the front overhang.

Jones had been an oil-well driller, then spent some time in the Hollywood movie-making business—though in what capacity is unclear. He was already infected with tuberculosis when he arrived at the creek, but he got along fairly well in spite of it. He would send out once a year to Meyers Cove for fifty pounds of good Southern tobacco—he liked to smoke natural leaf—hardly a cure for his consumption.

Jones had only three horses, but he did ranch the place. He had about fifteen of the seventy-four acres in hay; he also grew corn and wheat. He planted peaches, apples, grapes and currants. In October, 1927, he made homestead proof on the place.

Some of the trees had just begun to bear when he decided to sell out. He went down to Arizona and died a few years later near Salt River.

Fred and Daisey Paulsen-Tappan bought the place for $1,200. Fred was from Iowa, and Daisey was born in Pineville, Oregon. Her father had hunted geese and egrets for the markets there. Daisey had first come into the Middle Fork when she was seven, and she was every bit as competent in the backcountry as any man who ever lived there.

The Tappans extended the cabin by enclosing the porch. That became the kitchen. They built a barn, chicken house, and corral out on the flat in front of the house, next to the big ponderosa pine tree.

They planted additional fruit trees and put in a large garden. Daisey grew strawberries, blackberries, raspberries, peanuts, muskmelons, and watermelons. She said the rockchucks would make a little hole in the melons next to the ground and then hollow out the entire melon, which appeared edible until she tried to pickone. She grew corn for her chickens and canned all her fruit and vegetables. Deer were a plentiful source of meat. Between chores she looked after her boys and fought the bears that swam the river to feast in the orchard.

The Tappans had a few cattle, some horses, and cows. Since the stock could not be left out for the winter, they packed in a hay rake, ditched water out of Grouse Creek for

The Tappans at Meyers Cove ready for a ride to Grouse Creek.

Daisey and her boys haying the field below Grouse Creek, c. 1933.

irrigation, and hayed the upper and lower fields behind the cabin. Although the snow did not get too severe, the hillsides were dangerously icy. It was usually the 10th of March before the Tappans could let the cows out again.

Self-sufficient as the Tappans were, Daisey said they still had to buy horseshoes, leather, and clothes. Three hundred dollars would easily see them through the year. To get the money, Fred could work lookout or trail crew for the Forest Service, or work in the Yellowjacket mines.

In later years the Forest Service cut off the Tappan cattle range, so when the two boys were old enough to go to school (about 1933), the Tappans moved out. After they left Daisey said, "You know, it was three years before I could sleep without the sound of that river and creek. It was just too darned quiet."

One might think life was easier once the Tappans left Grouse Creek. Consider: they lived at a mine near Yellow Pine, Idaho—halfway between the town and the airport. Two dog teams hauled mail and freight between the town and the airstrip, and Daisey ran one. She would sled the boys three miles to school in Yellow Pine each morning, pick up mail and supplies, sled six miles up to the airport on Johnson Creek to make the delivery; pick up mail, freight, and groceries from the pilot and mush six miles back to Yellow Pine. There she would pick up the children and sled home to make dinner.

In her later years Daisey lived on her ranch in the Pahsimeroi Valley of Idaho, still looking after cattle and felling her firewood with a chainsaw—at age seventy-six. She died in 1984 and is buried at Challis.

Fred Tappan died in California in 1975.

Bob Simplot acquired the Tappan Ranch and sold all but the five acres with the cabin to the Idaho Fish and Game Department. When he got around to surveying it, he found the Fish and Game Department had left him only a bit over three acres.

TAPPAN ESTATE

AUCTION

Near Challis, Idaho

Saturday, June 1, 1985

Starting at 10:30 A.M.

LOCATION: 6½ Miles North of Challis on Hwy. 93. Watch for Auction Sign.

Owner — The Daisey Tappan Estate

Lunch Will Be Served.

TERMS — Cash or Approved Check

TOOLS

5 Metal Framing Squares
13 Hand Saws
3 Boxes of Miscellaneous Bolts, Nuts, Cable Clamps
5 Irrigating Shovels   3 Pitchforks
2 Scoop Shovels   2 Pruning Shears
2 New Shovel Handles   2 New Axe Handles
1 New Pitchfork Handle   1 Splitting Maul
1 Pick   1 Wire Stretcher
1 Garden Hoe   2 Horn Saws
4 Old Grub Hoes   1 Post Peeler
1 Mounted Electric Motor
1 PTO Tractor-mounted Belt Drive
1 Weed Scythe
1 Hand-pump Weed Sprayer
1 Axe
5 Wool Shears   3 Hack Saws
2 Wood Drills   11 Claw Hammers
2 Nose Tongs   4 1-lb. Hammers
5 6" Stove Pipe Joints   2 Sledge Hammers
1 8"; Stove Pipe Joint   1 Tri Square
5 Old Wash Tubs   3 Hand Drills
13 Chain Saw Chains   5 Pipe Wrenches
Miscellaneous Wrenches
Miscellaneous Sockets
Ratchets
Screwdrivers
3 Pair Tin Snips
1 2' Level
100 Miscellaneous Files
6 Pliers   7 Grease Guns
3 Crow Bars   2 Pair Vise Grips
1 Riveter   8 Planers
17 Oil Cans
12 Misc. Heavy Duty Drill Bits
3 Electric Extension Cords
1 Old Air Compressor
1 Electric Motor
1 Old Pump Motor
1 Ox-ygen Bottle
1 Buzz Saw
5 Bags Cement
2 Garden Hoses
2 Pry Bars
1 Poulan Electric Chain Saw
5 Gas Chain Saws

REAL ESTATE

PAHSIMEROI PROPERTY
Location — 22 Miles up the Pahsimeroi Valley.
Approx. 34 Acres.
17 Irrigated, 17½ Dry Grazing
Property will be auctioned to the highest bidder at 2:00 p.m. the day of the sale. On terms.
Auctioneer is Agent Only.
No Guarantees Implied or Expressed.

HOUSEHOLD

1 Plywood Closet
1 Old Barrel Stove
4 Cream Cans
2 Desks, miscellaneous
1 Shelving Stand
1 Old Wood Trunk
1 Dresser
1 Ironing Board
1 Electric Heater
1 Cream Separator
2 End Tables
Assorted Cast Iron Pots and Pans
13 Lanterns
1 Old Desk
1 Ice Cream Maker
1 Leather Kit
22 Cans of Paint
1 Stainless Steel Milk Cans
10 Fish Poles
1 Large Bellows
17 Old Suitcases and Trunks
1 Chest of Drawers
1 Gun Rack
1 Hand Operated Phonograph
1 Hi Fi
1 Box Springs & Mattress
1 Hand Operated Sheep Shearing Outfit
2 Rolls of Tar Paper
5 Meat Saws
1 Meat Cleaver
2 Old Radios
2 Carbide Lights
1 Chest-type Freezer
1 Refrigerator
1 Electric Cook Stove
1 Roll-away Bed
1 Metal File Cabinet
1 Oak Dresser with oval mirror—a real dandy!

GUNS

2 Antique Pump Action 22s
2 Model 94 30-30s
2 Shotguns
2 30-06 Rifles
1 .243 Rifle
1 .270 Rifle
1 .44 Ruger 44
1 .357 Magnum
1 .22 Pistol

AUCTIONEER'S NOTE

This is over a 50-year accumulation of Antiques and Collectables, by a well known pioneer to this country, the late Daisey Tappan.

TACK

3 Leather Stirrup Covers
9 Old Leather Halters
2 Bridles
7 Rope Halters
15 Horse Collars
17 Saddle Blankets
2 Sets of Harness and miscellaneous
4 Pack Saddles (3 Sawbuck, 1 Decker)
1 Bareback Riggin'
2 Stirrups
1 Saddles
1 Box Horseshoes
6 Single Trees
2 Shoeing Hammers
3 Boxes Miscellaneous Tack

ANTIQUE MACHINERY

1 Model A Farmall Tractor
1 Old Farmall Tractor
1 Old Combine
1 Manure Spreader
2 Buck Rakes
2 Dump Rakes
2 Horse-drawn Hay Mowers
Several Plows
1 Disc
1 Buzz Saw
1 Ripper
1 Snow Plow
1 Furrow
1 Grain Planter
Old Wagon
1 1976 Chevy 4x4 Pickup — Sells "As Is"
1 GMC 2-Ton Truck
1 1958 GMC ¾ Ton Pickup
1 1965 IHC 1 Ton Truck
    All Vehicles Sell "As Is"

MISCELLANEOUS

1 Metal Shed — 20x24', 480 square feet. Like new.
1 10x46' Paramount Trailer House. Good shape.
Lots of Motor Oil
Garbage Cans
Fruit Jars
Steel Posts
Barb Wire
Wagon Wheels
Antique Fiddle, Bow and Case
Truck Rack
2 50 gal. Barrel Gas Tanks
And Many, Many More Items Too Numerous to Mention.

All Items Offered
To The Highest Bidder and Must Be
Settled For the Day of the Sale.

WE WELCOME EVERYONE —
SEE YOU AT THE AUCTION!

Sale Handled By:

JR. Baker - Auctioneer

Clayton, Idaho

838-2232

FULL
AUCTION
SERVICE
TRUST

WE ARE NOT RESPONSIBLE
FOR ACCIDENTS!

Daisey Tappan's estate reads like a western list-poem:
hornsaw,
handsaw,
hacksaw,
buzz saw,
meat saw,
chainsaw;
shoeing hammer,
claw hammer,
sledge hammer,
splitting maul;
13 lanterns,
13 guns;
10 fishing poles,
and so forth.

193

The Tappan Gulch Fire, which scarred this area, began September 13, 1987, as the result of a hunter's campfire left at the mouth of Tappan Gulch. Suppression crews fought the fire, but in three hours it grew to 2,000 acres. The Forest Service decided to let it burn as a "monitor" fire. Effects visible for miles along the river are the result of that decision. By November 3 the fire had burned 4,160 acres—half of it categorized as "ideal" and half of it as "devastation."

The highest peak looking west across the river is Bear Creek Point, 8,629 feet.

MILE 57.3 *Tappan Island Camp* can be used in an emergency.

MILE 57.8 *Tappan I.*

MILE 58.2 *Tappan Falls* or Grouse Creek Falls (Helfrich) or Tappan II. This rapid can be scouted from the right bank. It becomes increasingly severe as the water level drops.

MILE 58.5 *Tappan III.* Marked by a large boulder off the right shore.

MILE 58.7 *Tappan IV.*

MILE 60.2 *Camas Creek* and campsite appear on the right.

Camas is a blue flower which grows in meadows on the upper reaches of this stream. It is a member of the lily family and the bulb of the plant, when dug in the fall, was an important source of food for the Indians.

The Camas Creek trail is the route to the Yellow Jacket Mine and to Meyers Cove. Before the Forest Service worked on it in 1923, it was a rough and narrow trail. An indication of how rough is contained in Billy Wilson's recollection of his father's cattle drive down to the Middle Fork from Meyers Cove in April, 1919. They pushed 350 head down the trail, and it took three days and three nights to cover the fourteen miles.

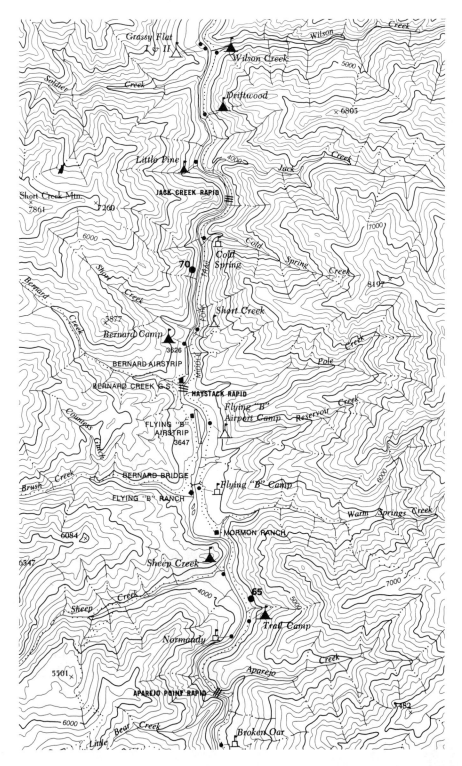

Grassy Flat
I & II
Wilson Creek
Wilson   Creek
Soldier
Creek
5000
Driftwood
× 6805
Little Pine
4000
Creek
Jack
JACK CREEK RAPID
Short Creek Mtn.
7861   7260
17000
6000
Cold
Spring   Creek
70   Cold
Spring
8197 ×
Short Creek
Bernard   Creek
3877
Bernard Camp
3626
Creek
Pole
BERNARD AIRSTRIP
BERNARD CREEK G.S.
HAYSTACK RAPID
Flying "B"   Creek
Airport Camp   Reservoir
Countess   Gulch
FLYING "B"
AIRSTRIP
3647
Brush   Creek
BERNARD BRIDGE
Flying "B" Camp
FLYING "B" RANCH
Warm Springs Creek
6084
MORMON RANCH
6347
6000
Sheep Creek
7000
Creek
Sheep   4000
65
5000
Trail Camp
Normandy
5501 ×
Creek
Aparejo
APAREJO POINT RAPID
5482
6000   Bear Creek
Broken Oar
Little

Charles Theodore Wilson Metz, born in 1864 and a native of Ohio, lived up Camas Creek at the mouth of Goat Creek. He first visited the site in June, 1906, and returned in the spring, 1916, to build a cabin there.

He used his 152-acre homestead as a base for his thirty-mile trapline on the divide between Morgan Creek and Camas Creek. It usually took him ten days to snowshoe the line. In the summer at his place he plowed twenty acres for grain, and kept thirty-five acres in tame hay and twenty acres in pasture for his nine head of horses. In 1928 he obtained his final homestead certificate.

Metz was well-educated, having taken considerable schooling by correspondence. In his mid-sixties he left Camas Creek to go to Chicago for some instruction in electrical engineering. He never made it back to his acres at Goat Creek on Camas Creek.

Elmer Keith, well-known ballistics expert and big game guide, camped for a couple of weeks with the Zane Grey party across from the mouth of Camas Creek. The party of ten included Grey, his son and daughter, and their spouses, plus two secretaries and a Japanese cook. It required seven packers to haul their personal belongings, grub, tents, hammocks, and canvas bathtubs for the two-month expedition. A fire closure was invoked while the party was headed for Camas Creek, so they camped until Keith obtained a letter from Herbert Hoover allowing the party to proceed.

The group rode down to the Mormon Ranch, then to Waterfall Creek, forded the river and traveled up Big Creek. They killed goats and deer before packing through Cold Meadows and up Monumental Creek to Thunder Mountain. The trip returned by way of Marble and Camas creeks to the Ramshorn Ranch. Grey's checks bounced and Keith never did receive full payment for the outfitting work. He did receive an autographed copy of *Thunder Mountain*, which was more than anyone else received.

Zane Grey (right) party on the trail to Williams Lake, fall, 1931. The two-month trip required 7 packers and 57 horses. Photo courtesy of Velma Ravndal.

George Tagahashi, Grey's chef, prepares a string of trout. He was the "peacemaker" for an otherwise troubled trip.

(It was not that Pearl "Zane" Grey was impoverished. Before he died in 1939, the dentist-turned-writer wrote more than eighty books. Sales totaled 30 million copies—incomparably more than any other author of his time. His romantic novels of the west created a new literary genre—the Western.)

MILE 61 *Johnny Walker* camp on the left bank.
MILE 61.2 *Kaufman's Cave* on the right.

The cave is a little way up from the river, partially obscured by brush, but right on the trail.

Clarence Kaufman was a Scotsman who was a miner in his youth. He came down to the Middle Fork, built a wooden door for the cave, and lived what must have been a rudimentary existence there. He got sick one summer, went out to a doctor, and never returned. Kaufman had a burro which could be seen grazing around the area for years after that.

Frank "Slim" Love was the next resident of the cave. He came to Idaho about 1915. He had a few horses that he looked after, and he did a little trapping—collecting bounty

Frank Love with his pet coyote. Photo courtesy of Esther Yarber.

money on coyotes. He also had a tent-shack at Big Aparejo Creek and spent some time there, as well as at a spot up on Duffield Creek.

One morning in August, 1942, Fred Paulsen got word that there was a dead packrat in a trap in front of Love's door—the canyon equivalent of newspapers piling up on the front porch. Paulsen went down and looked for Love's saddle, but it was not on the pole where it belonged. He figured Love had probably gone off to check on his horses.

When Paulsen returned the next day from hauling supplies to Pistol Creek, he was informed Love still had not appeared, so Mel Shepherd and he went searching.

They discovered Love up by the Seafoam Ranger Station pasture, where he had fallen from his horse and rolled down the hill with some ropes still on his arm. Since he had been dead almost two weeks, the sheriff told them to bury him there. The grave was marked at a later date. Papers found among Love's possessions revealed he was born in Cleveland, Ohio, in 1882.

Yellow Pine as it looked during the mining boom. Scheelite and stibnite were mined to recover strategic minerals tungsten and antimony. Open pit mine began in 1938, tungsten was discovered in 1941. In 1942 the mines employed 700 workers.

MILE 61.4 *Pool Camp* on the right side.

MILE 61.6 *Big Bear Camp* on the left side.

MILE 61.8 *Big Bear Creek* flows in from the left.

MILE 61.9 *Funston Camp* is located on the left.

MILE 62.2 *Broken Oar* is the small campsite on the right.

MILE 63.1 *Aparejo Rapid* and Little Bear Creek, which flows out from the left.

MILE 64.8 *Trail Camp* is the large site on the right in the timber.

MILE 65.5 *Sheep Creek* on the left. Camp is just above the mouth.

Every river canyon seems to have a murder mystery: Hells Canyon has one, so does the Main Salmon. The murder on the Middle Fork occurred at Sheep Creek. It happened thus.

Charles Ernst was born in 1887 at Hailey, Idaho. His father, John, was a miner at Leesburg, Idaho, and Charles was there by the time he was seven years old. At sixteen he moved to Clayton, Idaho, and about 1910 he met Frances Cooper, six years his junior. The Salmon newspaper reported that "[she] was raised on the Salmon River [on her father's ranch at Clayton]. She is blonde in complexion and not uncomely in appearance." The couple married in 1911 when she was eighteen, and they had a son named Charles, Jr. They lived on Peach Creek near Salmon, Idaho, for a while. Once the baby was a year old, the Ernsts left from Challis, Idaho, to take the Camas Creek trail down to the Middle Fork country, where they planned to prospect. Charlie established a placer claim about a mile and a half below the mouth of Camas Creek, and they revisited it sporadically.

Ernst was not the kind of man one could take lightly; he would just as soon settle a quarrel with a gun. He killed mountain sheep in the winter, dragged them across the road and hung them up in front of his house in Challis. All the game warden Tom Donahue could say was, "There's no way to talk to that man. If I go up there it's kill or be killed."

Old Bill Sullivan was trapping at the Cinnabar mine one winter and got into an argument with Ernst. Charlie went for his rifle in the cabin corner and Bill had to throw a pan of hot gravy in his face. No whiskers grew on the scarred patch of skin, and Charlie used to tell young Bill Sullivan, "Look at what your Dad did to me; I should have killed the son-of-a-bitch."

In July, 1917, Charlie and Frances went down to the Middle Fork to work their placer claim. They traveled downriver past Sheep Creek, where a young man lived in a cabin. His name was Julius "Jake" Reberg and he came to the Middle Fork in about 1914 from Minnesota. He had a few horses and cattle, and was raising hay on the flat. He also had an inconsequential placer claim up the creek. Wayne O'Connor of Salmon had worked with Reberg and knew him well. He recalled that Jake was "one of the most agreeable and trusty of men, a good and obliging neighbor and a steady citizen. He was liked by everybody in that country who ever had dealt with him."

Jake wrote, in a letter to his brother Frank in Minnesota, dated January 6, 1915:

" I had a very nice time New Years & hope you had the same. I am 80 miles from the railroad. I'm in the live stock business. It's paying. Cattle is paying 50% on the $100 and horses also. The winters very mild hear. I ain't feeding any stock yet. I am waiting for the spring to come so I can go bear hunting. That is one of my greatest enjoyment. This is a mountainous country where I live. I have an up to date house and up to date cook. Please write soon."

But Reberg had a problem that requires an historical explanation.

World War I began for Europe in August, 1914, but it was a prosperous period for the U.S., and isolationism and neutrality were the prevalent public sentiments. It was not until April, 1917, that Congress passed a war resolution, largely the result of German U-boat attacks on unarmed American ships. In mid-May Congress passed the first Selective Service Act: all men age twenty-one to thirty (inclusive) were

required to register for the draft on June 5. Almost 10 million men registered that day. Jake Reberg was not one of them. He, along with 337,000 others who did not answer the call, were branded as "slackers." If caught, the penalty was one year in prison.

It should be noted that there was some resistance to the draft among farmers and ranchers. To go off for eight months of military training, leaving crops and livestock, often meant that there would be nothing left when one returned. In 1917 the Speaker of the House protested that "there is precious little difference between a conscript and a convict."

Reberg, thirty years old at the time, and six months to the day from being thirty-one, hoped that officialdom would simply forget about him and his little ranch in the canyon. He told folks he was older than he was. But people talk.

Although Charlie Ernst had registered for the draft, he was exempt by reason of his wife and child. He and Frances, however, had heard the rumors, and as they looked over Reberg's place they admired it in comparison to the spot where they were camped. The hot July day may have germinated a conspiracy.

By September 24 Frances had made more than the acquaintance of Jake Reberg. She had visited without Charlie, carried on extended conversations, and with Reberg had driven cattle up to Meyers Cove (also known as Three Forks). According to her, when Charlie returned to the placer camp and learned of the "cattle drive" he flew into a rage and threatened to kill Reberg.

Back in Challis at September-end, Frances filed for divorce, alleging cruelty and nonsupport. The divorce decree was obtained on November 12, giving Charlie custody of their four-year-old boy, while she kept visitation rights. The Challis *Messenger* later reported, "A great deal of comment was occasioned by the actions of the couple prior to and after the divorce proceedings, for they seemed to be on very friendly terms." By November 16 she was living with Reberg, in her words, "in expectation of becoming his wife and moving to Montana."

However, Reberg in a letter to his brother John, dated October 23, 1917, already refers to Frances as his wife:

"My wife's gone to town. Now I'm in the country after my cattle. How is your wife getting along out there? I will come and visit you. Hoping to here from you very soon.
J. C. Reberg
Meyers Cove, Idaho"

A second letter to his brother revealed new plans:

" Nov. 17, 1917
Dear Brother John,
We are well and hope you are the same. We have sold out in Idaho cattle and horses and ranch and we will go to Montana now. Please do not write to Meyers Cove. I do not know what may post office will be next. I don't know if I will be drafted in army are not.
J. C. Reberg
Meyers Cove, Idaho"

On December 16 Charlie Ernst stopped at Meyers Cove to pick up mail for residents down in the Middle Fork canyon. When he was questioned about the contents of a gunny sack he was carrying, he said it contained a carbine (Winchester 32). He encountered John Pearson from the Mormon Ranch on the trail, and when Pearson asked where he was headed, replied that he was looking for evidence. Then he asked, "Is he there?" Pearson said he did not know. On December 20 Ernst was seen passing back through the Cove, and it was noted that his carbine was missing.

Albert Kurry, who lived at Brush Creek a couple of miles downriver from Reberg, and who wintered some horses with him, stopped by and asked Frances his whereabouts. She said he had gone fishing. After other visits, finding his horses neglected and not seeing Reberg and knowing of Ernst's visit, Kurry became concerned and mentioned his suspicions to the postmaster at the Cove, who in turn passed the word on to forest ranger Jack Oquin. On January 3, 1918, the ranger left for the Cove to investigate. The outcome was carried in a letter to his supervisor:

"I went to Meyers Cove on the above date [Jan. 3] and Andy Lee, who also had some horses with Reberg, said that he would go down with me and on the 4th we went down to the Mormon ranch, via Reberg's place, and Mrs. Chas. Ernst was there and we asked her several questions as to where and why Reberg had left and she told us that Reberg had gotten afraid that he would be locked up and taken in as a slacker, she told us that he went down the river and that he took his rifle and a small amount of grub and plenty of matches and salt, and that she didn't fear that he would starve. I asked her if he took along any snowshoes and she said that he did not. I asked her when he left and she said that he left on the 23rd of December, and she said that she put him across the river and that he went down this side. She went with us to help round up the horses on Jan. 5th and I questioned her at some length regarding Reberg, she said that he was only 31 years old on Dec. 4th, 1917, and said he told her when he left not to tell anyone where he had gone till after the week had passed and then he didn't care what she told except that he didn't want her to tell anyone where his people were. She said he was also afraid that the officers were going to get after him for living there with her without marriage, and she said that she had the money to go to Montana and get married and was willing and urged him to go but that he then said that he had lost his homestead right, and that if they married that they would lose the claim and wanted her to file on the squatters claim when the survey was accepted. She said that he began to get uneasy soon after she went there to live with him and began backing down on all his promises. All her story, however, laid the main reason for his disappearance on the fear that he would be arrested for being a slacker.

Reberg told me last fall that he was 33 years old and he told Chas. Sherman that he was 34. Now the most suspicious thing connected with his disappearance is the well known fact that Chas. Ernst, the former husband of the woman, with whom Reberg was living, went down there on Dec. 16 and was met on the trail by John Pearson, and Ernst, supposing that he was about to meet Reberg, got off the trail behind a rock and was ready to hold Pearson up when he saw his mistake. No one knows that Ernst had any business at all down there and he took a rifle in there and when he came out four days later he had no gun with him according to the people of Meyers Cove.

I asked Mrs. Ernst if she knew that the whole circumstances of the case pointed to the fact that she and Ernst had killed Reberg. I also asked her to explain how with Ernst already declaring he would get Reberg and his going down there without any business whatever carrying a rifle and coming out without it could create any other suspicions. She then declared that Ernst had always been sneaking around trying to kill someone when he was not justified. I then said, "But you know that if you, as you say, put Reberg across the river on the 23rd that Ernst didn't kill him don't you?" and to this she gave no answer, but went to talking to Lee regarding saddling the horse to change the subject. She sent a telegram to John Reberg in Sauk Rapids, Minnesota, saying Julius never sold his place, he is missing and thought to be dead. Come at once and signed Frances Cooper.

She said she was on the square with everybody and that Ernst had made a hell on earth for her for the last six years and that she was not implicated in anything but what she could and would show the whole community. She then said that she would get Ray Dryer [at Mormon Ranch] if he would to look after the stock, and when Reberg's brother John came they could investigate all they pleased. She then went on back to the Reberg place and said she would round up everything as best she could and come out and go to Salmon as soon as she could.

My recommendations in this case would be to take Chas. Ernst into custody pending a thorough investigation by the proper county and state officials and to keep the woman in the case under surveillance to see she didn't skip the country. It is my belief that Reberg was over the draft age and he never seemed to be worried about it saying that his only regrets if drafted was that it would ruin him financially, but his disappearance without getting something for his stock of which he had about 10 head of cattle and 10 to 15 head of horses and some farm machinery don't make his former attitude and the story of his leaving as told by Mrs. Ernst seem at all probable."

On January 10 Sheriff Frazier of Salmon, Lemhi County, learned of the suspected murder—apparently from a letter sent by Frances—and set out on horseback to investigate. The following day the Lemhi County undertaker and coroner W. C. Doebler was ordered to the site by the county prosecutor. (It was an eight-day round trip.) Doebler met the sheriff and Frances at Meyers Cove and spent the night of January 13 at the Mormon Ranch; Frances talked a good deal.

The next morning Doebler summoned a coroner's jury of six settlers there and they traveled up river to the Reberg ranch. (Having crossed the river, they were now in Valley

County.) Frances showed them where the guns were hidden and directed them to the grave about 350 yards from Reberg's one-room cabin. In his deposition, William Doebler described his findings:

"There was about three feet of rope tied around the body. We then proceeded to raise the body, the jurors were sworn over the body and an inspection was then made by the jurors. We found one bullet hole which entered the right side of the abdomen and came out on the left. We then buried the body in the same grave the best we could as there was no lumber there to make any box. We got some hay, put [it] in the bottom of the grave and we took a blanket and wrapped the body and laid some timbers over the body to keep the ground off of the body. The grave was then filled. We then proceeded to the Ray Dryer ranch in Lemhi County and an inquest was held there."

The jury found that Julius Reberg had come to his death on December 18 by means of a gunshot wound at the hands of Charles Ernst with criminal intent. Sheriff Frazier, Frances Cooper-Ernst, and Coroner Doebler returned to Salmon. (Curiously enough, on January 14, while the coroner's jury was meeting down on the Middle Fork, prosecuting attorney John Rees in Salmon was mailing a letter to Reberg's brother in Minnesota that stated, "Your brother...has been murdered by one Charles Ernst sometime in December last.")

Deputy Sheriff Shaw went from Salmon to Challis and arrested Ernst, who made no attempt to resist and made no statement. The Salmon *Herald* disclosed, "Friends of Ernst say that he has always borne a good reputation except per-haps for a disposition to indolence. He and his father John have been employed at the Clayton [silver] mine. Owen Swift knew the family when they formerly lived on Wood River. It is said of Charles Ernst that he is not of an excitable disposition at all nor do his clear eyes reflect any sinister light, but it is known that he charged Reberg with being the cause of breaking up his home."

Ernst was accompanied by his boy, "a bright little fellow of four years." The sheriff's kindly wife tried to take custody of the child, but he "screamed at being separated from his prisoner father and there was nothing to do but take him back [to the cell]." His mother Frances, who never saw him while he was in Salmon, went with company to a movie that night.

The suspects were held for the arrival of the Valley County Sheriff F. C. Sherrill enroute from Cascade, Idaho. Sherrill had to travel 600 miles by train to Salmon to pick up his prisoners and 600 miles back. It is only about 100 miles in a straight line, but by train through Boise, Twin Falls, Pocatello, Armstead, Montana, and Salmon, it is a lot longer. Cooper and Ernst were taken to Cascade.

On January 17, Frank Reberg, Jake's brother, arrived to transport his effects and remains home to Minnesota. (The body was not brought out for another month.) He met Frances but was hardly cordial.

On January 19 she wrote Andrew Lee, who was down at the Mormon Ranch on the Middle Fork:

" Dear Friend,
Am sending this by Frank [Reberg] who came instead of John. If there is anything you can do to help him in any way please do it and I will pay you for your trouble. I can see he has no use for me and oh if he only knew how a kind word or look from him would brace me up in this awful trouble he would not treat me so. He thinks I am bad all through. I can see that. I am giving up all hopes now of trying to fight it out alone as E has a lawyer and his Old Father is here. They are working to lay the crime on me and the lies they won't tell about me won't be worth telling. I have got to send for my Mother as I have stood about all I can stand now and there is no use to try to stand it alone any longer. Frank seems just to want to give the ranch away. Try and get him out of that idea if you can. Well there is nothing else I guess so I will close with best wishes.
Frances Cooper"

Reading between the lines, one has to wonder how self-serving was this letter? Did Frances intend that Frank Reberg read it? (He did.) She knew she was unable to pay Lee anything. And why was she still so concerned with the disposition of the ranch? In any event, by January 20 she was corresponding with Frank in a familiar, even friendly, manner from Cascade, Idaho:

"Dear friend Frank,
Well the preliminary hearing came out OK. I will get a good lawyer when the main trial comes on the 4th of June and I feel sure that cur will be sent over as I was able to get the best of the deal all the ways around and he had a good lawyer here too.
...Well if there is anything you want to know in regards to any thing I know anything about I will be pleased to help you. With kindest regards to all.
Frances Cooper"

The preliminary hearing was held on January 25 before L. S. Kimball, Probate Judge for Valley County. Frances Ernst's deposition ran twenty-three pages and portions of it are crucial to the story. She testified about meeting Reberg:

"Q. It was kind of a case of love at first sight with you and Reberg then was it?
A. No.
Q. When did you first fall in love with him?
A. I didn't fall in, I just naturally got to liking him about the time I went to Challis.
Q. It didn't take you long?
A. Oh, quite a while.
Q. You met him about the first of July and when was it you first agreed to marry him?
A. About the latter part of September."

Frances went on to explain that the reason she and Reberg did not get married was because of talk she had been hearing in Challis about the trouble Charlie was going to

209

make for Reberg, who had alienated her affections. "I thought ...there would be less trouble if we didn't get married. I didn't want Mr. Reberg to get killed if I could help it."

She was asked why she gave up her baby at the divorce.

"A. Well, one [reason] was that Ernst had always said if I took the child away from him and therefore left him subject to the draft he would commit wholesale murder on everyone that he could—the child and myself and everyone he had a grudge against. The other reason was that he had procured some letters that I wrote to Mr. Reberg and those letters might cause a bigger trial than I was financially able to stand at the time."

Further testimony in the deposition revealed that Frances had obtained a bill of sale from Reberg on "about November 18" for all the improvements on his place. She said he "just wrote this thing out in case he had to dodge the officers on this draft business and also that it might help if someone kicked about me living down there." On December 8 Frances sent the bill of sale to Charlie and under oath explained the act by saying Charlie had requested either that or $150, and she did not have the money.

Finally, she gave her version of the events on the morning of December 18:

"A. Well that morning about eight o'clock Mr. Reberg stepped outside of the door to wash his hands, he was standing by the step at the door washing his hands, and I was standing inside of the cabin near the window; I heard a shot and I jumped to the door where I could see Mr. Reberg. He seemed to have half fallen when I seen him but he got up and came in the cabin. I closed the door and he walked around behind me and looked out of the window. Then he went over to the other window and picked up the rifle and threw a shell into it and stood by the door with the rifle to defend himself if anyone came in. I was standing in front of him and he said, 'I am going to die, you will have to take the gun.' I put my arm around him and tried to hold him up but he slipped to the floor and he said, 'I am dying now, honey, good-bye.' He remained conscious about a minute and a half longer after that; from the time he lost consciousness until he died was about ten minutes. I stayed there with him about ten minutes longer after that, then I got my rifle and went outdoors to look for Ernst. I knew it would not do to be seen out there with a gun that he could see, so I went back and got the revolver. I started down the trail near the creek. Ernst jumped out of the brush along the bank near the creek and took my gun away. He asked me if he had got the son of a bitch. I said, "Yes, you've killed him." He made me go with him to get his horse and he brought it back and tied it back of the stackyard. Then he made me go into the cabin with him where the body of Mr. Reberg lay. He kicked the body and called it all kinds of vile names, then he drug it out to the strawstack and covered it with straw. He came back into the cabin, then washed his hands, and ate some breakfast. He stayed around there the rest of the day until about four o'clock; then he said he would have to take the mail to Pearson's and Kurry's. He got his horse, the mail, and what guns there was. He threw Mr. Reberg's gun away, and went on to Pearson's and Kurry's with the mail. He cached the other guns up the creek. He came back about dusk and made me get him some supper, then he waited until about eleven o'clock, then he went out to dig the grave. In about three-quarters of an hour he came back. He got an old white horse that was there, put the saddle on it, got a rope and tied it around the neck of the body of Mr. Reberg and drug the body out to the grave. He threw the body in and covered it up, then came back to the cabin, unsaddled his horse, and went in the cabin and ate some lunch and went to bed. He stayed there that night and the next day until about noon. He got his horse and made me go up the creek with him as he was afraid someone might see him there. We stayed up there until evening. Then he got the guns he had cached and came back to the cabin. He stayed there that night again and the next morning he left for Meyers Cove. He made me go along with him and he took the gun he had killed Mr. Reberg with, some rubbers Mr. Reberg had been wearing and some socks and cached them in a cave near his placer claim. He had taken what other guns there was along but no ammunition. He made me go as far as the mouth of Camas Creek, then he let me go back. I did not see him anymore after that."

Frances was questioned closely about why she did not send word of the murder to the sheriff. She defended the three-week delay by saying that she was afraid Ernst would find out before the officers could get there; that she did not consider Jack Oquin of the Forest Service an officer or "competent person to handle the situation" and therefore told him the story Ernst had instructed her to tell; that she could not send a letter through the post office at the Cove because the postmaster would open it, as she did other letters. "I notified the officers as soon as I found out for sure they were not coming in." (She sent a letter on January 7 by the stage driver at Forney to the sheriff at Salmon.)

Charles Ernst had his preliminary hearing the same day as Frances, before the same judge, who ruled that he was to be held for trial on a murder charge. Bail was set at $5,000 for each defendant.

At this point, the Salmon newspaper observed: "Several circumstances appear in the state's evidence which would tend to confirm the innocence of Ernst, and but few people hereabout will believe that the defendant is guilty."

The Challis Messenger was more voluble: "Thus is drawing to a tragic close a tale of two men and a woman—the eternal triangle which has been enacted for ages to come— the primal lure of even the beasts of the field to rend, tear, and kill for sole possession of its mate. Even with the damaging evidence of guilt which is hanging over the accused like a dark cloud, we cannot help but feel that possibly new developments might occur as the case progresses which will throw an entirely different light on the whole deplorable affair." Obviously, rumors were widespread, and some folks had reason to believe that Charlie did not pull the trigger. The tale was far from drawing to a close.

On the first of February Frances took the train back to Salmon. The next day she again wrote Frank Reberg. In part, she told him that she had to go back down to the Middle Fork, and then she added the most incongruous postscript in the history of Idaho correspondence:

"...I must go back in there myself and will come out when they bring Julius out. Oh my god it seems sometimes like my heart will break and I just can't go on another day. Oh if I could just have my own sweetheart back for just a little while again. We had planned so much on that trip back there together and now they are sending him back there like that to that poor little Mother and those sweet little sisters that I once thot would be my sisters but all that is gone now the little home that we loved so well and the dear little plans we made are gone forever and oh I wish I was with him too. If I could just be with some of you and talk to you a little while I might feel better. I know you felt more or less hard at me and I did not blame you for you had no way of finding out much about me as no one knows me here but I am not a bad women. If I had been Julius would not have loved me like he did if I had been bad. Well I must close with kindest regards to all I remain
Yours Very Truly,
Frances Cooper

P.S. A man was stabbed near to death here tonight and Sheriff Frazier is out now trying to catch the man who done it."

Two days later she wrote again. The disposition of the ranch remained on her mind.

" Dear Frank,

I have been talking to quite a few people about the ranch and there seems to be lots of them that would like to buy it. If you would put it in care of Sheriff Frazier and have him put it up for bids I think you will do much better than you are doing now and it won't cost you any more than it would this way. No one here wants anything to do with Bureson as he is an ex-bootlegger and a big wind jammer and no one trusts him. Then all he is thinking about is what money he expects to get out of you. Do as you like of course but I thought I ought to warn you any way.
As ever,
Frances Cooper"

On February 14 she wrote John Reberg with admirable considerations:

"Dear John,

Julius's body is now here in Salmon and will soon start east. You boys may be able to bear to look at it when it gets there but whatever you do don't let the Mother & sisters see it for it will only make it ten times harder for them. Burson never would have brought the body out if I had not went down with him and seen to it that he did and he is not dealing fair with you in selling the ranch but I have done all I can to help you in that line as I must go home to my Father & Mother until it is time for the trial. Now John there is one favor I would like to ask of you and that is that you hire Lawyer Whitecomb here in Salmon to help with this case. You must do that much for Julius's sake any way. I would not ask you to do it if I could raise the money to do it but my Father & Mother are not well off. They have not even got enough to keep them in their old age unless I help them and the way things are for me now it is hard for me to borrow any money and there must be another Lawyer to help me in this case. Whitcomb is the best lawyer. In fact please write to E. C. Frazier about this and see what he thinks. If you want keepsakes it looks to me like you would like some of his

214

graphiphone records. He had some that he liked very much. There is also a very fine set of deer horns nailed on the cabin. It was the first deer he ever killed and I would think some of you boys would want them. If you do, write to John A. Pearsons, Myers Cove. He was one of Julius's best friends/ and tell him and get him to send them to you. I am sending you the last picture Julius ever had taken. It was taken about two months before he was killed and shows his little home too.

If there should be any thing you want to write to me about my address is Frances Cooper, Ybar City, Flo., R2 Box 334 N"

While out on bail, Frances entrained from Nampa for Ybar City, near Tampa, Florida, the home of her parents, arriving March 2. It appears that while she made no secret of it, not everyone was certain where she went. At the time, according to her letter of April 30, 1918, to John Reberg, she intended to return for the trial. After acknowledging receipt of a letter from him and from his sister Mary, she wrote:

"I wish John that you would try and come out for the trial if you can for Ernst will sure try to blacken Julius's name and we must not let him get away with anything like that. Julius never done him any harm and was not the cause of me leaving him as i tried to leave him before I was seeing Julius and would have left him just the same if I had never seen Julius as he never made a living for me and was always mean. He is half crazy and a fiend on top of it. Lots of people are going to make a mean talk because he did not register for the draft but that was not because he was a slacker. He was not fit to pass as he could not hear good. He just did not want to have to go over to Salmon every time something came up about it. He did not mean to do wrong. He always spoke so lovingly of all of you and he seemed to think you would be the best one to send for if anything went wrong. Well I must close with best wishes for all. I will start back for Idaho on the 10th so if you want to write me about anything send letters care of E. C. Frazier, Salmon, Ida. Don't be afraid to write to Frazier about anything you want to know as he is a good man. That country don't look very good to a person when they first go there but it is a good country and an easy country to make a living in. Julius liked it and he loved his little home he had there.

My Father and Mother never were very good to me and now they want to say mean things about Julius so I am never coming back here. As soon as the trial is over. I am going to join the red cross and go to France at once. It's the only good place for me now.

Yours Very Truly
Frances"

Ernst, also out on bail, and with no star witness to testify against him, went to work in logging camps between Cascade and McCall, Idaho, while making regular reports to the sheriff. In winter, 1919, he married a woman named Margaret who had a four-year-old boy by an earlier marriage.

Then eighteen months after the preliminary hearing, Frances wrote two letters to the former prosecuting attorney for Valley County, F. M. Kerby. One letter confessed that she killed Reberg, the other gave details.

"Dear Sir,

Have just heard that Ernst is in jail again, also that he is married. I was so angry at him for awhile for ever sending me near Reberg that I wanted to give him a good lesson but I want to live right and do right now so please wire me ticket and $20 for expense so I can come at once. I was the one that killed Reberg. We won't need a trial to clear this up as I can explain it all. I have no money or I would not ask you for it. Please help me to do what is right and oblige.

Yours very truly,
Frances Cooper
Ybar City, Florida"

One theory purports that she "got religion" at a revival meeting in Florida. But the story becomes ever more curious. On April 18, 1919, Sheriff Ed Smith, with expense money furnished by the county commissioners, left to get Frances. He was back with the prisoner at least by mid-June because the Cascade paper chronicles his trip down the South Fork of the Salmon River to investigate a shooting by "Dead Shot" Reed. Something had happened to Frances, however. She may have fallen in love with the sheriff and he with her. More scuttlebutt. The Cascade *News* remarked elliptically that the sheriff's efforts would shortly be vindicated. Frances, however, recanted her recent letter-confession. (It was Mark Twain who quipped that he had given up lying because the field was full of amateurs.)

In mid-July prosecuting attorney R. B. Ayers went to Lemhi County to investigate the evidence in the case. It was beginning to look like there might be a trial.

On July 21 Frances appeared before Justice of the Peace D. J. Cain in Cascade and waived her right to counsel and to a preliminary examination and asked that she be bound over to the District Court for trial. The prosecuting attorney consented. It was charged that she did deliberately kill and murder Julius Reberg; that she conspired together with Charles Ernst; that the gun was held in the hands of one Charles Ernst.

At 5:30 PM Charles Ernst was arrested and brought to court by the sheriff and the murder charge read. He, too, waived his right to a preliminary examination and time to prepare, and asked to be bound over for trial.

The defendants were arraigned July 29 before Judge Charles Reddoch at the District Court of the Third Judicial District in Valley County (Cascade). On July 31 Charles Ernst pleaded "not guilty." Finding him without funds, the court appointed Boise lawyer T. S. Risser for the defense. The trial date was set for Monday, April 4. Charles Ernst's co-counsel, L. E. Glennon, arrived belatedly from Salmon.

On the appointed day, jury selection began. By now, of course, World War I was over. Nevertheless, a question was put to the jurors concerning the American loyalty of the dead man and whether his disloyalty in evasion of the draft would prejudice them.

The trial attracted such a crowd that "seating was little more than sufficient for the ladies present." On August 5 the State made its opening statement, and Frances Cooper Ernst testified for two days. She was one of fourteen witnesses for the prosecution.

On the afternoon of August 7 the defense opened its case with Charles Ernst taking the stand in his own defense. According to the Cascade newspaper, he contended that he had gone to the Reberg ranch to obtain evidence of illicit relations existing between his former wife and Reberg; that he found out what he desired to know for a proposed prosecution of Reberg; that the woman was drawn there under a hypnotic spell put upon her by Reberg; that as soon as Ernst appeared the spell was broken and the woman shot Reberg. Ernst testified that he had disarmed the man and covered him with a revolver in self-defense before she fired. He said that he then sought to protect her because she had been his wife and was the mother of his child. Six witnesses, including his father and Albert and Lulu Kurry, testified on his behalf. The court then recessed until August 11.

When the trial resumed after the weekend, both sides made their closing arguments and summations to the jury. The judge gave his instructions at a little after 8:00 PM and the all-male jury retired to its deliberations.

At 4:00 AM Tuesday the jury reached its verdict. Judge Reddoch was called from his bed, went to the courtroom, and had the jury brought in. Only the court officers, counsel, and the defendant were present. The verdict was delivered by the foreman and read by the clerk: "We, the jury, find the defendant guilty of murder in the second degree." (The Salmon paper commented, "It was said that all but one juror contended for first degree murder against Ernst.") The judge dismissed the jury and announced a recess until 4:00 PM August 12.

Upon reconvening, Judge Reddoch pronounced sentence: "...for the term of not less than ten nor more than twenty-five years in the state penitentiary." Frances was promptly arraigned and charged with manslaughter. She waived her rights, pleaded guilty, and requested judgment forthwith. The prosecuting attorney pointed out that she was the chief witness for the state and that such cooperation was normally recognized by the court. Judgment was then pronounced: "...for the term of not less than five nor more than ten years in the state penitentiary." Cost of the trial was $5,000. On the morning train the next day, the sheriff took both defendants to the state prison in Boise.

Charlie Ernst; Frances Cooper.

While the trial record has been lost, some bizarre aspects of the case were detailed in the Salmon *Herald* a week later—details drawn from witnesses who had testified at the trial and had now returned home to Lemhi County. In discussing the antithetical nature of the two defendants' accounts of the killing, the paper reported:

"Here the matter might have hung, had not some previous strategy been employed to procure additional testimony. Herein the prosecution proved itself master of the intricate situation. A Dictaphone had been installed in the Cooper room at the hotel, and stenographers, two in number, had taken down the conversations that passed between Ernst and Cooper while in a supposedly private interview. Also, a hole had been cut into the wall of the room and a third witness to the talk had his head intruded into the room, hearing everything. [Note: It is not clear whether this happened in Salmon or Cascade.] This was introduced proving collusion and complicity of the two main defendants.

Aside from this diverting evidence, there was no time that the testimony of either of the principals was shaken. They told radically different stories, but each was well fortified as to details. A letter written by Cooper to Ernst some time ago, but after the tragedy had occurred, was the only ray of hope afforded Ernst's counsel that her tale might be queered. Summed up, it is proved by the trial that both were guilty, and in collusion, that both of them on the stand lied like Huns hoping by opposing testimony to gain a clearance for each.

It is rendered fairly clear that Ernst shot Reberg, in the presence of the woman, and it is not improbable that they were equally guilty. Most people believe that the case was nothing if not cold blooded, premeditated murder, and that one or both of them should have been hung.

A prison sentence for murder is not fair or just to society because the murderer is quite invariably liberated in a few years, by pardon, that he may prey further upon society. It is safe to predict that a long petition will be sent to Boise, in less than a year from this date, praying for the pardon of both these persons."

Uncannily prophetic words these proved to be.

In early April, 1921, Frances Cooper, while in prison, told the state pardons board that she wished to confess that she, not Charlie, had killed Reberg, but she refused to tell her story in the absence of the governor. The next day the hearing was moved to the governor's office. The Cascade *News* reported its version of her confession:

"In her confession before the pardon board Mrs. Ernst gave an account of herself and her husband homesteading in a wild and almost inaccessible part of Lemhi County. She described her life there as a "prison." Reberg finally came along and after becoming acquainted with Mrs. Ernst told her that if she would divorce her husband he would marry her. This, she said, she did, and went to live with Reberg, who refused to marry her. [Note: In her deposition she said that Reberg never revealed the slightest reluctance to marry her. Furthermore, in his October letter to his brother, Reberg called her his wife.] Ernst heard where his former wife was and went to Reberg's cabin, arriving on the day that Reberg and Mrs. Ernst were having a quarrel.

At this point the story told by the two inmates of the penitentiary varies. Mrs. Ernst says that Reberg went outside and came back threatening to kill her for telling her former husband where she was. He reached for a rifle from the wall and a scuffle ensued in which she took the weapon away from him and the two scuffled out the door together into the yard. Here, according to Mrs. Ernst, she freed herself from Reberg and in a stooping position fired at him without placing the rifle to her shoulder.

Her husband's story of this incident is entirely different. He confessed to the pardon board that he gave his wife a rifle after she and Reberg came from the house. He stated, however, that he thought he took all the cartridges from the magazine but carelessly must have overlooked one. He says that the shot from which Reberg died was fired from behind him as he was advancing toward Reberg."

Boise public defender T. S. Risser made a statement to the board on behalf of Charles Ernst, referring to the two letters Frances had written from Florida where, under no duress, she had confessed to the murder. "Mr. Risser also mentioned a fact," wrote the Boise *Statesman*, "which in the opinion of the pardon board is the key to the whole difficulty. When Mrs. Ernst came back from Florida to participate in the trial of her (ex) husband, it is alleged that a certain officer influenced her to 'stick' her husband so she would get off lightly." [The "certain officer" is a reference to Sheriff Edwards.]

In July Charles Ernst, represented by a lawyer, received his own full hearing before the pardon board. On August 4, 1921, the Statesman reported that Ernst was granted an absolute pardon (July 30) "based upon confessions recently made by Frances Ernst." The account continues, "Attorney D. M. Cox of Cascade representing Ernst presented petitions in the prisoner's favor signed by more than 650 residents of Valley County. Upon being set at liberty, Ernst took his departure for the home of his mother at Williamina, Oregon."

Frances Cooper-Ernst was paroled in March, 1923, and pardoned in April, 1924. From Florida she asked the board of pardons for permission to remarry and leave the country.

There is more. Ernst went to work haying for Old Bill Sullivan in Clayton. They got into an argument when Ernst said the American flag "wasn't no good" and they soon had the hay wagon overturned.

Ernst went back to the Middle Fork and moved into the Mormon Ranch cabin. Billy Wilson owned the place and rode twenty miles down there to tell him to leave. On the way he had a Pauline revelation and decided he had better let old Ernst alone. Ernst starved out and moved to Leesburg, Idaho, just west of Salmon.

In 1942 at Leesburg he found some rich placer-gold ground. The Richardson Company was working the claim next to his, and Ernst told their employee Stanley Wood, "Whatever you do, don't *ever* get on my land." If Wood had known Ernst better, he would have heeded his words.

One September morning, while Wood was clearing road with a bulldozer in order to move dragline equipment farther up the creek, a shot was fired from ambush. The bullet hit his tractor seat and fragments pierced his hip. Wood was taken to the Salmon hospital. A rifle with corresponding caliber was found in Ernst's nearby cabin, and it was sent to the FBI lab in Washington, D. C. for examination.

In October, 1942, Charles Ernst was charged with attempted murder. Although he only admitted to "shooting at a deer," and his court-appointed attorney argued that the evidence was circumstantial, the jury convicted him of assault with a deadly weapon. He was sentenced to no less than one, and no more than two, years in the state penitentiary and was again received at Boise. He was pardoned nine months later, dying of tuberculosis.

One night soon after his release he came to visit his old friend, Bill Sullivan. They talked most of the night. Ernst planned to leave in the morning, but Mrs. Sullivan insisted he stay while she made him a cake for his birthday.

Twenty months later the Salmon newspaper carried a two line notice: "Charles Ernst, age 58, died [March 21, 1945] at the Hamilton [Montana] hospital following a long illness. He is survived by wife Margaret and son John and daughter Velma."

So the mystery abides. Only one detail is as clear as Middle Fork water: Frances Cooper-Ernst could out-lie any fisherman.

Reberg's grave in Minnesota.

In 1922, John Bernston (see Mile 66.2, Mormon Ranch) filed on 110 acres at Sheep Creek through a desert-land entry. He had arrived at the location in 1919, but in December of that year the land was withdrawn from entry for inclusion in the Idaho National Forest. Upon Bernston's appeal, however, his entry was allowed because the Forest Service had no objection. (He caught the tail-end of the we're-here-to-help-you era.) He installed a cable crossing over the river at a cost of $200, cleared rocks, dug irrigation ditches from the creek, built a wooden flume, harrowed the ground, planted alfalfa seed, fenced twenty-five acres, and tended the fields from 1919 to 1926. From 1926 to 1929 there was no cultivation or residency on the site. George Crandall, from downriver at Brush Creek, looked after the place and pastured his cattle on it. In 1930 Bernston received final proof at a cost of $1.25 an acre.

MILE 66.2 *Mormon Ranch* on the right at Warm Springs Creek.

Like many of the other ranches along the river, the Mormon place was used by packers, miners, and trappers wintering their stock. It was on the trail to the Yellow Jacket mines, to Meyers Cove, and to Big Creek.

The "Mormons" were the Beagle brothers: Perry, Bill, and Ben. They were farming the ranch in 1900. In July, 1902, the Salmon paper reported that, "The Beagle Ferry at the mouth of Brush Creek near the Mormon Ranch is making regular trips." Dimensions given for the ferry are twenty-four by twelve feet.

The best account of where the Beagles came from and how they got to the Middle Fork is related by Basil d'Easum in an extensive piece that followed an interview with Perry Beagle in 1912 in Salmon. (Perry was the eldest brother and regarded as the leader by the others.) The article was carried in the *Statesman*, and reprinted in the Lemhi *Herald* the same year.

According to Perry, in May, 1843, the Beagle parents and their five children (Perry was eleven years old) joined a train of 110 wagons in Missouri that was setting out for the Whitman colony in Walla Walla. The Beagles were members of Jesse Applegate's company.

The wagons reached Fort Hall (Idaho) in August. They followed the Snake River to Burnt River and thence to Walla Walla (Washington), where some of them spent a month making boats to proceed down the Columbia River.

They left their livestock with Hudson's Bay factor McKinley and floated to The Dalles, portaging their supplies and letting the boats down with ropes. They followed the same procedure at the Cascades. At Fort Vancouver, the end of their six-month trek, they were welcomed by the famous

Dr. McLoughlin. The Beagles reassembled a wagon and pushed south to a valley now known as Willamette.

They had farmed for scarcely five years, when gold fever smote the region. James Marshall had been a member of the party a year ahead of Beagles', and they may have met him in Willamette Valley just before he left for California to get some Mexican horses. He fought in the War with Mexico, then in January, 1847, discovered gold at Coloma while digging a millrace. William and Perry Beagle and fifty others rode horseback to the new camp. Fortune smiled on the Beagles in the goldfields.

In January they went to Sacramento and whipsawed lumber for a hotel. Wages were $20 a day, but meals and board cost $10 a day.

The account continues:

"From that time on to the present moment, the placer mining fever has had full possession of Perry Beagle, and his story is a record of the gold discoveries in the west. After his California experiences, he returned to Oregon, where he took part in the Rogue River Indian wars of 1855 and gold strike, on the south fork of the Salmon River [Oregon], and struck out for the gold fields of Idaho. Beagle washed the first pan of dirt at what was afterwards Canyon City [Colorado]. This was while on a journey to Warren [Idaho]. At Pine Creek, Auburn [California], and Sumpter [Oregon], Beagle successfully placer mined. At the latter place Beagle averaged $9 a day from the diggings.

In the fall of 1862 Beagle and his wife (whom he married when he was 19 and she 14 years old) came to Idaho Basin and bought a third interest in a claim for $140. After the third day they averaged $100 a day each from this claim. When Beagle began to think that the claim was playing out he sold his third interest for $2,500. But the night before the deal was completed Beagle hired two men to work with him all night and they took out $681 that night.

He then went to Grande Ronde valley [Oregon] and later bought a mule train and ran a pack train into Idaho Basin.

After this he tried farming again for 11 years in the Willamette Valley. But in 1876 he was back again in Idaho and during the Nez Perce outbreak [1877] built a strong fort at Moscow [Idaho] and was captain of the garrison.

At the present time he and his two brothers are living on a ranch about 70 miles from Salmon. Often he visits the little town, with his pockets full of candy for all the children who know and love him. An active, clear-eyed, very lively man is Perry Beagle. He declares he is going to live to be a hundred; the clean story of his clean life, free from the forms of dissipation which have wrecked many old-timers, is sufficient to warrant his belief. Today, at the age of close on 80 years, he can jump into the air and crack his heels together three times before he touches the ground. He is immensely proud of that fact and always ready to perform it when some skeptic doubts his ability."

In May, 1909, R. H. Woolard from Forney, Idaho, filed a homestead entry application on the fifty-nine acres at the Mormon Ranch ranger station. He found that there was only one granite boulder large enough to use for a metes-and-bounds description. Woolard did not take his filing to patent, and either he or Perry Beagle sold to Bob Ramey of Loon Creek in summer, 1913.

Ramey sold to Lee Wyatt in the fall, 1914, and he in turn sold to John Pearson and Ray Dryer in 1917, a year after the location was surveyed. The Salmon *Herald* reported in July, 1918, that John Pearson had been in town and said that they would put up about eighty tons of hay on the place that year. "He says his family and that of his partner, R. L. Dryer, are well and happy, and that prospects of their district are excellent. They have none of their sheep there now, all being on Pahsimeroi [Idaho], but they expect to have 1,000 of them on the ranch this winter. They could have wintered the entire band there last winter without difficulty."

In April, 1919, Issac Wilson of the Pahsimeroi bought the ranch, along with the Reberg place at Sheep Creek. Wilson was the father of Billy Wilson and the father-in-law of John

Bernston. The Salmon newspaper reported that Bernston and the Wilson boys "are all of an interest with the father and will run 1,000-1,500 cattle over the new ranges. Bernston moves to the Middle Fork this spring, up from Salt Lake City where he had been in contract work in a big way." The winter of 1919 proved to be the worst that ever struck the Middle Fork (see Mile 33.5).

John Bernston was born in Christiana, Norway, in 1890. He immigrated to Liverpool, England, then in 1907 to the U. S. via the port of Boston. He was 5'4", fair complexion, brown hair and blue eyes.

Bernston was in Salt Lake City sometime before 1917—a carpenter who became a building contractor there. He married Erma Wilson, and they had children. In 1919 he became a naturalized citizen and in May moved his residence to the Mormon Ranch. They lived in the house built by Wyatt in 1914. Over the next four years, the Bernstons were gone six months at a time (winter) to perform construction work in Salt Lake City. It was a difficult time to try to make a backcountry livestock operation pay.

By 1922 they had established a twenty by thirty-foot log house with two rooms; a barn the same size of stone and logs; a log milk house, poultry sheds, storehouse, and stone cellars, and fencing around fifty acres of oats and alfalfa.

Bernston received his homestead title in 1922 and his desert-land entry title in 1930.

Remains of the stone cellars are still apparent. Several graves lie on the flat halfway between the cabin and Bernard bridge. Ben and Bill Beagle are buried there, and Mrs. Lee Wyatt. A fourth grave is that of Alvah Beedle. As a homestead witness for Bernston in 1922, Beedle wrote that he was seventy-three; that he had known the Mormon Ranch since 1893 but did not locate there until Bernston did; that he had his own place with cattle nearby (Pole Creek, downstream) and went to check on them every two to three months. Beedle therefore must have been a caretaker for Bernston.

The Mormon Ranch is now an administrative site for the Idaho Fish and Game Department.

Beagle brothers used this shed as a chicken coop. Warm Springs Creek was diverted through the floor of the nearby spring house.

MILE 67 Brush Creek-Flying B Ranch, or Flying Resort Ranches on the left.

When Captain Bernard's soldiers arrived in 1879, the Sheepeater Indians had six large lodges at this location. Miners erected a log cabin on the place some time afterward.

In 1900 two brothers were living at Brush Creek when the Laing family came through (see Mile 68.3). They later sold their squatters' rights to Albert Kurry.

Kurry was one of three brothers who came into the Middle Fork country with horses in 1912, having heard about the area from Cougar Dave Lewis (see Mile 78.2), whom they had met at Pittsburg Landing on the Snake River. Kurry's parents homesteaded Kurry Creek in Hells Canyon.

Albert Kurry was married; his wife Lulu was a school teacher and musician. Henry Kurry was a bachelor. At times the brothers kept their cattle together; later Henry moved his stock over to the Mormon Ranch. They had a cable-basket for crossing the river.

In April, 1919, the brothers drove a herd of 100 cows from Salmon down to Brush Creek. They went into the winter of 1919 with 300 head. By the following April, they had only thirty left. In June Lulu died at the ranch; her last request was to be buried in Boise. They packed her body by horse twenty miles up Camas Creek to Meyers Cove. Then Charley Sherman hauled her non-stop with a team and wagon sixty miles to Salmon. Packed in ice, she was taken by train almost 600 miles to Boise.

After the funeral, Albert returned to the Middle Fork, bringing his brother Henry along.

The Middle Fork survey had been completed in 1917, and Albert had filed on 160 acres under desert land entry and acquired title in 1920. The brothers labored hard to rebuild their cattle herd. A 1923 copy of the Salmon newspaper reported that "the Kurry brothers grow nectarines, peaches, plums, apples, dewberries, raspberries, strawberries—the cellar so full of fruit and vegetables hardly room to enter it." In 1926 Albert obtained title to an additional 160 acres. The same year, he sold his cattle to Chuck Davis and Bill Foss, but Henry stayed on at Brush Creek a while longer.

George Crandall and his wife bought Brush Creek to raise cattle. Mrs. Crandall was about twenty years older than George and had the purchase money. The Crandalls had carpeted floors and a big gramophone, but it was a lonely life for her—she might see two or three women in a year. In sixteen years she never left the place. In 1936 when the Hatch-Swain-Frazier trip came through, Mrs. Crandall took Frank Swain aside and asked him, "Tell me, do they really have talking picture shows?"

George toiled hard. He fenced the place, cutting thousands of poles up in Deer Heaven. But they never realized much money from their livestock business.

Finally the Crandalls sold and moved to Phoenix, Arizona. George was apparently murdered for the money that he inherited from his wife. His body was never found.

George and "Ma" Crandall, Brush Creek, visited by 1936 Hatch trip.

Albert Kurry photographed at Whitebird, Idaho, 1912. He was the first rancher at Brush Creek.

A. A. Bennett bought the ranch from the Crandalls and converted it to the Flying B Ranch with the intention of making it into a guest and hunting operation similar to what it is today.

Bennett was one of the legendary Idaho backcountry pilots. He had flown for six years in Alaska, making him one of the earliest bush pilots there. In the early 1930s Bennett Air Transport planes carried mail, equipment, and passengers to the remote mining communities of Stibnite, Yellow Pine, Atlanta, Deadwood, Knox, and Warren. During winter, 1932, when Yellow Pine lost its fuel oil because a snow-covered pipeline broke, Bennett's Zenith cabin biplanes and Stearman hauled 12,000 gallons in thirty-gallon drums in less than a month!

From 1932 to 1934, Bennett was a partner with the famous Bob Johnson, as they flew mountain mail and freight contracts from Boise. He had flown with Johnson in Missoula before starting Bennett Air.

In 1940 Bennett had a flying school in Salmon. Then in 1941-1942 he served as state Director of Aeronautics. By 1944, after he bought Brush Creek, a newspaper reported that he was flying in a bull rake, bulldozer, and sawmill—in pieces, of course.

Approximately 150 families own shares in the Flying B, using it as a vacation spot and donating their labor for its upkeep. It is operated in conjunction with the Root Ranch (fifty air-miles northwest of the river, homesteaded in 1919), once owned by movie actor Wallace Beery.
The two operations were consolidated under the name Flying Resort Ranches, but the name has never taken hold with river people—the historic spot on the banks of the Middle Fork is still known as the Flying B.

MILE 67.1 Bernard Bridge

The cables for this bridge were flown in from McCall by Bob Johnson of Johnson Flying Service. No airstrip existed at the time. According to Bill Sullivan, the cables weighed 1,800 pounds and had to be wrapped around the outside of the plane. Johnson made it with the first load. The day had warmed up by the time he arrived with the second load, however, and he had to come in under full power. He damaged the undercarriage of his plane and had his license suspended briefly.

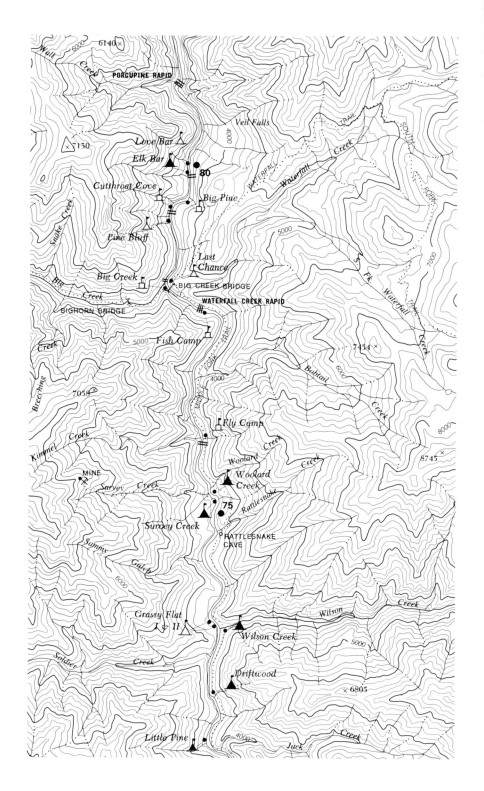

IMPASSABLE CANYON

MILE 68.1 *Haystack or Rattlesnake (Hatch) Rapid.*
Haystack marks the beginning of Impassable Canyon.

The rapid is scouted from the left-hand shore. It may be named for stacks of hay on the fields at the Flying B, or for standing waves in high water, which are called haystacks.

A boater drowned here in 1970, when he became entangled in a rope after the boat in which he was riding wrapped on a rock.

In June, 1980, veteran boatman and outfitter Eldon Handy drowned in Haystack on high water after being thrown from his sweepboat when it struck a rock. He owned Salmon River Expeditions and had boated the Middle Fork for thirteen years. His body was recovered five miles downriver and was helicoptered to Salmon.

Handy, who was only forty-seven years old, was buried in Jerome, Idaho, the town where he lived all his life. He was survived by his wife, two daughters, and three sons.

Pole Creek enters on the right. Al Beedle lived in a comfortable house on the creek. He did well there for several years. Beedle was formerly a stage driver between Salmon and Armstead, Montana. He is believed to be buried on the Mormon Ranch, having committed suicide.

MILE 68.3 *Bernard Creek* on the left.
The creek is named for Captain Reuben F. Bernard who, in 1879, had command of the army chasing the Sheepeaters. At this point the soldiers had lost the Indians' trail and Bernard with fifty-six men began his retreat to the Boise Barracks, going by way of Loon Creek.

The first settlers on the creek found large mounds of deer bones, evidence of meat hunters who were furnishing game for the miners.

Flying B Ranch (left), looking north downriver, across Bernard Creek bridge.

The first family on the flat was the Laings, with their children Dave and Jenney, who were in their early twenties. The Laings traveled from Indian Valley, near Cambridge, Idaho, hoping to settle at Brush Creek, but found that the site had been occupied by squatters who had arrived two weeks earlier. Here is a portion of Jenney Laing Lewis's version of that trip made in the summer of 1900:

"Our party of father, mother, brother David, a guide by the name of Carl Schodell, and myself left Washington County the 13th of July, 1900. Our outfit consisted of 29 pack horses, two burros, 48 head of cattle, and about 30 loose horses. A person who has never done any packing or traveling with a bunch of stock can hardly imagine the task we had taken upon ourselves. Many of the pack horses had never been packed until the day we started. I helped get them all packed that first morning and saw them start, then went to round up the cattle for it was supposed to be my task to drive them. I had only driven the cattle a mile or two when I overtook the packtrain. Two of the horses had decided to unload, and as a consequence the contents of their packs were scattered over an acre or two of ground. Looked pretty discouraging for a beginner, but we loaded up and made another start. That first day we traveled 12 or 13 miles, but as the days passed we got used to such mishaps and the horses became resigned to being pack animals.

Our first really exciting experience happened on Big Creek, between what is now Cascade and Knox. At this time there was a very poor trail through there. It was the custom for David and Schodell to drive the packtrain, father the loose horses, mother the two burros with kitchen equipment, and I drove the cattle. The packtrain would go ahead until they found a good camping place and the rest of us would manage to connect with them some time before dark. That day I guess mother must have started a little ahead of the rest with the burros, and a little later father must have overtaken her. Some way they missed the main trail. When the rest of us got into camp, nearly dark, none of us had seen father or mother. When it was dark and still they hadn't come in, we began to feel much worried. We built a big fire to guide them should they be in sight of camp and about 10 o'clock, when they still hadn't shown up, David started out to find them.

He finally located them by their campfire way up a mountainside. But they could not very well come down to our camp. So they had to make the best of things for the night without bed, but they had enough saddle blankets so that with a good fire they were able to keep fairly comfortable. As David was returning to our camp, his horse walked off a bank into a ditch and fell heels up into the air pinning David under him. The horse could not get up with him holding the saddle and he could not get away from the saddle for some time. But finally he worked himself loose from the horse and was able to get the horse back on its feet. It was after midnight when he finally got back to our camp.

One of our most trying experiences happened between Warm Lake and Pen Basin. It had rained the night before and so we had not planned to break camp until after breakfast. But David and I had driven the cattle over the summit and left them to drift down the other side while we went back, had breakfast, and helped pack. Then mother and I started on ahead of the packtrain to round up the cattle. We had only driven them a short ways when a big cow started to act queerly, and from what I'd heard of it, I knew she was poisoned. I jumped off my horse and tried to bleed her, but no blood would come. In less time than I am taking to tell this, she plunged headlong down the mountainside. She had hardly gone when we started to see others showing signs of the deadly poison. We did not try to doctor any more of them but used all our efforts to get them out of that place so that any which hadn't eaten the poison might be saved. Soon the men came up with the train and they turned the horses loose and began to help us. By dark we had them worked off the mountainside but had left 14 behind that were unable to travel. The pack horses had drifted along too, but we managed to round up some of them and get them unpacked. But when we went to bed we had seven packs still on the mountainside. That night was the most discouraging I ever passed through, for we did not know by morning if we would have any cattle left. However, with the coming day we found that no more cattle had been poisoned. And during the day all but two that were down came into camp. We were also able to find all the horses that had packs on all night.

We struck the Middle Fork of the Salmon at the mouth of Sulphur Creek below Bear Valley. There our guide left us. We had been finding out that he did not know the country as well as he had claimed and we let him go and were joined by an old prospector who had just been in the country where we were wanting to go. In Bear Valley we sold our cattle, except five cows, so that we were not quite so encumbered. From Bear Valley we went by way of Cape Horn, Seafoam, Greyhound Mountain, and across Rapid River, finally reaching the land of our dreams the 13th of September, having been two months on the road."

The Laings spent two weeks at Thomas Creek, then went down to the Mormon Ranch to see what the prospects might be for winter feed. They then went back to Loon Creek and visited the town of Salmon, waiting until dark to enter because they were ashamed of " looking so seedy."

A log cabin on Bernard Creek provided winter shelter for the Laing family. All the cooking was done in the fireplace. The next year the mother and father moved to Salmon, but Jenney and David stayed on the place.

Jenney soon married a mining engineer, and their first baby, Orrill Lewis, was born in 1904. The family moved back to Indian Valley the following year, where Orrill lived until her death.

A.D. "Asa" Clark was the next resident at Bernard Creek. He packed a string of milk cows from Boise Valley to Thunder Mountain in the boom days, and made it pay well. He was on Bernard Creek before 1916 because the survey plat done that year marked his cabin.

Clark had about twenty head of matched, white-faced sorrel horses with white legs. He would pack them tied head-to-tail and carry his supplies down from Meyers Cove.

At one time Clark had been financially secure in Boise, then he suffered losses. One March he went out from Brush Creek to Boise on business and never returned. Perhaps he simply recouped what he had lost.

The Forest Service packed lumber in from Yellowjacket by way of Warm Springs Creek and built a guard station on the foundation where Clark's cabin used to sit.

In 1988 the Bernard Creek fire burned this reach of the river.

MILE 69 *Bernard Creek Landing Field.* A state-owned airstrip.

MILE 69.6 In 1983 a 7.2 earthquake, with its epicenter near Challis, jolted the Middle Fork country. A huge rock rolled into the river here and made what had been an easy rapid into a more difficult one because of the ferry to the right required at the lower end.

MILE 71 *Jack Creek Rapid.* The 1930 USGS maps called this Senk Rapid. W.C. G. Senkpiel was a topographer on the survey and must have met a mishap here. At low water, stay right of center.

MILE 71.7 *Little Pine Camp* on the left. In the upper meadow an inconspicuous plaque on a stone memorializes Eldon Handy. The eddy is where his body was recovered.

MILE 72.4 *Driftwood Camp* on the right, a fine site with sand and trees. Oregon guides call this camp "Table Rock" because Prince Helfrich always set his table on the large boulder.

MILE 72.8 *Soldier Creek* drains the canyon on the left. Lee Wyatt built two cabins on this creek when Leesburg was still an active mining center in the Salmon River Mountains.

In 1904 he and Joe Walker came down to the river by way of Wilson Creek. They filed the Brown Beauty group claim and quarried several tons of ore. Wyatt built a small wooden arrastra to grind gold ore that he packed from Sammy Gulch. They reportedly built a waterwheel to gear the arrastra. After fourteen months, they had a single gold bar. Wyatt and another partner, Gibbtown Mamie, even wintered on the stream.

MILE 73.2 *Wilson Creek and Camp* on the right. For years T. H. "Snowshoe" Johnson owned a mining claim on Wilson Creek. He did a lot of packing on the Pistol Creek trail, and often wintered at his cabin on Wilson Creek.

MILE 73.4 *Grassy Flat Campsite* on the left, on the large open bench.

MILE 74.3 *Sammy Gulch.* Tommy Kenyon had mining claims here. His small mine is on the knoll that overlooks the river. Kenyon lived in the mine until he built a cabin on the up-river side of Survey Creek.

In February, 1938, Kenyon broke his leg. He dragged himself up to the Crandall Ranch at Brush Creek, but it took him several weeks to get there. The Crandalls were able to arrange medical attention for him. Kenyon finally traded his mine for three acres near Boise.

MILE 74.7 *Rattlesnake Creek and Cave* on the right.

No camping is permitted in the cave; woodsmoke has already obscured the Sheepeater pictographs.

MILE 75 *Survey Creek Camp* on the left.

The Survey ford is just below the camp. Nephi Bates had a mining claim up Survey Creek and one spring came in with his pack stock to do some work. The water was high, but he was impatient to cross from the east shore and decided to attempt it. His horse lost its footing and Scheiss drowned. His relatives came in to help search for his body and found it several days later. He was taken to Ririe, Idaho, for burial.

The ruins of a cabin built by Tom Brummet can be found on the trail just across Survey Creek. Brummet was a miner active here in the early 1900s. He may never have finished the cabin; it appears to have been tented-over rather than roofed. He was the same man who later had a placer claim at Loon Creek hot springs. Brummet died in 1943 and is buried in Hamilton, Montana.

The flat above the high-water mark and just below the backeddy was known as Nolan Bar, after miner J. M. Nolan, who later made a mineral discovery near Yellowjacket. Three unmarked graves are located on the bar, the eddy being a natural place to catch a body.

Base logs are all that remain of Brummet's Survey Creek cabin.

242

The grave with the large flat rock is that of Ted Dillon. In May, 1902, he was crossing the river at Little Creek with two boys from Mahoney Bar when in a boat when it upset. Sixteen-year-old Dillon, who could not swim, drowned. The other graves are believed to contain the remains of two Forest Service packers, one of whom may have drowned at Bernard Creek.

MILE 75.2 Woolard Creek and Camp on the right. Named for prospector and miner R. H. Woolard, who lived at the Mormon Ranch in 1908-1909. The site occupies a spacious grassy bench just above the mouth of the creek. Pictographs may be seen on the downriver side of the trail where it cuts the creek.

MILE 75.5 Kimmel Creek on the left. Fly Camp is on the right, just below this stream.

MILE 77.7 Fish Camp on the left.

MILE 77.9 Waterfall Creek Rapid. Straightforward in high water; left or right of center in lower flows.

MILE 78.1 Waterfall Creek. The trail which goes up behind the falls about one half-mile, led to a cabin, since burned, used by Tom Brummet in the thirties.

Many years ago a fire burned through the Waterfall Creek-Bobtail Creek area all the way to the Bighorn Crags. When Bill Sullivan was hiking through the drainage looking for an Indian cave, he stumbled across a puzzlement: He found a heart and diamond blazed on a tree, and nearby, in a shallow grave, numerous charred bones which were later identified as human. He also found the charred remains of a riding saddle, three pack saddles, thirteen boxes of exploded shells, and the butt plates from a .405 Winchester, a .303, and a .30-30 Savage made about 1900. It looked like the old forest fire might have been started to conceal foul play. The site is such that it would not have been possible, in his experienced opinion, to get a horse to it. The mystery is undispelled.

In 1981 Forest Service and volunteer archaeologists did a test excavation of a suspected pithouse depression on the Waterfall site about 300 feet above the river. They found

Late Prehistoric projectile points (arrowheads), and Middle to Late Archaic scrapers, drills, and faunal remains. At a depth of one meter they had still not reached the occupation floor.

MILE 78.2 *Big Creek* disembogues on the left, just below the bridge. In 1957 structural materials for the Big Creek and Waterfall Creek bridges were flown by Aircraft Services, Boise, into landing strips at the Flying B and Bernard Creek. (Some of the steel beams are fourteen feet long and weigh 640 pounds.) Austin and Ralph Smothers hauled the supplies downriver in a motorboat, averaging five trips a day for two weeks.

This stream, with headwaters below Profile Gap almost fifty miles from the river, drains a large area.

In 1981 the same archaeological team that tested the Waterfall site excavated a small dry cave at the mouth of Big Creek. The excavation yielded fifty projectile points, scrapers, a drill, knife blades, pottery sherds, shell-bone beads, freshwater mussel shells, ungulate bones, and fish vertebrae. The assemblage appeared more Great Basin than Plateau.

In 1985 University of Idaho archaeologist Frank Leonhardy conducted a month-long excavation at the mouth of a cave on Big Creek, six miles from the river. He found ten times more mountain sheep bones than deer bones, and only a single elk bone. He theorized that the native winter diet was eighty percent mountain sheep, and that there were three times as many sheep as deer at the time of occupancy.

Two hundred yards upriver from the mouth of Big Creek, John Cherry had his camp on the narrow bench. Ed James, in *Hanging and Rattling*, writes, "Cherry had trained to be an attorney-at-law, but he told me that people as a whole were just plain no good—the high ones and the low ones—and he and his partner decided to spend their lives on the Middle Fork and Main Salmon. He was known as the 'Wild Man of the Middle Fork,' and he and his partner got all the gold they wanted by cleaning the crevices in the bedrock when the river was low during the fall of the year."

A four-mile hike up Big Creek, with a gain of 800 feet in elevation and a view of the Bighorn Crags, brings the hiker to Soldier Bar landing strip. The grave of Harry Eagan, casualty of the Sheepeater War, is located at the east end of the field. Vinegar Hill, site of the famous battle, is another ten miles up the trail.

A notable figure on Big Creek, "Cougar" Dave Lewis, built his first cabin at the mouth of Goat Creek, just downstream from Soldier Bar.

Lewis was born in 1844 in New Orleans, Louisiana. Of Welsh descent, he was a slight man, 5' 7", 130 pounds. He claimed to have served in the Union army at Vicksburg; to have been been a volunteer at the Modoc uprising in northern California in 1872; and to have been a scout in Montana with Captain Benteen in 1876.

"Cougar" Dave Lewis with his hunting dogs.

It is beyond ambiguity that sometime before 1877 Lewis traveled from Oregon with the Henry Jones' family to Idaho's Camas Prairie near Grangeville. He probably hired out as a civilian packer during the Nez Perce War that year. During the Sheepeater War of 1879, Lewis handled the ammunition train —two mules—for the army. He was on Big Creek when the Indians ambushed the soldiers.

After the war, he located on the Jewett Ranch at Slate Creek, near Riggins, Idaho, and from 1881 to 1894 raised horses. Then he rode back to Big Creek and, probably finding Soldier Bar occupied, squatted at Goat Creek and built himself a small cabin. When John Conyers and his wife moved out of Soldier Bar, Lewis moved up two-and-a-half miles and took possession, hosting a housewarming party there at age sixty-five.

Lewis largely supported himself on Big Creek by hunting cougars for the $50 state bounty and whatever he could get for the pelt. He always had three or more dogs that slept beneath his bunk—he used them to tree the lions. In 1922 the Boise *Statesman* reported that Lewis had collected $1400 in bounties for the year. He saved the bounty tokens as his currency. Lewis maintained that he and his cross-terriers had killed at least 300 cougar in his hunting years—only a search of state records would reveal whether he was stretching the blanket.

He did have other sources of income: he packed for miners and for the Forest Service during fire season; he sometimes guided sheep hunters; he did blacksmithing on his forge for neighbors; he looked after John Conyers' cattle during the winter; and he claimed a small pension for military service.

Lewis was friendly without being loquacious; an ardent reader in the winter; a Republican. He lived alone in a log fifteen- by-fifteen-foot cabin under a roof insulated with six inches of dirt. In 1923 he was visited there by Francis Woods, a Forest Service surveyor:

"We rested at his cabin for a couple of days. The cabin, I remember, had an outside kitchen area, a living quarters built of logs and an additional room.

The second day he said he was going to take his cougar dogs and hunt for some meat for them.

We noticed he never went into the second room of the cabin. While he was away, we looked into the room through a window. There were cobwebs and dust everywhere. On the wall near the door was a large framed picture with its face to the wall. We just had to see the picture. We cut a small pole, four or five feet long, and opened the door to the room very carefully and pried the picture away from the wall, but not far enough to make it fall. It was a portrait of a beautiful young woman. For the past sixty years I have been intrigued by the picture with its face to the wall. What a mystery"

[Note: The portrait was that of a woman on a ranch in Oregon who had received and rejected his marriage proposal.]

In 1928 Lewis, with the assistance of friends, finally received a homestead certificate for his sixty-three acres. The homestead spans the mouths of Rush, Trail, and Sheep creeks.

Five years later he met Jess Taylor by chance when the two of them were hunting in the area. Taylor was invited to stay at the cabin. In fall, 1934, Taylor bought the ranch for $1,200.

Walt Estep, who had mining interests on Ramey Ridge and assisted Lewis in legal matters, witnessed the sale and agreed to carry the deed to Cascade to record it. Three miles west of the ranch, he was murdered—perhaps for paying too much attention to another man's wife. The Valley County sheriff had to come in to recover the body; he found the deed and finally recorded it.

In June, 1936, Lewis contracted pneumonia and managed to ride to Edwardsburg for help. He was placed in an ambulance that set out for Cascade by way of Yellow Pine. Enroute it had a head-on accident with a truck. Lewis died the next

Lewis on "Old Belle," 1932.

Lewis at Soldier Bar a year before he died.

248

day, age ninety-two, at the Veteran's Administration Facility in Boise. He was buried in Yoncalla, Oregon, where his brother lived.

Jess Taylor, a ship's carpenter during World War I, had been ranching in eastern Idaho in the 1920s. He left the Lewis place in the hands of a caretaker while he worked as a building contractor in Boise.

Following World War II, Taylor and his wife Dorothy moved back to the ranch intent on making it a hunting resort. The Taylors worked like they were working for themselves. With a pair of Percheron draft horses, a slipscraper, and a log drag, they sanded out an airstrip. Two year later, in 1950, the first plane landed.

From 1948 to 1950 the Taylors built a log house uphill from the landing field. Then they added a duplex for hunters. Having been a contractor, Taylor built things to last. He poured concrete foundations and installed metal roofs and indoor plumbing.

Jess Taylor went to the regional U. S. Post Office in Pocatello, Idaho, and was able to persuade the administrators to establish an air route for mail service to Middle Fork and Main Salmon backcountry ranches. Johnson Flying Service, and more recently Arnold Aviation, thereby provided a regular flow of supplies and guests to these remote locations.

The Taylors made steady improvements on the place. They grew vegetables and fruit for their guests and hay for the horses and mules. The Taylor Ranch acquired a reputation as a hospitable and comfortable retreat.

After eighteen years, the Taylors sold the ranch in 1968 to the University of Idaho as a field station for wilderness research. The sale was brought about by Maurice Hornocker, who had used the ranch, while associated with the University, during his five-year study of mountain lions. Forty-six lions were captured and marked, then recaptured at intervals. Their kills were examined, as well. The study concluded that elk and deer populations were limited by winter food, and that predation by lions was inconsequential in determining

Big Creek, 1937.
House (left). hotel,
store, bar.

ultimate numbers in the herds. As a result, mountain lions
were removed from the bounty list by the state and categorized as "big game" animals with a hunting season—although
it must be noted that there is no "hunt" in shooting a large
animal out of a tree.

And how ironic that the animal whose slaughter was for
so long the mainstay of the location, eventually became the
opening for its preservation.

One other haven on Big Creek must be mentioned: five
miles farther west upstream from the Taylor Ranch, and one-
quarter-mile north up Cabin Creek, its tributary, is the
Caswell Ranch. The Caswell brothers— Ben, Dan, and
Lou—were from Michigan. Ben and Lou settled at Cabin
Creek in 1894. They may have intended to ranch the site,
but they were compulsive prospectors and they were broke.

In August they discovered surface indications of gold on
Thunder Mountain. So much for ranching. They still hunted
and trapped in the winter, but in the short summer season
when water was available, they rockered for gold. Brother
Dan came down from Montana to join them. By 1899, with

250

sluices and a small hydraulic nozzle, they had recovered thousands of dollars worth of gold.

But miners have to sell or ship their dust--in Boise word leaked out and the Thunder Mountain boom was underway. In 1900 the Caswells sold one set of claims for $100,000; in 1901 they sold another set for $125,000, then sold their ranch site to John Conyers, and moved out.

Dog team carrying the mail in Big Creek country, 1929. Photo courtesy of Margaret and Ken Twiliger.

Roosevelt on
Monumental
Creek, tributary of
Big Creek.

Roosevelt after a
slide dammed the
creek and flooded
the town.

Conyers shifted his headquarters one mile farther north up the creek, where he grew garden produce, hay, and cattle. In 1910, after Thunder Mountain had gone belly-up, Conyers sold to Mel Ables, who patented the location in 1913 as a homestead. Ables expanded the holdings into the largest cattle ranch in the drainage. Then in 1920 he died—the victim of an unsolved murder.

The Ables' holdings, combined with another homestead, were purchased in the 1950s by Rex Lanham, an executive of Harrah's Club, Reno. He named the homesteads Cabin Creek Ranch, and set about making them into a hunting and fishing resort.

In 1957 he walked a D-9 Caterpillar from Chamberlain Basin to the site and carved out a reliable airstrip. (Lanham was a pilot.) First-rate guest houses were constructed and plumbed. The creek was dammed for a Pelton wheel generator. Then equipment poured in: tractor, truck, jeeps, hay balers, backhoe. It became the most mechanized ranch in the backcountry.

In 1973 Lanham sold Cabin Creek to the Forest Service for $1.6 million and retired. Most of the machinery and buildings have been removed.

Blackie Wallace packing two lengths of pipe to Snowshoe Mine on Crooked Creek, tributary of Big Creek. In a similar manner, 20-mule teams carried 2,600 feet of 3/8-cable to the Yellow Jacket mine on Camas Creek.

Rock spire and capstone that named Monumental Creek. Note men at base.

MILE 79.2 *Cutthroat Camp* on the left, just above **Cutthroat Rapid.** The USGS map in 1930 named this Lewis Rapid in honor of Cougar Dave Lewis.

MILE 79.9 *Elk Bar Camp.* Andy Anderson called this site Paradise Bar. In 1978 it was the second camp used by President Carter.

MILE 80 *Lower Elk Bar* or Love Bar, separated from the upper camp by a pair of rocks.

MILE 81 *Veil Falls and Cathedral Cave.* In a cave near this location Andy Anderson and Barry Goldwater found a stick with "Bob McCollom L. H. Atkins 1889" carved into it.

MILE 81.3 *Wall Creek* flows out of the canyon on the left. The rapid at Wall Creek was called so on the 1930 USGS map. Since 1940 it has been called Porcupine on Forest Service maps, but it is known to most boatmen as Wall Creek Rapid.

MILE 82.8 *Redside or Golden Creek Camp* on the left. Porcupine Rapid. The rapid at Golden Creek, just below the camp, has been labeled "Redside" by the Forest Service, but most boatmen consider this a misnomer repeated with troublesome frequency. The conflict will never be resolved now. Most Oregon guides refer to the rapid as Eagle Rock, after a similar obstruction on the McKenzie River in their state. Elwood Masoner called it Sevy's Rock because District Ranger John Sevy (Bob Sevy's father) wrecked here in the early 1960s. Suffice to say that at certain water stages the opportunity for stamping a boat on the center rock is genuine.

MILE 83 *Redside Rapid.* Considered the "real" Redside, but it does not appear on USFS or USGS maps. It has also been called Little Porcupine, Loin of Pork, and Corkscrew (Masoner). "Redside" is the colloquial term for cutthroat trout.

MILE 83.3 *Weber Rapid.* Named for Carl Weber, a Eugene, Oregon, guide who began rowing the Middle Fork for Hindman and Helfrich in 1942, and who dumped his drift boat here in 1946.

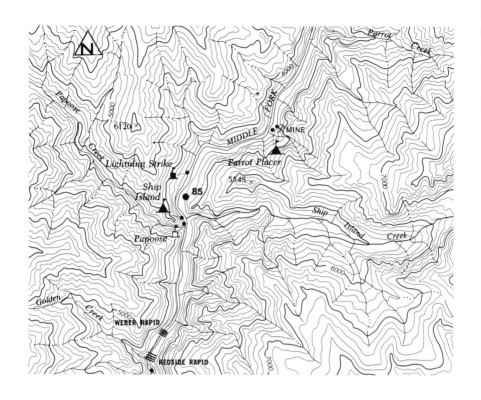

On June 28, 1942, Eliot DuBois here had his most serious mishap on his Middle Fork solo. He chose not to scout the rapid, and what happened next is best told from his own point of view:

"The bow plunged into the boil of foam, and instantly the boat [foldboat] was wrenched over with me underneath, head down. A good modern kayaker might have rolled up, but I had neither the training nor the equipment for that manuever. My only option was to bail out, and that proved very difficult. As I struggled to get free of the small cockpit, I wondered if I would drown, and if so, how far downstream would the debris drift before being caught in an eddy, and how long would it be before anyone found out what had happened.

With a mighty struggle, I broke loose and came to the surface, just in time to get a breath of air before being pulled under again and dragged through a long series of standing waves. In a hundred yards, I was in calmer water but could see another rapid ahead. 'Now you've done it,' I said to myself...I looked around and discovered the boat a few yards upstream, floating bottom up."

DuBois recovered his boat and paddle and paddled ashore. He discovered that the turnover had destroyed his spray deck—a vital detail of the boat's design. Once he had taken stock and wrung out his clothes, DuBois was ready to sail on. But first:

"Something remained to be done. Suppose I didn't survive the last thirteen miles. I wanted to leave at least some record of of my having made it this far., and of having lost my spray deck in an upset. I found a pencil and a piece of paper in my duffel bag, sketched a little map showing where I had upset, and scribbled a brief account of what had happened to me. I then decided that having upset in the drop, I had the right to name it. I would call it Lenore Rapid after the girl [he was dating at the time]."

The note was deposited in a Band-aid box in a rock cairn well above the rapid. Eighteen years later, it was returned to DuBois. A woman whose raft had dumped in Redside found it after she swam ashore. (For the "rest of the story," see *An Innocent on the Middle Fork*.)

On high water, June 25, 1970, a three-boat party of Los Angeles businessmen guided by Everett Spaulding also met trouble here. The passengers had joined the boats at Indian Creek four days earlier. Boatman Troy Teague in a McKenzie boat, and Ken Smith in a sweep-raft, overturned. Tom Brokaw, longtime host of the "Today" television show, and network anchorman, was in Smith's raft and wrote of the experience:

"Suddenly I noticed that Teague's boat appeared to be stalled in the middle of Weber Falls. It was sinking.
Later, Stone described the scene. He said a huge wave broke above them and practically filled the right-side of the boat. Teague yelled out, 'Shift your weight, shift your weight,' and he began frantically pulling on the oars, trying to move to calmer waters.

But it was too late. Another wave rolled over the other side. All three men were swept into the raging water.

Doumani turned to signal Spaulding, and I began coiling a length of rope and assembling loose lifejackets. Downstream I could see Stone and Harmon neck deep in the middle of the river, racing in tandem toward another set of rapids. Teague was off to the side and behind them heading for the same rapids.

Suddenly we had our own problems. The raft flipped over when hit by a powerful wave as it plunged into Weber Falls. As I tumbled into the water I was stunned by the ferocity of the current. In a lifetime of swimming I can't recall a greater struggle to break back through the surface, even with the assistance of a lifejacket."

Smith, Brokaw, and friends swam ashore and were rescued the next morning by helicopters. The body of twenty-nine year-old Ellis Harmon was recovered at the mouth of the Middle Fork. He was a tax lawyer, dedicated conservationist, and the father of three daughters, ages four years, two years, and eight months. Troy Teague was fifty-eight, an experienced Oregon guide. His body was never found.

MILE 84.7 *Papoose Creek* threads the defile on the left. Lieutenant Farrow's men captured an Indian woman with her baby on the headwaters of this creek at the close of the Sheepeater War. The baby's cries kept the men awake all night.

MILE 84.8 *Ship Island Camp* on the left. **Ship Island Creek,** just across from the camp, drains Ship Island Lake in the Bighorn Crags. The lake is named for a small ship-shaped island. The creek drops 4,000 feet from lake to river.

258

The charred logs and blackened snags that occur along the right side of the river from this creek north to Cliffside Camp (mile 90) are the result of a lightning strike the afternoon of July 17, 1979, just north of the creek, within a mile of the river, which began a blaze that burned for three and a half weeks. Initial attempts to suppress the fire with helitack crews and smokejumpers were unsuccessful because of wind and the steepness of terrain.

As the fire spread over the first two days, the situation was reassessed, and a decision was made to let it burn rather than risk lives and money under such extreme conditions. The burn was monitored by a biologist stationed on Stoddard

Roaring Creek fire cloud.

Ship Island fire on Roaring Creek, 1979.

Creek lookout, at the head of Nugget Creek on the west side of the river. His assessment, coupled with that of a fire team, was that while the fire might have short-term deleterious effects on elk and deer range, it was improving the Rocky Mountain bighorn habitat without inflicting unacceptable resource damage. It was also believed that, in any event, the Bighorn Crags would serve as a natural barrier to the fire's eastern advance. But unconstrained fire is less predictable than the weather, and the weather went awry. With wind, Ship Island fire switched from servant to master.

At this point, the Forest Service attempted limited control action on the ridge above Ship Island Creek and on the north and west flanks of the fire as it moved into Tumble Creek.

Fire analysts for the Forest Service now realized that the unusual burning conditions increased chances the blaze might escape their projected northeastern perimeter, and that the likelihood of fire spotting across the Middle Fork was growing as well. Fire camps were established at Stoddard lookout and Horse Heaven (nearest trail points) and later at Cove Creek on the Main Salmon. Taking advantage of breaks in the weather and slightly more suitable topography, 250 men were committed to the containment. Aerial support and infrared surveillance were utilized.

Capricious wind and weather again combined to frustrate the firefighters. The burn, which had engulfed only about 3,000 acres in ten days, now doubled its size over the next four days. On August 5, the conflagration spurted out of the McGuire Lake area between Parrott and Tumble creeks and poured into the Roaring Creek drainage. Trees on the upper half of the creek, and those around Roaring Lakes, burned like grass in a prairie fire. Only another turn in the weather—from spotty rain to steady downpour—granted a reprieve to thousands of acres in the Goat Creek region.

The Ship Island fire was declared controlled on August 15 at 10,480 acres. Suppression costs included one life and almost a million dollars.

Those who boated through the 1979 "summer of fire" will never forget it. For two weeks, the smoky pall that obscured the afternoon sun cast an eerie, surreal light across the Middle Fork canyon. The feeling is best captured in a poem by Scott Greer:

All day the trees were heavy with flowers of smoke,
Their charred perfume of withered cones and needles
Staining the sombre skies we travelled under,
Tainting the light we knew, the air we breathed.

The burning oils of death had steeped the day;
Lightning had sown the green with a thousand seed
And heavy slopes returned their lives to the sun
In a sudden explosion of bright and mortal being.

—Dark illuminations in August noon;
Grey waves roiling, of wind and smoke,
Parted to a column of black through the dusk,
A great cone of mountain, a charred and dying slope.

As the forest was unburdened of its ghostly flowers
Their sweet and hopeless scent grew on the air,
On tongue and lips and eyes and it was neither
Catastrophe nor covenant nor prayer—

It was our nature cast against the sun;
Our senses guttered in the terrible wind
As all the slow fuses went blazing, charred and one
With the ravager who soars towards the end.

MILE 85.3 *Lightning Strike Camp* on the left.
Goat Mountain (9,607') can be seen downstream to the
northeast.

MILE 86.5 *Parrot Placer Camp*

MILE 87.9 *Nugget Creek* enters on the left. Parrott
Creek, which drains Parrott Lake, enters the river just above
on the right.

"The more I see of people, the more I like my dog."

Earl K. Parrott was the hermit of the Middle Fork, and
his hermitage was a log dugout just above the rim of Impassable Canyon. Of all recluses along the river, his story seems
to contain the most imaginative appeal and much of that
appeal must lie in the beauty of the place in which he chose
to hide. As with most hermits, the details of his life are
elusive, but this much is now certain. Parrott's parents,
Joseph and Sarah (nee Stanton) immigrated from England to
Canada in 1864, and then to America five years later. According to the census in 1880, they resided in Wilsburg (now
Blanchard), Iowa, just north of the Missouri border. The
town of 150 persons was located on the Omaha and St. Louis
railroad (later Wabash), and had been platted a year earlier.
Joseph Parrott, educated in England and Germany, was
the town's first postmaster and druggist. His wife tended shop
as well. In 1880, he was fifty-two, she was forty-nine. The
couple had ten children: six boys and four girls ranging from

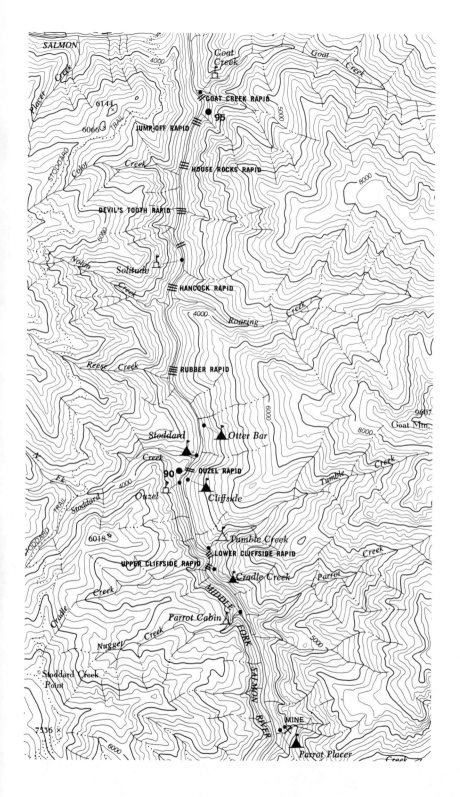

SALMON

Goat
Creek

Goat Creek

4000

Placer Creek

6144

GOAT CREEK RAPID

95

6066

JUMP-OFF RAPID

5000

STODDARD TRAIL

Color Creek

HOUSE ROCKS RAPID

8000

DEVIL'S TOOTH RAPID

6000

Notch

Solitude

HANCOCK RAPID

4000

Roaring Creek

Creek

Reese Creek

RUBBER RAPID

6000

Stoddard

Otter Bar

9607
Goat Mtn.

8000

Creek

90

OUZEL RAPID

Ft.

4000

STODDARD TRAIL

Stoddard

Ouzel

Cliffside

Tumble Creek

6018

Tumble Creek

LOWER CLIFFSIDE RAPID

UPPER CLIFFSIDE RAPID

Creek

Cradle Creek

Parrot Creek

Cradle Creek

MIDDLE FORK SALMON RIVER

Parrot Cabin

5000

Nugget Creek

Stoddard Creek
Point

7536

6000

MINE

Parrot Placer

Creek

263

five to twenty-nine-years-old. Earl was the seventh sibling. Blanchard was known for its excellent school, and Earl, who was then ten years old, attended. When he was old enough, he assisted at his father's store. In 1888, at age sixty, Joseph sold the drugstore and moved the family to Orange Park, Florida.

Earl, now eighteen, and his brother Allen, younger by two years, engaged in truck farming with fruits and vegetables. During their spare time, they taught themselves telegraphy with a wire run from the house to a shed.

Though the first telephone exchange had opened ten years earlier, the telegraph had been around for fifty years, and Western Union was the first monopoly and largest corporation in the country. Its most valuable and inseparable partner was the railroads, which had agreed to lay telegraph lines along their right-of-way and provide office space in depots for telegraphers employed by the railroad and Western Union. In return, Western Union transmitted messages regarding the railroad business without charge and gave priority to railroad messages. This marriage made the railroads a safe and efficient transportation network.

After two years practice with a telegraph key, Earl obtained employment with the Jacksonville, Tampa, and Key West Railroad, and Allen joined him a few months later. According to Allen, Earl left the railroad business in 1898 because he became color blind (being able to discern the color of railroad signals was a necessity for such telegraphers).

The rest of Earl's story—pieced from letters, diaries, newspapers, and interviews—becomes less certain. Earl alleged that the telegraph carried early word of the Yukon Gold Rush (1897-1898), and he went north to seek his fortune. It may have been so.

His brother said, however, that he thought Earl went directly to Idaho because he heard from him in 1898 by letter addressed from Dixie, Idaho (just north of the Salmon River), and from Warren, Idaho (just south of the Salmon), a short while later.

If Earl did go to the Yukon, it was a brief stint. He was seen in Lewiston, Idaho, about 1900, and he may have gone to Warren at the invitation of saloon keeper Charlie Bemis. He filed on a homestead (later known as the Rushton place) in 1908 on Rock Creek, a tributary of the South Fork of the Salmon, but did not patent it. He had a cabin and barn there. One clue suggests that around 1910 Parrott may have gone home to Florida for a visit.

Following the sale of his Rock Creek acres to Earl Rushton, Parrott spent the winter of 1916 at the mouth of Elk Creek on the South Fork of the Salmon with Brad Carrey, uncle of Johnny Carrey. Although Johnny remembers that Parrott was intelligent and industrious, he was also stubborn, aloof, and lacking in humor. Nor was he fond of children. He lived in a sturdy tent with his possessions kept in wooden boxes, and his chief occupations during those months were tanning hides and panning for gold. He left with the melting snow.

Some evidence implies that Earl Parrott located his roost above the rim of the Middle Fork in the early 1900s, perhaps at the time of the Thunder Mountain boom, and began preparations for full-time residency. Certainly he was established there by 1917, living like a hawk with wind under its wings. At that time he had a little brown riding mare, half a dozen burros, and a dog. Perhaps he liked animals. In any event, for the next twenty-five years Earl Parrott became about as self-sufficient and self-reliant as it is possible for a person to be.

In early April, 1919, he visited the town of Salmon in the company of August Motzell and Jess Root. Root had a homestead at the head of Whimstick Creek in Chamberlain Basin (about seventeen air miles west of Parrott's place), and needing witnesses for the final proof on his ranch, brought the two men along to testify to U. S. Commissioner Merritt. They had come four days upriver on foot to Shoup, where they caught an automobile ride to Salmon. The town newspaper took note:

"They are sturdy men, just as would be looked for in the last frontier of the wilderness where they have set up homes. They told *The Recorder* that most settlers like themselves in that country live lonely lives of bachelors, always in hopes, however, that they may be able a little later along to induce life-partners to come and make real homes....After arriving here they ascertained that Capt. Harry Guleke would have a transport down the river [Salmon] early this week, so they waited for passage that way."

Earl doesn't appear again until summer, 1923, when Francis Woods was working as a member of a Forest Service survey crew along the Middle Fork. As the three-man mapping party hardscrabbled through the country, locating the mouths of tributaries entering the Middle Fork, they had an encounter of interest:

"One day we spotted a small cabin and noticed smoke coming from the chimney. We decided to stop and have lunch with the occupant. He was busy at a stove cooking some kind of berries. The mixture had not come to a boil. Above the stove, lying on a shelf, was a big cat. When he saw us he made a pass at the cat, knocking it into the fruit. Reaching into the pot, he pulled the cat out and ran his hand over it, draining the berries back into the pot. He then threw the cat out the door. Needless to say, we did not stay for lunch."

Another chance meeting was recorded April 11, 1928, by Jim Gipson, who was bivouacked at Nolan Creek (five miles up the Middle Fork from its confluence with the Main Salmon) with Henry Weidner, the two of them having left a scow at the mouth of the Middle Fork. It was a cold and windy day, blowing snow before breakfast was over, and Gipson decided to stay in camp. A stranger, who must have spotted his smoke, joined him.

"An old prospector by the name of Parrott, who makes his headquarters on the Middle Fork a couple of miles above where we are camped, came down and spent the day with us, an odd character of about 65 who hates to leave his hills. Like most of the Salmon River settlers he is a southerner. His trip to Mountain Home [Idaho] after wild burros. Dates everything by the Thunder Mountain Boom [1900-1905]. Another nick in his gun when he gets hurt or sick. Wes [Weidner] and I try our hands at panning gold, but find it too cold and tiresome. I talked with him by the fire and rather sympathize with his philosophy of life. He says coyotes increasing. Believes my project for stocking the Salmon River country with buffaloes is a good one and thinks well of the idea of heavily salting the licks. No coyotes in the hills when he came here 35 years ago."

It was the boating parties that came down the Middle Fork in the 1930-1940 period, however, that revealed most of what is known about Parrott's lifeway.

In mid-July, 1936, the Hatch-Swain-Frazier expedition was floating past Nugget Creek when someone spotted a small log structure and what appeared to be bear tracks on the beach. They rowed ashore and were incredulous at finding a tiny shed with a note on the door:

"Dear Oliver, the cork came out of that bottle of Poison and alot of it spilled in here all over this stuff. I don't know if it would be safe to use it, but be careful. Better not monkey with it. Come on up. Parrott. You remember what the druggist said, a very little of it would kill a horse. Be careful how you stir things up, you can breath enough to kill you."

Inside the small, crude shed the men saw cornmeal, a frying pan and plate, a gold pan and blanket. Finding a trace of trail leading to a ladder which stood against a rock wall, they went up the ladder and began the two-mile, 2000-foot ascent to the canyon rim. Log ladders along the way helped them up the cliffs.

267

The men came up into a hanging valley and followed the trail with rising curiosity and arrow-through-the-throat expectancy. Coming around a turn, they suddenly saw a small cabin and a garden that looked like an exhibit at a state fair. No one in view. On approaching closer, they found the cabin was actually a partial dugout, rumped into the bank. Smoke feathered from the chimney, and another note was tacked over the door:

"Some of everything in this garden is poison. Nothing in the house is poison. Help yourself."

Swain called several times but received no answer. The men sat down outside the cabin to await the owner's return. One of the party went over to pull a carrot from the garden and was startled by a voice from the sky: "What do you men want down there?" Peering from a crowsnest of poles and goat skins in the fork of a ponderosa pine was the hermit. Persuaded that they meant him no harm, he came down with the agility of a monkey.

The parties surveyed each other until Swain broke the silence by saying, "Dad, you sure have a beautiful place here." "I like it," Parrott replied. Everyone relaxed as the hermit moved his hand from the butt of a Colt .45 slung under his arm. Each man felt as though he had just made it across a river on horseback.

The boatmen explained how they had rowed from Bear Valley and recounted their adventures. But Parrott learned more about them than they discovered about him.

Parrott was about five feet four inches, muscular, blue-eyed, and clean shaven. He wore an old buckskin visor, buckskin shirt, tattered denim trousers with buckskin suspenders, and shoes with tire-tread soles and buckskin tops.

All of the men agreed that his garden was the most extraordinary they had ever seen. He irrigated it from the creek, fenced it with poles to keep out the deer, and raised corn, beans, potatoes, sweet potatoes, cabbage, beets, carrots, peppers, squash, cucumbers, raspberries, strawberries, watermelons, peaches, and apricots. He selected the best from each crop for next year's seeds, and dried and stored all the produce, even the berries. He kept his potatoes in a small root cellar. His major storage containers for corn and beans were large yellow pine logs, which he split and hollowed. He would put one half on top of the other horizontal half, having smoothed the faces where they met so perfectly that not even an ant could get between them. For meat, he would kill a deer with his .30-30 Winchester from his platform in the trees.

Elaborating, Parrott said that the only supplies he needed were salt, matches, tea, and bullets, which he obtained by a seventy-mile trip to Shoup once a year. (In earlier times, before the Salmon River road, he hiked to Warren.) Parrott would go down canyon to the mouth of the Middle

Parrott in 1936 about to sample one of Frazier's cigars. He said he packed the pistol in case he broke his leg.

Fork, making the trip in two days. Later he used the Stoddard Creek trail to the pack bridge across the Salmon River.

For these necessities, he traded the gold dust he panned. In 1936 Doc Frazier estimated 100 cubic yards of placer tailings had been worked on the Nugget Creek beach. He said Parrott "worked his placer every day in the summer, including Sundays," but such seems highly unlikely, given the demands for growing and storing food. "The most he ever got out of one pan of gravel was $97. At first he thought we were there to rob him of his gold, but reasoned we would not come in a bunch and in daylight."

Though small, with a three-by-four-foot bed, his cabin was "neat and clean, he swept the dirt floor with pine boughs, his bed was out of poles covered by a bear skin, his cover was a mountain sheep and a great white goat's skin, his pillow was a mountain goat kid's hide." The door hinges were wooden, set in knot holes.

The only tools observed on the place were an axe and a cross-cut saw. (In 1946 Hack Miller found a brace and bit.) Parrott would cut enough wood from dead pines to last all winter. He said he did not move around much once the weather turned icy for fear of getting hurt; at such times he would sleep almost twenty hours a day.

Although he had never heard a radio, Parrott knew the day of the month. Frazier again: "I had seen no calendar and asked him how he kept the day and the month. 'What else have I got to do?' was the terse response. He had a sundial out in the yard that told him the time and the equinoxes." (No one else reported a sundial. Hack Miller on a later trip said he saw a pocket watch in good repair in a tobacco can and a current almanac on a shelf.)

When a camera was explained to Parrott, he consented to have his picture taken, though he called it "a peck of foolishness."

The rivermen learned that the following day was Parrott's birthday; so they invited him to join them for dinner at the boats. To their amazement, he ran down the ladders face-out, beating them to the boats by twenty minutes.

Parrott obviously enjoyed their food. "Frank opened a Hormel canned ham, and did his eyes bug out, again the biscuits, canned butter and canned milk, canned pears for desert." They gave him what items they could spare: cigars, some salt, surplus containers, a spade for his garden. As they said their good-byes, Parrott told the men that they were his first visitors in thirty-seven years. His hermetically sealed world had been perforated.

After their completion of the 1936 trip, Dr. Frazier, with Mack Corbett, published an article in *Field and Stream* magazine about their meeting with the "Hermit of Impassable Canyon." Earl Parrott's brother Allen, now in Portland, Oregon, read of the encounter in the July 24 edition of the *Oregonian,* and promptly wrote Frazier and got the name of a packer who could take him to see his brother—he had not heard from Earl for twenty-five years.

Ray Mahoney packed Allen to the Stoddard Creek lookout and then went down to inform Earl, who told the packer to have Allen come down to his place if he wanted to visit; he was not going up to the lookout. Because of this unwanted publicity, Parrott was most unhappy with Dr. Frazier.

Unaware of the hermit's acquired animosity, Frazier and Swain stopped to visit him when next they ran the Middle Fork, in early July 1939. Doc Frazier recalled the meeting this way:

"As we rounded the bend above his diggings, we saw the old man bent over his gold pan, he did not hear us because of the roar of the rapids until the prow of our boats landed at his feet. In an instant he had whipped out his gun and had us covered. Recognizing who we were he started to lower his gun. His expression changed, and he said I have a notion not to let you come ashore. On being asked why, he said you told that brother of mine where I was and I had to lie to him about coming out last winter. Besides that he brought two of those forest fellers in with him. We told him we had brought him some salt and other supplies. Let me see the salt was his

Parrott at his
dugout above the
river, 1936.

immediate reply. We undid the waterproof hatch on the boat
and set out a 5 gallon keg of salt. When he saw it he gathered
both hands full of 'sal' [salt], and as he let it trickle back into
the keg through his fingers, he said, now I will not have to go
back to that old store for years. As he repeated handling the
salt, tears came to his eyes and he said he was sorry about the
way he had greeted us. Wait here and I will go up and get you
some garden stuff. We camped with the old gentleman that
night. Sitting on a rock after supper I pecked [Morse code] his

name on a rock with my geologist hammer, two or three times before I attracted his attention. I'll be dammed, I have not heard that in 40 years. How did you know I knew the code? Your brother told me. That was enough to set him off. 'I'll have to leave this place for it will be overrun now.' "

Since Hack Miller's account states that the group hiked up to Parrott's cabin and met him there, Frazier must have resorted to literary license.

Charles Kelly's diary from the same trip has additional useful insights:

"July 5—Parrott's cabin on the river is very small but weather tight. Looks like a boar's nest. He lives above during the growing season to look after his garden. In the fall he works his placer here or above about a mile (up river), and climbs the cliff twice a week to see that everything is all right above. We found his trail overgrown and dim. Climbed the face of the cliff about 1500 or 2000 feet, very rocky and narrow, with ladders in several places. His garden is very fine. All kinds of vegetables. Has had no new seed since 1900. Potatoes that weigh more than 1 lb. each. Strawberries growing wild. Wild roses all around his garden. No domestic flowers. Cabin is small, built half in the hillside, but is tight. Makes his own shakes. Two very small windows, no glass. Fireplace and bunk, a few dishes and tools. Bunk is about 4 feet square. No supplies in cabin except a few potatoes. Soap covered with dust. [Note: Since Parrott was clean-shaven, if he did not use soap, how did he shave?] Everything made of split logs. No sawed lumber. Few nails. Makes his own shoes and buckskin clothes for winter. Enjoys tobacco but don't drink. Goes out once a year. Packs in about 30 lbs. of stuff— overalls, tobacco, ammunition, salt, etc. Lives on 8 cents a day outside expenses. Pans enough gold to buy necessities, but no more. Said if he knew we were coming he would have hidden out. Don't like company. Says he used to go two years without seeing anyone, but now hunters disturb him every few months. Deer eat lettuce out of his garden sometimes, but otherwise don't bother. Game not so plentiful now. He eats meat only in winter. Don't like dried meat. Kills a bear in the fall for its grease. Has to go five miles now to hunt deer in the fall. There is a new forest guard station [Stoddard Lookout, 1933] 5 miles from him. Country is getting too crowded. Used to go 70 miles for supplies. Now goes 10 miles to CCC camp [on the Salmon River] and bums a ride to town. Gets mail at Shoup, Idaho if and when. Has not seen a movie in 15 years. Dying calf expressions of actors make him sick. Don't like radio. Would rather hear the coyotes howl. Only question he asked us was 'Who is going to run for president?' [Note: Parrott inveighed against Roosevelt because he felt the CCC was going to ruin the river and fishing; he said he was going out to vote for Landon.] No taxes to pay. Gov't makes him sell gold dust through buyers, they take $3 an oz. He gets only $17 to $19 for his gold. Once made 2 oz. a day for 7 months on the Salmon River. Cunningham says he was once disappointed in love. Also lost his money in a bank failure. That's why he's a hermit. [Note: Parrott told one informant that he put his money in the Weiser, Idaho, bank and it went broke. He would have taken his money via Warren, and the distance would have given him more privacy than the Salmon bank. Both banks in Weiser failed in 1924.] Drinks tea but no coffee. Dries all his vegetables. Raises corn every 3 years. Eats only corn bread. Has no use for women. Won't live with his brother because he would be bossed by a woman. Uses no candles or artificial light. Reads little. Sleeps outside between two big trees in summer. Carries .45 Colt with him everywhere, to kill himself in case he falls and gets broken leg.

July 6—Parrott had supper with us last night, then climbed back up to his cabin. Came down again just as we finished breakfast. Seemed more friendly. Doc gave him a keg of salt, and some gallon tin cans with lids. I gave him a box of cigars. Seemed to enjoy them. Posed for pictures. Panned some gold for us. ... [He] came down to Butts Bar [Salmon River, below the confluence] and met John Cunningham [sweepboat pilot]."

And Willis Johnson notes a few details more:

"..It is almost unbelievable how he exists. About all he has to buy is 30 lbs. of salt, tea, and tobacco. He uses one box of matches a year and makes his own shoes; wears no socks or underwear and doesn't own a coat. Just a dirty pair of overalls and shirt and his shoes which are made of buckskin and old tires, which he never takes off. His garden is very neat and well-kept, his potatoes are the most perfect ones I have ever seen...he cooks in an open fireplace."

In addition to the salt, the men gave him fishing line, hooks, and Corona cigars.

Parrott must have sensed that his way of life was fast becoming an anachronism. The following summer his domain was invaded yet again, and visitor hours were becoming ever less tolerable. In August the Zee Grant party with three foldboats was boating through Impassable Canyon at 10:00 P.M., having grievously miscalculated the length of the canyon. In his article about the trip, Zee recounted the unexpected meeting:

Parrott's irrigation ditch.

Parrott at his
garden, 1939.

"...just as we were positive that at last our objective was
at hand, a campfire gleamed on the east bank [Parrott Placer
camp], so we quickly beached our boats and hailed it. But no
answer came in reply. Aller left his boat and walked up to the
fire. At first he could not find its maker, but shortly he
sighted an old man quivering behind a rock. The man did not
speak until Aller strode over and touched him. 'Hello! Hello!
Hello! Who are you?' The poor man surely thought Aller was
a river ghost. In ten years, he might have seen other men four
or five times in the Impassable Canyon. Now, here was
someone coming up out of the river itself, in the middle of
the night. During this brief conversation the old man never
stopped shaking. He told Rodney of five rattlesnakes he kept
there, which, we later learned, was a story he had told before
to others that he might be rid of them. Although it was
difficult to get any information from the terrified old man, we
did learn that the junction with the Salmon was still six to
eight miles away [sic. ten], and so we decided to camp at the
next available spot. We discovered later that the man to
whom we had given the scare of his life was Earl K. Parrott,
famous hermit of the Middle Fork, who has lived there for
years, eking out a meager existence by placer mining."

As surely as a placer streak, the old hermit's stay on the Middle Fork was playing out, along with his solitude.

In March, 1942, Parrott appeared at a mountain sheep study-camp on Reese Creek on the Middle Fork. He was in pain from what was to be diagnosed as an enlarged prostate gland. One of the men rode to Stoddard Creek lookout and telephoned Shoup, Idaho, upriver on the Main Salmon, for a packer. Earl Poynor, who was packing for the crew, took a packstring to the Reese Creek cabin on the Stoddard Trail. Parrott was waiting there with a small tote bag. As the packer guided him out, Parrott confided that while some people thought he was rich, he had never accumulated more than $600 in gold dust.

The men followed the Stoddard trail down to the Stoddard pack bridge and crossed the Salmon River below the confluence with the Middle Fork. The doctor from the CCC camp at Ebenezer Bar (up-river) met them at the mouth of the Middle Fork, and Parrott was taken by car to Salmon.

It is not clear whether Parrott had surgery, but he lived with sweepboat pilot Cap Guleke for a period until alcohol and arguments required other arrangements. Parrott went downriver to Shoup, where Mr. and Mrs. Emmett Reese provided a comfortable home for him in a little cabin at their ranch on Pine Creek. There he remained until his health failed and he had to be nearer a doctor. He was transported back to Salmon and cared for by the Department of Public Assistance. Dr. O. T. Stratton of Salmon noted that Parrott had, since 1942, "lost compensation." Then he was moved to Lewiston, Idaho, in the hope its lower elevation would prove beneficial.

Before long he was back in Salmon, because the Salmon *Recorder*, February, 24, 1943, reported:

"A sanity hearing was conducted before Prosecuting Attorney Fred Snook in probate court Monday morning. C. W. Lyons was appointed to represent Earl Parrott, and Dr. Owen Stratton and Dr. John Mulder were the examining physicians. They pronounced the defendant sane.

The case was the result of an episode that disturbed Mr. Parrott's neighborhood one day last week. He claimed that dogs were running across his porch and were bothering him at night, so he fired at them with a rifle. The bullet glanced and went through Captain Harry Guleke's house, allegedly narrowly missing Mr. Guleke. The sheriff was called and a complaint resulted."

Mercifully, no trial was ever reported. Later in the year, Parrott had a cerebral hemorrhage, followed by hemiplegia (paralysis on one side of the body). In September, 1944, he suffered another stroke. Thereafter he was unable to walk or talk, but he was well cared for at the Silbaugh nursing home until his death on August 15, 1945. On the certificate of death, Dr. Stratton listed the cause as "Occlusion of coronary artery. Had lesion of aortic valves." Parrott had been at the Silbaugh home 300 days. He was seventy-five years old.

Funeral services were held at the Doebler chapel on the afternoon of August 20, and then his body was laid to rest in the Salmon cemetery.

In 1945, Swain and Frazier again floated the Middle Fork. Doc Frazier wrote:

"When we came to the old hermit's place, no work had been done on the bar, weeds had grown up around the little overnight shack, the trail had not been used. We went up the canyon wall to his cabin, the garden had dried up, the cabin door was ajar, and we were sure we would find the old gentleman's body. We looked around the place and over all of the ledges as we went back to the river, not a trace was found of him. We were sure that his good "Doctor" had not let the old man suffer. Enough to say—we were sad."

Hunters who used Parrott's place after his death vandalized it while looking for his gold. Lee Bacos, a river guide, burned the storage logs for firewood. When outfitter Bob Sevy first visited the cabin in the mid-sixties, he found letters wedged between cabin logs that revealed Parrott had a paranoid fear of rats. Sevy left them and they too disappeared. The shelter largely went to ground, finished off in 1989 by a forest fire; grass and brush have taken the garden, but three dwarfed peach trees still bear fruit on their gnarled limbs.

In 1988 Bruce and Diane May, having made a Middle Fork trip and learned of Parrott's life, decided to have a tombstone made for his unmarked grave. It was in place, along with flowers, for Memorial Day that year.

Earl Parrott's memory lives in the name of a creek, a lake, and a river campsite.

Earl K Parrott

(Sign plainly, with full Christian name.)

When hermits die
They close their eyes. They never hear
The parson sermonize how somewhere
There is hope where no hope was.

> *Hermits*
> —James Galvin

MILE 88.4 *Cradle Creek* on the left. Named for Parrott's sluice box. Cradle Creek Rapid is just below the creek.

MILE 88.7 *Cliffside Rapid.* Tumble Creek enters on the right. One of Parrott's alternate cabins and gardens was located on the bench just below the mouth of Tumble Creek.

MILE 88.8 *Tumble Creek Camp* on the right, just below the mouth of the creek.

A human drama which occurred one and one-half miles up Tumble Creek deserves commemoration, though it happened more recently than most events related in this book. It is a story of risk and fortune, courage and fate.

July 26, 1979, the Ship Island fire was out of control. Jim

Camp, age forty-three, fire management officer for the Payette National Forest, and Kyle Pattee, twenty-nine, fire officer from Targhee National Forest, were supervising a twenty-four-man crew that was using shovels, pumps and chain saws on the slopes of Tumble Creek. Camp and Pattee were directing their men from the vantage of Helispot 10—a level landing pad notched into the 100-degree incline of the hills near the stream. As they observed the blaze sluicing downhill, they saw a spot fire erupt on their side of the creek. The creek was intended to be part of the fireline, but the new burn gathered uphill momentum. Camp radioed crew members to retreat to their safety zones, as he and Pattee mounded fire equipment into a salvage pile and prepared to make their stand—they had no place to run.

In years past, a firefighter about to be overrun by flames could only bury himself in a hole. Today a firefighter is required to carry a fire shelter—folded in a thin three-pound packet belted around his waist. In an emergency, he can shake out the aluminum foil-glass cloth heat deflector, lie down and slide beneath it. If there is oxygen, his chance of survival increases by about 400 degrees. In minutes, such an emergency arrived for Camp and Pattee.

The fire shelter is more envelope than tent. Camp and Pattee bellied down in the dirt beneath their foil pods. Communication continued between them until intense heat warped their radios. By then, there was little left to talk about. The firestorm, fed by winds funneled up the canyon, roared through the surrounding trees and brush like a mountain torrent. Both men were fighting for their lives. Embers ignited the gear pile: gas cans and chain saw exploded, backpacks and bedrolls burned, cans of food ruptured, pelting the thin foil that shielded their prostrate bodies.

Camp remembers moving four times. The superheated air was so hot he could scarcely force himself to breathe, even between clenched teeth. With gloves on, he tried to hold the edges of the tent which contracted and billowed in the gusty turbulence that accompanies unrestrained fire. Faced with withering heat and choking smoke, he had to stifle an over-

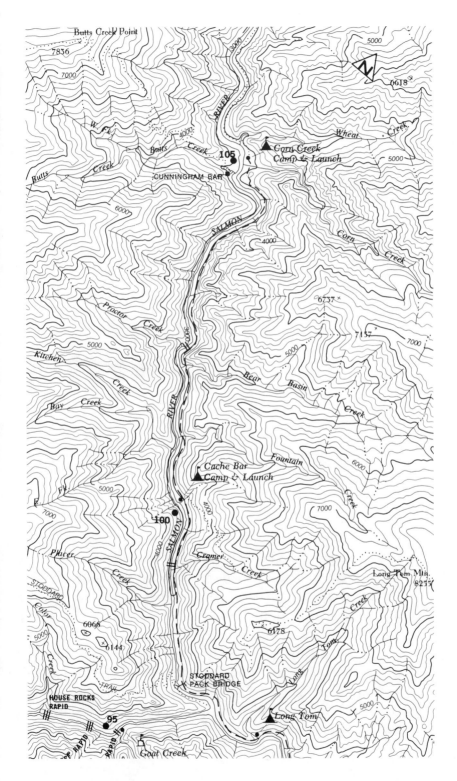

Butts Creek Point

7836

7000

W. Fk.

Butts   Creek

Butts   Creek

6000

Proctor   Creek

Kitchen

5000

Bay   Creek

E. Fk.

7000

5000

Placer

STODDARD

Color

5000

6068

6144

TRAIL

HOUSE ROCKS
RAPID

95

RAPID

RAPID

Goat Creek

RIVER

4000

CUNNINGHAM BAR

105

SALMON

4000

RIVER

4000

SALMON

100

Cache Bar
Camp & Launch

4000

Cramer   Creek

STODDARD
PACK BRIDGE

5000

6000

Corn Creek
Camp & Launch

Wheat   Creek

5000

Corn   Creek

6737 ×

7157 ×

7000

Bear   Basin   Creek

5000

6000

Fountain

Creek

7000

Long Tom Mtn.
8255

6178

Long   Tom   Creek

5000

Long Tom

6618

5000

5000

283

whelming urge to jump up and run. The inferno swirled over them for almost an hour.

When the fire receded and the crew reached their supervisors, they found Pattee, a veteran of over 300 fires, lifeless beneath his shelter. He had moved at least once, but he had no gloves to hold the scorched aluminum edges of his floorless cover. The coroner's report listed the cause of Pattee's death as "inhalation of hot air and lack of oxygen." It was a tragic accident in a risky business—another dimension to the second word in Forest Service.

Camp, married and the father of three children, survived with minor burns on his head, hands, elbows and knees. He was kept overnight for observation in the Steele Memorial Hospital at Salmon. Fewer than two weeks later, Camp was back at work on another large fire.

M I L E 89.2 *Ouzel Camp* on the left.

M I L E 90 *Ouzel Rapid - Cliffside Camp* on the right. The rapid is named after cinclus, a small bird with the ability to fly underwater. It is sometimes called a "dipper."

M I L E 90.1 *Stoddard Creek* trails out on the left.

This creek is probably named for early relatives of Smith "Smitty" Stoddard, a Middle Fork backcountry pilot whose flying service operated out of Salmon. Smitty was killed while flying outfitters into Indian Creek. Stoddard Bar Camp is just below the creek.

The most spectacular Sheepeater pictographs on the river are located a short distance up this creek.

M I L E 90.5 *Otter Bar Camp* on the right.

M I L E 90.9 *Rubber Rapid* In high water Rubber has the largest waves on the river. The derivation of its name is uncertain, although it is known that the USGS crew in 1930 had some rubber boats in the canyon.

M I L E 91 *Reese Creek* on the left. Reese Creek is probably named for the father of Emmett Reese. He and Emmett had a cabin here and ran winter traplines up toward Chamberlain Basin. Emmett became well known for his cattle ranch with registered Herefords at Pine Creek on the Main Salmon.

M I L E 91.9 *Nolan Creek* enters on the left. J. M. Nolan was an early-1900s placer miner who worked from Survey Creek to this creek.

M I L E 92.3 *Roaring Creek* on the right. **Hancock Rapid.**

The rapid is named for Monroe Hancock, Salmon River sweepboat pilot. His wife recalled that Monroe remarked it was not really fair to have named the rapid after him since he had never taken a dip in it.

M I L E 93.3 *Devil's Tooth Rapid.* Called Scoop Rapid on the USGS map in 1930. Oregon guides refer to it as Digger Hole. "Digger" Larsen was a Eugene, Oregon, mortician; a storyteller and a friend of Prince Helfrich.

M I L E 93.8 *Color Creek* runs out on the left. Traces of gold are called "color."

MILE 93.9 *House of Rocks Rapid.* A tight squeeze on low water.

MILE 94.3 *Jump-Off Rapid* or Whoops (Hatch) or Chuck Hole (Helfrich). The Oregon name commemorates Chuck Elliot who spilled here.

MILE 95.1 *Goat Creek Rapid.*

MILE 95.2 *Goat Creek* splashes in on the right. Horse Heaven lookout—elevation 8,086 feet—is about four miles from the river, on the east ridge of Goat Creek. A " fly shed" or stock barn used by the Forest Service survives on the peak. While being used by employees during the Ship Island fire in 1979, a verse was discovered written on one of the boards inside.

> There's nothing like a little cabin
> to weather out a storm—
> build a fire, plug up the door
> and it will keep you warm.
> Here's to the Forest Service—
> my credit they do earn.
> Thank you for this cabin that you
> forgot to burn.
> > J. Lish Oct. '77
> > —Caught Out

MILE 97 The confluence with the River of No Return.

The log cabin on the downstream-side of the confluence was built in 1930 by Clyde and Don Smith. Gus Peebles, with his dog King Zog, lived in it from 1935 to 1945. He had a cable-box to cross the river. River folk liked to stop and visit with him.

Born in Lovilla, Iowa, in 1873, Peebles had gone to the Yukon Gold Rush in 1898, then he worked as a marine engineer on a steamboat on the Kootenai River for ten years, before following the same occupation in Alaskan waters. He also worked on a cargo ship in the Atlantic during World War I. In 1946 Peebles died in Hamilton, Montana, and is buried in Salmon.

A KIND OF HERMIT RACE

The Sheepeaters: Mountain Shoshoni

Here we found a few Snake Indians [Mountain Shoshoni-Sheepeaters] comprising six men, seven women, and eight or ten children who were the only inhabitants of this lonely and secluded spot. They were all neatly clothed in dressed deer and sheepskins of the best quality and seemed perfectly contented and happy. They were rather surprised at our approach and retreated to the heights where they might have a view of us without apprehending any danger, but having persuaded them of our pacific intentions we then succeeeded in getting them to encamp with us. Their personal property consisted of...a small stone pot and about 30 dogs on which they carried their skins, clothing, provisions, etc. on their hunting excursions. They were well armed with bows and arrows pointed with obsidian.
—Osborne Russell, Journal of a Trapper, July, 1835, Lamar Valley, Yellowstone.

...these belonged to a kind of hermit race, scanty in number, that inhabit the highest and most inaccessible fastnesses. They speak the Shoshoni language and probably are offsets from that tribe, though they have peculiarities of their own, which distinguish them from all other Indians.
—William Bonneville, September, 1835, Wind River Range, Wyoming.

There also exists another band of Tookooreka or Sheep Eaters a branch of Shoshonees who live almost entirely in the Mountains very seldom visit the white settlements.
—Luther Mann, Jr., 1867, Fort Bridger, Wyoming.

A few wretched Sheepeaters are said to linger in the fastness of the mountains about Clarke's Fork; but their existence is very doubtful.
—Earl of Dunraven, 1870, Yellowstone Expedition.

A knowledge of the Sheepeater Indians and of the campaign waged against them is essential to any understanding of the Middle Fork country. Familiarity with their Plateau culture enhances appreciation of their pictographs, enlightens perception of the skills required to survive in the regions they occupied, and lends meaning to the geographical names which recall their struggle: Sheepeater Hot Springs, Indian Creek, Vinegar Hill, Ramey Ridge, Soldier Bar, Bernard and Papoose creeks. The Sheepeater story shares a recurrent, poignant pattern found in other native-American histories— white encroachment trespasses on an existing culture, resistance to that intrusion is repulsed with greater aggression, and broken fortunes follow the natives into exile.

Since National Park Service historian John Hussey has written the most straightforward summary of the Sheepeater culture available, it is included here.

The Sheepeaters

"The earliest trappers and explorers through the vast region now comprising southern Idaho, western Wyoming, northern Utah, and eastern Nevada made little effort to distinguish between the several groups of Shoshoni-and Paiute-speaking natives encountered there. To most of them these various peoples were simply "Snakes." The shifting habitats and personnel of these Indian groups made for utter confusion among the observers.

Alexander Ross, veteran and chronicler of the first fifteen years of the Columbia Basin fur trade, admitted that the traders of the North West Company, "with all their experience," possessed "but a very confused idea of the Snakes, both as to their names or numbers." It was not until he himself had visited the Snake country that Ross could gather more detailed information; and even then, he admitted with rare modesty, "it cannot be fully relied upon as entirely correct."

The confusion became worse in later years as trappers, travelers, and settlers applied such names as "Bannocks," "Sheepeaters," "Salmoneaters," "Shoshonis," "Paiutes," and

"Buffalo-eaters" to various bands or groups of these peoples, not realizing that these units changed composition frequently and adopted different habitats and eating habits with the seasons. The situation was somewhat clarified when trained ethnologists applied themselves to the problem, but the picture is not entirely clear to the present day.

This lack of knowledge is particularly noticeable in relation to the Indians who inhabited the broken, rugged area of central Idaho from the east-west course of Salmon River southward to the ranges forming the northern boundaries of the Snake River Plains. These natives, often termed the "mountain Shoshoni," retreated into the jagged fastness of their homeland when miners and settlers invaded the outward fringes, and the newcomers had little opportunity, or desire, to become acquainted with them. And when the remnants of the Sheepeaters were settled on the Fort Hall Reservation in 1880 there were so few left that little comprehension of their prewhite culture could be obtained. Thus the leading authority on the Indians of Idaho [Sven Lilijeblad] must still admit that "the distribution of the mountain Shoshoni is imperfectly known."

These mountain Shoshoni were the inhabitants of the Sawtooth Range when the region was first visited by Europeans. Although evidences of aboriginal occupation are found rather frequently in the Sawtooth Mountains and in the rugged country around them, the number of Indians in the region was never large. It has been estimated that the Shoshoni groups in the entire vast mountain districts of central Idaho and southern Montana, including the Lemhi bands, numbered only about 1,200 before they were disturbed by Europeans.

In the summer of 1855 Nathan Olney, a special agent of the Oregon Indian Superintendency, made a particular effort to determine the composition and numbers of the "Snakes." At Camas Prairie, near the present Fairfield [Idaho], he was told by the Indians that one of the three principal groups of the Snakes was made up of the "Too-koo-ree-keys or Sheepeaters," who numbered 300.

By 1875, after the white man's diseases and persecutions, as well as attacks by other tribes, had reduced their numbers, the mountain Shoshoni population almost certainly was not more than 500. When the Indians of central Idaho from the Sawtooth Range north to Salmon River were rounded up by the Army in 1879, only fifty-one were found. Allowing for a few families that eluded the troops and remained in the region and for those which moved quietly off to join other Shoshoni peoples on reservations, it is evident that the Sawtooth area was very sparsely inhabited by Indians.

The mountain Shoshoni, or Sheepeaters as they came to be called by the whites, belonged to the language group known to anthropologists as the Northern Shoshoni, which, in turn, is a branch of the Uto-Aztecan family, the speakers of which range from the Yellowstone area to Guatemala. In fact, nearly all the Shoshoni-speaking peoples of Idaho are now generally classified as Northern Shoshoni. As one authority states, from the northern limits of the Shoshoni, along the Middle Fork of the Salmon River and on the upper Salmon River drainage, south to Great Salt Lake, and from the northward bend of Snake River east to central Wyoming there existed no linguistic, cultural, or political borders.

No one knows when the Northern Shoshoni entered the present Idaho, but not so long ago it was believed by authorities that they moved into the Snake River drainage from the south at a relatively recent date. Some scholars believe this move may have been in the last thousand years. However, recent archeological excavations in the general area reveal a cultural continuity extending back at least about 8,000 years. Regardless of when they came, these people brought with them the culture of the Great Basin, marked by an economy based on seed and root gathering, skillful basketmaking, employment of clothes and shelter covers woven from plant materials and animal skins, and the use of specialized stone utensils. They were seminomadic and had no political organization other than loosely composed family or village groups. As these Shoshoni moved into the mountains north of the Snake River Plains they gradually imposed upon their basic culture the specialized Plateau cultural traits found among their northern neighbors, particularly the Nez Perce, who shared much of the same environment.

Further and more drastic changes came about the middle of the eighteenth century or slightly earlier when the Shoshoni Indians of the present Idaho obtained the horse. This innovation led to greater mobility, to the development of organized bands to conduct buffalo hunts, and to contact with the Plains Indians to the eastward. Those Shoshoni who adopted the horse, such as those of the Lemhi Valley on the east and those about the lower courses of the Boise, Payette, and Weiser rivers on the west, rapidly superimposed on their old culture many features of the Plains Indian way of life, including the use of tepees, the wearing of tailored skin clothing, and the practicing of certain ceremonial dances.

The mountain Shoshoni of central Idaho, however, were a relatively conservative and isolated group. Very few of them adopted the horse, except perhaps for temporary hunting expeditions with their eastern and southern neighbors; and thus the mountain Shoshoni or Sheepeaters became a recognizable group, readily distinguishable from the other Shoshoni of Idaho. Their neighbors tended to laugh at their "slow, singsong speech" and old-fashioned ways.

As with all the Shoshoni, groups of the mountain dwellers moved about frequently and subsisted for intervals on particular kinds of foods obtainable in particular localities. Such groups were often named temporarily after one of these foods. For instance, families joining the Lemhi Indians for a trip to the buffalo country might be called "buffalo eaters," but when at home at the fishing villages on Salmon River these same people were known as "salmon eaters." When hunting in the western mountains, they might be designated as "deer eaters."

In general, however, the people who inhabited the mountains were known to the Lemhi and other Shoshoni as the "mountain-sheep eaters," although "salmon eaters" was also a commonly used designation. The mountaineers called themselves "tukudeka," or "mountain-sheep eaters"; and this name, shortened to "Sheepeaters," was used by the miners and settlers who invaded their homeland.

By the time the first whites reached Idaho they found living among the Shoshoni in the Lemhi Valley, along the Snake, and on the Boise, lower Payette, and Weiser rivers another people who came to be called the Bannock. These Indians spoke the Northern Paiute or Mono-Bannock tongue, which, like Northern Shoshoni, belonged to the Shoshonean branch of the Uto-Aztecan linguistic stock. Probably these Northern Paiutes were latecomers. It is believed that they moved into the Snake country from southeast Oregon about the end of the eighteenth century. Presumably they had already acquired horses from the Shoshoni and had begun to hunt with them. They apparently preferred to join only those Shoshoni who shared the new culture.

The Shoshoni seem to have welcomed the Northern Paiutes. They called the newcomers "Panaite," or "our friends." Hence the term "Bannock." Groups of the Bannock and Shoshoni began to band together for buffalo hunting, for defense against the Blackfeet, and for other purposes. Even when separated, they utilized the resources of the same geographical regions. By the time of white settlement the speakers of the two languages were quite well mixed within the groups and bands in parts of Idaho, with some predominantly Shoshoni bands even having Bannock chiefs. In fact, says Liljeblad, "one cannot properly speak of a Bannock and Shoshoni tribal division" during the historic period. The two lived together in social, economic, and political union under joint leadership and with common cultural conditions.

The true mountain Shoshoni or Sheepeaters—exclusive of the Lemhi and other former companion groups who broke away upon the adoption of the horse—apparently did not attract the Bannocks. There were few if any of these newcomers among the Sheepeaters when first observed by Europeans; but during the Bannock disturbances of 1878 it seems certain that a number of these Northern Paiutes took refuge in the mountain Shoshoni bands.

The social and political organization of the Sheepeaters followed the simple pattern that characterized the Shoshoni prior to the introduction of the horse. The only community organization was the small, loosely-knit family or village group. Most often these groups consisted of only two or three families under the informal leadership of an old and experienced man. But occasionally twenty or thirty families wintered together at favorite fishing places; in such cases a headman, recognized because of his prestige, directed such community activities as demanded cooperation. There were no formal chiefs, even of villages.

These small family groups moved about from place to place as the food supply changed with the seasons. Even when several families camped together during the winter they often broke apart into smaller units during the summer. The composition of the groups shifted frequently. Families and individuals joined or broke away at unpredictable intervals. Those individuals and families that acquired horses usually moved off to join their distant cousins in the Lemhi Valley.

Intercourse between family groups was informal in nature, consisting largely of seasonal economic cooperation in fishing or hunting. There were no territories or natural resources that were the exclusive property of any group or individual. The fishing places, the hunting grounds, and the meadows where roots were found were open to all. With no territorial rights to defend there were few quarrels or wars. The groups were so isolated that there were no large ceremonial gatherings; festivals were limited to family or village dances.

In the Sawtooths vicinity the principal village was Pasasigwana, situated at a warm spring in the mountains north of the present Clayton, about thirty miles east of Stanley. Here some thirty families traditionally wintered together. Among other villages were one on the upper Middle Fork of Salmon River, one near the junction of the Middle Fork and the main Salmon River, and two or three on the upper Salmon River above the junction of the Lemhi River.

During the summer these villages generally broke up, and groups of two or three families wandered about on foot gathering seeds, bulbs, and roots and hunting game. Favorite places for such activities were on the headwaters of Salmon River, the East Fork of the Salmon River, the Lost River Range, and the Salmon Range. During July, 1831, Warren Ferris and a party of American trappers encountered a group of "Root Diggers" in Stanley Basin. They had no horses and were hunting elk, deer, and bighorn and catching salmon. In August, 1879, miners reported seeing a group of thirteen Indians at the lakes in the Sawtooth vicinity. The natives were fishing, but since they had "ponies" they may have been non-Sheepeaters who were simply passing through the mountains.

One Indian trail used in these wanderings crossed the Sawtooth Range by way of the present Smiley Creek. And certainly there were other frequently used routes over the mountains, to the Wood River drainage, to the South and Middle Forks of the Boise, and to the South Fork of the Payette.

According to Alexander Ross, the mountain Shoshoni, or 'Snakes" as he called them, seldom ventured onto the open plains for fear of attacks by the Blackfeet and other enemies from beyond the Rockies. In fact, noted Peter Skene Ogden in 1825, "Nature has been most provident in affording Shelter to the poor Mountain Snakes if it were not so long since the War Tribes would have destroyed them all." It was to avoid such exposure, said Ross, that the Sheepeaters did not keep horses.

Contrary to common belief, the Sheepeaters fared better economically than most of the Shoshoni. The foods available to them were varied and sometimes abundant. Salmon teemed in the upper waters of Salmon River and were readily caught by dams and weirs, as well as by hooks, harpoons, clubs, and baskets. Some of the fish traps were large structures built as a result of community effort under the direction of a head man. The salmon were split and dried, and then pulverized and stored for winter use.

294

Photographed by William Henry Jackson, this is the only known group-picture of Sheepeaters, and it was taken in 1871 near the Idaho-Montana border.

Unlike most other Shoshoni, the Sheepeaters were basically a hunting people. Elk, deer, and mountain sheep were the principal game and were preferred. Antelope were rare, and by the early 1830s buffalo had retreated to the Big Lost River, at the southeastern fringe of the Sheepeater homeland. Bear, mountain lions, coyotes, and smaller animals were killed if opportunity provided—the mountain Shoshoni had few food prejudices.

One authority has said that the Sheepeaters were "the most skilled hunters on foot of all Idaho Indians." They were so successful, in fact, that they could afford to bypass the grasshoppers and other insects which made up a substantial part of the diet of many Shoshoni.

Communal drives, except for sage hens and water fowl, were not frequent among the mountain dwellers. They preferred to hunt big game as individuals or in groups of about three men.

Such hunts were conducted at all seasons of the year, light snowshoes being used in winter. Animal skins and heads were worn as disguises in stalking game; and specially trained dogs were often employed. Deer and antelope ordinarily were stalked and ambushed, but the larger elk were shot from ambush at night or harried in deep snow.

The Sheepeaters made excellent bows of mountain-sheep horn. Arrows were often poisoned with a mixture composed of wild iris (*Iris Missouriensis*) root and other ingredients. In winter, however, these Indians were able to kill deer in the deep snow with knives and spears without the necessity of risking the loss of arrows.

In addition to fish and game, the mountain dwellers had available most of the food plants employed by other Idaho Shoshoni as well as a few additional ones. Camas, the great staple of the Pacific Northwest Indians, grew in the prairies at lower elevations; and the Sheepeaters occasionally made long trips on foot to gather supplies. While journeying southward from the Salmon River drainage in 1831, Warren Ferris came across some natives, probably mountain Shoshoni, cooking camas roots in underground ovens.

The single-leaf pinon pine, a mainstay of most Shoshoni diets, does not grow in the mountains of central Idaho, but the Sheepeaters gathered the seeds of the limber pine (*Pinus flexilis*). After being picked by the women, the nuts were carried back to the winter village in buckskin bags. When desired for eating, a quantity of seeds was ground to flour on a metate and boiled to porridge.

Not much information is available about the domestic utensils of the Sheepeaters. Probably, like the other Shoshoni and like their Nez Perce neighbors, they made excellent baskets, both twined and coiled. The Shoshoni in southern Idaho made a crude but effective pottery, but it is not known that the mountain groups practiced this art.

Similarly, there seems to be little data concerning the homes of the Sheepeaters. Alexander Ross in 1824 noted that the mountain Snakes "always" built their winter houses among the rocks and in the woods; and in another place he mentioned "wigwams among the caverns and rocks." He also was told by an Indian that the Snakes never built their winter houses underground.

From these remarks it can be inferred that the Sheepeaters did not erect semi-subterranean winter lodges as did their Plateau-culture neighbors to the north. Probably they continued the ancient Shoshonean habit of building conical pole lodges thatched with bundled grass, bark, or tule mats.

But in the matter of clothing the Sheepeaters had made a decided break from the old Shoshonean practice of wearing woven rabbitskin blankets or garments woven from grass or bark fibers. Even before the Plains influence began to be felt in Idaho, the mountain Shoshoni wore tailored clothes of various types of animal hides. In 1831 Warren Ferris encountered Indians on the westerly sources of the Salmon River who were wearing "robes and moccasins made of dressed beaver skins."

The Sheepeaters had a reputation as furriers of great skill. They tanned by rubbing animal brains into the skins; and it is said that their success was due to using two brains per hide as compared with the one brain used by most other Indians.

A high degree of delicacy was shown in selecting the types of skins for the different articles of clothing. Women's gowns were made from mountain-sheep hides, men's breachcloths from antelope skins, hunting moccasins from badger or elk hides, while the best grades of soft moccasins for men and women were manufactured from deerskins.

Coyote fur was used for leggings and for men's fur-lined winter caps. Headbands, though not frequently worn, were fashioned from fox fur.

Ordinary blankets were made from antelope skins with the hair left on. When the fur wore off, snowshoe rabbitskins were sewn to the hides.

The finest blankets, however, were created from wolf hides. These products were works of art, considered the apogee of Sheepeater handicraft. They were generally worn as robes.

Such handicrafts gave the Sheepeaters an opportunity to trade with their neighbors and, later, with the whites. Small groups sometimes went great distances on foot to Camas Prairie and other meeting places to exchange dressed skins, otter furs, and service-berry arrow shafts for horses and other exotic items. Buffalo meat was an item much desired by the mountain Shoshoni.

Social conformity was usually enforced by ridicule. Marriage was a rather informal affair, easily contracted or dissolved. Plural marriages were permitted, but men generally married sisters in such cases. The Sheepeaters differed from most Shoshoni by being more tolerant of cross-cousin marriages.

Religion involved a somewhat abstract idea of a supreme power that made itself manifest in nature and man but was variously conceived in accordance with individual experience with it. A person attempted to achieve rapport with the supernatural from his subconscious mind, as revealed by dreams and visions. Such experiences placed the individual in touch with his guardian spirit. Fear of death was another aspect of religious belief. Pipe smoking, conducted in combination with prayer and meditation, was a religious act. There were no great ceremonials or festivals among the mountain Shoshoni, but there were dances for men and women which were thought to bring health and natural abundance.

By remaining in their mountain strongholds, the Sheepeaters largely managed to avoid the first miners who began to invade the fringes of their territory during the early 1860s. The discovery of gold in the Boise Basin 1862 and then along the South Boise River during the next year started this invasion. And, in 1866, prospectors discovered gold on Panther Creek and established Leesburg, west of the present Salmon City. Then mines were opened on Loon Creek and on the Yankee Fork of Salmon River near several major Sheepeater fishing villages.

These developments brought miners to the heart of the mountain Shoshoni homeland. Trails between mining camps crisscrossed the entire area; prospectors worked up every stream. The Sheepeaters, generally peaceable and shy, retired farther and farther into the remote corners of their mountain fastness, particularly in the region now known as the River of No Return Wilderness north of the Sawtooth Range, and in the Sawtooth Range itself. Some of them, seeing their food supplies reduced, moved eastward to join other Shoshoni in the Lemhi Valley.

The miners were apprehensive at the presence of the Sheepeaters, the general sentiment being that all Indians were dangerous and their proximity inimical to "progress." For a number of years there were no serious troubles between the newcomers and the natives, although isolated murders and horse stealings were blamed on the Indians. Occasionally the miners "retaliated" by killing such natives as they could find. And in defense of their actions they spread the report that the Sheepeaters were mongrel race of robbers and murderers, made up of "outlaws" from a number of tribes.

Then, during the time of the Nez Perce War of 1877 and the Bannock War of 1878, the Sheepeaters, together with all of the Indians of Idaho, showed a certain "restlessness," and a few incidents, attributed to them but never proved, occurred. During June, 1878, small groups of natives stole some horses from ranches in western Idaho and killed three settlers who went in pursuit. This murder, which occurred near the falls on the North Fork of the Payette River a short distance north of the present town of Cascade, was blamed on "the Sheepeaters and their renegade Bannock recruits." In August of the same year two more whites were killed in Round Valley, "presumably" by Sheepeaters. Despite patrols by troops from Camp Howard near Grangeville, the perpetrators of these deeds were not apprehended; and uneasiness on the part of the settlers mounted. In 1879 the miners and settlers in the remote mining camps of central Idaho finally found an excuse to rid themselves once and for all of the few Indians who still inhabited the rugged region between the Sawtooth Mountains and the westward-running course of the main Salmon River. During February of that year five Chinese miners at Oro Grande, on Loon Creek about twenty-three miles north of the present Stanley, were murdered by persons unknown.

The white settlers in the region put the blame on the Indians. It was reported in the press that the raiders numbered twelve "warriors" and two boys. The culprits, said the settlers, were "probably" some of the few hostiles of the Bannock War of 1878 who had evaded United States troops and were thought to have taken refuge with the Sheepeaters on the Middle Fork of Salmon River. Through the Indian agent at Lemhi, the settlers requested military protection. Meanwhile, two more white ranchers on the South Fork of Salmon River had been killed. Again it was concluded, but not proved, that the Sheepeaters were guilty."

Prologue to War

Though gold miners had no compunctions about traveling through Sheepeater country at this time, there were a number of whites who had observed the financial benefits realized by civilians in the path of a military campaign against the Indians.

A confidential report from Colonel Frank Wheaton, the Commanding Officer, District of the Clearwater, to Brigadier General O. O. Howard in April, 1879, intimates as much. Of a Boise City merchant, identified only as Moore, Wheaton wrote:

"[he is] deeply interested in U.S. contracts, and anxious for another Indian War in the Boise Country; he stated that he had then some 25 thousand dollars worth of Government vouchers from last summer's campaign [the Bannock War] and hoped to secure more this summer. Some citizens of northern Idaho really dreaded an amicable settlement with Moses [a Yakima chief], fearing that it might avert or prevent an outbreak of Indians this coming summer. They evidently dread the prospect of a peaceful year, and yearn for serious hostilities, openly envying Eastern Oregon's good luck in having an Indian War and its concomitant shower of green backs, all to itself in 1879."

On May 1, Brigadier General O. O. Howard, commanding the Department of the Columbia, received orders to dispatch troops to "ascertain who the murderers were; and, if Indians, to apprehend them, and bring them to Boise."

Accordingly, General Howard sent orders to Captain Reuben Bernard at the Boise Barracks to deploy Troop G, First Cavalry, on or about June 1; the troop to proceed to Challis and operate from that point upon any information obtainable.

Boise Barracks, 1870.

These orders were subsequently altered to exclude Challis when it was reported that no Indians had been seen in that area. At the same time, Colonel Wheaton was directed to send a similar force from Camp Howard to join Bernard as soon as possible. It was Howard's intention that when the two commands came together, Captain Bernard was to be in charge.

In compliance with their orders, Troop G, First Cavalry, of about sixty men under Bernard, left Boise Barracks to travel in a northerly direction. A detachment of the Second Infantry, mounted and numbering about fifty men under First Lieutenant Henry Catley, moved out from Camp Howard on a southerly course toward Warren and the South Fork of the Salmon.

Additionally, General Howard ordered Lieutenant Edward Farrow of the Twenty-first Infantry with seven enlisted men to recruit twenty veteran Umatilla Indian scouts. They were to travel under independent command from the Umatilla Agency (in Oregon) across the Snake River at Brownlee's Ferry as soon as possible. Farrow's scouts left July 1 and arrived at Payette Lake July 19.

Howard obviously believed that Nez Perce warriors were returning from their refuge in Canada and that some Bannocks had eluded capture at the battle of South Mountain. He feared these Indians might join with the Sheepeaters and renew an outbreak of hostilities.

The campaign which followed is explained through first-person accounts from the diaries of men who fought in the war: Captain Reuben Bernard and Private Edgar Hoffner ,who served under Bernard; Lieutenant Henry Catley and George Shearer, who served under Catley and wrote his recollections three months later; and William Brown, who served under Lieutenant Farrow.

Most of the journal entries have been excerpted in order to maintain interest and avoid repetition.

The Sheepeater War

This is the longest I have ever been without anything to eat...

MAY 31, 1879, Capt. Bernard. Marched 35 miles-Camped at Idaho City following the stage road all the way. The Command consists of 2 officers and 62 enlisted men, one scout, one guide, and 10 packers with 60 days rations.

JUNE 1, Capt. Bernard. Marched 40 miles. Camped on the East Fork of Payette River a mile above the bridge.

In descending the mountain to the river where we are encamped we came down for 4 miles. The river is a very swift and clear stream in a deep narrow canon. Grass very poor.

JUNE 2, Capt. Bernard. In crossing Hot Creek we lost two boxes of hard bread and a sack of salt and one of sugar, the mules falling in the swift water and being rolled over and over until the cargo comes off and is carried away by the swift current.

JUNE 3, Capt. Bernard. In arriving at the head of the canon (Deadman's Canon) we found a perfect plain covered with snow varying from 6' to 2' deep. Where it was shallowest, the stock would break through, giving much trouble. We walked and led our horses for about 8 miles. Arriving in camp we found the snow melting and the streams rising very fast.

Rain commenced to fall about noon, continuing all night. When it turned to snow, the packtrain not getting in, we were without tents, breakfast or anything to eat, tho we had all the wood we wanted and kept big campfires all night.

JUNE 3, Pvt. Hoffner. My Bunkey is Jim Sexton formerly an Attorney of Philadelphia. Booze got him so he went soldiering. We fared as follows. Had venison, hard tack, bacon and tea for dinner. Tea and hard tack for supper, others being less fortunate, having only wind pudding for dinner. Marched 27 miles today.

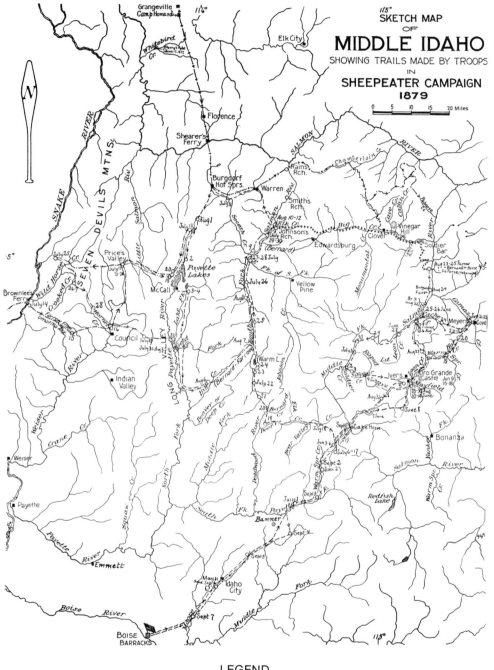

SKETCH MAP
OF
MIDDLE IDAHO
SHOWING TRAILS MADE BY TROOPS
IN
SHEEPEATER CAMPAIGN
1879

0   5   10   15   20 Miles

LEGEND

—+—+—+ Catley's first march to Vinegar Hill, then he returned to Warrens, and Johnson's Ranch.

— — — — — Bernard

———•———•— Farrow

++++++ Bernard's consolidated command down Big Cr. Aug. 14-20.

For movements of Forse and McKeever (supply) dates of camps are indicated where space permits; otherwise by circle in trail, thus O.

JUNE 4, Pvt. Hoffner . The boys are loud in anathematizing mule teams in general, ours in particular. The majority are taking in a quantity of wind, but for all that trowsers have to be reefed in at the waist. The only bedding that we have is a saddle blanket and overcoat, with pine twigs for mattress, and the canopy of heaven for shelter.

JUNE 4, Capt. Bernard. Remained in camp waiting for the packtrain. Rained and snowed all day. Streams rising very fast. Bridging the Cape Horn Creek so the packtrain can cross when it arrives. The day has been very unpleasant one—no packtrain yet.

Everybody is commencing to look a little serious upon the question of something to eat, tho the men have killed many grouse, fool hens and ground squirrels.

JUNE 5, Capt. Bernard. Rained all day. The packtrain or a portion of it came in about sundown with about one half of its cargo, leaving the other half so they can go back for it. The train has had a hard time wallowing through the snow. They have lost two more boxes of hard bread and other rations and all Lieut. Pitchers clothing and blankets in the stream. He goes back to look for them. This is the longest I have ever been without anything to eat.

While we were three days without rations or blankets and in the rain and snow all the time I did not hear a cross word or complaint in any way.

JUNE 6, Pvt. Hoffner. Lieutenant Pitcher is as happy as a June bug, having recovered his blankets. We sigh for a summer breeze.

Vel me no see da trail, me no see anything dat I know...

JUNE 7, Pvt. Hoffner . Off again. Broke camp at 6 A.M. The ground was covered with snow. Came near loosing my bunkie last night. He was on guard about 1/2 mile from camp, and it being dark, lost his way trying to get to camp and got stuck in a mud hole about two feet deep. By sheer grit got out and came to me covered with mud and a woe begone

expression on his usually smiling countenance. He asked for a cup of tea, which I soon got for him.

JUNE 7, Capt. Bernard In crossing Trail Creek we lost two more boxes of hard bread by a mule being carried down the stream. Snowed hard all day and night. Where the ground has thawed out it is so soft that the mules often mire down.

JUNE 8, Capt. Bernard. While we were crossing the mountains Johnny the Guide came to the conclusion that he was lost. I asked him why he thought so, he said: "Vel me no see de trail, me no see anything dat' I know." I said: "How do you expect to see a trail where the snow is 10' and 12' deep?"— "Vel me no see de blazes on de trees." I said Well

Johnny I don't think we are lost because there is no other way for us to go but to follow this Canyon. As we moved on the little Dutchman discovered some blazes on the trees which made him quite jubilant.

JUNE 8, Pvt. Hoffner. Broke camp at 6:30 A.M. Found the trail in such condition that we had to take the side of the mountain a portion of the way. The snow was so deep thro' the canon we had to pass thro' that we chose the lesser evil and made our trail over rocks and thro' snow two feet deep. I see some tenderfoot shake his cranium. Know ye my friend the snow was so hard that the crust held up our horses. Where it was not, the horses lunged or rolled thro' packing it pretty well. Snow fell part of the day in the forenoon, but in the afternoon Old Sol showed his bright face.

JUNE 9, Pvt. Hoffner. Oro Grande was a lively mining town 2 yrs. ago [1877]. It is now mostly in ashes having been burned in Feb last [1879] by the Noble redman special pets of US Interior Dept. There were no white men here at the time, but a few Chinamen who were murdered by the Indians. There was a garden here when we arrived with a fine lot of onions. We threw out a skirmish line and charged. In 10 mins. there was not an onion left to tell the tale. Not one sickly onion top left to tell that there had ever been a garden there. Part of the fence was left, which is accounted for by there being a lot of cord wood piled up. Bill of fare for dinner: Fried onions, tea and venison.

JUNE 9, Capt. Bernard. The Indians killed and robbed the Chinamen and burned the town [Oro Grande]. One of the Chinamen after being killed had frozen in such a shape that he could be set up on his hands and feet on all fours. In this position the Indians put an old pack saddle on him and loaded him up with picks and shovels as miners load a pack mule. In this shape the Chinaman was found.

JUNE 10, Capt. Bernard. Some men came over from Bonanza bringing the latest papers and news of very rich mines being discovered. With the white that came over was a Chinaman that owned the gardens we got the onions out of. He charged us $25 for them which was paid.

JUNE 10, *Pvt. Hoffner*. Two of us went hunting. I got a squirrel that was so near starved that it could not get out of our way. (game non est comatable).

JUNE 11, *Pvt. Hoffner*. Went hunting today. Saw no game, returned to camp tired, hungry and disgusted. Washed clothes in water as cold as ice then had supper, fried onions, venison steak, scouse, which is concocted as follows, stewed hard tack and bacon fat (soldier's name for this: Son of a B). Had troubled water for coffee. At 6 P.M. it began to rain and as a natural consequence we got everything more or less wet (some more). We put up shelter tents inside of wickiups and were more comfortable. The rain still keeps pattering so we are compelled to do without fire which would be comfortable as it is cold. We sigh for a cottage by the sea, for a cabin in the wood.

An Infantry man mounted reminds me of a monkey on a goat.

JUNE 12, *Pvt. Hoffner*. The rain it raineth all last night, and was showery all this day. The boys are all cheerful, some singing, some conversing in groups of past, present and future, while I pore over my journal and try to get down an idea. But my ideas have flown back to childhood's happy hours when in a snug and comfortable home with parents, a brother and sisters. Bah, such thoughts unman me, so will close and join the most hilarious group. Oh the heart of a man often bleeds when the face wears a smile.

JUNE 13, *Pvt. Hoffner*. Our supply train arrived this P.M. consisting of 41 pack mules with escort of nine mounted Infantry of Co. A 21st Infantry. An Infantry man mounted reminds me of a monkey on a goat. We now have more blankets and rations and a supply of reading matter, which we have been wishing for while lying in camp.

JUNE 14, *Capt. Bernard*. Marched 3 miles camped just below the burnt town. Several miners have come in from Montana and are prospecting for gold. They go around with pick, pan, shovel, and rifle. Rained all day. Streams are rising fast. Lt. Pitcher has been quite sick for several days; in fact he has been sick ever since he killed the 3 deer and now Robbins is sick with the same disease. It is what they call mountain fever.

Pitcher is getting better while Robbins is now delirious. It is a bad place and bad weather for sick people. I am the doctor and have nothing but Cathartic and quinine pills to give them while this and brandy is our supply of medicines. I wouldn't know how to use but very few other medicines if I had them. As night comes on the rain changed to snow.

JUNE 15, Pvt. Hoffner. This morning on waking up we found the ground white with snow. Broke camp at 5 A.M. Marched to Oro Grande, thro' a beating rain which continued all day, accompanied by Heaven's artillery. You people of low lands have no idea how loud thunder can roar or how bright flashing the lightning is on the mountain tops. On arriving at camp we turned our horses out to graze and then turned our attention to putting up shelter tents for ourselves.

A cavalry man's first duty is to his horse, next his own comfort. After putting tents up and acoutermenta under cover, I laid me down to read a Sea novel.

JUNE 18, Capt. Bernard. Sent Lt. Pitcher with 25 men 8 miles down the Canon to build a bridge across Loon Creek. Returned in the evening without having completed it. When they would fall a tree across the stream it would break in two and be carried away. Several more lost in this way; at last they got one to remain, tho at such a late hour in the evening that they could not complete it.

A man came in today from the Yellow Jacket mining district where he has been all winter. He reports Indian signs on Camas Creek about 70 miles from here—northeast. The man has a rifle and 18 cartridges, 2 blankets and about 30 pounds of flour and says he has eaten nothing but bread and salt with an occasional grouse for six months. He is looking well, is cheerful ragged and dirty, so we will march in the morning complete Pitchers bridge and go to the place where the man says he seen the Indian signs tho I don't believe his story at all.

Reuben F. Bernard,
Captain First
Cavalry.

it began to hail, stones as big as quail eggs...

JUNE 19, Capt. Bernard. The streams having
fallen we were enabled to cross without having to complete
the bridge. After following the Loon Creek Canon for 10
miles we turned to our right up the deep, narrow, rocky and
brushy canon that Hot Creek flows through.

    The stream is deep narrow and rapid. The trail which
was an old one and very dim crossed the stream many times.
Rain fell at intervals all day. When the pack train came in we
found we were out two mules and four cargoes consisting of
bacon, hard bread, sugar and coffee. From our losses our 60
days rations are going fast. The Hot Springs near camp are
splendid bathing places, several of them flowing over falls
forming a perfect shower bath.

JUNE 20, Capt. Bernard. Marched 16 miles.
Camped on Camas Creek.

    Fording our losses were only two cargoes and one
mule—the mule being killed by rolling down the mountain
into the stream. The losses were hard bread, bacon and horse
shoes. We will now soon find whether the Indians are here or
not. Grass very good. No rain today, but wood ticks by the
thousands are found everywhere and annoy men and horses
very much.

JUNE 21, Pvt. Hoffner. After a march of 10 miles
we came to the junction of the Challis, Salmon City, and
Warren's Diggings Trail. Sometimes called Washington. We
turned on the Warrens Diggings Trail, followed it a mile,
then camped. Just before getting in some men and ponies
were seen moving, and the order was to dismount, tighten
cinches then remount and charge. The horses seemed to
enter into the spirit of the men and fairly flew over the
ground in pursuit of the Indians, as we supposed camped in
front. These proved to be a few prospectors who were badly
scared. They saw us on the charge and hid in the rocks,
thinking we were Indians.

At 4 P.M. it begun to rain, wind to blow and thunder to roll. It blew great guns, for awhile playing the mischief with our shelter tents. After a half hour it begun to hail, stones as large as quail eggs. Some of the boys were hit in the head with stones which they say were as big as a water bucket. After it quit hailing we had a snow balling game. My bunkey brought from the miner's cabin cinnamon, dried peaches and soda. Voss killed a fine buck, so venison for supper. Marched 12 miles.

we have come from ten feet of snow to roses and rattlesnakes...

JUNE 25, Capt. Bernard. Marched 16 miles. Camped on the Middle Salmon at the mouth of Loon Creek. For the first six miles we had hard work on account of the softness of the earth from the rain and melting snow. As we neared the top of the mountain the snow became very deep and in places quite steep. One of our pack mules rolled from near the top to the bottom, a distance of about six hundred yards, the cargo and aparejo was lost and the mule reported dead. The following day it came limping into camp considerably bruised up by his roll, tho will recover. After once on top the mountain the whole country was deep snow for about five miles. It was hard and gave us no trouble. This side of the mountain is very steep. We go down rapidly. Within a distance of ten miles we have come from ten feet of snow to roses and rattlesnakes. Since we came into camp five rattlesnakes have been killed. Johnny killed two deer after we came into camp. Our first trout were caught today. They are nice ones weighing from a 1/2 to 1 1/2 pounds. The streams are very full of water. The Middle Salmon is a beautiful stream, it is about three hundred yards wide, with a very steady but rapid current. Loone Creek is about fifty yards wide and has such a rapid current that the water is white as foam. We are now camped in a small valley where the grass is splendid and as we can not well go ahead or in any other direction except back on our trail we will remain in camp for awhile to allow our stock to graze and rest. We will also bridge Loon Creek by falling trees from each shore to a small island in the stream.

JUNE 25, Pvt. Hoffner. There were a number of fine mountain trout caught in Loon Creek this P.M. by use of bacon for bait. It is evident that these are not Jew fish as they take bacon greedily. Voss killed two deer near camp an old one and a fawn so plenty of fresh meat.

My bunkie and I had the misfortune to have our blankets opened by one of the half civilized packers, and five pounds of tobacco, a Spanish dictionary and quite a lot of paper covered novels and novelets as well as a few minor articles taken. If cussing could kill, there would be a vacancy in packers ranks. We consider the loss of the tobacco the greatest as we are two hundred miles from our base. There has been an Indian town here at some time as there are a number of wickiup skeletons standing. Marched 12 miles.

JUNE 26, Pvt. Hoffner. Today we rest. Tried fishing and concluded that as fishermen am not a success. Some of the boys were more fortunate getting quite a string of Salmon. All I got was a bite on the hand by an ant. Day fine.

JUNE 27, Capt. Bernard. Moved camp one mile. The company crossed the stream on their horses, the water running over the backs of many of the smallest horses, the mules all had to swim, many of them being carried a long way down stream. One of the mules did a thing today that showed that an animal has more sense than we give them credit for. As one of them was being carried down stream it struggled to the shore where the bank was so steep it could not get out, the water being so deep and swift that it could not keep on its feet. It took hold of a strong snow bush with its mouth and held fast until ropes were got around it to assist it in getting out. When the mule was safe on the bank of the stream the packers and soldiers gave three hearty cheers for the mule. After going into camp the men went back and carried everything across to the opposite side where it was loaded on the mules and brought to camp. Two of the mules fell off the

Charlie Whirlwind
Shaplish, Umatilla
scout.

narrow trail, rolling into the stream, losing their cargoes, two thousand rounds of cartridges and two hundred pounds of horse shoes. Robbins, Ramey and I went up the river to see if we could find a crossing. Robbins took my horse and swam him to the opposite side of the Middle Salmon, then went up about three miles and swam back again. He says he is the best horse he ever had in the water, so there is no show to cross without swimming and to do this we would lose all our rations. A raft can not be handled on the river, it is so very swift.

Mosquitoes thick as redheaded children in Utah...

JULY 1, Capt. Bernard. When my blankets were being rolled up in the morning a rattlesnake about 16 inches long was found snugly coiled in them. As the morning was quite cold the snake was very inactive. He was gently laid in a campfire to get warm.

JULY 2, Pvt. Hoffner. We found a log across the trail and, not being able to get around it because of the river on one side and a rocky mountain on the other, we jumped our horses over it. It was about 4 feet high. Two of the pack mules were unable to make it, so did the next thing, by rolling into the river and swimming to the opposite side, mulelike, with the exception of two which went out a short distance and gave up the ghost, losing 2 boxes of hard tack and two sides of bacon. Col. Bernard and Lt. Pitcher had their blankets and rations soaked and a number of the boys had their blankets wet. Curses loud on all sides on mules and this Godforsaken country.

JULY 3, Pvt. Hoffner. Robbins and Ramey, a guide not mentioned before, who joined us at Oro Grande, went out to try to find a trail, as we do not know our exact location. In fact, we are lost. They discovered 7 small lakes on a mountain, also snow in abundance but no trail. But know the general course and will get out somehow somewhere.

JULY 4, Pvt. Hoffner. The Glorious day of Independence. The day in which our friends in the East are in Holliday togs and the kids frightening old men and nervous women with fire crackers and infernal inventions, while we are roaming. We wonder if there is one who gives us a thought.

We rest for a few days, as much as the mosquitoes will let us. They, like a creditor, put in their bills at a most unreasonable moment.

JULY 5, Pvt. Hoffner. This has been the roughest days march that I was ever on. We are camped on West Fork of Loon Creek, about two miles from the place we camped in June while waiting for our supply train. Very cold over coats in requisition, fire comfortable. Fortunately wood is plenty. Heavy frost last night. Old Sol smiled his sweetest today. We have lost 9 mules and sixteen pack loads of supplies while crossing mountains and streams. Marched 21 miles.

JULY 6, Pvt. Hoffner. We passed through two of our old camps. One two miles N.W. of present camp, the one where we first fasted. There are several Catholics in our command who if told by the Priest to fast a certain time, would do it, but they are the greatest grumblers when forced to fast through unforeseen circumstances.

JULY 7, Pvt. Hoffner. One of the boys was out four miles and wounded a bear, and was following it up to finish it when he heard a noise in the brush in his rear. Turning his head he saw two half grown cubs following him. He concluded the bear meat was too expensive for a soldier and left a clear field for the cubs. Bunkie and self had a present of a quarter of deer. Quite a frost last night, day fine. Mosquitoes as thick as redheaded children in Utah.

JULY 8, Pvt. Hoffner. An old man with his dog came from Bonanza on his way to Idaho City, having failed to make a strike. We divided with him and his dog. Two men sick with Mountain fever, and no doctor in camp. The Col. has a few pills and other drugs. Pills go for every case from boils to saddle blisters, and sich.

316

JULY 9, *Capt. Bernard*. We were camped on the main trail from Boise to Bonanza. Parties were passing to and fro every day, many of them brought us newspapers from Boise, Idaho, and Bonanza. Several deer were killed. While at this camp five of the men got very sick with mountain fever and had to be sent home.

JULY 11, *Pvt. Hoffner*. Two men passed this evening for Banner City. Ramey returned from a two days' visit to Bonanza, his home. When Mark Twain was in Venice he called a gondelier who asked Mark where he wished to go to. Mark said he wanted some place where there were no Americans. The gondolier said, after studying a minute, that he could not take him there, as Heaven he believed was the only place where there were no Americans. I begin to think the same is true of the tramp, as we have seen several in our rambles.

JULY 13, *Pvt. Hoffner*. Two men passed on their way to Boise City, with pack animals. Two passed, going to Bonanza with six pack animals. Three this morning with pack horses for Bonanza, and two for Banner with two. An old man came in on his way to Idaho City. He was with some others with pack animals and they left him behind. Man's inhumanity to man, makes countless thousands to mourn. Ramey went to Bonanza with dispatches. Patched my overalls today. Light rain this evening.

I cannot see how men can get so turned around in the mountains...

JULY 15, *P Hoffner*. Four men with six pack animals passed going to Banner this morning. Two on horseback for Idaho City. One had a soldier shoe a horse, paying for it with salt, a part of which fell to my share. Our sugar has gone where the woodbine twineth, and the whangdoodle mourneth for it's first born. Ramey returned with salt. Now we can eat salt and fill up with water.

Henry Campo,
Umatilla scout,
1923.

Joe or
Henry Campo

JULY 16, Pvt. Hoffner. Three men sick with fever, and the man with broken arm started with Brodenstein to Boise. 100 miles on horseback. Two men passed on horseback for Bonanza. I got some flour this evening, and made a loaf of bread for supper, having a cup of clear water to wash it down with. Flies and mosquitoes getting in their work.

JULY 17, Pvt. Hoffner. Two of the boys went fishing or rather hunting, killing a bear, and part of which I had for supper. It was like boarding house steak, tough.

JULY 20, Capt. Bernard. Marched 12 miles. Over snow and rocks. Country very rough. Rained all day and snowed at night. Killed ten deer, I killing five of them, one of them being a very large one; it had 11 prongs on each horn. One of the men killed one equally as large tho it had but 9 prongs on each horn. This camp was made high up in the mountains on a small tributary of the Middle Salmon River.

Very little grass, which caused our stock to scatter during the night. This detained us in camp an hour or so looking for them.

JULY 21, Capt. Bernard. Marched 10 miles. Camped on the East Fork of the South Salmon River in a splendid meadow of good grass. Here we saw and killed our first salmon, they were fine fish weighing from 20 to 50 pounds.

JULY 22, Capt. Bernard. Marched 15 miles. Camped on same stream, tho in the rocks and timber with very poor grass. Here we caught many very fine trout. Sent Pitcher and Johnny in one direction and Robbins and Ramey in another, to find a way out. All got back with a story of having discovered lakes and rivers of wonderful sizes, the streams all running in the wrong direction. The two parties stories about the country not agreeing at all. I can not see how men can get so turned around in the mountains.

JULY 24, Pvt. Hoffner. After a seat in the saddle for three hours we arrived at our camping ground. Quite a lot of fallen timber which we had to partially clear away by cutting and piling so we could unpack mules (Uncle Sam's Canaries), and cleared a road to get animals over the creek, the outlet of

Wat-is-kow-kow, Sergeant, Umatilla scout.

the lake, so they could graze. Had to clear a spot for cooking, after which we placed some logs across the creek, it being very narrow and midsides to the horses. Like Thompson's colt, we had to cross the stream to get water. Creek water hot. Up stream we found a spring of clear cold water, close to the lake. We washed clothes, then a number of us made rafts by cutting logs and lashing them together with ropes. We launched and went out into the lake taking a bath in the same. Water milk warm and blue black. The depth we failed to find. Sounded forty feet but no bottom. The lake covers about five hundred acres, surrounded by snow capped mountains. I enjoyed the row and bath as much as a school boy his holiday in the country with his uncle.

JULY 25, Pvt. Hoffner. Found huckleberries on a hill side so lunched on berries. Very sultry till 1 P.M. when it begun to rain, which cooled the air and put us in the best of spirits. Lost two mules, played out. We are camped on south Fork of Salmon River. Marched 25 miles.

JULY 27, Pvt. Hoffner. About two hundred yards above the mouth near an old log cabin, we found several ruins of old buildings and ground excavated, showing that miners had been here in quest of gold. If I had at present just what my horse could carry in his saddle pocket, I would bid goodbye to this expedition and take the back trail.

We lost a mule loaded with horse shoes. One mule tumbled over a precipice two hundred feet, with blankets. It was recovered, but slightly hurt. Marched 16 miles.

I fell in. Am not a success as a fisherman...might pass as a Baptist.

JULY 29, Pvt. Hoffner. Before crossing the stream we passed some buildings and a field in a pretty flat where onions and potatoes were growing, but no one occupying the house, the owner having been killed by Indians. There is an old unoccupied ranch near the bridge. After going down the river a short distance we found it impossible to cross with pack train, without getting every thing wet and possibly losing part as water is deep and swift. We turned and camped in timber near the ranch just mentioned, getting orders not to touch any of the timber, potatoes and onions. This was strictly obeyed, until dark. Then we had an understanding with the guard that was guarding the vegetables. Put a lot of hungry soldiers in close touch with vegetables, and they will have pats in spite of orders. There was formerly a bridge across the river, below us on the Warren trail, but nothing remains but the abutments. High water swept it away. Fine string of fish was caught, I tried my luck here. Found a large rock on the river bank, which I thought a fine place. I got on the rock all right, but in turning my feet slipped and I fell in. Have no idea how deep it was, as I failed to touch bottom. By a little exertion I managed to get on land with hook, pole and bait. Was wet, cold and disgusted. Am not a success as a fisherman. Might pass as a Cambelite or Baptist.

[At this time Catley's detachment sent from Camp Howard had proceeded to Warrens where they were held up by deep snow until late June. The following month his men worked their way down the South Fork of the Salmon, then across to the canyon of Big Creek where they encountered fresh sign of Indians.]

The Indians opened fire...

JULY 28, George Shearer. On the afternoon of
July 28th 1879 between the hours of one and two o'clock
P.M. Mr. White, one of the Packers of Grostein's packtrain
which was along with Lieut. Catley's Command came in and
said to Dave Monroe, one of Lieut. Catley's scouts, that he
had seen Indians signs during the morning about eight miles
below our Camp on "Big Creek." The Indian Signs consisting
of two Indian horses out grazing and moccasin tracks made
that morning he supposed; soon as Dave Monroe heard this
he started off to find Lieut. Catley, who was fishing, when he
found Lieut. Catley and told him what Mr. White had said,
Lieut. Catley replied to him. 'Keep quiet with your foolish
story you have lost me two bights' or words to that effect.
Lieut. Catley never returned to Camp for nearly an hour or
more after Dave Monroe told him what Mr. White said.
When Lieut. Catley returned to camp he called up Mr. White
to his tent and asked about what he told Dave Monroe. Mr.
White told him the same story as Dave Monroe had told
Lieut. Catley already. Lieut. Catley said "if he had more time
he would go down that evening but it was too late to start" or
words to that effect.

Lieut. Catley then with his Command following as before
stated without throughing [throwing] out any advance guard
in front of flankers on both sides of Big Creek on the ridges,
but went right into the canon where the Indians had gone
just about two hours before him. When he had advanced
about two Miles in this manner the Indians opened fire on
his Command from the opposite side of Big Creek about one
hundred yards off; after the Indians had fired instead of him
giving any Commands to his men he jumped from his horse
and got behind a large tree, which was near where he got off
his horse; the men seeing him dismount and go behind a tree
did the same without any command and tried to git shelter
the best they could, some behind their horses and others
behind brush, which was along Big Creek and which afforded
shelter.

Prvts. James Doyle II and A.R. Holmes Company "C" 2 Infantry were endeavoring to git shelter behind their horses but both were badly wounded. When I sawh Lt. Catley and the men gitting behind shelter I dismounted and stood alongside of him a few minutes expecting Lieut. Catley to give some orders; finding he did not give any, I went down near the bushes seeing that I could not do any good where I was.

just as we were in the greatest danger...

AUGUST 2, Lieut. H. Catley [covering July 28-31]. Having marched into the Big Creek country (Big Creek is a large tributary of the Middle Fork of the Salmon River), I found fresh Indian signs, which led me down Big Creek through a deep and rocky canyon, and the signs becoming fresher, I was obliged to follow their trail (which I believe to be the only way through that country), or give up the pursuit.

The result was that on the 29th day of July my command struck an ambuscade, from which, after determining that it was impossible to do anything, the Indians being lodged in a point of rocks across the creek, where they had so fortified themselves that their exact location could not be discovered, I ordered a retreat. The first intimation I had of their presence was a few words spoken by one of their number, which was immediately followed by a volley. Two men, Privates Doyle, 2nd, and Holm, of Company C, 2nd Infantry, were seriously wounded, but gotten out from under fire and carried about two miles back up the creek, to a point which I selected as one that could be held, where I met the packtrain coming down the creek.

Here I camped, and the next morning, putting the wounded men upon hand litters, I moved up a ridge which I thought would lead me into the mountains somewhere near the route I had traveled to Big Creek.

In this I was mistaken. It proved to be an impracticable route, and, being encumbered by the wounded men, I was unable to take and hold the points ahead of me, although the

Indians were endeavoring to reach them first. They secured a high rocky point ahead of me, and I fell back to a similar point, the wounded and the pack-train arriving there at the same time. There were then Indians ahead and behind. I ordered the packtrain unloaded, and the men to take such cover as they could find in the rocks and behind the cargo, and hold the position if the Indians attempted to approach.

The Indians, seeing this determination, set the base of the mountain on fire. The wind was high, and the terrible roaring of smoke and flame seemed to approach us from every direction.

First Sergeant John A. Sullivan, Company C, Second Infantry, then took a party of men and worked bravely and hard to get a space burned off around us large enough to prevent the fire from reaching our position. This effort, and the fact that the wind seemed to shift just as we were in the greatest danger, alone saved the command.

That night, after the moon had got down, we moved down the side of the mountain, which was so precipitous that it was impossible to bring more than a very small portion of our baggage with us. Officers and men threw away the greater part of their effects, and I ordered most of the public property abandoned, so that the train might be as lightly loaded as possible with what was absolutely necessary. Some of this was lost in descending the mountain by rolling and straying of the mules. At daylight we were ascending a ridge running parallel to the one we left, and which was found a fair route.

As I had not a sufficient command to establish and hold a camp to take care of my wounded men, and being crippled in every way by the loss of supplies, animals, equipage and clothing, I took up my march for Camp Howard, to which point it will be necessary to return and refit, if the command is to keep the field.

I shall order the purchase of sufficient rations at Warrens to last to Camp Howard, and continue my march in that direction as rapidly as the jaded animals and men can travel; at present both are exhausted from fatigue. No ammunition fell into the hands of the Indians. I think they got Private Doyle's rifle.

The McCoy family haying on Big Creek with Vinegar Hill in the background.

George Shearer: Lieut. Catley, I think, acted as a coward and is totally unfit to take command of any body of troops. As to the conduct of Lt. Webster every where I sawh him, he seemed to be cool and collected. I never got to see him much, as he all ways was left behind in charge of packtrain. Lieut. Catley's men behaved very well, and seemed to be willing to obey any Order given to them, they did not seem to be excited in the least.

[As soon as he learned of Catley's defeat, Colonel Wheaton, commander of the District of the Clearwater, dispatched Captain Forse, First Cavalry, with twenty-five men of his company to turn Catley back toward the South Fork. Pvt. Hoffner at this point continues his diary with Troop "G," First Cavalry under Capt. Bernard.]

The boys are whetting their knives on their boots...

JULY 30, Pvt. Hoffner. Today a few of us took a tramp to a house where a man had been murdered. It is like a charnel house, the man having laid in his gore for a few days before being found. The stench is horrible. From my observations I conclude that it was very convenient to have some

Indians in one's neighborhood in case of a crime being committed. It gives one a chance to shift the blame on the Indians.

JULY 31, Pvt. Hoffner. After leaving the ranch we begun the ascent of a mountain five miles from the base of the summit. Fortunately the trail is good, having been worked. After a march of 10 miles we reached Warrnen's Diggings, a small mining town, where we made a short stay. There is a hotel, blacksmith shop, two or three general merchandise stores and two saloons one of which was floating "Old Glory." There are about two dozen dwellings, a few whites, one white woman and one china woman. Here we found a wagon road, the first we have seen since June 1st. After leaving Warrens' three quarters of a mile we left the road, taking the Indian Valley trail, which is broad and well kept being travelled continually, so it is necessary to work it.

A messenger just came in with word that Lieutenant Farrow with a few soldiers and Indians are on the trail of the Sheep Eaters. We are to follow and join as soon as possible. The boys are whetting their knives on their boots, their eyes snapping fire. The few hairs on the head of my Bunkie standing on end. I asked him if he was intent on scalping an Indian, if he was really intent on murder. His answer was 'No, D-mit. Do you see that piece of bacon Uncle Sam saved for this campaign? I mean to carve it for supper.' Being interested in said piece of bacon, I unsheathed my knife and scraping a portion of the rust off of it, discovered the letters B. C. Truly a venerable piece of meat to feed men. Think of it, ye bloated Government contractors and shoddy aristocrats, whose wives order their Phantom to the door so that Jemima may go out to the Perade ground to see the soldiers, and say, "Oh Mr. Colonel, make them trot so we can see the funny little boxes [Infantry cartridge boxes] hop up and down." Such an occurrence actually took place at the home station for the benefit of an old woman by the Major in command who was sweet on the daughter of the old woman. Only the company of Infantry was in the circus.

326

Edward S. Farrow,
Lieutenant.

[Lieut. Farrow was on the trail of some miners and by the time he was able to get word of his mistake to Capt. Bernard, the Captain's men had already traveled an unnecessary seventy miles.]

AUGUST 1, *Pvt. Hoffner*. We here struck a creek about 25 feet across, where we saw a number of salmon, fifteen of which we shot. They average 25 pounds each, and on an average of two and a half feet in length. Marched 6 miles and camped on the bank of a small creek on the edge of a small prairie. Those of our party who have been reconnoitering returned this P.M. reporting that the Indians which Farrow was preparing to attack proved to be white men, supposed to be horse thieves. As we have lost no horse thieves, we will allow them to follow their innocent amusement.

The bushes are full of drying clothes...

AUGUST 4, Pvt. Hoffner. This morning a Courier arrived from Lieutenant Catley's [2nd Infantry mounted] which is on Big Creek, between South and Middle Forks of Salmon River, stating that the Sheep Eaters had given them a warm reception. In fact had demoralized them. The boys have been in the Southern States since the Civil War, herding Negroes, and being unused to being given a volley of lead from an unseen foe, were taken by surprised. Two soldiers were wounded, several mules, blankets, rations etc., were captured. Col Bernard immediately sent a messenger to Boise Barracks for our Post Doctor, and all Cavalry at Post of G Troop 1st Cav able to get into saddle and meet us at the South Fork of Salmon River, also for supplies to be sent to North Fork of Loon Creek, on the Middle Fork of Salmon River. Today is wash day. The bushes are full of clothes drying.

> Capt. Bernard August 4.
> To
> Lieutenant H. Catley
>   Commanding-Detachment
>   2nd Infantry
>   Near Warrens Idaho Territory
> Sir
>
> I have received the news of your affair with the Indians. I will cross the mountain and go down the South Salmon to Elk Creek when I will expect to meet you with your command—when we will cross over to the Indians Position you

should at once send for supplies to Camp Howard to come to you at or near the mouth of Elk Creek on the [South Salmon] when I will meet you as soon as I can hear from Boise. If you are out of Provisions supply your command by purchasing in Warrens sufficient to do until supplies from the Post can reach you.

Lt. E. S. Farrow with 30 scouts will probably be with me.

Respectfully yours,

R. F. Bernard Captain 1st Cavalry—Commanding

the Indians lay in ambush...

AUGUST 5, Pvt. Hoffner. Broke camp at 6:30 A.M. Lieut. Farrow of 21st Infantry and four Umatilla Indians came into camp last night. They belong to his command being with us.

AUGUST 6, Pvt. Hoffner. Broke camp at 7 A.M. Marched twelve miles arriving at North Payette River, near Payette Hot Springs, forming junction with Lieut. Farrow's party. We marched a short distance down stream, below the springs, passing a large rock which has the names of three civilians inscribed on it who were killed by Indians at this point on August 20th 1878. The names are Healy, Monday and Grosclose. The Indians lay in ambush on a small hill where there are a number of large rocks on either side of the trail. It is a narrow defile of fifty feet in length to pass through, only wide enough for one to pass at a time. An enemy can be within ten feet unseen. We halted for a short time on the river bottom, crossing three small creeks after remounting and leaving the river. We then took to the hills. The first was high and precipitous. After descending we brought up on a creek bank with solid bank walls of granite on either side almost perpendicular for one hundred feet, and about 25 feet wide at the bottom....

Camped for night—and I get numerical strength of allies which consist of Lieut. Farrow 21st Infantry, and Lieut. Brown 1st Cav. Two enlisted men, twenty Umatilla Indians, which are clothed as Infantry men, rationed and paid as white soldiers, together with four civilian packers and 18 pack mules. The outfit is mounted on ponies.

[The Umatilla scouts had two ponies per man.]

We now present a fierce warlike appearance...

AUGUST 7, Pvt. Hoffner. Broke camp at 6 A. M. Marched through some marshes, over rugged hills, through streams, thick brush and fallen timber, passing through a burning forest, fired by Sheep Eaters, stately pines falling on all sides. Sport, our company dog, which followed the supply train from Boise Barracks, joining us on July 18th, ran hither and yon, through the hot ashes, getting up on a log now and then to ease his feet. The poor brute was badly burnt when he at last sat up on his haunches and set up a piteous howl. One of the boys picked him up and carried him in front of him on his saddle. After getting through the fire we came to the head waters of the South Fork of the Salmon River, only a few miles from a hot lake. We followed the river a mile and camped on a small flat in timber. It was with difficulty that we got thro', in places the prostrate timber being so thick on the ground. We passed a number of wikiups, old ones. There were no signs of the noble Red Men here. Jack Frost last night. Marched 33 miles.

AUGUST 8, Pvt. Hoffner. Our trail led through some fine timber and good agricultural land, over some high, precipitous mountains crossing several creeks. Passed on a mountain side, which is now on fire, a place where we camped in passing through here before. It is a blackened mass. Grass and timber that was down is entirely burned. We neglected to put out our camp fires, and by that neglect were obliged to march twelve miles further than we would have done. Experience is a good teacher, tho' a little severe at times. We camped on a flat of a hundred acres, more or less, in good timber a short distance from the river on a creek. The water here is as clear as crystal. Grass is good. An Indian belonging to Farrow's company shot a couple of Salmon, of which part fell to me. 'Tis better to be lucky than rich. Marched 33 miles.

AUGUST 9, *Pvt. Hoffner*. The trail that we followed was dangerous in places. If a horse missed his footing there was a chance of a tumble of two hundred feet for him and his rider, into the river. My horse (Sprightly) fell once, but by springing out of the saddle, I saved him and myself an immersion, if not a broken neck.

Our pack train did not get in tonight, so we have to sleep with saddle blankets and overcoats for covering and saddles for pillows on the blackened ground. Very few have anything to eat tonight. Crossed several precipitous hills. Day sultry. Marched 22 miles.

AUGUST 10, *Pvt. Hoffner*. Broke camp at 6 A.M. Bill of fare for breakfast, a piece of bacon placed on the end of a stick and cooked over a fire, a cup of undressed tea, and a few pieces of hard tack. Most of the rest had wind pudding. We had ours in the saddle bag. After marching four miles, we halted on a bench or table land by the side of a creek turning our horses out to graze and waiting for the pack train, which came at 2 o'clock. We then had lunch, resaddled and mounted. After a march of six miles we camped at an old ranch in a small valley, near scattering timber, on the South Fork of the Salmon River. There is a field of potatoes here. We made free with them, taking what we could dispose of. Four mules were lost yesterday by falling over a precipice. Flour and all soft bread we had and 2000 rounds of cartridges went with them. One horse gave out and was left on the trail. The pack train did not get in camp until 9 P.M. The mules are nearly given out. Thunder began to boom and a light rain fell. Two men just got in bringing letters and papers from Boise. They have been searching for us since July 25th. Marched ten miles.

AUGUST 11, *Pvt. Hoffner*. Lieut. Catley 2nd Infantry and forty men and a Lieut. of his command mounted on a sorry lot of ponies, joined us today. Day sultry, light rain.

AUGUST 12, *Pvt. Hoffner*. Robbins returned from Boise City with mail, our post doctor Wilcox, two sargents, and two privates of G Troop 1st Cav. They had a tough time for three days with nothing to eat but a salmon. A party of

Umatilla Indians who are camped a half mile below us went reconnoitering today. Lost four pack mules by falling over a precipice. Troop D 1st Cav joined us today with 24 men. We now present a fierce warlike appearance. Wash day.

have been roughing it so long we are anxious to get back...

AUGUST 17, Pvt. Hoffner. We had a very high, precipitous and rocky mountain to pass over. A pack mule with load overbalanced and went end over end down the mountain side like a shot, bringing up on the creek bed with a broken neck, after a fall of three hundred feet. The packers recovered the load. A saddle horse was left to keep the mule company, being fagged out. After leaving this point the marching was fair. Passed several wickiups, one of which had about two cords of wood piled near it, probably for winter use.
AUGUST 18, Pvt. Hoffner. We crossed an extensive flat, covered mostly with tall coarse grass, commonly called Saw grass, where Sheep Eaters have been holding out, and where Lieut. Catley was chased by them to a bald mountain. There is a flat of large dimensions with tall willows and cotton wood along the creek. There is sufficient room for two or three hundred men to lie under cover if necessary, and where no officer would have taken his men if not rattled. The 40 that Catley had were sufficient to rout the three times in number of Indians, that drove him to the hills, if they had taken to the brush. An Indian is not going to take desperate chances. They would have left after exchanging a few shots, if the soldiers were under cover. But the boys were in a panic, and made for the mountain away from water. They remained on the hill until near morning, when they muffled the bell on the bell mule and stole away. They managed to get the two wounded men away. We joined the party [2nd Infantry] after they left the hill....

There we unbridled the horses and let them graze for a couple of hours. Robbins, Ramey and Lieut. Pitcher, mean time going down to the creek to reconoiter, and get word from Farrow, whether or not they had got word about the Sheep Eaters. But meeting an unfavorable response, they withdrew and joined us. Soon after Farrow with his Umatillas joined us.

The last five miles we marched as often as we could on the gallop, expecting to find work when getting to Catley's run. We would like to get it over, having been roughing it so long we are anxious to get back to our post. There is a fish trap here in the creek, constructed by making abutments similar to a bridge, then laying poles across, then stakes are driven in the creek three or four inches across leaning across the poles fastened by withs. Mr. Lo gets a pole and attached an iron hook, sharpened, to the end, and imitates Patience on a Monument, until the fish come. They can be plainly seen as the water is very clear, and he hooks the fish nine times out of ten. Quite a string of small trout were caught this P.M. Marched 12 miles. [The "mountain away from water" to which Hoffner says Catley ran with his men and remained until near morning is known as Vinegar Hill, on the north side of Big Creek.]

To reach the summit, a man would need a balloon.

AUGUST 19, Pvt. Hoffner. Broke camp at 6 AM crossing the creek, marched one and one half miles when we halted and let our horses graze for a while. Robbins, in the mean time, going ahead to find the whereabouts of Farrow's command, and learn the location of the Sheep Eaters if possible. After an hours absence he returned with word that the Umatillas had surprised the Sheep Eaters and had them on the run about two miles in advance of us. We then mounted, putting spurs to our horses and going at a gallop where the trail would permit. In places it was too rough, and besides we had the creek in front of us to be forded. We passed through a narrow canon which the Sheep Eaters have fortified on either sides, by walls of rock with loop holes.

This is where Catley's command was started on the run. No blame can be put on them for running out of this, but they should have stopped after gaining the flat mentioned before. The breast works are on the bluffs. A party of fifty could have held four times the number attacking. After passing this canon a short distance, we ascended a precipitous hill, after which we found a comparatively level of perhaps three hundred acres, covered with grass and sage brush, surrounded by sage brush and surrounded by rugged mountains. To reach the summit, a man would need a balloon.

After marching a short distance we came to the camp where the Hostiles were surprised, at the base of a rockey hill near a fine spring. Finding the Umatillas [four of them] with a lot of plunder which they had captured, such as buckskin, beads, blankets, pots and pans. There are ten wickiups, four being the average village. This makes the band to be about 40, the Umatillas say that they saw but 18 bucks, no squaws nor papooses, nor ponies. Being without ponies at this point, it was an easy thing for them to escape, as they could climb the hill side.

We turned our horses out after getting to this camp, to await developments. Gathered up every thing that we could find and consigned to the flames. The four Umatillas whom we found here have gone to their own command. A messenger from Farrow came stating that he is in hot pursuit of the hostiles, they having got their ponies. They are throwing away their blankets and all other articles that can hamper their flight.

We rolled his body in blankets and buried him...

AUGUST 20, Pvt. Hoffner. Broke camp at sunrise, troops G and D 1st Cav ascending a high hill precipitous and high as a mountain. Catley's taking back trail to south Fork of the Salmon to meet their supply train, being short of rations. We left our pack train in camp with 20 men including packers. G and D Troops had gone about five miles from camp when we heard firing. An but a few went back as fast as their legs could carry them, leaving their horses with the few who staid behind. The mountain being so steep, a man could get down quicker on foot than by horse. In ascending we saw four Indians on ponies on the opposite side of the canon, and heard them whoop. Two of G Troop stopped in rear to adjust their saddle girths when they were fired on by two unseen Indians. The firing then opened on the guard and packers in the camp which we had left. The Indians had been concealed on the hill by rocks and brush. They waited till all but one of the animals had been packed. It was a good scheme if carried out, as by driving the guard and packers away, they would have made a haul of rations, blankets, and other things. But the guards were old Indian fighters and did not run.

One of Catley's men who was left with us was shot through both legs. As soon as we got back our doctor put him under chloroform and amputated one leg, but he died in a few minutes. Catley returned as soon as he could after the ball opened. One of our men and a packer carried the body to the shade out of reach of the bullets. One of Catley's men who has been in the service for 18 years ran behind the bluff along the creek, and was not seen until evening. A couple of Cavalry men drew their revolvers and threatened to shoot any who ran during the fun. Col. Bernard sent a dispatch to Lieut. Farrow by two of Troop G requesting him to return. One of our horses was shot and killed, three wounded in the skirmish and one mule poisoned by some unknown cause. We could not see if any Indians were shot, as they were so well concealed. The name of the man killed was H. Eagan. He leaves a wife and daughter. We rolled his body in blankets and buried him. No shot was fired and no word was spoken, but he was left to rest as peacefully as if there had been pomp and ceremony. No more, old Comrade, will you be called to fat bacon and bean soup, to climb mountains nor damned by civilians for a lazy lout. We camped on the field in skirmish line at intervals of ten feet, with clothes on and pistols and cartridges around waists and carbines loaded and lying by our sides ready for action at a seconds notice. The hostiles have signal fires on the mountains on two sides of us. Marched ten miles today.

Shot three mules and four horses...

AUGUST 21, Pvt. Hoffner. Broke camp at 6:30 AM taking the same trail that we started on. D Co. in advance, pack train next and hungry Co. G in the rear. After we had marched a mile from camp an Indian gave a whoop but we did not see him. After getting three miles from camp we saw four Indians on ponies in a canon, with a deep creek between us. The trail is very bad, rocky and precipitous. After a march of eight miles we saw a small lake between hills. Passed snow drifts four feet deep and waded one three feet deep. Shot four mules and three horses that gave out. One mule lost footing and rolled end over end about three hundred feet down the side of the mountain. The pack came off. Sir mule gained his feet, shook himself, faced the pack, flopped his ear, gave a wink and walked off to graze . A bruised eye and cut on his chest were the only injuries.

The Umatillas overhauled the hostiles and had an engagement with them, capturing an old buck and releasing him. Captured 18 ponies and a few mules. The Sheep Eaters are getting short of feed so they killed two mules and feasted on mule steak.

We camped in a canon, heavily wooded with a precipitous mountain on one side and a hill of loose granite on the other. There is a small creek through the canon. This is where the Umatillas and the Hostiles had the skirmish. The Umatillas are with us and well pleased with themselves. Marched 14 miles.

AUGUST 22, Pvt. Hoffner. Broke carnp at 11:30 AM. Curses both loud and deep because of losing horses. 24 of Troop G horses, my own included among them, are missing. They strayed during the night, some mules with them. Searches all morning but did not find them. The majority of us were on foot, our saddles on extra horses. Some who were mounted went in search of the horses after we moved out of the camp. All of Troop G who were mounted took the advance, as skirmishers on either side of the trail, the pack train following while we unfortunates on foot brought up the rear. The Umatillas were somewhere in the lead, having started early in the morning. We saw fires on a mountain side about three miles from our last camp on the west. Three miles from our last camp on the west is a lagoon about three acres in size. After marching about three miles, mostly down a mountain side, over rocks and through a creek, into a dense thicket, word was passed that the party that was looking for the horses had over taken the rear of the command with the horses. I unsaddled the played out horses that I was leading and waited on the side of the trail until Sprightly came up. I was glad to see him. After getting our horses we forded a creek and ascended a high precipitous mountain.

This morning we had a fall of snow for a few minutes, followed by rain which lasted two hours. Then Old Sol came out smilingly. Three horses were shot on the trail, having given out. Marched 6 miles.

Those Indians must be defeated, or trouble will extend...

AUGUST 23, *Pvt. Hoffner*. The last of our meat went this evening, where the Woodbine twineth. It is fish, go hunting or go hungry. Marched 12 miles.

August 24, Captain Bernard received the following message from General Howard:

CAPTAIN BERNARD,

In the Field:
Guard has been sent to Warrens. Indians have been encouraged by apparent misconduct of Catley. Possibly he may redeem himself under your eye; but his precipitate retreat before inferior numbers is astounding. Sorry for Farrow's unavoidable mistake. Think we will aid you materially. Must leave details to your discretion. Those Indians must be defeated, or trouble will extend.
　[Signed]
　　HOWARD,
　　Commanding.

AUGUST 24, Pvt. Hoffner. Broke camp at 7 A.M. leaving the Umatillas with five days' rations, they to go back on the trail to try to catch the Sheep Eaters, we to rejoin them after we get suopplies.

Ascended a high precipitous mountain. Immediately after crossing the swift creek three pack mules and one horse fagged out in the ascent and were shot. Several more horses weakened, but the boys had such fondness for them that they walked, and by resting frequently, got them into camp. Camped in small willows on a small creek, good grazing. We had some experience in fighting fire, which got started in the grass from a fire that had been built for cooking. Last night we had rain. Went fishing and lost hook as well as my angelic temper. Marched 16 miles.

the instruments of torture were...lost.

AUGUST 25, Pvt. Hoffner. Broke camp at 6:30 AM, taking back trail for a mile and a half to the summit after which we crossed several precipitous hills and had two miles of rocks to pass over. One mule gave out. The pack was transferred and his muleship was left to his fate. A pack horse fell over a precipice and was so badly injured that he was shot. The medicine chest and instruments of torture were in that and lost. Robbins and Ramey went to the mouth of Loon Creek, about five miles distant, and returned with word that the supply train was not there, so hunger stares us in the face. Marched 15 miles.

AUGUST 26, Pvt. Hoffner. Broke camp at 7 AM. Parted company with D Troop they going back over the trail by which we came to rejoin the Umatillas. We divided rations with them. After accomplishing what they can in the way of quieting the Sheep Eaters, they will go South to the South Fork of the Salmon River for supplies, then to their station at Camp Howard in Idaho.

After crossing some rough, rocky hills and small streams we arrived at our old camp at the mouth of Loon Creek.

[At this point Bernard realized that his supplies were exhausted, his stock worn out and famished, so he requested permission from General Howard to return to Boise and refit in order to continue the battle. Bernard had covered 1,168 miles, fought snow for thirty-seven days, and lost sixty-three head of stock.

Howard agreed, ordering Forse and Catley back to Camp Howard.

Lieut. Farrow used the period September 2 to 16 to get resupplied from Camp Howard. He then set out again in pursuit. His officer, Lieut. Brown, resumes the narrative at that point.]

the dog was found hanged...

SEPTEMBER 17, Lieut. Brown. We left Rains' Ranch, following Catley's original trail until the afternoon of the 20th, when we left it, striking out east and north for the section south of Salmon and west of the Middle Fork. Fortune smiled on us, for, before noon the next day we came on a party of two squaws, a papoose and two boys about eight and seventeen years old. We took them in, except the older boy, who, though hotly pursued, made his escape. Farrow made a short stop, while I took ten scouts and, going forward, soon struck fresh signs in shape of two recently occupied camps and the trail of a hunting party of about eight men (four of them mounted) heading north. Farrow with the remainder of the command overtook us at sundown, just as we arrived at the north edge of the general plateau overlooking the main Salmon, apparently about ten miles distant.

About dark, leaving here our packs and horses, and each taking a blanket or overcoat, we started on the trail afoot, losing it, as I had predicted, after going about two miles. We then made for a ridge about half a mile distant, and, on reaching it, heard a dog bark about three-quarters of a mile distant. Scouts were sent out to more definitely locate the camp, while we waited, suffering considerably from the cold.

Starting again about 1:30 AM, Farrow and I each took half our force and made our way stealthily to the camp, surrounding it at daylight. As we gradually closed in we could see four horses and the place where the camp ought to be, but no fires—the Sheepeaters had escaped! The hostiles, realizing that the barking of the dog had revealed to us their whereabouts, had put out their fire, left four of their horses, stabbing one in the shoulder with a butcher knife, leaving the knife in, so the horse had to be shot. They had here about six hundred pounds of meat, partly cured. Our pack train and "prisoners," some four miles distant, were sent for. We spent the remainder of the day alternately sleeping and feasting on venison and elk meat. Shaplish was sent out with a white flag and with one of the squaws to induce the hostiles to come in for a parley. Peo and To-it-akas found the trail of several horse and foot tracks leading east. About two miles from camp the dog, whose barking had revealed to us their camp, was found hanged directly over the trail, where we would be sure to see it. The dog had paid the supreme penalty for his watchfulness and for giving the alarm! It is possible, too, that the boy who had escaped may have reached the camp and warned them.

papoose kept the entire camp awake with its wailing...

SEPTEMBER 23, *Lieut. Brown*. We started out on the trail, which took us in a complete circle to a fine meadow on our trail of the 21st. Here we made a base camp about 8 miles west of the Middle Fork, started civilian scout Bright and Private Smith to Warrens with dispatches and for flour and fifteen horses. After dark, leaving campfires burning brightly to indicate presence of the full command, Farrow and myself with sixteen of the command, taking with us the squaw who had the papoose, started again on the trail. The following day we camped in a gulch now marked on maps as Papoose Gulch, so called because the papoose of the squaw

William C. Brown,
Lieutenant.

whom we sent out to bring in her people, retaining the
papoose to insure her return, kept the
entire camp awake with its wailing. We discovered enroute a
lake to the north of us. Two camps, each several days old and
each containing four to six lodges, were found. The squaw
failed to get us in touch with her people, and we returned to
our base camp on the 25th. About two hours after we returned we were startled by a loud yell in the timber half a
mile from camp, and soon we discovered a hostile who evidently wanted to 'parley.' Lieutenant Brown and Wah-tis-
kow-kow left camp and approached him. But he moved, so
that they, in following his movements, were soon out of sight

341

of camp. When within one hundred yards it was discovered that he had a rifle and he was warned that as we were unarmed he must drop it. He then asked who Lieut. Brown was, and Watiskowkow replied that he was the Tenas Tyhee [Little Chief]. Our scouts subsequently said that had the reply been "Hyas Tyhee" [Head Chief] he would have shot us, as he might easily have done, and made his escape. However, he left his Henry rifle, approached, shook hands, and was brought into camp to Farrow. During the parley in camp we discovered at his back a revolver which he had failed to leave with the rifle. There he said his name was Tamanmo [War Jack], part Bannock and part Nez Perce, and successor to Chief Eagle Eye. He said that he was at the Manheur Agency when the Bannock War broke out and, not being able to get back to Fort Hall, had participated in the outbreak and subsequently joined his friends here. He was tired of fighting and wanted to quit. He had crept down in the bushes last night close to our camp, and so learned that our Indians were Cayuses; said that he and four others had planned to steal some of our horses tonight, therefore we should guard them well. Farrow told him to go out and bring in his people, that it must be an unconditional surrender, that no one not guilty of murder would be harmed. Tamanmo wanted a fresh horse, saying he had two "played out" horses hid near by in the timber. He was given one, and when his two jaded horses were driven in, either better than the one he got, we knew he would "play fair."

Tanmanmo said that part of the hostiles were at the mouth of Big Creek, and that he would either have them in or come himself tomorrow. Kept white flag out today and put on a strong guard at night.

White flag still out...

SEPTEMBER 26, Lieut. Brown. Remained in camp. Tamanmo with a Weiser named Buoyer came under white flag for a talk. Tamanmo, who has only been here about a year, is not well conversant with the country and had not succeeded in finding his people; says there are nine men with their families near here who belong here and know the country. The mother of the children whom we got on the 21st is Buoyer's squaw. Another party, consisting of twelve men, women and children, are scattered through the country near here, and all are to be hunted up. Buoyer went out again, leaving his gun in camp.

Courier David R. Munroe left for Warrens with dispatches for General Howard, stating Indians were suing for peace, and, if we failed to collect them all, we would start in again.

SEPTEMBER 27, *Lieut. Brown.* In camp. Considerable rain today. White flag still out. Command placed on half rations pending receipt of supplies from Warrens.

SEPTEMBER 28, *Lieut. Brown.* still in camp. Rain, sleet and hard snowstorm. Night cold and hard on animals.

SEPTEMBER 29, *Lieut. Brown.* still in camp. Snow melting off slowly. Later learned that Capt. Winters, First Cavalry, had left Camp Howard via Elk City for Mallard Bar, on account of report of fifteen Indians seen near there.

SEPTEMBER 30, *Lieut. Brown.* Marched twenty miles [or less] camping where Lieut. Brown left Farrow to go scouting in advance on the 21st. Buoyer came in.

OCTOBER 1, *Lieut. Brown.* Marched five miles and camped where we halted on 21st ult., where the creek turns to the east. Snow last night and rain nearly all day today. Tamanmo with another Indian [Weiser] came in this morning ahead of four lodges, consisting of eight men and twenty-four squaws and papooses [nearly all Sheepeaters], and doing justice to the occasion by liberal use of feathers and paint. A few still are out. Farrow is to wait a few days for Buoyer to bring them in. The muster roll reports thirty-nine surrendered up to this date. Later surrenders increased this to fifty-one, of whom fifteen may be classed as warriors. [Their arms October 1st consisted of two Henry carbines, one Sharp's carbine, one Springfield carbine, calibre .45; one Springfield breech-loading rifle, calibre .50; two muzzle-loading rifles, and one doublebarrelled shot gun.] The aggressive part of the campaign being at an end, Farrow thought best to send Lieut. Brown to Warrens in advance of the main party, carrying dispatches and arranging for rations and forage. The command was nearly out of rations, moreover it was incumbent on us now to feed the prisoners. Capt. Forse and Lieut.

Muhlenberg, with twenty four men, had left camp Howard the previous day [September 30] with rations which reached Warrens about October 6th or 7th. The matter of supply, etc., rendered it advisable that the prisoners be taken back via Camp Howard, Forts Lapwai and Walla Walla, and Umatilla Agency. They arrived at the latter place in due time. Farrow and his scouts were justly given an enthusiastic reception by the Indians, as well as by the citizens of the nearby town of Pendleton. The scouts were furloughed from November 6th until December 9th, their date of discharge, while the prisoners were taken by Lieut. Farrow to Vancouver Barracks.

There is not a rougher or more difficult country for campaigning in America...

OCTOBER 5, Pvt. Hoffner. So ends the never to be forgotten campaign of 1879. A number of animals made useless, and men badly used up.
We marched 1,258 miles, passed through sections where no humans beings had ever set foot in before. Were 117 days in the saddle.

General Howard October 9.
[TELEGRAM]
 Vancouver Barracks, Wash., Oct. 9, 1879.
ADJUTANT GENERAL,
Military Division Pacific,
Presideo, San Francisco.

My Annual Report indicated a failure in the main object of the expedition against the Sheepeaters and renegades located between the Little Salmon and Snake Rivers.
Now it is reversed, and the expedition has handsomely been

completed by Lieutenant Farrow and his scouts having defeated the Indians in two skirmishes, capturing their camp, with stores and stock. He has finally forced the entire band to surrender, and will deliver them as prisoners of war at this post.

Lieutenants Farrow, 21st Infantry, and W. C. Brown, 1st Cavalry, with their seven enlisted men, citizen employed, and Indian scouts, deserve special mention for gallantry, energy, and perseverance, resulting in success. There is not a rougher or more difficult country for campaigning in America.

Please add this to my report.

HOWARD, Commanding Department.

Private Harry Eagan's grave on Soldier Bar. Erected in 1925, the marker reads, "Killed in action here during an attack by Sheepeater Indians on rear guards and pack trains of Co's C, 2nd Inf., and G

Epilogue

Reuben Bernard: Fought Apaches in Arizona and New Mexico, promoted to Major of the Eighth Cavalry.

Reuben F. Bernard, Lieutenant Colonel, 1892.

Edward Farrow: Awarded brevet of First Lieutenant for service.

William Brown: Awarded brevet of First Lieutenant, later retired as a Brigadier General.

Edgar Hoffner: Died in California.

Henry Catley: Tried by a General Court-martial and found guilty of misbehavior in the presence of the enemy.

Sentenced to be dismissed from the service. Sentence set aside by President Hayes on the advice of the Judge Advocate General.

The Sheepeaters: Subjected to personal interrogation by General Howard at the Vancouver Barracks in November, 1879. During the questioning they willingly admitted the attack on the Rains' ranch, but vehemently denied any connection with the murders of the five Chinese miners or the deaths of Johnson and Dorsey. The captives were moved to the Fort Hall, Idaho, reservation the following year.

Perhaps as many as half of the Sheepeater-Bannock-Weiser Indians frequenting the Middle Fork mountains avoided capture. In spring, 1880, there were reports of sightings in Indian, Council, and Long valleys. Miners on Squaw Creek related an encounter with a group of twenty Indians who threatened them with death if they revealed their location to soldiers.

The Weiser band eventually settled on a secluded spot along the the Payette River, south of Long Valley, the site of a traditional summer camp. Eagle Eye's band joined them, but chose Dry Buck Valley, south of High Valley, near Timber Butte, in the mountains well above the river. They were there sometime earlier than 1888.

These remaining Sheepeaters caught and smoked white-fish and salmon at Payette Lake, hunted, gathered huckleberries; with time, they even built log cabins and frame houses, kept chickens and pigs, planted fruit trees. Eventually white families became tolerant, even sympathetic. A few of the Sheepeaters, less shy than others, were employed at nearby sawmills.

In 1898 Idaho Senator George Shoup, who had participated in the Indian massacre at Sand Creek, Colorado, wrote the Commissioner of Indian Affairs urging that the Payette and Camas Prairie bands be coerced onto the reservation.

Indian Inspector William McConnell visited the Payette band and responded that he would ask the government to purchase a small tract for them in the Payette canyon, where they were better off than on a reservation. Shoup's suggestion was dropped when local white settlers voiced opposition to ousting the bands.

But as their headmen died and pressure from encroaching farms grew, the Indian families finally capitulated. Some of them moved by hoseback to the Lemhi reservation—only to be evacuated in 1907 to Fort Hall on the Snake River in eastern Idaho; others journeyed directly to the reservation at Fort Hall. Their lineage survives in their descendants there.

On the Middle Fork, the Tukudeka have vanished like swallows in October, and even their name comes hard to the tongue. But their rouge pictographs and sequestered shelters remain a legacy entitled to courteous regard—an elegaic effort that can partially opaque the shame.

Bannock summer tipi.

Takuarikas, a Sheepeater, photographed in 1902 at McCall, Idaho. A young woman at the time of the war, she was taken to Fort Hall reservation after the conflict ended. In summer she joined Weiser Indians while they hunted and fished from a camp south of Payette Lake.

Shoshoni tipis, Fort Hall, Idaho.

Bannock camp near Fort Hall.

NATURAL HISTORY

Fish

First visitors and settlers of the Middle Fork described
the early fishing as remarkable. Three and four pound trout
were common; salmon in side streams, such as Sulphur Creek,
were "thick as blackberries in July." As late as 1955, it was a
simple matter to catch more than a hundred fish a day,
ranging up to sixteen inches. Since that time, the fishery has
experienced an unfortunate skid, but is on its way back.

A number of reasons explain the decline. Dredge mining
on the headwaters affected water quality. In 1956 the Forest
Service attacked spruce budworm on the river and its tributaries with massive aerial applications of DDT . This action
undoubtedly had some effect on the aquatic food chain.
Army Corps of Engineer and Bureau of Reclamation dams on
the Columbia and Snake rivers have exacted a tragic toll on
the salmon and steelhead populations. At the same time,
boating numbers have grown. Before stricter regulations,
fishermen among them accounted for the thousands of fish
each season. The single most restorative action for the fishery
has been the adoption of a "fish for sport" attitude on the part
of anglers—the use of barbless hooks and the release of their
catch at water-level (with wet hands in order to preserve the
mucous coating that protects fish from fungus and bacteria).

Three species of trout are resident in the Middle Fork:
Dolly Varden, rainbow, and cutthroat. Dolly Varden are the
largest and are found the length of the river.

Rainbow are also widely dispersed. The six to seven-inch
rainbows caught between Boundary Creek and Rapid River
are actually immature steelhead which rear in the headwater
streams for two years, then migrate to the ocean. Most will
spend two years in the sea before returning to the Middle
Fork in the fall. By then they may weigh up to ten pounds.
After spawning, the steelhead, unlike the salmon, can repeat
their ocean odyssey.

The cutthroat of the Middle Fork is a unique trout strain that has adapted to the specialized habitat. Research has shown that they spawn and rear primarily in the river's tributaries and perform a seasonal emigation from the Middle Fork each year before subzero temperatures occur. They overwinter in the warmer Salmon River or lower reaches of Impassable Canyon. As the water warms in the spring, the fish migate back up the Middle Fork, spending the summer months in the glides and large pools. Cutthroat of three or four pounds were caught thirty years ago, but today a fish over fourteen inches is considered large. Because of its slow growth and low reproductive rate, the west-slope cutthroat is unable to survive heavy fishing pressure. It has been protected for this reason.

Chinook salmon, which spawn in August and September, utilize Middle Fork tributary streams. After one season in the river, six-inch smolts head for the ocean where they spend one to three years. They journey back to Idaho in the spring and early summer to spawn on the headwaters of the Middle Fork.

Fishing Marsh Creek, Bear Valley, 1922.

FISH

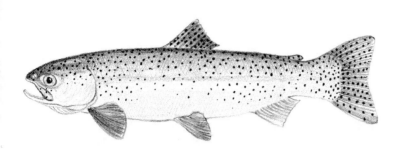

RAINBOW TROUT. Body color variable. Back olive to greenish blue, belly white to silver. Sides may show pink streak, white tip on pelvic and anal fin usually evident. Irregular spots on back, sides, head, dorsal fin and tail. Native. (Steelhead are ocean-run rainbow.)

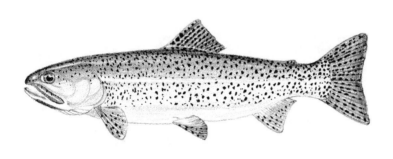

WESTSLOPE CUTTHROAT. Body color variable. Back steel gray to olive green. Sides may be yellow brown with red or pink along belly. Red or orange slashes on underside of lower jaw. Teeth on back of tongue. May hybridize in wild with rainbow. Native.

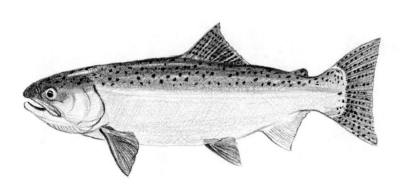

CHINOOK SALMON. The number of anal fin rays in all salmon exceed 12—in trout they never do. Adults generally 18 to 40 inches in length. Dark olive on back, shading to brown on sides. Teeth well developed. Native.

DOLLY VARDEN.
Olive green to brown above and on sides, shading to white on belly. Upper body with yellow spots and side with red or orange spots. Tail slightly forked. Native.

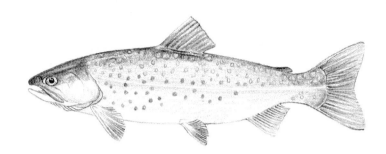

REDSIDE SHINER.
Dark oliver or brown on back, silvery on side and belly. Dark lateral stripe on side from snout to tail, lower sides reddish. A minnow species, the lower Middle Fork shiners are believed to be the largest in the state. Native.

WHITEFISH.
The Middle Fork species is Prasopium Williamsoni. Back brown, shading to silver and white on sides and belly. No spots. Body cigar-shaped. Large fleshy adipose fin. Mouth small with no teeth. Scales large. Native.

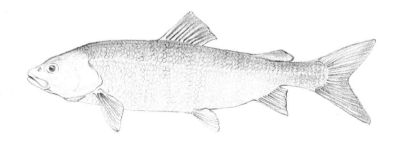

354

FLOWERS

TRILLIUM:
Grows about a foot tall, with a single blossom above green leaves. Flower has three white petals that gradually turn pink. Found in cool, moist shade along tributary streams.

OREGON GRAPE:
A Barberry that grows close to the ground, found throughout the canyon. Green leaves are stiff and prickly like Holly. Yellow flowers grow in clusters at the ends of the stems. Bitter blue berry makes good jelly.

RIVER LUPINE:
Perennial, about two feet high, with branching stems bearing tall spires of flowers. Open flowers are blue and purple.

HAREBELL:
Graceful plant with slender stems, six inches to a foot tall. Flowers hang on threadlike pedicels, are less than an inch long, and are violet or blue.

355

STAR FLOWER:

Grows three to six inches tall with a six-petalled white flower. Prefers shade; grows in groups.

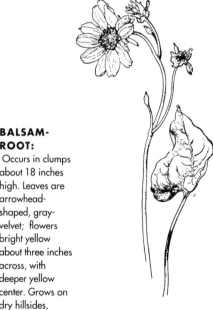

LARKSPUR:

Twenty to thirty purplish-blue flowers in a crowded cluster along the branching stems. Grows ten inches to two feet tall. Upper sepal, resembling a petal, is prolonged into a spur at the back of the flower. Poisonous to cattle.

BALSAM-ROOT:

Occurs in clumps about 18 inches high. Leaves are arrowhead-shaped, gray-velvet; flowers bright yellow about three inches across, with deeper yellow center. Grows on dry hillsides, common below Thomas Creek.

SCARLET PAINT BRUSH:

Grows on a rough stem a foot or so tall, with roughish dark green leaves. Yellowish bracts tipped with red, flowers bright red.

FIREWEED:
Perennial, grows two to five feet tall, alternate leaves. Purplish-pink flowers droop on their stems. Found along upper portions of the river. So-named because plant flourishes in burned-over areas.

MONKEY-FLOWER:
Three to six inches tall, bright yellow, monkey-faced flowers grow on the tips of slender stalks. Likes moisture.

SHOOTING STAR:
Smooth, reddish stem about a foot tall, springing from a cluster of rootleaves. Five to fifteen flowers grow atop the stem. The four petals are purplish-pink; corolla has a yellow and maroon ring and maroon point.

ARNICA:
Most common yellow flower in the canyon; has a hairy stem six inches to two feet tall, velvety leaves, some of which are heartshaped. Flower heads usually single, about two inches across, bright yellow rays.

357

TREES

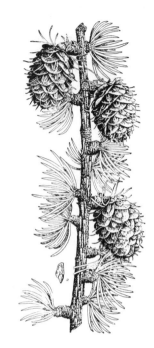

**PONDEROSA
PINE**

WESTERN LARCH

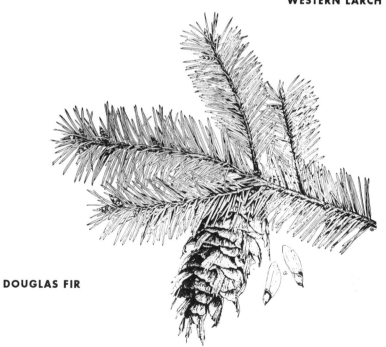

DOUGLAS FIR

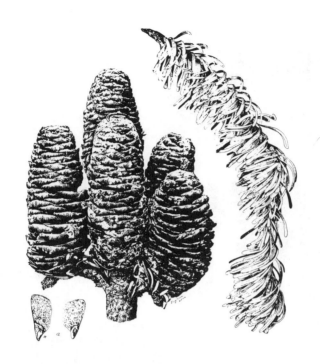

ALPINE FIR

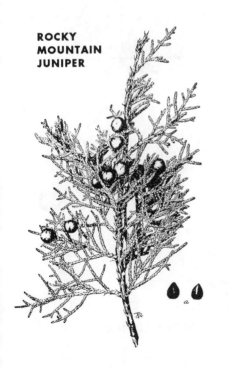

WILLOW

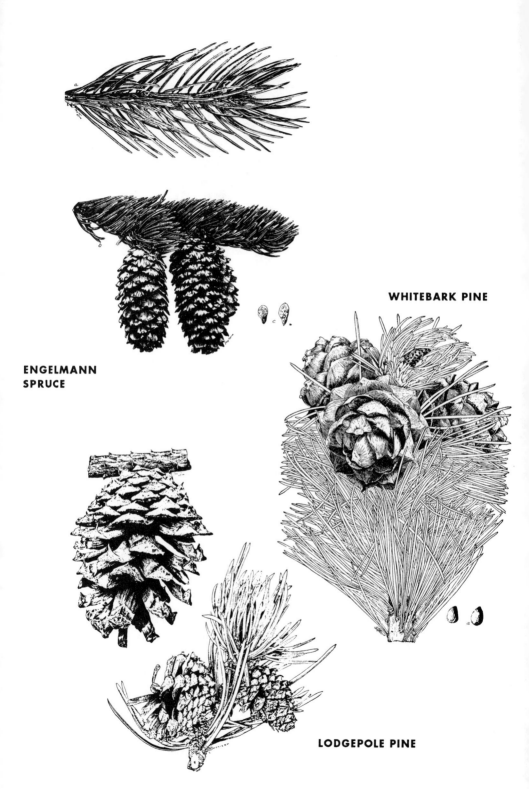

WHITEBARK PINE

**ENGELMANN
SPRUCE**

LODGEPOLE PINE

BIRDS

JUNCO

SPRUCE
GROUSE

SPOTTED
SANDPIPER

LEWIS WOODPECKER

361

SPARROW HAWK

CHUKAR

KINGFISHER

MAGPIE

VIOLET GREEN
SWALLOW

WATER OUZEL

CLIFF SWALLOW

MERGANSER

MOUNTAIN
CHICKADEE

363

**GOLDEN EAGLE
-ADULT**

**GOLDEN EAGLE
-IMMATURE**

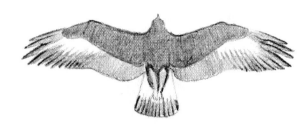

**BALD EAGLE
-ADULT**

**BALD EAGLE
-IMMATURE**

OSPREY

364

TRACKS

OTTER

COYOTE

DEER

MOUNTAIN SHEEP

BLACK BEAR

MOUNTAIN LION

365

MIDDLE FORK BIRD LIST

American Kestrel
Blue Grouse
Ruffed Grouse
Chukar
Spotted Sandpiper
Red-tailed Hawk
Common Nighthawk
Common Flicker
Violet Green Swallow
Barn Swallow
Cliff Swallow
Tree Swallow
Black-billed Magpie
Common Raven
Common Crow
Clark's Nutcracker
Black-capped Chickadee
Mountain Chickadee
Dipper
American Robin
Mountain Bluebird
Cedar Waxwing
Pine Grosbeak
Mourning Dove
Black-headed Grosbeak
Evening Grosbeak
Dark-eyed Junco
Chipping Sparrow
Brewer's Sparrow
White-crowned Sparrow
Song Sparrow
Kildeer
Screech Owl

Great Horned Owl
White-throated Swift
Rufous Hummingbird
Belted Kingfisher
Lewis Woodpecker
Williamson's Sapsucker
Hairy Woodpecker
Downy Woodpecker
Western Kingbird
Hammond's Flycatcher
Dusky Flycatcher
Western Flycatcher
Western Wood Peewee
Olive-sided Flycatcher
Red-breasted Nuthatch
Pygmy Nuthatch
Brown Creeper
Canyon Wren
Hermit Thrush
Swainson's Thrush
Veery
Golden-crowned Kinglet
Ruby-crowned Kinglet
Warbling Vireo
Yellow-rumped Warbler
Yellow Warbler
Western Tanager
Lazuli Bunting
Pine Siskin
Osprey
Bald Eagle
Golden Eagle
Common Merganser

BIBLIOGRAPHY

Brimlow, George F. *Cavalryman Out of the West. Life of General Carey Brown*. Caldwell, Idaho: Caxton Printers, 1944.

Brown, William C. *The Sheepeater Campaign, Idaho—1879*. Tenth Biennial Report of the State Historical Society of Idaho for the years 1925-1926: 25-51.

Carrey, John. *Sheepeater Indian Campaign (Chamberlain Basin Country)*. Grangeville: Idaho Free Press, 1968.

Domnick, David D. *The Sheepeaters*. Annals of Wyoming 36 (2): 131-168, 1964.

DuBois, Eliot. *An Innocent on the Middle Fork*. Seattle, Washington: The Mountaineers, 1987.

Goodwin, Victor and Hussey, John. *Sawtooth Mountain Area Study Idaho (History)*. U. S. Forest Service, National Park Service, 1965.

Hardin, Major C. B. *The Sheepeater Campaign*. N.Y.H.: Governor's Island. (Reprinted from the Journal of Military Service Institution, July-August, 1910 25-40) .

Hultkrantz, Ake. *The Source Literature on the "Tukudika" Indians in Wyoming: Facts and Fancies*. In "Languages and Cultures of Western North America," Earl H. Swanson, Jr., (e.p.), 246-264. Pocatello: Idaho State University Press, 1970.

Knudson, Ruthann. *A Cultural Resource Reconnaissance in the Middle Fork Salmon River Basin, Idaho, 1978*. Ogden, Utah: U. S. Forest Service, Intermountain Region, 1982.

Liljeblad, Sven. *Indian Peoples of Idaho*. Manuscript on file, Idaho State University Museum, Pocatello, 1957.

Midmore, Joe. *Middle Fork History*. Reno: Harrah's, 1970.

Murphy, Robert F. and Yolanda. *Shoshone—Bannock Subsistence and Society*. Anthropological Records, 16 (7): 293-338, 1960.

Parker, Aaron F. *Forgotten Tragedies of Indian Warfare in Idaho*. Grangeville: Idaho Free Press, 1925.

Pavesic, Max G. *Archaeological Overview of the Middle Fork of the Salmon River Corridor, Idaho Primitive Area*. Archaeological Reports No. 3. Boise: Boise State University, 1978.

Rossillon, Mary P. *An Overview of History in the Drainage Basin of the Middle Fork of the Salmon River*. Ogden, Utah: U. S. Forest Service, Intermountain Region, 1981.

Schearer, George M. *The Battle of Vinegar Hill* . Idaho Yesterdays 12 16-21, 1968.

Swanson, Earl H., Jr. *Ancient Camps and Villages of the Middle Fork*. Naturalist 23 (2): 29, 1972.

Trenholm, Virginia C. *The Shoshonis, Sentinels of the Rockies*. Norman: University of Oklahoma Press, 1964.

Wells, Merle W. *Gold Camps & Silver Cities*. Moscow, Idaho: Idaho Department of Lands, Bureau of Mines and Geology, 1983.

Yarber, Esther. *Land of the Yankee Fork*. Salt Lake City: Publishers Press 1963.
Yarber, Esther. *Stanley Sawtooth Country*. Publishers Press 1976.

GRATITUDE

Every effort has been made to check the names and facts in this book. But as anyone who has listened to witnesses under oath in a court of law knows, nothing is so fallible as human memory. In many cases we were forced to choose between conflicting stories, taking that which seemed most plausible or cross-checked reliably. We did this without intending any disrespect for our sources, realizing that at times we may have accepted half truths without hearing the proper half. Such are the limitations of oral history.

Obviously even so modest a work as this could only have been accomplished with invaluable help from many people. Sincere thanks to

Pearl Carrey, Jerry Hughes, Jim Campbell, Chuck Bartholomew, Billy Wilson, Frank and Vonda Swain, Hack Miller, Daisey Tappan, Fred Paulsen, Bob and Don Smith, Don Hatch, Steve Schaefers, Bob Sevy, Vera Claussen, Art Selin, Eliot DuBois, Jenny Lewis, Bill Sullivan, Royce Mowrey, John Marshall, Dave Helfrich, Earl Perry, Jed Wilson, Andy Anderson, Ted Anderson, Ed Budell, Larry McGowan, Fred Shiefer, Emma and Lafe Cox, Sister Afreda Elsensohn, Earl Poynor, Catherine Beckley, Patti Hornback-Reynolds, Johnny Peterson, Mary and Milt Hood, Bob Cole, Peter Gibbs, Carole Finley, Dock Marston, Bill Bernt, Melvin Hughes, Dean Snell, Chris Neher, Clay and Marcia Wood, John Little, Pat and Susan Conley, Elwood Masoner, Eldon Handy, Dave and Sheila Mills, Steve Lentz, Sven Liljeblad, Max Pavesic, Dennis Baird, Dorothy Morton, Ted Trueblood, Al Dunham, Gordon Reid, Les Bechdel, Randy Stone, Mark McKane, Al Busby, Jack Bills, Florence Smothers, Esther Yarber, Marjorie and Jim Collord, Roscoe Dodge, Idaho State Historical Society, Utah State Historical Society, Colorado University Historical Library, U. S. Forest Service.

INDEX

RAPID CHART

MILE	NAME	RATING	APPROACH
2.3	Sulphur Creek	1	Log jam and small island appear on left. Take right channel always.
2.7	Sulphur Slide	3	Low water: enter right center and work left.
4.0	Ramshorn	2	River narrows between two cliffs with a massive rock in the middle. Take left channel.
5.4	Velvet Falls	4	Approach: Velvet Creek enters Middle Fork on right just above falls. Take left channel.
8.3	Chutes	2	Approach: Log jam on right. Take left channel, but beware of big rock at channel entrance.
11.5	Power House	4	Approach: Cottonwood trees and old waterwheel on right. Work middle channel in upper section. Work left after making first right hand corner. Work hard left in lower portion to avoid headwall at end of rapid.
18.0	Artillery	1	Run right center.
19.6		1	River flows around island. Take the right channel.
20.0	Big Snag	1	Work left to avoid shelf rock exposed in the lower water.
22.6	Pistol Creek	4	Enter rapids in the middle of the stream. Work hard right after sharp left hand corner to avoid hitting wall on the left.
32.0	Marble Creek	2	Approach: Just below Marble Creek Camp. Run either far right or center chute to avoid exposed shelf rock.
32.7	Ski Jump	1	Large boulders in river, run left side.
36.2	No Name	1	Approach: River flows around island. Take left channel.
37.5	Jackass	2	Pull right on low water.

MILE	NAME	RATING	APPROACH
44.8	No Name	1	Approach: Low water exposes rock shelf below Pine Creek Flat. Take left side.
47.0	No Name	1	Approach: Island below Cox Camp. Take right channel.
47.8	No Name	1	Low water exposes rock shelf. Take left channel.
48.5	No Name	1	River flows around island. Take right side of left channel.
58.2	Tappen Falls	4	High water: run far right side of the river. Low water: run 10 feet from the right bank.
58.5	Tappen III	2	Run left of center until you pass large boulder in center of stream, then work hard right to avoid rock shelf exposed in low water.
58.7	Tappen IV	1	Low water: run left side.
60.7	No Name	1	Approach: Camas Creek on right. Low water: run left.
63.1	Aparejo	1	Enter in center: Work far left avoiding rocks on right.
68.3	Haystack	3	Large boulders scattered the width of the river. Enter on left side. Work to the center avoiding rocks on both sides.
71.0	Jack Creek	1	Low water: run right of center.
77.9	Water Fall Creek	2	Approach: Big Creek Bridge (steel span) is visible just above rapid. Enter center then work either left or right to avoid large boulder in center of river.
81.3	Wall Creek	2	Approach: Rapid just below Veil Falls. High water: run center. Low water: enter on the right. After passing rocks on the left, work to the left, work to the left to avoid wall on the right.
82.8	Porcupine	4	Approach: Massive rock on the right and one in the middle. In high water run far left. In lower water run between large boulders in the center of the river and the right side. Large rock at the end of the white water, but possible to go to either side of it.
83.0	Redside	4	Run either far left or left center.

MILE	NAME	RATING	APPROACH
83.3	Weber	2	Low water: run right side working left.
88.7	Cliffside	3	Wall on the left: work right to avoid the wall. As water moves away from wall move in close to wall on the left side for second portion of rapid.
90.0	Ouzel	1	Wall on the left: work right to avoid the wall.
90.9	Rubber	4	Big waves: enter in the center. Work left after floating through tongue to avoid rocks on the right side.
92.0	Hancock	4	Approach: Roaring Creek is on the right. Run first portion right of center. Run big waves in the center after making right hand turn, but work to the left when approaching the wall on the right side.
93.3	Devil's Tooth	2	Run right of center.
93.9	House of Rocks	2	Run left side.
94.3	Jump Off	3	Low water: run right side.
95.2	Goat Creek	1	Low water: run left of center.

Design: Temel West; Boise, Idaho
Mechanicals: Roger Cole

Front cover photograph: Larry Harrel
Rear cover photographs:
1926 Weidner expedition; courtesy Vera Claussen.
Daisey Tappan; Molly O'Leary.
Earl Parrott, "Hermit of Impassable Canyon"; Hack Miller.

OUR TRIP

CAMPSITES

DAY 1

_____

DAY 2

_____

DAY 3

_____

DAY 4

_____

DAY 5

_____

DAY 6

_____

DAY 7

_____

DAY 8

_____

GUIDES

_____

_____

_____

_____

_____

_____

_____

TRIP MEMBERS

_____

_____

_____

_____

_____

_____

_____

_____

_____

TRIP MEMBERS

_____

_____

_____

_____

_____

_____

_____

_____

_____

MEALS

DAY 1

_____

DAY 2

_____

DAY 3

_____

DAY 4

_____

DAY 5

_____

DAY 6

_____

DAY 7

_____

DAY 8

_____